OF DECEPTION AND DIVINITY

Death and Destiny Trilogy, Book 3

N.D. Jones

KUUMBA
PUBLISHING
CREATIVE MINDS.
PASSIONATE HEARTS

Baltimore, Maryland

kuumbapublishing.com

Kuumba Publishing
1325 Bedford Avenue #32374
Pikesville, Maryland 21282

Publisher's Note:

Book Layout © 2014 BookDesignTemplates.com
Cover Design by Atlantis Book Design
Concept Art Design by Phu Thieu
All art and logo copyright © 2017 by Kuumba Publishing

Of Deception and Divinity/ N.D. Jones. -- 1st ed.
ISBN-10: 0-9975293-7-7
ISBN-13: 978-0-9975293-7-1

DEDICATION

This book is dedicated to Barbara Jones.
Daughter
Wife
Mother
Grandmother
Friend
Lover of God
Lover of Books

PROLOGUE

Over 500 Years Earlier
Primordial Waters of Nun

Apep slithered through the ancient waters, his fifty-foot orange-and-black body of scales and strength gliding toward the shore and the battling witches. Forked tongue preceded lethally sharp fangs. He could taste his win in the black, smoky air, succulent and satisfying.

The sky opened and rained down bolts of lightning. The waters roughened, swirling in a vortex of magic and menace.

The god of war, chaos, and death dipped deep below the water's surface, avoiding the blazing inferno the water witch had turned the liquid pool of life and death into. Ah, yes, Apep did so love fire witches, even more so when they came undone. And this one, well, her sinful soul would make a delicious meal for Ammit, the Eater of Hearts, the Devourer of the Dead.

Blessed war raged above him, damned souls below, sinking into the depths of Nun. The souls would find no peace in Duat, the realm of the dead and Apep's home, which Ra dared to cross over each night, shining his sun in the most reprehensible of places.

But not tonight and not for the next five centuries. Ra would lose, and Apep's influence in the mortal world would expand and deepen. No one could stop him. Not Ra, not without Ma'at by his side. Now, all he had was Sekhmet. And the cat goddess wouldn't be enough, had never been enough to thwart his violent toxicity, the saccharine addiction of chaos, falsehood and disorder mortals so loved.

Leaving behind the heated water, Apep came ashore. Marble-black eyes glistened with anticipation.

A thirty-foot tidal wave rose from Nun, a whirl of vicious water. Water spikes formed as it churned, harnessing the lethal intent of its mistress.

Wind whipped. Thunder crackled. And fire rampaged.

They spared nothing and all was dark, including the hearts of the dueling witches.

Whatever humanity they once claimed had bled away with each spell cast and life taken. They cared not for those sacrificed in their brutal battle to the death. Apep doubted if they recalled why they fought at all, but fight they did, with malevolent skill and gods-given magic.

The swirling spikes of water crashed onto the shore, the water witch's eyes blazing bright blue with power and murder. It didn't stop, moving at a speed the god's snake eyes could barely track.

Yet the path was clear, and the fire witch, surrounded by hundreds of balls of fire, stood her ground, an immovable force ready to meet an immovable force.

Slam. The spikes of water crashed into the balls of fire, up and over, drenching the fire witch's rotating weapons of war. The spikes of water pushed the fire witch back.

"Into the water with you," the water witch screamed. "To your death." Hands raised, palms out, the witch shoved against the night air, forcing the swirling spikes deeper into the balls of fire.

Back the fire witch went, her fire magic and endless lightning bolts no match for the water witch whose element of power soaked her feet and fueled her spells.

"Into the water. Into the water. Into. The. Water."

Fireballs of protection keened, then exploded, a roaring of fire witch magic too weak to hold form and shield its mistress.

The churning spikes of water closed in, piercing fire-hot skin but dissolving under the heat of the fire witch's molten body.

But the damage had been done, the fire witch's balls of protection were no more. The witch was nearly drained of magic and energy.

The water witch snarled, sensing her victory, the same as Apep. Blue eyes as cold as the primordial waters from which she drew upon watched as liquid binds wrapped around the fire witch's body, tentacles slowly pulling her away from land and into the wet, waiting embrace of Nun.

Apep slunk closer to the battle unwilling to miss the fall of Ra's hope.

Desperate and cursing, the fire witch dug her fingers into the marshy ground, breaking nails and bones as she fought against the gripping tide of water drawing her to her death. Wet, red-gold hair clung to scalp, green eyes glistened with fear and vile screams of retribution scorched the wetland around her.

She knew. Yes, she knew.

Just a few more feet.

"Into the water with you!" The water witch yelled her spell over the top of her shrieking enemy and the thunderous rapids of the river, eager to add one more soul to its ravenous maw. "Into the water with y—"

Blood spurted from an arm suddenly ripped in two. The water witch howled her disbelief and pain. Cherry liquid escaped her mauled limb, and her face twisted in agony. She lifted her other arm, and her trembling lips spat a spell at the beast before her. The water witch's severed arm hung from the predator's mouth. The teeth clamped around it were long, thick, and bone-crushingly sharp.

Out her spell went, shards of water slamming into the black-and-gray fur of the gigantic cat, knocking him back but not down.

The cat ducked and dodged the next attacks, running with a swiftness that angered and confused the water witch.

Apep moved even closer, his anger leaving a swath of slimy scales in his wake. Up he went, shedding the lower half of his body and taking on the form of a two-legged male, his head still that of a hissing snake.

He'd seen this creature of Sekhmet's twice before. Apep smiled, as much as one could with the head of a snake. "It won't work, brother."

The god glanced upward at the starless sky. "The Mngwa is too late. Your fire witch has already failed. She is more *isfet* than *ma'at*. I win."

But he hadn't. Not yet. Not with the Mngwa stalking the water witch and keeping his massive body between her and his mate. His mere presence fueled the magic of the fire witch and granted her precious seconds to regain her strength and composure.

A couple of minutes, that was all the fire witch had needed. And the blasted cat had given it to her, willing to die for his witch, even though she'd killed many in her thirst for victory and vengeance.

Apep glanced back to the ancient waters. The rapids were beginning to calm, the chains on the ocean floor forming and preparing to reclaim its prisoners. He could hear the shrill screams of Mami Wata as she watched on from the Realm of the Gods, her water witch unable to stand against the combined might of Oya's chosen one and Sekhmet's Mngwa.

The god of chaos and disorder crept forward, black eyes traveling from the water witch and to the fire witch, making her way to her feet, protected behind the bulk of her familiar.

The beast roared when his mistress stood to her full height of six feet, hands and eyes on fire, chest heaving, and magic coalescing.

A towering wall of water rose from Nun, raced toward the shore, heeding the command of its water mistress. Liquid hands shot forward, grasping and clutching yet finding only layer upon layer of sizzling fire.

Fire and water grappled, linked in a deadly, violent clench. Chaos and disorder at its finest, *isfet* personified.

No, Ra would not win today. Nor would Oya secure her freedom and Sàngó the return of his consort. Mami Wata, well, the goddess of water and its creatures would simply have to wait for the fall of Ra and the ascension of Apep, of *ifset*. A seat beside the new King of Gods would be her reward, the mortal realm Mami Wata's betrothal gift.

Oya dropped from the sky, her physical form snatched from the Realm of the Gods by Nun's power-dampening chains. The chains yanked the goddess down and into her watery prison for another five hundred years. Her fire witch had broken too many of Ma'at's divine principles for the goddess of wind, thunderbolts, and fire to do anything other than succumb to her endless punishment.

Water and fire engulfed the land, the battling witches the epicenter of the disaster, their magic out of control, their minds on nothing but killing the other.

Apep cast his eyes upward one more time. There, plummeting toward Nun, a mystical chain around her ankles, the other working to secure the struggling goddess' wrists, was Mami Wata. Beautifully naked and cursing Ra with each downward spiral, Mami Wata raised her free hands and shoved the fleeting embers of her godly power outward and toward the dueling witches.

The second chain captured her wrists, hauling the mutinous goddess into Nun and to her waiting prison, Ra's cruel irony for a water goddess whose very existence aided Apep's coup.

A howl of abject horror had Apep's head and eyes lowering. Gone was the mountain of swirling fire. Gone was the wall of ice water. Gone was the Mngwa. His body, turned inside out, was now nothing but bloody chunks of organs and innards, a puddle of gooey hair and blood where once a mighty cat had stood.

Mami Wata's fleeting magical energy still sparked in the air around the dead beast, the fire witch's shield broken beyond repair. What was left of the mortal's sinful heart was no more. Her mate was slaughtered right before her eyes, the witch powerless to protect him.

"No, beloved. Please, don't die. Don't die. Nooooo!"

She bellowed her heartache to the quiet night sky. Tears soaked the remains of her mate over which she hung her head, shoulders shuddering from endless tears, knees, and hands in the mud, defenses down and open for attack.

The water witch didn't disappoint. A tide of water grew behind the weeping fire witch, forming hundreds of spikes as it barreled toward its prey.

It struck, and Apep waited for the sobs of mourning to morph into cries of pain and misery. Instead, an explosion of fire and fury sent him and the water witch flying backward.

"All your fault. If it's the last thing I do, I swear, I'll kill you."

Everywhere he looked there were flames, untamed and hellfire hot. Not even the ancient waters of Nun dared to challenge the inferno, the water witch no longer able to command the element.

Apep heard her screeched spells from smoke-filled and burning lungs, frantic and futile.

Dropping to the ground, Apep returned to his preferred corporeal form, the fifty-foot snake. Slithering away from the fiery tempest, Apep rejoined Nun. The water was far too hot for comfort, the fire witch's magic unchained, her broken and bleeding heart a threat to every living creature.

Ra was a fool. Fire witches were too destructive, impatient and soft-hearted to defeat anyone, much less their base instincts.

Every five hundred years, in the year of Ra, a fire witch born to the Temple of Oya and a water witch born to the Temple of Mami Wata will mark the beginning of the end and rebirth. Ma'at demands balance, and these witches will bring both destruction and another five hundred years of peace for mortals. All the old will be washed away like sand after an early morning tide. Pray for Oya's fire witch and her invincible Mngwa, for they will be all that stands between mortals and a liquid grave with serpents. Pray for Mami Wata's water witch, whose desire for power will know no bounds. Mortals cannot know love without hate, good without evil, fire without water. The Day of the Serpents will be upon you, repent your sins before it's too late.

Ra's decree over a thousand years ago, whispered in the ears of pre-ternaturals, was passed along like an inevitable but unwanted disease, from one generation to the next. Ra was a shrewd god, indeed, seeing the profit of the war between Oya and Mami Wata for the gods of the realm. Yet such benefits were outweighed by the cost Ra had not antic-ipated but eventually paid.

From a safe distance, Apep watched as the fire spread, the water witch morbidly silent. Yes, Ammit would devour many heart-souls tonight, beginning with the shattered heart of Ra's fire witch. The woman was no legend but a wonderful blight on the human realm.

Slinking down and away, Apep began his journey home where he'd wait, impatiently, for the next fire witch to be born. Would she be as gloriously chaotic as her predecessors? Apep knew she would, knew that not even her mate would have the power to constrain her fury.

Five hundred years, yes, five more centuries and another battle between water and fire and Apep's coup would be complete. The Reign of Isfet was a foregone conclusion, and the Day of Serpents would be his rise to King of Gods.

CHAPTER ONE

Baltimore, Maryland

Sanura wrapped her arms around Makena's shoulders and hugged her mother from behind, burying her face in the older woman's thick black hair, the locks in a curly blowout reminiscent of 1960s Angela Davis. "Thank you for doing this."

Admittedly, Sanura and Assefa's upcoming trip to the Sudan was a flimsy reason for a family dinner. But Makena loved a full house and an excuse to spoil her family with her great cooking.

"It's no trouble, sweetie."

"Smells good, but I think you made too much." Sanura stepped away from Makena, tempted to snag a slice of garlic bread to tide her over until dinner. Even at twenty-nine, Sanura knew her mother would have no compunction slapping her hand for the offense.

"I doubt that. Mike alone could eat everything in the refrigerator. Now, hand me that onion and a utility knife."

Sanura had no idea what a utility knife looked like, so she handed her mother one of the smaller knives from the knife block, which she took politely. But Makena's raised eyebrow was all the silent judgment required.

"I mean, Assefa and Zareb may not get here in time and I haven't heard back from Cyn, although I left her three voicemails about to-night's get-together."

Assefa and his FBI partner, Zareb Osei, were out of town on bureau business. Gone a week, the men, as of Assefa's last phone call, were driving back from New Jersey, the small band of cannibalistic dwarfs "dealt with." He took no pleasure in killing, even when the execution was sanctioned by the Chief of the Preternatural Division of the FBI and the criminals were unremorseful murderers.

After peeling the yellow onion, Makena held it on the cutting board and set to work. "Why haven't you heard from Cynthia?"

"I have no idea. She's been distant lately, and I don't know why."

"You know how she gets right before the new school year begins."

Yes, Sanura knew. As Head Mistress of Sankofa Preparatory School's lower school, Cynthia Garvey, Sanura's best friend, involved herself in every aspect of the running of the school. She knew every new student, teacher, and parent, every budget item and broken locker, every approved textbook and refurbished computer, every donated musical instrument and disgruntled staff member.

Head Mistress Garvey was, without a doubt, a busy and micromanaging water witch, but none of that, Sanura suspected, had anything to do with why Cyn had barely spoken to her since early July. It was now mid-August.

Makena held the cutting board above a pot of boiling water. Using the knife, she slid the diced onions into the pot, replacing the lid and reducing the heat. Wiping her hands on a dishtowel, Makena turned to Sanura.

"She's busy. You're busy. She has a family, and you now live in Virginia with six men."

Makena smirked at Sanura when she glowered at her, not finding humor in the way she described her living arrangement. Yes, well, six men in the most technical sense. Assefa and his clan of legend, Zareb, Omar, Rashad, Manute, and Mr. Siddig.

"Six men. Who knew you raised such an indecent fire witch, Makena."

"Shut up, Rachel."

"I'm just saying. I mean, you do live with six men. And one is old enough to be your father."

Sanura whirled around. Rachel stood in the dining room, a few feet from the kitchen, hands on her petite hips and brown eyes sparkling with mischief.

"You leave Mr. Siddig out of this. And no one asked your opinion."

"If I waited for people to ask my opinion, I'd be as old as High Priestess Katherine."

"By the gods, Katherine Spencer is dead and no longer High Priestess of the Witch Council of Elders."

"Exactly. As old as that." Rachel, dressed in skinny black jeans, a baby blue serenity shirt buttoned up to her neck and black heels, looked casual and classy in her late summer outfit. At five feet, she strained to see behind Sanura and to what Makena had cooking on the stove. "Makena, may I have—"

"No, go sit down and be patient."

"Damn, that never works."

Sanura shoved Rachel as she made her way out of the kitchen, through the dining room, and into the spacious living room. "I don't know why you even bother. You know how she is."

"Yeah, but I only wanted a slice of garlic bread. I missed lunch, and I'm starving."

Rachel patted her flat stomach, pouting up at Sanura.

"That's wasted on me. I have no more power over what happens in Mom's kitchen than you do." They flopped onto a couch, Sanura's long legs in front of her, Rachel's pulled onto the cushion, her shoes off and on the floor. "Have you talked to Cyn lately?"

"Yeah, she observed my Introduction to Ancient African Writing Systems class."

Sanura blinked at her childhood friend. "That makes no sense at all. You teach foreign language to middle-schoolers, and school hasn't officially started yet."

"I'm piloting a two-week professional learning course for Sankofa faculty at the upper and lower schools. Ten guinea pig teachers are in my class. Apparently, having a rich Sudanese as the Witch Council of Elders' alpha has opened up coffers we've never had access to before."

"Wait, you're telling me that the were-cat-witch African immigrant communities have shared—what?"

"Their precious family texts. Some of the communities, anyway. Mainly the ones on the East Coast." Rachel smiled, and Sanura was certain she hadn't seen her friend smile in quite that way when talking about work. She was damn near glowing. "Oh, my gods, Sanura, you should see all the documents, magically preserved and in great condition. I'm not even a third of the way through all of them, and I've been at it since late July."

Only a lover of languages would get so excited over old, dusty books written in dead languages. But Rachel Foster, a level one earth witch, was unmatched in oral and written languages. To her, this windfall of ancient writings probably felt like winning the Mega Millions.

"Not in a professional capacity. Have you spoken with Cyn after-hours or on the weekend? Had dinner? Seen a movie?"

"Of course, why wouldn't I?"

Of course, why wouldn't she? They were friends, after all. But Sanura and Cynthia were also friends and her friend, the past month and a half, hadn't made a single effort to reach out to her despite Sanura's own efforts.

"Damn, girl, you look like someone just told you Assefa was creeping around on you."

Sanura's head snapped up, her concerned thoughts of Cynthia having pulled it down. "What in the hell kind of thing is that to say?"

"I don't know. It got your attention. Besides, Assefa wouldn't do something like that, so it's a perfectly harmless joke."

"You need a filter... or a muzzle. Something to calm you down and shut you up. You're terrible."

"Only around the people I love and trust."

Rachel leaned over, smacking her lips loudly as if to kiss Sanura's cheek, but she pushed her away, laughing. "Like I said, terrible."

"Maybe, but do you know what's truly terrible?"

Sanura didn't bother answering Rachel's question and was seriously reconsidering braving Makena's wrath by stealing a slice of garlic bread and shoving it into her friend's mouth.

Rachel pointed to the dining room and the person seated at the table.

"He's been sitting there, just watching her cook. The man is the head of a secret division of the FBI, wears a gun on his hip and has a devilish smile that makes me think he's a hell spawn on vacation, yet he gets this I'm-a-harmless-puppy-so-please-take-me-in-and-let-me-sleep-at-the-foot-of-your-bed look whenever he's around Makena."

Sanura refused to look in Ulan Berber's direction. In fact, she'd been trying, very hard, to ignore the man's presence. He'd arrived about an hour ago, with two dozen long-stemmed red roses for Makena, the crimson color matching his tie. And, yeah, the man did remind Sanura of a hell demon, always in an exquisitely cut black suit with red silk tie and handkerchief.

"He's damn near salivating, which is funny because Makena is not at all interested."

Sanura twisted to look at Assefa's uncle, who, to the were-cat's credit, wasn't salivating. But he did look like a man very much interested in a woman. And that woman, to Sanura's continued annoyance, was her widow of a mother. Who, damn him, Sanura could no longer say with certainty that Makena was unaffected by Ulan's persistence and charisma. Makena and Ulan weren't dating, but her mother did seem to enjoy his company and conversation.

"At least he's a handsome puppy-dog. Dangerous, but handsome."

She glowered at him when he reached down, retrieved a slice of garlic bread from a small plate in front of him, and took a pleased bite. His eyes twinkled with self-satisfaction and arrogance when their gazes met.

He winked.

Fire magic sizzled in her fingertips and Sanura made to rise, but Rachel's hand around her wrist had Sanura reconsidering murdering her mate's uncle. She was pretty sure killing a family member wasn't the best way to endear her to Assefa's family, whom she would meet in a couple of days.

"As far as Sam's replacement, your mother could do a lot worse than Ulan."

"You're not helping."

"It's been almost four years."

"I know."

"Then get over it already and let your mother enjoy the attention of a handsome man. Makena deserves it."

"I know."

"I don't think you do."

She knew her mother was sometimes lonely in the big house by herself. Hence, tonight's dinner. She knew Ulan Berber respected and genuinely liked Makena. And she knew Samuel Williams would not want Makena to spend the rest of her days lonely and alone.

Sanura knew all of that. But playing witness to the quiet, seductive courting of her mother, well, a fire witch could only take so much.

"Anyway, you don't have anything to worry about. He'll be the rebound guy, the sexy, good-looking were-cat she fucks then tosses away."

She got up and walked away from Rachel.

"What? What did I say? Where are you going, Miss Sensitive?"

CHAPTER TWO

Sanura closed the security door behind her, shutting out Rachel's mocking laughter. It wasn't Makena's style to throw anyone away, especially someone she cared enough about to be intimate with. She didn't think Makena was anywhere near that point yet. But Ulan, like Assefa, possessed a seemingly endless supply of patience.

So much had changed since her father's death and even more once Assefa entered Sanura's life. She couldn't have them both, Sam and Assefa, no matter how much she wished otherwise. Holding onto the jaguar spirit of her deceased father, transferred to her after Sam's death, was no way to honor his memory. He'd sacrificed what should've been a long life so his daughter could find love and safety in the protective heart of her mate, the Mngwa of myth.

Sanura smiled when a four-door sedan parked behind her car. A minute later, three familiar faces alighted from the dark-green car, one carrying a bottle of wine, one hoisting her handbag on her shoulder, and the third bounding up the steps with a boisterous, "Hi, Aunt San."

Gen flung herself into Sanura's arms, squeezing her tightly as if she were the one nearly six feet tall instead of five-feet-one and ninety-five pounds. Sanura hugged her niece with the same enthusiasm and affection.

"Good to see you too, Gen." Sanura stepped back from the fourteen-year-old, taking in her graphic tee. The girl was forever sporting a shirt with some anime or manga character, most of which Sanura had never heard of. Today it was *Attack on Titan*, which she knew since she'd watched a few episodes with Gen and Rashad the last time Cynthia visited, bringing Gen with her. That had also been right before Cyn stopped answering Sanura's calls.

"Nice shirt."

"Thanks, Rashad sent it to me." Gen beamed, not a blush in sight at her crush on the twenty-year-old college student. "Is he here?"

"Rashad's too old for you." Eric reached around his sister and, with the hand not holding onto the bottle of wine, grabbed Sanura around the waist and pressed a kiss to her cheek. "Good to see you. It's been too long."

Sanura ignored the unintended opening. Now wasn't the time to get into how come it had been a while since she'd seen Eric and his family.

"Six years isn't even that much of an age difference."

"It is when you're under eighteen." Eric stared down at his sister, who glared back with a mix of defiance and uncertainty. "He also has a girlfriend, not that it matters. Rashad's too old for you, end of discussion."

To Gen's credit, she didn't huff, stomp her feet, or even mumble teenage nonsense under her breath when she stalked away from the three adults and into the house. But she did sigh dramatically, yanking out her cell phone and no doubt texting one of her girlfriends about how unfair life was living with an overprotective brother.

"She's ridiculous." Eric ran a hand through his light-brown hair, his gray eyes reflecting the male frustration of raising a teenage girl who thought herself grown and all-knowing. "Gen wants to date. Can you believe that? She's just beginning the tenth grade, for Sekhmet's sake."

Cynthia rubbed the middle of her husband's back, sympathy and humor rimming her eyes. "You sound eighty instead of thirty. Gen will be fifteen the end of September. It's pretty much in her job description to be ridiculous and to test boundaries. But she's a sensible girl. Don't worry so much."

Eric glanced over Sanura's shoulder and to the open front door. "Is Rashad here?"

"No. He decided to attend a pre-back to school party with a bunch of his Howard U friends and his girlfriend."

That bit of news had Eric's shoulders relaxing and his grip on the wine bottle loosening. "Good, because I really didn't want to spend the evening ungluing Gen from Rashad's side. And I really don't want to be around the day Gen figures out that Rashad is kind to her because he's a decent guy who thinks of her as a cute little sister and that's it." Eric turned to his wife and kissed her cheek. "That's what a sister-in-law is for."

"Gee, thanks." Cynthia gestured with her chin to the front door. "Why don't you go inside and give the red wine to Makena. Let her know Sanura and I will be in in a few minutes."

Eric looked between the two women, as surprised as Sanura that Cynthia wanted to have a private word with her. But he did as his wife asked, closing the door when he entered the house instead of leaving it wide open as Gen had done.

"You want to walk around and sit on the deck in the backyard?"

It would be more comfortable and private than standing on the front step. Not that many people were out on the quiet street. Besides, there were low bushes that ran the length of the walkway, providing a semblance of privacy.

"Here's fine."

Cynthia sat on the step below where Sanura stood, holding her giraffe print designer handbag on her lap. They both wore slacks, so sitting on the step wasn't as unladylike as it would've been if they were in skirts. They used to sit like this all the time when they were girls. As Sanura joined Cynthia on the step, she didn't recall the concrete being so hard and unforgiving on her behind.

Sanura didn't speak. She had no desire to rush her friend and knew it counterproductive to do so. So, she waited, running down a mental checklist of all the things she'd packed and still needed to pack. She and Assefa would be gone for only a long weekend, but Sanura didn't want to forget something important, like her birth control pills or the black bikini lingerie she purchased a week ago. Assefa hadn't seen it yet, and she couldn't wa—"

"I had a miscarriage."

Sanura's rambling brain skidded to a halt, backed up and then paused. What had Cynthia said?

"Almost five weeks ago. I started bleeding and cramping, and it wouldn't stop." Cynthia's light-brown fingers clutched at her handbag, her blue eyes on the darkening street and not the speechless woman to her right.

Shit. Cynthia had been pregnant? Sanura had known she and Eric were trying to conceive. But a miscarriage. Hell.

Sanura wanted to reach out to her friend, to pull her into a much-needed embrace. But the way Cynthia held herself, in a tense ball of stress and sadness, Sanura remained where she was.

"Three times, Sanura. Gods, three times."

She knew. The first miscarriage occurred six months after Eric and Cynthia were married. The second a month before Eric's rapist of a brother violated Rachel, his witch but not the were-cat she wanted as her mate. Tough times for the friends, but they'd more or less had gotten through the traumas together with Sanura playing the dual role of friend and psychologist.

Cynthia reached into her bag and pulled out a couple of tissues, and wiped harshly at her tears.

"I don't get it. What's wrong with me?" Tears ran down Cynthia's freckled cheeks, her face turned to Sanura, eyes a heartbreaking shade of depression blue.

"Oh, sweetie, there's nothing wrong with you." Scooting closer, Sanura tugged Cynthia to her side with a single arm, letting her friend rest her head on her shoulder. "Nothing is wrong with you. You know Mom's story."

Cynthia sniffled and nodded. "Two miscarriages before you came along."

Sanura stroked Cynthia's hair, sandy-brown dreadlocks pulled back in two braids.

"Both you and Eric have been to several doctors, including from our witch community. There's no physical or magical reason why the two of you can't conceive, or you carry your baby to term."

"Then why does this keep happening to us, to me?"

"I don't know. I wish I did." Being the fire witch of legend was of no use at times like these. What good was her high magic level when she couldn't spare her friend pain, find the answer to her sister's concern?

Sam and Makena had taken in a sixteen-year-old Cynthia when her mother had passed away, leaving them legal guardianship over a child whose father had abandoned his wife and daughter when Cyn was a little girl.

There was nothing they wouldn't do for each other. But this, the pain of repeated loss and sense of failure and guilt, didn't fall within the domain of magical fixes.

"Eric doesn't know, does he?"

"I didn't even know I was pregnant, hadn't noticed I missed my period."

Ah, hell, what a horrible way to find out.

"Eric was on rotation at the fire station when it happened and Gen at her friend Jalia's house for the weekend. I handled it on my own."

She'd handled it on her own, which meant she'd driven herself to the emergency room, no one at her side, no one to hold her hand and no one to cry with her. Cynthia should've called Sanura, Eric, Makena, someone, dammit, instead of suffering alone and in silence.

She lifted her head from Sanura's shoulder. "Don't be mad. I couldn't talk about it. I didn't want to talk about it, not with you and definitely not with Eric. I knew what your advice would be. I didn't need or want a psychologist. Sometimes, Sanura, I just need you to be my sister and let me do the wrong thing because it's all I can handle at the time."

Sanura understood, despite how helpless it made her feel to stand by and do nothing while her friends hurt.

"I should've called, though. I shouldn't have let so much time go by without calling."

"No judgment, Cyn. No blame. I was worried, knew there had to be a reason why you were distant."

"But my distance and silence hurt you."

"I'm a big girl. It's fine."

Cynthia wiped the last of the tears from her eyes. "As witches, we get only one male who can impregnate us, all others are biologically incompatible. It's so rare for a were-cat to father a child by more than one witch. But Eric's father did. What is that, Sanura, a one in a billion chance?"

She had no idea, but she grasped Cynthia's point.

"It's unfair. A drunkard like Mr. Garvey, who didn't give a shit about his sons, managed to have three children by two different witches. And Eric and I struggle to have one. Just one, Sanura. Fuck, and we can't even do that."

After Eric's mother escaped her abusive, alcoholic husband, filing for divorce and sole custody of her sons, Eric and Stephen, Mr. Garvey, years later, married a young Chinese woman. Genji Zhou-Garvey was the product of that union. Like Cynthia said, a biological rarity in the witch-were-cat community.

Knowing her friend had emotionally bottomed out for tonight, Sanura hugged her tightly for long minutes. "I love you, Cyn."

"I know. I love you, too. I'd never do anything to hurt you." Cyn wrapped her arms around Sanura. "Never. Please know that."

She did.

CHAPTER THREE

Assefa spotted Eric's and Sanura's cars when Zareb pulled up, parking his SUV across the street from Makena's house. In the driveway, next to Makena's silver Audi Coupe, was Ulan's high-performance Mercedes Sedan.

"Uncle Ulan is here."

Zareb snorted. "Did you think he would pass up a chance to eat one of Makena's delicious meals and further ingratiate himself into her life? Chief's so obvious. It's embarrassing to watch."

"There's nothing wrong with letting a witch know you're interested."

"Yeah, well, some women have a way of making a man lose his mind when they're around. I thought Chief was better than that." Zareb punched Assefa in the shoulder. "I already know you aren't. Sanura has you wrapped around her pretty little fingers, and you don't give a damn." Zareb's gaze swept past Assefa and to the house. "Dammit, I was hoping she wouldn't be here."

Assefa followed his best friend's frowning eyes. On the front step sat Sanura and Cynthia, heads together and talking. Their reunion pleased Assefa because he did not like seeing his witch unhappy, which she had been without her friend in her life.

"She's married."

"Shut up."

"And her mate is probably in the house."

"Are you trying to pick a fight?"

"No, I'm trying to prevent one." Assefa snapped his fingers in front of Zareb's eyes until he tore them away from Cynthia Garvey and focused them on him. "She's Sanura's best friend, and she's a happily married witch. Whatever is going on between the two of you, pretend it doesn't exist."

"It doesn't exist because nothing is between us."

A lie. True, Zareb hadn't slept with the woman. Assefa was also fairly certain Cynthia would never betray her husband with another man. But the lack of physical contact didn't mean that nothing was going on between them. Cynthia and Zareb found each other attractive, which wasn't surprising since they were both good-looking people. The problem was that Zareb was attracted to her, no matter how much he denied it. From what Sanura told him about the night of her birthday party when Cynthia met Zareb, the water witch returned the were-cat's feeling of attraction.

The last thing anyone needed was Eric catching Zareb stealing glances at his beautiful wife. The way he was doing now, watching her from the truck with the same obvious longing he'd accused Ulan of a few minutes ago. Zareb, despite what he thought of himself, was no different from Assefa. They both wore their hearts openly for the women they wanted. In this case, however, Zareb would have to stow his tender emotions for the water witch. Which, clearly, wasn't sitting well with the Bengal tiger.

"She's sad."

"Who's sad?"

Zareb pointed his finger in Cynthia's direction.

Assefa looked at the women again. "She's just talking to Sanura. I can barely see her face with that big bag on her lap." She did sit hunched in on herself, so, Assefa supposed, that could be what Zareb used to draw his conclusion. But Assefa didn't think so, not with the concerned way Zareb watched Cynthia and the certainty with which he'd spoken the words.

"She's upset. Probably been crying."

Assefa swore under his breath. None of this was good. "Why don't you drive home?" Before Zareb could protest or question, Assefa opened the door and slid from the truck. "I'll ride back with Sanura and give your excuses to Makena and the others."

Zareb frowned but didn't argue. The man had to know the little obsession he had with Cynthia could only end badly. The less they saw of each other, the better. Affairs were messy at best, bloody at worse, especially when witches and were-cats were involved.

His jaw ticked and his eyes darted, once more, to Cynthia, who now stood, waving at the two of them. Zareb waved back but stayed in the truck. "She's mated," he said, more to himself than to Assefa.

"I'm glad you realize that."

Zareb squared his shoulders and put the truck in drive. "But she shouldn't be. Not to him." A forceful hand slammed against the steering wheel, followed by a low, bitter growl of, "To hell with her. She made her decision."

Not daring to wade into those hostile waters, Assefa pushed the door closed. Zareb pined after no woman, especially not a mated one. Right now, if his friend wanted to awaken to a hot, sexy body in his bed, he could make it happen. Women found the tall, dark, bald-headed Sudanese just that appealing. So, this thing with Cynthia had nothing to do with sex.

He waited for Zareb to pull away from the curb before he strolled across the street and straight to his smiling fire witch. Before he had a chance to greet either woman, Sanura had her arms around his neck, body pressed into his and hugging Assefa as if he'd been gone months instead of a single week.

He waved at Cynthia, who shook her head at Sanura's sweet, exuberant welcome. Then she stared down the street, in the same direction Zareb had driven, thoughtful yet dreamy. When she returned her gaze to Assefa and caught him watching her, a guilty blush formed.

"Hi, Assefa. I'll, umm, see you two in the house. I haven't said hello to Makena yet." Cynthia dashed up the steps and into the house, the scent of ashamed disappointment trailing after her.

"So, you two made up?"

"We did."

"Do you want to tell me?"

"Later."

"Why did Zareb drop you off instead of joining us for dinner?"

"For the same reason Cynthia ran into the house after watching his truck disappear down the street."

He hugged his witch, loving the unabashed way she'd greeted him and the feel of her warm, curvy body against his. "Missed me?"

"You know I did."

The kisses began at his ear, soft, little nibbles to his lobe, then his cheek and jaw, traveling down to his neck and the high collar of his gray dress shirt. Circling back up, Sanura continued, finding the left side of Assefa's face and gifting it with the same sweet attention as the right. By the time she reached his mouth, his hands had dropped to her hips. His breath was hot, heart thudded, and lips parted for her sublime tongue.

Sanura kissed him with the same enthusiasm as her welcome back hug. Hands moved to her bottom and pulled her into him. For the first time since meeting Sanura, Assefa was grateful the woman didn't wear one of her dresses, showing off, to exquisite effect, her long sexy legs. If she had, if he'd been able to feel the silky-softness of her legs rubbing against his as they kissed, his greedy hands would've relished taking full advantage, exploring terrain they knew so well.

By slow, regretful degrees, Assefa pulled out of the kiss, remembering they'd shared their first in this very spot about four months ago. Their eyes met, and Assefa knew Sanura recalled the same memory.

Her hands came to his cheeks, cupping his face, voice tender and sincere when she spoke. "Back then, you were so much of what I wanted and everything I was afraid to have."

Assefa knew she spoke the truth. Still, they shared only a partial mate bond. Her fire spirit had claimed his Mngwa as mate, but Sanura hadn't yet accepted his binding bite.

Her heartfelt grin had Assefa smiling in return, unwilling to ruin the moment and Sanura's confession with his foreboding thoughts.

They'd made it through the summer without any more deaths linked to them, Mami Wara, the water witch of legend, or the prophecy. But Assefa didn't trust the silence. Too many had died because of the water goddess' machinations. For Assefa, it wasn't a matter of *if* something would happen but *when*. The Day of Serpents would come.

"We'll be ready. And we'll fight. Together."

Yes, Sanura was made for him. She knew Assefa in a way unexplainable by science and the laws of nature.

She was right. They would fight, not because they had no choice but because their protective nature would allow for nothing less. Yet Sanura was also wrong. They were not ready. And he feared, no matter what they did or how well they planned, when the lull finally gave way to terror and war, it would take more than togetherness to save the world and themselves.

By the time they made their way into the house, everyone was just sitting down at the table. Makena sat at the head of the table and Ulan, predictably, claimed the chair to her immediate right with Cynthia to her left. Next to Cynthia sat Eric and across from the couple was Gen.

Assefa held out a chair for Sanura. He sat to Sanura's left and on his other side was Rachel. The petite woman smiled at him and said something about Sanura being "too sensitive" and not being able to "take a joke."

Well, he'd heard what Rachel Foster considered "jokes" and he'd yet to laugh at one of them. Besides being as bright and as adorable as a woodland faerie, the earth witch took far too much pleasure in poking fun at people, unaware or simply uncaring where her barbs landed.

Glancing around the table, Assefa couldn't help but feel blessed. The assembled group were only a small portion of the friends he'd made since moving from the Sudan and to America. His band of brothers had come with him, and Ulan was already there, but the Williams women, the Garveys, Rachel and even Mike, filled a void in his life and heart he hadn't known needed filling.

They were a true family, loving and accepting each other, faults and all. In two days, Assefa, Zareb, and Sanura would be in the Sudan with Ulan joining them a couple of days later. They would celebrate the birthday of Ulan and Jahi Berber, and Assefa would finally introduce Sanura to his family.

The thought thrilled and frightened him, for so many reasons. But one reason mattered more than the others. It was this, the easy way everyone in Sanura's life got along, the way they could gather and laugh without fear of stepping on a landmine, the detonation exploding in an emotive shower of ego and obstinacy.

Sanura patted his knee under the table, her touch letting him know he'd gone quiet and introspective far longer than he'd realized. Dinner was over and everyone, except him, were stuffing their mouths with homemade apple pie. His own plate of pie and ice cream sat in front of him, cinnamon sprinkled on top, a shining spoon on the rim of the plate.

He dug in, not one to let dessert go to waste. Makena smiled when he helped clear the dishes after a second helping of dessert, with melted chocolate and whipped cream. Gods, the woman really was one fine cook.

"One more round," Rachel whined. "Just one more."

Sanura shook her head. "It's late, and we have a long drive back to VA. Besides, you only like *Cards Against Humanity* because it's as insane as you are."

Once Gen had slinked off to a guest bedroom, cell phone in hand, earbuds in and gossip echoing her escape from the adults, Rachel had run out to her car and returned with a black box with white cards. From there, it was all downhill, the cards and combinations crude and obscene yet strangely funny. But Sanura was right, they had more than an hour drive ahead of them, and they should be going.

"Okay, okay, what about a song? You could sing something for Ulan since it's his birthday in a few days."

The request was made of Sanura, and all eyes turned her way, which Assefa didn't understand.

When Sanura said nothing, her face falling, Rachel gestured to the acoustic piano in a corner of the living room. It was a lovely instrument he'd paid little attention to and never saw anyone play. He'd assumed, like the treadmill and heavy bag in the basement, that it belonged to Sam and Makena had held onto it for nostalgia's sake.

Apparently, he was wrong, and Sanura could not only play piano but sing…?

"Come on," Rachel pleaded, clasping her hands in front of her dramatically and blinking up at Sanura as if she would erupt into tears of disappointment if she refused. "Just one song. I haven't heard you sing since… since…"

"Sam's funeral, you forgetful imp." Cynthia rolled her eyes. "Sanura hasn't sung since Sam's funeral. You were there. Why in the hell are you even bringing that up now? We don't ask her to sing anymore. You know that. Gods, Rach, sometimes…"

Rachel appeared both remorseful and ashamed, her eyes falling away and down.

"It's okay, Cyn. Rachel didn't mean any harm. She never means any harm."

Cynthia glowered at Rachel, who seemed unable to make her mouth work to offer the apology he saw in her glassy eyes. No, the woman hadn't meant to cause Sanura pain, but she often spoke without thought, which made her comments no less injurious.

"Sanura I—"

"It's okay, Rach. I'm not upset." Sanura leaned down and kissed Rachel's cheek, then whispered something in her ear Assefa couldn't hear. The shorter woman nodded and hugged Sanura.

And just like that, the tension in the room dissipated. Even Cynthia, who looked as if she wanted to slap Rachel for her insensitive prodding of Sanura, sighed and calmed.

His tricky witch. She'd used calming magic to bring a quick resolution and prevent an argument among the friends.

Five minutes later, they were at the front door.

"Have a safe trip." Makena hugged first Assefa and then Sanura. "Call me when you arrive and when you return."

"I will, Mom." Sanura hugged her mother again before taking hold of his hand and pulling Assefa out of the house.

He listened for the telltale sign of Makena locking the door, then the subtle scent of ward magic going up to protect the house and the sole occupant within.

The Garveys, Rachel, and Ulan were already in their cars, headlights, and engines on. Sanura waved to her friends before using her key fob to unlock the doors for them. They climbed in, Sanura tossing her purse in the back seat before buckling up.

Ten minutes into their drive home, Assefa turned to her. "So, you can sing and play the piano. It would've been nice to know that about you. Anything else I don't know that you want to share?"

CHAPTER FOUR

Sanura waited for the garage door to lift completely before driving her car into her space. Assefa's silver Benz was there as was Mr. Siddig's and Omar's vehicles. Manute's spot was vacant, which she expected. The cheetah, per Assefa's orders, had traveled with Mr. Siddig to Delaware. After Joanna Blackwell's death, Dahad Siddig had been restless, his grief profound.

The trip had been Sanura's idea. The older man needed a distraction from his thoughts of loss and love. More, Mr. Siddig's sense of purpose and self-worth had taken a heavy blow with the death of his witch. When Assefa mentioned his desire to bring more were-cats into the Sankofa community, Sanura remembered a small group of unaffiliated cheetah shifters in Delaware.

Her father had made a couple of overtures to the alpha, but the man had been intimidated by the size and might of the Sankofa community and by Sam himself, an imposing six-three jaguar shifter. But there was nothing obviously threatening about either Mr. Siddig or Manute, no matter that each shifter was as vicious and trained in battle as were-cats twice their size.

The trip would serve multiple purposes, which Assefa had understood. The men were due to return home soon, although unlikely before Sanura, Assefa, and Zareb departed for the Sudan.

Sanura reached behind her and grabbed her purse from the back seat. After locking the doors, she noticed another empty parking space.

"Where's Zareb?" She'd assumed the agent would've driven straight home after dropping Assefa off.

"I don't know. But I doubt that he's alone."

They stared at each other across the hood of Sanura's car, letting their shared thought go unsaid. Better Zareb find a sex partner who wasn't Cynthia than do something stupid and ruin a marriage.

Cynthia would tell Eric the truth tonight, about the baby and miscarriage, which would free her friend of guilt and lies of omission. Yet one lie would remain between the husband and wife, no confession made about unexplained and unwanted attractions, about illicit and wistful desires. Because, in an unguarded moment when Cynthia spotted Zareb in his truck, staring at her, the witch's magic had flared to life, her water spirit awakened and interested.

Sanura had pretended not to notice, standing when her friend did, Cynthia's arm going up to wave at the man who should not have the kind of impact on her that he did. She'd explained Cynthia's distance these past few weeks. She'd given Sanura permission to share her secret with Assefa since she planned on revealing the truth to her husband when they returned home.

Sanura would've kept Cynthia's confidence, of course, but was glad she didn't have to. As it was, she hadn't been completely honest with Assefa when he'd asked about her singing and playing of the piano.

"Let's take a walk before going in."

Shrugging off his blue suit jacket, Assefa tucked it in the crook of his arm before taking Sanura's hand and walking away from the house. By silent agreement, their stroll steered clear of the Potomac River, which buttressed Assefa's property. Too much had happened down there, mainly the death of Gayle and Callum Livingston, Assefa's friend, and housekeeper and her mate.

"There's space in the living room for a piano. I could move the—"

Sanura tugged Assefa behind a tree and kissed him, enough to silence his offer.

"Thank you, but I don't need you to buy me a piano. In fact, Assefa, you don't have to buy me so many gifts. Don't get me wrong, I love and appreciate everything you do for me but you spend too much.

Everything I want, I don't need. And I don't expect you to go out and buy me a new piano because you now know I can play."

She thought he would frown or even argue, but Assefa only wrapped his arms around her and smiled.

"And that's why I don't mind splurging on you."

"Because I don't want you to?"

"Precisely. You never ask me for anything, not even subtle little hints. You live within your means. Your car and clothes, all very nice, but within your means. You buy what you can afford on your professor's salary."

"Okay, what am I missing?"

He kissed her. "There's not one piece of jewelry, painting, or item of clothing I've bought you that you couldn't have purchased yourself, including the piano that I *will* buy for the living room."

"I can't afford a five thousand dollar piano," which an acoustic piano like her father's would likely run her. It had been Sam's piano, her father the one to teach Sanura how to play, his grandfather having taught him. Sanura would also teach their children, but that was a conversation for another day.

"Do you even know how much you're worth, the value of Sam's rental properties?"

Sanura knew, but how did Assefa?

"Mom handles Dad's businesses. She has a team of managers, lawyers, and accountants. I stay out of it unless she needs me to sign something."

She had never wanted her father's money. She'd rather have him instead. And yes, she knew how much Sam had left her in his will as well as the value of each apartment building he'd owned. Just because she didn't actively involve herself in the business, it didn't also equate to a lack of knowledge.

"You buy so little and ask for even less, which makes me want to spoil you. That's not how I grew up, which you will soon see. We Berbers ask for everything and get even more in return, much of which we don't deserve and haven't earned. But you have access to so much but never touch it. I respect that, and your parents for raising you to value friends and family over money and power. If it makes you uncomfortable, though, I'll curb my gift-giving."

She knew he would if she asked him. But he'd shed light on the reasoning behind his extravagance. His expensive gift-giving, no doubt, an example set by his father. Assefa's gifts weren't attempts to buy her affections or assuage a guilty conscience, or any number of questionable reasons why some men bought expensive gifts for women. For Assefa, he gave so freely because he found a partner who wanted nothing from the billionaire but himself. Still, Sanura didn't want him buying her so many presents.

A piano would fit her plan perfectly, which Rachel's big mouth almost ruined. She did miss playing, the act soothing. Her memories of sitting on her father's lap as a girl were vivid when she immersed herself in the music and the feel of the keys under her long fingers.

"I'll buy it."

"But—"

"I'll buy it. If you do, it'll be so expensive I'll be too afraid to touch the thing. I'll purchase something nice but within reason."

Despite what she'd said earlier, she could afford to buy a piano, even a five thousand dollar one, on her salary. Not that she intended on spending that much on a piano. Then again, it would be an investment in the musical upbringing of their future children.

They rarely spoke of the future, and not only because of the prophecy. Assefa didn't yet believe in a happily-ever-after for them. He didn't know if Sanura was willing and ready to give away her last physical connection to her father.

As much as Assefa believed in her, he still lacked true faith, which was painful yet understandable. Soon, however, he would believe. Sanura would make sure he did. Beginning now.

Grabbing his suit jacket, she dropped it to the grass, along with her purse. And, before he could ask what she was about, Sanura undid Assefa's belt, button, and zipper.

"Ah, sweetheart, what are you doing?"

"I think that's pretty obvious. I'm witch-handling your orgasm-giver."

He couldn't help himself, Assefa burst into laughter. "My what? Have you been talking to Zareb because that sounds like something he would say about his penis?"

"Of course not." Her sure, warm hand stroked him and Assefa closed his eyes. "But it is, which makes me one lucky fire witch."

With Sanura's hand down his boxers, sure fingers around his "orgasm giver," Assefa felt like the lucky one.

"We shouldn't be doing this outside."

"Why not? The property is protected by a four-element ward, and everyone is away from the mansion except Omar, who's probably holed up in his room reading a book no one other than him and the author has heard of."

"True but—"

Her left hand skated up his chest, popping buttons as she went. Her right hand was still doing amazing things to his throbbing penis, which was beginning to weep thankful tears from her balls-tightening up and down motion.

"Sex outside is on your list."

Assefa's eyes flew open. "What list?"

Pushing the fabric of his shirt out of her way, Sanura bent and claimed a nipple, biting and sucking and making all kinds of nasty, delicious sounds against his chest.

"The list you have in your head." A soft squeeze to his penis, her finger gliding over the wide tip. "Not this head, but the other one. The one that's trying to figure out how I know about your list."

He did want to know because, damn her, he had one and it sure as hell wasn't written down.

"All men have a list of places they want to have sex with their girl-friend or wife." She flicked her tongue over his collarbone, faux-brown eyes lifting and watching him watch her enjoy his taste on her tongue. "And you, Special Agent Berber, are no exception."

There was something both arousing and humbling about how well his witch knew him. Without a doubt, he'd fantasized about making love to Sanura outside. A short skirt or dress normally factored into his daydream, not the sexy, tight, but long white jeans she wore today.

In his dreams, she was on all fours, dressed rucked up to her waist and Assefa—

To her knees Sanura went. Her eyes lifted to his, fingers gripped, and she kissed the tip.

Okay, Assefa was a flexible man. Let it not be said that a Berber was incapable of making on the spot adjustments to a plan.

Sanura kissed him again, lingering then opening her mouth and sucking on the head. Damn, just the aching head. Those amazing eyes of hers, her natural green hidden behind the magic of her moonstone, still gazed up at him.

Their eyes locked. Assefa was incapable of looking away from the love he saw with each inch of him she swallowed. When he was in her mouth as deep as she could take him, Sanura closed her eyes. His head tipped back against the tree as Sanura pleasured him, fulfilling an un-spoken fantasy.

She devoured him, taking him deep and then pulling all the way back, tongue rimming the bulbous head before gliding back down his shaft again.

Yes, just like that. Keep going. Keep. Going.

One hand settled on her shoulder while the other in her hair, ruining the asymmetrical curly updo she'd likely spent a fair amount of time to get just right. Gods, he was close.

Sanura drew away and Assefa wanted to whimper.

Standing, Sanura tugged down her blush off-the-shoulder top. She twisted him, so he was behind her, and she was facing the tree. Lifting one of his hands to the button of her jeans, she encouraged him to pull down her pants.

He did, with Mngwa speed and hunger.

Sanura dropped to her hands and knees, ass bare and inviting. She glanced over her shoulder, eyes sultry with lust and challenge. "Claim your witch. Go big or go home."

Assefa claimed his witch. He was big. She was loud. Afterward, fingers linked, they walked home together.

Omar was neither reading nor in his bedroom. He was, however, waiting outside Assefa and Sanura's suite, appearing uncomfortable when he saw them, looking and smelling of sex.

Slipping past the tall man and into the suite with a quick and self-conscious, "Hi, Omar, have a good night," Sanura left the men in the hallway.

"Is there something you wish to say to me?"

Assefa had a good idea why the man was there, and he damn sure wasn't going to make it easy on him by stepping in and giving the lion shifter an order from his alpha. It was past time for Omar to man up and put his life and family in order.

"I assume there's room on the plane for one more?"

"Perhaps, depending on who wants it and why."

"You know why I want it."

"Five years, Omar."

"I know."

"You ran."

"I know."

"If you hurt her again—"

"She was the one who refused to see me the last time."

True, but the weak excuse wouldn't take Omar far, especially not with the person who mattered the most to him.

"We depart at nine. Be ready."

"I'm already packed."

"That's not what I meant." Assefa opened the door and stepped inside the suite, Omar's soft, "I know," his troubled retreat.

CHAPTER FIVE

Khartoum, Sudan

"I heard the prodigal son is returning, and he won't be alone."

Tracey Kemraha shivered, the Grimba Forest not the most appealing place to meet. Yet the darkness and lateness of the hour, combined with the remote location, made this a smart meeting place. They were surrounded by towering trees, muggy air, and long-awaited anticipation. No one could see them together, which made tonight's outing, so close to the eve of their plan, both dangerous and important.

The tall, arrogant man, dark eyes devoid of any emotion except contempt, stared at her, his green-and-black military fatigues blending into the forest in a way her royal blue outfit did not. She despised him, her means to an end, just as much as he loathed her.

"I see you still know far too much that takes place within the presidential compound. I would guess a spy if I didn't believe you were capable of finding out all you needed to know by yourself."

His sneer and slight baring of teeth reminded her, intentionally, she knew, of his power and standing. Out there, and all alone, there would be little Tracey could do if he decided to wrap his hand around her neck, breaking it as easily as he did the trust of those who dared to love the pampered prince.

If given enough time and physical space, she could defeat the werecat in a one-on-one battle. But shifters like him understood the limitations of witches. She didn't bother stepping away from the predator. He would only follow, guaranteeing she'd have only a second to begin a spell. Then he would be on her, ripping her throat out with fangs or claws and leaving her bloody, dead body to the scavengers.

"I have my means, but I don't know anything about the woman Assefa's bringing home. What can you tell me about her?"

She hadn't seen Assefa in years. Not that he hadn't been home since he'd departed for the States. He had. But he'd come and gone, and never sought her out, which angered Tracey. He was hers. It was time he stopped running, returned home for good and made her his mate. Yet, if the rumors were true, Assefa wanted his family to meet a woman he'd met in America.

"I need you to get as much information as you can on the extent of their relationship and anything else you can dig up about her. She's obviously a witch. Assefa would never bring a full-human before the general supreme. I need to know how powerful she is and who trained her."

He said nothing, just continued to stare down at her from his height of six-five. Chiseled and dark, he was a handsome were-cat, but his soul was ugly, mind cruel and heart ice-cold. She hated him, truly, deeply, and with a desire to commit bodily harm. If he were anyone else, and she didn't need him, a suffocation spell would put an end to his heartless existence.

"You know the prophecy."

Observant eyes cast over her head and to the trees and blackness behind her. He scanned the landscape for anyone foolish enough to make themselves known to the vicious were-cat.

"Do you think he found her?" Black eyes lowered with his question.

What was it with the Sudanese and their obsession with the prophecy? Even a monster like him believed it, and he didn't believe in anything but his own self-worth.

"I know what some ancient scroll says, seen the cave drawings near the Temple of Sekhmet, but I don't believe in the prophecy. I believe in making and controlling my own destiny and damn the old ways."

He smiled, gorgeous and treacherous.

"Mistress Kemraha would be disappointed." Reaching out, he made to touch her cheek, but fear and self-preservation had her rearing back and her lips parting to cast a binding spell.

Mocking laughter slapped the spell out of her mouth.

"You're enchanting, Tracey. You're so willing to sacrifice a mother's trust and reputation for the heart of a man who left you. Assefa never looked back, yet you still want him."

"Don't speak as if you're superior to me or ask as if your motives are purer than my own."

If possible, his eyes hardened even more because there had been no humor in them, not even when he'd laughed.

"Choose your next words carefully, or they will be your last."

His words were a snarled warning she didn't take lightly.

"I don't want to argue with you. We don't have to like each other or even agree with the other's motivations. But we do need each other. If we work together, we'll get what we both want."

Even the devil, when so disposed, listened to reason. The cold-hearted were-cat did as well, nodding his assent before turning on his booted feet and disappearing into the night.

When she reached her car, locking herself inside, Tracey's heart finally slowed. She was certain something had stalked her from the forest and to the side of the road where she'd parked her vehicle. Raising her second sight, she searched the darkness. The first two scans, Tracey saw nothing, just inky blackness and ageless trees. But on her third sweep, she saw it, saw them—rich golden-yellow eyes.

She gulped. He'd wanted her to see him, wanted Tracey to know he'd let her reach her car and live. *The three-legged son of a dog. Assefa should've killed him that night six years ago. He would've done the country a favor if he had.*

Wiping the sweat from her brow, she sighed with relief when those savage, threatening eyes vanished. She got it, tell no-one about him, or he'd finish the hunt.

Infuriated, Tracey jammed the key in the ignition and started the car. In a few days' time, she would have Assefa in her bed and under her spell. Once she did, once they were married, the deformed dog's ass would meet with an untimely and untraceable accident. And she would never have to see those scary golden-yellow eyes again.

"It's late. Are you sure you want to do this tonight?"

Sanura sat at the foot of their bed, body still tingling from the shower she'd shared with the man standing in front of her, bare except for a thick gray towel around his waist. She wanted to make love again, so tasty did her mate look—dark skin, broad shoulders, cut abs, and a shy dimple that came and went at its leisure. But she'd had him twice already. If they made love again, even a short session, they may just fall asleep before she did her duty to her familiar.

"I'm sure."

"You don't have to."

"He wants it. And so do you."

"What about what you want?"

"I want every part of our relationship, which you've already given me."

They'd engaged in the spirit fire three times since she'd gifted Assefa with her father's wedding ring and her promise. She would take him as her full-mate and eventually as her husband. Yet her failure to accept his claiming bite left his Mngwa without the full magic and comfort of her fire spirit. So, while the human side of Sanura and Assefa could bask in the physical pleasure of being together, their inner spirits were denied the same security and well-being.

"It's not guilt, Assefa." He'd never used the word before, but his insistence on posing the same question before each ritual made his unspoken concern clear. "It's my gift, part of my promise."

If she didn't have special plans for the final part of their handfasting, Sanura would pull him to the bed, push her hair away from her neck and let him bite her, no ritual, just his delicious fangs in her soft, willing flesh. But she did have plans for her were-cat, which made the spirit fire ritual both necessary and fair. Because no matter the reason, or deep her love, a partial mate bond was simply unfair.

"Your gift?"

"Yes. And it's free."

"Let it go, Sanura. I'm buying you a piano. End of discussion."

"'End of discussion?' That's a bit high-handed of you, Special Agent Berber?" She crossed her legs, relishing the fall of his admiring eyes and the tongue that peeked out to lick sexy, full lips.

Golden Mngwa eyes lifted to hers, and she thought he would forego the spirit fire ritual and pounce, making Sanura pay in the most sweat-inducing way possible.

"You're asking for a spanking."

"Maybe." She uncrossed, then crossed her legs again, the silk of her short robe riding higher and showing even more of her thighs.

Flat on her back she went, Assefa's bulky body on top, lips hard and hungry, tongue deep and demanding. His hands pushed her robe up and yanked his towel away.

Then he was inside of her, creating a different kind of spirit fire between them. Gods, what would sex be like with Assefa once they were fully mated? She couldn't imagine it being any better than this, them wanting each other more than they already did. They'd never leave their suite, this bed, expiring from exhaustion and an extreme case of hedonism.

Fifteen minutes later, he rolled off her, beautifully naked and breathing like he'd run a 10K.

"T-three minutes. Give me three minutes, then I'll shift."

He took five, which she also needed. Sitting up, she watched as Assefa slipped from the bed only to take his place in front of her again at the foot of the bed. For the ritual, no clothes were needed for him, and Sanura had never wanted any barriers between his fur and her skin, so she didn't put back on her robe.

The sight of his change never ceased to amaze Sanura. She'd never seen a were-cat shift as effortlessly as Assefa. Shimmered. That word always came to mind whenever she watched him go from man to beast. The molecules that comprised his body broke apart and reconfigured themselves so swiftly that even with Sanura's advanced second sight, all she ever managed to see was a twinkle of light right before his Mngwa appeared.

With a girlie squeal, she threw her arms around the humongous neck of her familiar. Gods, what a magnificent animal, Sanura's arms barely long enough to cuddle his neck.

I believe we did this earlier, sweetheart, Assefa spoke in her mind.

"Not like this." Burying her face in the thick black-and-gray fur of her Mngwa, Sanura smiled, loving the feel of him in her arms. "I missed you."

He knows. He missed you, too. And her.

Her inner spirit began to hiss and wail, wanting freedom from the cage Sanura kept her locked in, afraid to let the fire beast off her leash and what she'd do once emancipated.

But there, with the Mngwa, Sanura could give her inner spirit, if not absolute freedom, more than she'd had before they started performing the spirit fire ritual.

Releasing the nearly seven-hundred-pound cat, whose gigantic claws and teeth were capable of bloody, life-ending damage, she stepped away.

For long minutes, the Mngwa circled and eyed the floor of the bedroom, his golden orbs taking in the area with a critical, discerning gaze.

"For Oya's sake, Assefa, it's just a floor inside our private suite. How dirty could it be? Pick a spot and lay your big behind down."

He growled, showing lots of white, sharp teeth.

Sanura rolled her eyes and pointed to the empty floor space in front of her.

You could at least pretend to be afraid of my saber teeth. I am the predator of all predators, after all.

An arched eyebrow, hands on hips, and a foot tapping with impatience were all the response his statement deserved.

Selecting, purposefully, a location on the other side of the room, the Mngwa reclined in all his legendary glory.

"Suit yourself." Sanura made her way to the colossal baby and waited for him to lie on his side when she reached him.

Climb up on your magic carpet, my fire priestess.

Smiling, she did, stomach down, face pillowed against his strong, throbbing neck. One hand went to the top of his head, the other splayed on his chest.

Do you wish to go first tonight?

Always the gentleman. "No, you should go first."

After a week away, hunting serial killers, Assefa needed this part of the ritual far more than Sanura. Even with the lateness of the hour, and Sanura's fatigue, she would stay awake as long as it would take for Assefa to shore up his soul with the ideals of Ma'at.

The Mngwa's golden eyes stared off, looking at the closed balcony doors, but Sanura sensed he saw replayed images of the cannibal dwarves he and Zareb had punished.

I benefit without violence.

Ah, the second of Ma'at's forty-two ideals, principles of good, upright living that began with the ancient Egyptians. The idea of codified morals did not end with the forty-two ideals but could also be found under Mosaic Law and the Ten Commandments, religious systems of thousands of full-humans. Of the faithful, of those preternaturals, like Assefa and Sanura, and like those of the Sankofa community who believed in the principles of Ma'at, they strove to uphold the ideals in their daily lives.

Sanura began to caress the Mngwa's head, knowing how much Assefa detested violence, although his job, as well as his heart, demanded he protect innocents. She wondered if he would state the negative confession most closely aligned with the ideal. Sanura knew not to push. She understood Assefa had to see himself and his Mngwa as vessels for right and truth, not blood and death.

I have not committed murder, neither have I bid any man to slay on my behalf.

The first of forty-two Negative Confessions, declarations of sins one did not commit during their life, normally stated upon death before the gods of the underworld, the heart of the deceased weighed against that of Ma'at's white feather of truth. The soul would either be allowed to cross the Lily Lake to the Field of Reeds, to live eternity with their loved ones, or the heart-soul judged as unworthy of paradise and devoured by Ammit.

"Yes, that's it. Not murder, my Mngwa, but righteous justice."

A sweet purr of gratitude had Sanura scratching the back of the big cat's ears eliciting even more purrs from her familiar.

I do the best I can. I remain in balance with my emotions. I advance through my own abilities.

Old territory. These were three of Assefa's favorite principles of Ma'at.

I follow my inner guidance. I honor animals as sacred. I do good.

Yes, he did.

A lengthy silence followed, the Mngwa still staring off and Sanura's fingers working their way through the cat's dense fur.

I think that's enough for tonight, sweetheart.

"How do you feel?"

Better. With you, like this, alone and together, I feel so close to understanding our true purpose in life. But it won't quite come into focus.

This wasn't the spirit fire spell, but the prologue, as Sanura's come to think of it, to the spell itself. They began this ritual the night they'd returned from Baltimore, having completed the Oshun ceremony and receiving the blessings of their union from the Sankofa community of witches and were-cats. It had been a night of violence, blood, and lies, but also of love, friendship and hope.

She'd never heard or read about any other witch-were-cat couple doing what they now did, not every night but as often as they could. Sanura had known, instinctually, this self-created ritual needed performing.

Each time they engaged in the ritual, she grew even closer to Assefa but also closer to finally understanding her fire spirit. Unlike Assefa, who thought the answers they sought external and knew only by the gods, Sanura believed the truth resided within them.

She'd thought about tonight's ritual while Assefa finished in the shower. While the ritual, for Assefa, was an opportunity to purge his soul and clear his conscience, Sanura used it to speak her heart to the man she loved.

"I can be trusted. I am trustful in my relationships. I do the best I can. I follow my inner guidance." Her right hand fisted the fur over his heart. "I embrace the all."

A rumble of a laugh. *Not exactly subtle, sweetheart.*

True, but a man like Assefa didn't want or need subtle. He appreciated forthrightness and honesty, which Sanura had no problem giving him because she expected the same in return.

Knowing it was time to proceed to the next ritual, Sanura closed her eyes and began to chant.

"Woman to fire, fire to woman, rise. Woman to fire, fire to woman, rise."

Her hands began to heat, and the doors to her fire spirit's cell creaked.

"You're my soul, but he's my heart, rise. You're my soul, but he's my heart, protect."

The sound of wood crackling in a hearth grew, the cell shook, and the Mngwa rumbled under her.

"Fire to beast, beast to fire, rise. Fire to beast, beast to fire, be free."

Sanura's glowing, red hands gripped the Mngwa, her entire body an inferno of emancipated fire spirit magic. Out it went in a burst of red-

and-orange vapors. The magic spread, thickened and covered the purr-ing feline in the Fire Phoenix's mantle of warmth and love.

CHAPTER SIX

Through the fog, a glimmer of light glowed in the far-off distance. Sanura lifted her hand and reached for the light, drawing back when she met bitterness instead of warmth. Sadness and anger suddenly permeated the fog, the smell of the malevolent brew rancid and ancient.

"Who are you?" Sanura asked, taking a blind step forward.

"Who are you?" echoed back, a distorted version of Sanura's voice.

Another blind step. And another. She walked along an invisible path. The feeling of sand squished below her bare feet, the tiny granules sticking to toes. As she walked toward the beacon of light, Sanura repeated the same question of, "Who are you?" After several minutes with no response, she added, "What do you want?"

She repeated the questions and ignored the reverberation of her voice, the only reply. Then there was another sound, another voice in the fog.

Crying. A baby?

Sanura stopped walking, turned in the direction of the faint sound, and listened carefully. Not a baby. A whimpering woman.

She moved as swiftly as she could, noticing for the first time her stomach round and full. Her confused mind filled in the blanks. She carried twins, a witch and a were-cat.

Hands outstretched in front of her, she inched closer toward the sound.

Closer.

Closer.

Sanura halted when sand gave way to rough ground and sharp rocks that cut into her exposed feet.

The sound came again, but Sanura dared not move. But she saw the source of the weeping, a female figure on the other side of the ravine.

Sanura's eyes dropped to the huge chasm that separated her from the crying woman, its depth forbidding.

The woman's long, reddish-gold hair was wrapped around her body like a heavy shawl, hiding portions of her nude form. Bronze and beautiful, the woman sat at the edge of the ravine, her tears the source of the water Sanura had seen at the bottom.

Out her eyes.

Down her cheeks.

Into the ravine. No splash. Just a ripple of grief and hatred.

"Who are you?" Sanura asked again.

No answer.

She waited.

No answer, but the woman's tears had inconceivably filled the ravine.

Sanura stepped back from the river's edge, the rocks cutting even deeper into her feet. The weeping woman raised her face and looked directly at Sanura. She saw them, the woman's eyes.

Blood seeped from the corners, and the beauty Sanura once thought she saw was marred by a face contorted in unbelievable agony.

Sanura took three more steps back but refused to turn and run. She had her attention now, but damn if she really wanted it. Not like this, not when the woman, the thing, looked like death incarnate.

"Who are you? Why are you here?" Sanura asked again, now fearing the answer. "What is this place?"

The woman's head twisted, glaring at Sanura with heart-clenching curiosity, then a black python, that wasn't there before, appeared. It slithered from the bloody froth of river and found the woman's leg. Slowly, it inched its way from her ankle, up her thigh and to her shoulder, where it managed to glide its way between her shoulder blades and her impossibly long hair.

There it rested, its body curled around the woman's, its head falling to her midsection, stopping right above her pubic area and looking like the scariest fig leaf Sanura had ever seen.

With blinding realization, an image popped into her mind. A scene she'd seen many times in books, museums, and paintings. She didn't believe, wasn't a Christian. But still…

"Eve?"

The woman's eyes sparked to life, black giving way to fire red. Blood blazed from them. Streaks of red slithered and stained her face, her body, her snake.

"Not Eve," the woman growled her voice a thunderous cloud of magic and threat.

She placed one foot in the river, then the other, and Sanura gasped. The river held her weight, her toes, and heels as firm on the flowing liquid as a tree on the sturdiest of soils.

Sanura couldn't move. She tried, screamed at herself to take a step backward for each one the bloodied woman took toward her. Nothing. Was she paralyzed with fear? Or simply paralyzed?

Move dammit, move.

Nothing

Thirty more steps forward. No steps back.

Nearer.

She was so close Sanura could smell her breath, volcanic ash, and death.

The blood that ran from the woman now washed over Sanura, bringing with it the scales of the python.

The snake's forked tongue slipped in her ear, hissing a threat she'd rather not contemplate. The smell of brimstone assailed her nostrils, burning them and creating a liquid mix of tears and blood.

The snake spoke to her, but it was the woman's voice she heard. "Do you know me now?"

By the gods, she thought she did.

"You think you're better than me, can do what I could not? You think his love and strength will be enough to save you, to save him? Such a little fool you are."

The forked tongue withdrew, and so did the scaly beast.

Sanura didn't watch it glide down the dead woman's body and into the river of churning blood. She was too focused on the green eyes that reminded her of her own, if Sanura ever turned into a heartless monster, adrift and angry at the world.

Those lost, soulless eyes would likely haunt her waking mind, the damned creature already haunting her dreams.

"Why are you here? What do you want from me?"

"No paradise for the wicked, young one. No Field of Reeds. No peace, just a lake of fire, endless pain, and unforgettable loss."

Arctic lips dripping with blood pressed to Sanura's forehead, hot and contemptuous. "Say my name, sister. Claim me, by right and magic."

She didn't want to say her name. Didn't want to be there, across from the monster whose blood ran through Sanura's veins.

She felt one of her little ones move within. And though she was still paralyzed, Sanura gave an inward smile. They were with her, safe inside and hers to protect.

They didn't exist outside of this nightmare, but she loved them with a ferocity that made this horrific dream feel painfully real.

An inhumanely strong hand came to Sanura's throat. Nails pierced sweaty skin, and blood droplets formed and fell.

"I said say my name, sister, or I'll slit your throat before cutting your children from your womb."

Defiant tears bubbled and Sanura, with a strength that only surprised those who underestimated her, fought through the paralyzing magic enough to raise her hand up to and over her belly. It wasn't much, but she would fight for her and Assefa's children. Kill for them. But first, she needed to survive this unwelcome family reunion.

"Fire witch of legend." She spat the name on a revolted spray of blood and spit. Not a name, but a title, a morbid fate Sanura claimed with detested forbearance.

Her blood-stained lips lifted into a satisfied sneer. Then she licked the blood from them, smacking and smiling at Sanura with a childlike devilment that sent chills down her spine.

"You think you aren't like me, but you are. Just as I was like her, the one before me. She fought and failed. Drowned then burned. Even Ammit didn't want the foul taste of our impure heart-souls in her demon belly, casting us instead into Duat's fiery lake."

The fire witch of legend flicked her eyes down to Sanura's stomach and the hand that rested protectively across it. "We should never pro-create, pass along our curse to another. But we do. We always do. And it continues, the gods never satisfied with our sacrifice. Except one, but he doesn't care, not about our hearts or eternal souls."

Bloody tears of fire filled the green of the witch's eyes, her gaze lifting to Sanura's then back to her protruding stomach. "We had a daughter once, but we left her to fight, thinking we would save the world and return to our little one." The fire witch of legend's hand crept to her naked stomach, as flat as a board. "I should've protected her, protected him… from me."

The scent of sulfur rose from the river of blood, bringing the return of the blinding, debilitating fog.

"You can't win. You aren't made to win, no matter what Oya and Ra believe. You aren't better than me, and those babes must not be al-lowed to continue the legacy of the fire witch and cat of legend's curse."

Blood fire coated the other woman's face, a macabre mask that did nothing to conceal her deadly intent.

Wet scales returned with the bitter fog, but the fire witch of legend's python wasn't alone.

Five.

Ten.

Twenty.

So many, gods, there were so many of them.

They struck, biting into Sanura with vicious, merciless fangs.

The might of their bites and bodies sent her crashing to the rocky ground. On her back and without her magic, Sanura could do nothing when the first, second, then third, and gods know how many more after that, attacked her stomach.

Sanura fought, bled, cried. But she heard her, right when the first snake broke through her stomach enough to slither inside, ripping a scream of agony and horror from her.

"You're the last of us. Let the curse die with you. Trust me, this isn't the worst loss your heart can know. Die, sister, die."

Sanura tumbled out of bed. Thrashing, legs kicked at the covers, hands pushed up nightgown and searched. Closed eyes cried and mouth twisted in a silent scream.

Her hands flew over her body, hot with magic and searching for flesh-hungry snakes to destroy. When she found none, when her right hand settled on her taut stomach, belly button perfect and sealed, not a bloody, open wound ripe for scaly invasion, Sanura curled in a tight ball and sobbed.

It wasn't until she heard Assefa's voice in the hallway, speaking to Omar, that she forced herself up and off the floor. Stumbling, she made her way to the master bathroom, closing and locking the door a minute before Assefa entered the suite.

He would see the messy bed with sheets half on and half off, but she doubted he would think anything of it. At least she hoped he wouldn't because Sanura wouldn't know how to begin to explain her nightmare to him.

They'd started the night after he'd left for New Jersey and had gotten progressively worse each night afterward, with this dream being the worst of them all. Yet the first night of his return, she hadn't dreamt. She'd hoped Assefa's presence would ward off her nightmares.

It hadn't. The fire witch of legend was growing bolder, crueler, and more violent with each dream. Her mind was playing tricks on her. The prophecy and impending Day of Serpents was a mental stressor worming its way into Sanura's psyche.

Undressing and climbing into the shower, Sanura permitted cold water to cool down her body and wash away the fleeting embers of her bad dream. She wouldn't allow nightmares to ruin her trip to Assefa's home. He was nervous enough for them both.

A soft knock on the bathroom door. "Are you all right in there?"

Ducking her head under the spray of cold water, Sanura inhaled through her nose and exhaled out her mouth. "Bad dream."

She'd told Assefa about her childhood nightmares and the return of them the night they first became intimate. But those dreams had nothing on what she now experienced.

"You want to talk about it?"

Hell no. What she wanted to do, needed to do, involved getting dressed and driving to a pharmacy or grocery store and buying a half dozen pregnancy tests. She didn't think she was pregnant. Shit, Sanura was on the pill for Oya's sake, she damn well better not be pregnant. Not like this and not now because that would make her dream divinatory instead of frighteningly hellacious.

"We can talk about it later." Much later, preferably once they returned from the Sudan. "I'll be out in ten. But I need to run an errand before we leave for the airport. I won't be long or make us late."

She could detect the worry in the silence on the other side of the door, but Assefa simply said, "We need to be in the limo at nine, Sanura. Be back before then, please."

Sanura would, without two tiny passengers, she prayed.

CHAPTER SEVEN

Khartoum, Sudan

Assefa held Sanura's hand, his grip just shy of possessive. They made their way down the steps leading from the plane and onto the tarmac. The pilot bypassed the local airport, flying them to the general supreme's personal airfield, secured by an electrical fence, video cameras, and a well-trained squad of were-leopards.

He could smell the men's cat aura. Assefa always had that ability, the one that allowed him to ascertain a were-cat's inner beast by scent alone. It unnerved many of his classmates, made them even more skittish around him as if having the name Berber wasn't bad enough. It was enough for some, many preferring to steer clear of the second son of the House of Berber lest they somehow managed to raise the ire of his father.

Yet, there were others, alpha males, who thought to make a name for themselves by challenging the quiet and smaller Berber son. While his older brother, Razi, should've been a natural ally, he often led the gang of bullies. And bullies they were, cursing and pummeling anyone who didn't fit their definition of a Sudanese warrior.

Assefa snorted, opening the door to the limousine and ushering Sanura in. Like those Neanderthals knew what it meant to be a true Sudanese warrior. They hadn't, yet they'd persisted, terrorizing children, like Assefa, who were either too afraid or too proud to do more than quietly lick their wounds and hide their shame from everyone, especially their parents.

Sanura stared out of the car window, her right hand absently massaging his thigh. She was in her own world, taking in the passing, unfamiliar landscape. He wondered if she saw the city of his birth or whether her mind was still on the nightmare she'd had and the results of the four pregnancy tests she'd taken before they'd left the house.

He'd never told her how much he wanted children, although he suspected she knew. While now would be the worst possible time to conceive a child, Assefa couldn't help the pang of disappointment that seized his heart when she revealed four sticks with minus signs. The thought of watching Sanura grow round with their baby, the tattooed likeness of the child Assefa and his protective Mngwa on her belly, had him watching her with a depth of love and want that frightened instead of soothed for how much he desired a family with her. A life of peace and safety and unfettered joy, laughter, and tears of happiness, all the emotions he'd never known as a boy.

They'd arrived at the beginning of the rainy season, although no rain clouds threatened the dry day. But he could scent rain in the air, feel the moisture in his soul. This was his city, a beautiful, bustling metropolis with over six hundred thousand residents. Twenty-five million Nubians called Sudan home, most of them witches and were-cats. There were, however, communities of dwarves and other preternaturals who preferred not to hide their identity by living among full-humans. Thanks to Assefa's despotic great-grandfather and grandfather, full-humans no longer lived in the Sudan, forced to flee for their lives but having no true understanding for their expulsion. His father hadn't withdrawn the decree after becoming general supreme, seeing the importance and strategic advantage of having one country populated by the gods first creations.

"What do you think?"

Sanura turned to him, her brown eyes smiling. "It's lovely and huge."

It was at that. Skyrise buildings towered over the two-lane streets they drove down, cars jockeyed for position, speeding up to avoid each red light. In that respect, Khartoum was like most major metropolitan cities around the world, overpopulated, industrialized, bright, fast-paced, and exhausting.

But all of Sudan wasn't like the capital. In fact, much of the country was quite rural, farming an invaluable part of the economy. Yet it was the exportation and use of crude oil that helped his grandfather turn the country around financially. Instead of permitting full-human businesses to pillage their land for its natural resources, his grandfather, then his father, had managed to extract the reserve themselves. Assefa's father, Jahi Berber, had pooled the intellectual and physical resources of once warring people, bringing them together for a common cause. His motto: There's nothing a full-human can do that a preternatural can't match and exceed.

"You don't see this side of Sudan on the news." She peered out the window again.

"You thought you would see a typical war-torn country? Bombed buildings? Homeless littering the streets? Children begging instead of in school learning?"

Sanura continued to stare at the skyline, her silence his answer.

"It's been years since the last civil war, and, yes, the visual reminders of those horrible times are no longer present. My father spent billions repairing the infrastructure of the country."

Sanura settled against him, her tall, slightly muscular female frame a perfect fit between his side and left arm. She smelled like vanilla musk today, not her natural gardenia scent her moonstone covered, which she opted to wear. Neither of them was ready to have the prophecy conversation with his family, especially his father. So, Sanura's natural hair and eye color were concealed behind a magical spell, one that made her appear as nothing more than a gorgeous African American woman with adorable brown eyes, gleaming brown hair and flawless brown skin.

"If a facelift were all it took to heal wounds, this country would be a perfect specimen." Assefa leaned in, no longer able to ignore the tantalizing line of Sanura's neck, her thick hair twisted and pulled up in a neat, conservative bun. He kissed her neck, pleased when the vein there began to throb with each wet swipe of his tongue.

"A gilded cage?" An enchanting moan followed her question.

Assefa halted his ministrations and stared at her. "Not for the people but—"

"For you," she finished, or perhaps it was a clarification of her question.

"What makes you think so?"

They sat up straight, the scenery and sensual pleasure fading. Sanura's eyes were no longer smoky with satisfaction but probing and clinical.

"You have all the material trappings of success. I imagine there was little, if anything, you ever wanted but didn't receive."

True.

"But you shouldn't feel guilty about—" Sanura's gaze shifted to the window behind his shoulder, her eyes widening, jaw dropping. He knew what had silenced and shocked her.

Assefa turned, and it was as he'd thought. They'd just driven through the gates of the presidential compound. The compound claimed twenty-five acres of prime real estate his ancestor acquired after killing a Bengal tiger shifter in an alpha duel. To secure his new position and repress revenge plots, Assefa's ancestor had also murdered the former alpha's entire family, children included.

Except for one tiger baby. That were-cat had been taken into the Berber household and raised as a medja, a protector Each generation produced another Bengal tiger medja guardian and a Berber male he would serve and guard with his life. Assefa and Zareb never talked about how he came to be Assefa's medja, his bodyguard and servant. It was there, though, in the bloody history of their families, a touted honor for the Osei clan but a badge of shame for Assefa.

This was his family and legacy. On this stolen plot of land, Kashta Berber built an estate, the home an outstanding replica of the pyramids, covered by thousands of years of sand, in the ancient city of Meroe. It was told that Alexander the Great came to Meroe thinking to subjugate the people, only to find the warrior witch, Queen Amanishaketo, atop her beastly elephant, daring the full-human foreigner to challenge the strength of her people. Her wind magic had sent him home as swiftly as the sandstorm could take him.

Whether the story was fable or fact, Kashta Berber built a pyramid fortress, the design old yet materials modern. This physical link to the past had been Assefa's childhood home, an ancient city on a hill And, yes, his gilded cage.

"A pyramid home, Assefa."

"I know."

Disbelief had Sanura shaking her head and squinting her eyes at the huge building. "A freaking glass pyramid. You could've warned a witch." She laughed, a soft chuckle filled more with lingering surprise than true humor. "Cyn and Rach won't believe me."

"Trust me, I know normal people don't live in pyramids."

He should've better prepared Sanura for this ostentatious reality that was his infamous family and their unabashed display of power and wealth. Sanura would now see, know how different they were and what becoming a mate to a Berber would mean.

"You left this behind to play cops and robbers for the FBI."

Sanura's tone couched no judgment, just an acceptance for his choices. Besides his sister, no one else understood how someone in his position would leave all of this behind.

"Like you said, a gilded cage."

Just like that, the eyes of the psychologist were back. "Did you have an unhappy childhood?"

How could he explain how the absence of a mother was as powerful as the presence of one? How could she understand a son's yearning for warm embraces when Sanura's mother had always been by her side? Yet, Sanura had experienced the loss of a parent. Her father's sacrificed death was one she still grappled with during her quiet, reflective moments.

"I was different from the other boys at school. I didn't always fit in or make friends easily. I tended to stay to myself." She reached for him, Sanura's hand finding his cheek, her eyes a soft shimmering haze of female compassion. "Even in a country full of preternaturals, there is still fear of the strange and powerful."

"We should know better, but sometimes preternaturals are no different from full-humans who discriminate against each other on the basis of skin color."

Assefa's hand came to rest overtop of Sanura's. The heat of her gaze and love warmed him in places the desert heat couldn't begin to touch.

"Are you ready, my witch?"

"To meet the General Supreme of the Republic of the Sudan?"

"No, to meet my father, Jahi Berber."

"Semantics." Sanura nodded her head in the direction of the line of soldiers in black military fatigues, gun holstered at their side, were-cat eyes vigilant, stance rigid and ready to defend. "Tell me if I'm mistaken, but this is quite literally the House of Berber."

For better or worse, it was.

"I can detect the magic around the pyramid from here, no need to even use my second sight. This may be your home, but it's also a military and political installation. Jahi Berber may be your father, but he's also the ruler of this mighty country of witches and were-cats." Leaning close, she brushed her lips across his. "I may not want anyone to know I'm the fire witch of legend, but I've never felt more of a need to be her than I do right now. My fire spirit agrees. This place, this land, is old. With old land comes ancient and deadly magic and creatures."

For the briefest moment, Assefa considered having the driver turn the limousine around and return to the airfield. But the door had just opened, Zareb on the other side, his hand outstretched to Sanura. When he opened his mouth, suddenly questioning the wisdom of bringing Sanura home, she smiled at him with such sweet acceptance Assefa almost missed the fierce pulse of magic he felt through their partial mate bond.

When Sanura accepted Zareb's hand, permitting him to help her from the car, he had no idea of the devastating effect this weekend would have on all the important relationships in his life.

CHAPTER EIGHT

Sanura adored Africa, the continent large, diverse, and beautiful. But it was also old, the cradle of civilization. While Rachel, with her special earth magic, would be capable of communing with the flora and fauna of this great ancient-modern city, it produced the equivalent of an allergic reaction within Sanura. Her magical senses were abuzz with tingling vibrations from old and current aura signatures, from dead and restless souls and from treacherous and greedy magical pulses.

The forces, unseen and unfelt by everyone else, including Assefa, threatened Sanura's control. The urge to vomit after burning this pyramid to the sandy foundation soured her stomach and awoke her fire spirit. Too many ancient empires had this effect on her, particularly sites of great battles, horrendous deaths, and vile plots.

Sanura sensed them all, the magic and the dead calling out to her, whispering their chilling secrets, evil deeds, and bloody deaths. Not in words, not even through sight, but in the brush of magic against her aura, an uninvited stroke to her senses.

She gripped Assefa's hand harder, using his strength of spirit to keep Sanura from casting a spell that would obliterate every specter in this building, in this goddamn city of sand and ruins. She was too attuned to ever be comfortable there, not with her level of sensory awareness. On principle alone, Sanura disliked every powerful witch in this city. They had done this, created and maintained a dimensional abyss, a prison, as much as it was a place to hide their sins and secrets.

Assefa's sister had to know. He'd told Sanura Najja was a level six wind witch. Although, with being the twin sister of the cat of legend, Sanura suspected Najja's magic level was closer to that of Makena's, which would make her a hell of a lot stronger than a damn level six.

Which also meant the woman could not be ignorant to what dwelled beneath this pyramid of wonder and wrath.

For the last few weeks, Sanura had looked forward to visiting Assefa's ancestral home and meeting his family. Now she couldn't wait to return home, grateful her work schedule prevented an extended stay.

With a caution that had nothing to do with being a visitor to a foreign country, Sanura scanned the large foyer, taking in every detail. While the outside of the structure harkened back to a time of kings and queens, the interior was quite modern. Three vertical rows of square wall sconces decorated the angular walls. Fluorescent light beamed from honey art glass panels, the etched glass bottom panels giving off maximum light. Three mosaic wall sconces, with dark bronze bases and gold accents, triangulated to highlight a stainless-steel reception desk, three potted plants, two black leather sofas, seven black-and-white armchairs, four glass top round wooden end tables and one beautifully poised receptionist.

The receptionist's smile was pleasant, her frame tall and elegant in a black fitted dress that managed to be both professional and sexy. Her light-brown eyes twinkled with a little something extra when Assefa turned to her and spoke. For a second, a blue tinge formed in her eyes before disappearing. The same phenomenon happened to Cynthia's eyes when she saw something she liked or wanted. It was a sign of two things: the receptionist was a water witch, and she found Assefa attractive, desired him even.

How many times had this happened to Sanura since becoming involved with Assefa? Too many. Restaurants. Museums. Movies. Even the blasted natural food market not far from Makena's Mount Washington home, it never failed. Winks, lingering smiles, and soft feminine tones followed Assefa as if he were some sort of Pied Piper of sex-starved females. To make matters worse, the women ignored Sanura's presence at Assefa's side, she no more important to them than their obvious lack of decency.

"Nice to see you again, Chanya."

Assefa spoke to the receptionist in English, although everyone since they'd landed in Khartoum had spoken to them in Wolof. She didn't know whether they assumed she also spoke the language since she was there with Assefa, or whether they didn't care whether the American understood them or not. She appreciated Assefa's consideration, although he knew of her Wolof lessons with Rachel.

She hadn't mastered the language, but she'd learned enough to understand most of what the pilot, limo driver, and soldiers had said to them. Just as she understood the receptionist's reply to Assefa, delivered in Wolof and in such a sugary-sweet manner that Sanura had no doubt the woman spoke perfect English.

"It's nice to have you home, Master. Berber. The general supreme is in his office, awaiting you and your guest's arrival." Chanya's eyes shifted to Sanura, taking her measure in a single sweep of her body.

To her credit, the water witch's face revealed none of what she thought. But Sanura knew. She'd dismissed her and her witch level, probably wondering why "Master Berber," and gods how Sanura despised that title, would waste his time with a witch so beneath the mighty cat of legend.

Good. The less the local witches knew about her the better. Besides, Sanura had no intention of being there long enough to disabuse them of their assumptions. Because, to Chanya, and those of her ilk, Sanura, with her moonstone firmly in place, registered as witch prey, weak and vulnerable.

Chanya hit a buzzer and a set of glass doors opened to the left of her desk, which Assefa escorted them through, Zareb right behind them.

When Zareb moved to flank her, she wasn't surprised to see him smiling down at her. The were-cat was sinfully handsome and knew it. He also enjoyed flirting with her, especially in front of Assefa.

"Do you know how deceptively adorable you are?" He laughed and flicked the tip of her nose with his index finger. "The best part is that you aren't even pretending to be someone you aren't. This is really who you are, how you are, but not nearly *all* that you are."

"Leave her alone, Zareb."

"Come on, you know it's true." He nudged her with his elbow. "I mean, your gorgeous, that's no deception." His deliberate leer made Sanura want to roll her eyes. "But you're so much more than you appear, which is sizzling hot, by the way."

At that, she did roll her eyes.

"You make a were-cat want to—"

Assefa's growl had Zareb laughing but shutting up and falling back. He walked behind them as they made their way down the long hall and to a battery of elevators.

A single person stood in front of an elevator, dark of complexion and broad of shoulders. Another soldier, from his stern, unyielding bearing, not that the man wore a military uniform like the other soldiers she'd seen. Instead, he'd squeezed his massive body into a black suit and white shirt. How long did that tie of his must be to fit around that wide neck of his? Could he even breathe? What in the world was in the water in the Sudan because, for Oya's sake, every were-cat she'd seen was built like a tank, battle-ready and capable of inflicting major damage?

"Master Berber." The tank lowered his eyes when he'd addressed Assefa, unlike Chanya who'd held his gaze with a woman's appreciation. "The general supreme is expecting you." He nodded to Zareb. "Thank you, medja. Your services will no longer be required, while Master Berber and his guest are within these walls. You're dismissed."

She heard Zareb's rumble of a growl, a second before Assefa pulled her to the side and stepped between the men, his eyes on the tank, his back to his friend.

"I will say this only once." Assefa's voice, low and full of icy warning, chilled the air. "Never speak to Special Agent Osei as if he's a servant again." Assefa stepped closer to the man, whose eyes had dropped to the floor the moment Assefa began speaking. "Now remove yourself from in front of the elevator so that we can proceed."

Without another word, the large were-cat hastened to obey Assefa's cold command. It clicked, when they filed onto the elevator, the tank huddled in the corner as far away from Assefa as the small space would allow. The witches adored Assefa, his handsomeness and kindness, while the were-cats feared him, his intensity and might. Some, Sanura expected, feared him to the point of hatred.

A gilded cage indeed, and a dangerous one at that. No wonder Assefa had fled country and family.

Once off the elevator, the tank asked, with a meekness that even had Assefa grimacing, "Is there anything else you require, Master Berber? I'm at your service."

She didn't think Assefa wanted anything from the were-cat except for him to go away.

"Please verify that a guest room has been prepared for Mr. Omar Wek. I'd imagine he'll want to rest and freshen up after he's met with his father."

Ah, right. Omar's father was the Executive Chef to the General Supreme.

"Why won't you tell me again why Omar decided, at the last minute, to travel with us here?" Sanura asked after the tank pulled out his cell phone and climbed back onto the elevator, barking orders to whoever was on the other end of the line.

Assefa led the way toward a huge door at the end of the corridor. "Because I want to see how long it takes you to figure it out."

"To figure what out?"

"Omar's secret." Zareb flicked the tip of her nose again.

"Stop doing that." She shoved him away from her when Zareb made to squeeze her face as if she were a chubby cheek toddler, and he a doting grandfather. "So, the two of you know but won't tell me?"

"We kind of have a bet, Dr. Williams."

Sanura frowned at Zareb, knowing he'd called her that deliberately. Of Assefa's clan of brothers, only too-formal Omar referred to her as Dr. Williams.

They stopped at a set of doors, which were, at once, magnificent and intimidating. The doors were impractically high, extending from floor to ceiling. The country's flag, a white background with a black jaguar claw print in the center, was surrounded by a raindrop, a flame, an acacia tree, and a wind turbine. The lovely four-element design had been elegantly carved into the center of each massive door.

She reached out and glided a hand over the smooth grooves of the red-and-orange flame, ignoring Assefa and Zareb's conversation about Omar and their bet. A part of her caught sight of the two sentries stationed beside each door, wearing the same style of suit as the tank, their frames were just as wide. Wary yet respectful were eyes on Assefa and not the "deceptively adorable" woman who stood touching the only barrier between herself and their general supreme.

"I'll wait for the two of you out here," she heard Zareb say.

"Are you ready, sweetheart?"

To fly home, yes. To meet his father, hell no.

"I'm here, and he's waiting. We might as well go in."

Assefa bent to whisper in her ear, his lips full and warm. "Thank you for this. It means more than you'll ever know. I only wish I could've met your father. It would've been an honor."

Reaching for his hand, Sanura had never been prouder to stand by Assefa's side, as when one of the sentries pushed the doors open and ushered them inside.

CHAPTER NINE

Twenty-Four Years Earlier
Phoenix, Arizona

Water fizzed, pushing the white bubbles upward and toward the laughing, playing girl, only to have two anxious hands grab a fistful and pull them to a smiling face, blowing.

"Again, Grandma, again."

Sharon placed her right hand, palm down, an inch above the bathwater and recited a spell she'd learned decades ago. Ripples upon ripples of water and bubbles churned, heating the water in the process. Not too hot, but enough to prolong the private moment between Sharon and her beloved granddaughter.

More blowing of bubbles and laughter. This time of the night, an hour before her granddaughter's bedtime, was her absolute favorite. While her daughter, Christine, cleaned up from dinner and made lunch for the next day, Sharon took care of the little water witch, her father still at work.

At the thought of Andre, Sharon bit her lower lip, forcing down the frown her granddaughter would misinterpret as directed at her.

Her son-in-law was a problem. Hell, he'd always been a problem. From the first day they'd met, his dark-brown eyes had stared at her, challenging Sharon to comment.

She'd said nothing. Christine wouldn't have listened, even if she had brought up the obvious. A black man with a white woman wasn't that unusual in Phoenix, but it also wasn't popular either, especially among some of their full-human friends.

So, she'd attended their wedding, accepting their witch-were-cat mating long before they'd exchanged vows, their handfasting proving their biological compatibility. Andre's Bengal tiger was Christine's familiar, and she his water witch to love and to protect.

And he did love Christine, would lay down his life for her and their child. Wasn't that a mother's blessing? To have such a strong and devoted were-cat mated to her daughter, capable of producing mighty tigers to carry on his proud family legacy?

Sharon lifted her own family legacy from the cool bathwater. An hour of magical use was her limit. Patting the little girl down, making sure to dry every inch of the child before wrapping her in a light-pink robe, Sharon held her granddaughter's hand when they made their way out of the bathroom and to the pink-and-yellow bedroom across the hall.

Christine and Andre would have more children, now that the precocious water witch, crawling under her covers, pajamas on and sandy-brown hair combed and pulled back into a ponytail was in kindergarten. According to Christine, they'd waited for the "right time." Now, apparently, was the right time for them to expand their family.

If Sharon didn't act soon, her daughter would be pregnant again, with Andre even more determined to keep his family in Arizona. And while Andre Walker's powerful Bengal tiger genes would grant the couple strong sons, Christine had little to offer a witch daughter from the union.

Level two witches could not produce level five witch daughters, no matter the power level of the witch's were-cat father. Like produced like or even less, but rarely more. A high-level witch giving birth to a daughter with a low magic level was just as unheard of, although it did happen.

Sharon and Christine were level two witches, as were Sharon's mother and grandmother, as was the impatient girl waiting for her bedtime story.

But a level two witch wouldn't do and neither would Arizona. No matter what, Sharon had to convince her daughter to move to Maryland. That's where they needed to be, where her granddaughter would surpass every low-level witch in Sharon's pathetic family. Not a level five witch, or even a six or seven. Her granddaughter would be so much stronger than that, the mightiest witch of this generation.

She'd be the water witch of legend. All that stood between that glorious future was a loving but problematic father.

Grabbing a book from the nightstand, the one they began last night, Sharon kissed the child's forehead and began to read.

She didn't regret the pact she'd made with the water goddess, although Sharon had no desire to see her daughter and granddaughter in pain. But when Andre Walker would fail to return home tonight, no trace of the father, husband, and emergency room doctor found, they would be hurt by his abandonment.

But sacrifices had to be made, acts of loyalty offered up to Mami Wata in exchange for power and privilege.

Children were raised by single mothers all the time. Christine would eventually get over the loss of her mate. And the little one, fading with each word spoken, the long, warm bath, more than the story, pulling the child into slumber, would survive the loss of her father. Hell, in a few years, Sharon doubted the five-year-old would remember the man at all.

She read until the child fell asleep, a stuffed tiger clutched to her chest, a gift from Andre.

When Sharon turned off the overhead light and clicked on the nightlight, she took one last look at her granddaughter and smiled. With Sharon's help, she would make a magnificent water witch of legend, defeating Oya's fire witch and elevating all water witches in the process.

The Day of Serpents couldn't come soon enough for Sharon. As for Andre Walker, well, his Day of Serpents should be starting about now.

"Father, I would like for you to meet Dr. Sanura Williams." Assefa motioned to the approaching man. "Sanura, this is my father, Jahi Berber."

Sanura looked at the tall man, whose face she would recognize any-where, so strong was the father-son likeness. Uncanny really, almost to the point of being spooky. She'd always thought Assefa resembled Ulan, which he did. She'd assumed since Ulan and Jahi Berber were fraternal twins that Assefa would share the same level of resemblance to his father.

She'd been wrong. In the face, Assefa and his father literally looked like the same person with Jahi Berber's graying hair, goatee, eyeglasses, and over thirty years age difference inconsequential distinctions be-tween the men. The man's eyes were as enticingly dark as Assefa's, covered by wire-rimmed glasses Sanura assumed were more for politi-cal image than utility, for were-cats had preternatural vision. Those perfect seeing eyes of his were as observant as any predator, taking Sanura in, from her smiling lips to the hand linked with Assefa's to her pink-and-navy stripe sleeveless dress to the three-inch heels, which didn't begin to place her at his eye level.

Like Assefa, Jahi Berber's complexion was as lovely as Hawaii after sunset. That was where the similarity ended. General Supreme Berber had at least five inches on Assefa, placing him well over six feet in height. His shoulders, while broad, weren't as wide and linebacker thick as Assefa's. And whereas Assefa prided himself on wearing tailor-made suits, Jahi Berber gave off a much more relaxed energy. The man donned no suit or tie. Instead, he wore an all-black dashiki brocade pant set, the one-piece top falling nearly to his ankles with a matching black with gold-trimmed kufi atop his very dignified head.

People always told Sanura she was the spitting image of her mother, but she could never see what they saw. Looking at the two men, she now wondered if Assefa could see the almost frightening resemblance between himself and his father. Perhaps it was this physical similarity that had sent Assefa running away from home, fearing the family re-semblance was more than skin deep.

Sanura stood frozen, unsure how to best address the man the world thought of as Bloody Berber. He appeared normal enough, despite the blackness of the eyes gazing upon her, as unreadable as his son's when Assefa was in FBI mode.

A Berber male Assefa had told her countless times. Having now met three Berber men, Sanura could see his point. And while she'd yet to meet his older brother, Sanura doubted she would discern something different in his eyes than what she saw in Assefa's, Ulan's and Jahi's, dangerous, serious, intelligent.

She had no problem envisioning Assefa's grandfather and great-grandfather ruling this nation with an iron fist and a wickedly handsome smile, seducing witches and terrifying were-cats.

Shattering Sanura's wayward thoughts of despotic Berber regimes and men too handsome and powerful for their own good, her mind snapped back when Jahi Berber pulled her into an unexpected hug.

"It's my pleasure to meet you."

Stunned, Sanura did nothing while the man held her, firm yet gentle, his long arms wrapped around her shoulders, tall frame leaning down as if he would lift her off her feet. Then the sly jaguar sniffed her, subtle and quick, before releasing Sanura.

She pretended not to notice, knowing whatever answers he sought about her went unanswered. The look he gave her as he pulled away nearly hid his confusion. But she'd detected the slight shift in his aura, his inner cat interested in the newcomer whose smell he wouldn't have been able to identify.

Reaching for his son, Jahi took hold of Assefa in a crushing embrace, and Assefa returned the hug, holding his father just as tightly.

It was a beautiful sight, father and son. Assefa rarely spoke of his father, but Sanura had known, even in his silence, how much he loved and respected the older man. Assefa needed this visit more than he would ever admit, especially to himself.

He'd told her he didn't care what his father thought of him, his decisions and his American lifestyle. But that wasn't true. Assefa cared deeply for his father's good opinion of him, which included his choice of a life partner.

"Thank you for coming home, son, I've missed you."

Sanura went to step back, intending to grant the men a bit of privacy, but Jahi caught her left hand, stilling her movement.

"My son didn't exaggerate, young lady. You're beyond lovely, adorable in fact."

Sanura refrained from sighing her annoyance. What was it with Sudanese men and that word?

He held onto her hand, and Sanura was sure the man was still trying to figure out what in the hell he was missing about her.

"Any woman my son wants me to meet is a woman I'm happy to welcome into my home." Delivering her hand back to Assefa, he added, "And into my family. When's the wedding and how long afterward do I have to wait for my first grandchild?"

Assefa glared at his father, but Sanura found herself laughing, amused by his deliberate attempt to test and unsettle her.

"She has a doctorate in psychology, Father. Sanura won't fall for your tricks."

"How do you know? I've been told I'm very charming. Wouldn't you agree, Sanura?"

"I suppose when you're not smelling women without their permission."

"Ah, caught that, did you? I must be losing my touch. While we're on the subject, explain to me why you don't smell like a witch?"

They weren't on that subject, and Sanura wasn't going to have the moonstone and fire witch of legend conversation with the man.

"I'm a fire witch, Mr. Berber, as I'm sure you've been made aware."

"I have, and you may call me Jahi. After all, you're my son's mate, which makes me your father-in-law, even without a wedding American witches and were-cats are so fond of engaging. But I must admit, I'm looking forward to traveling to the States and bearing witness to your union."

Jahi clapped Assefa on the shoulder. "I wasn't joking about grand-children, son. I want them, sooner rather than later. Your brother refuses to even look for his mate and your sister—"

"What about me?"

They all turned, smiles plastered on the men's faces, Sanura the only one not having heard the woman enter the office before she spoke.

Between Sanura's nerves and the odd man that was Assefa's father, Sanura hadn't noticed the door that connected Jahi's office to the one next door.

"I wondered how long it would take you to finish with your meeting and join us. Have you seen your older brother? He was supposed to be here as well, to welcome Assefa home and to meet Sanura."

Before Sanura could process the utter wrongness of the woman's aura signature, much less the disapproving tone she'd detected in Jahi's voice when he'd asked about his eldest son, Assefa was across the room, hoisting his sister into his arms and swinging her around.

The tall, lean woman threw her head back and laughed, her arms wrapped around her brother's neck, joy palpable between the twins.

Sanura found herself grinning from the unabashed display of love between Assefa and Najja. Assefa's unchained adoration for his sister pulsed through their partial mate bond, thrumming with tenderness, trust, and safety.

The bond of twins, she'd once read, rivaled that of the bond between mates. Until this moment, Sanura hadn't agreed. But seeing Assefa re-united with his sister, his twin, Sanura had no doubt their bond would stand against anyone and anything.

"Put me down, you womb hog," she laughed.

"You told me to come home, and now that I'm here you think to boss me around even more." Assefa kissed her cheeks before settling Najja, with care, back into her motorized wheelchair. "You get more beautiful every time I see you." Assefa knelt in front of Najja. "So very lovely that I forget what an absolute menace you can be."

Najja Berber was beyond words like lovely and beautiful. Assefa's sister was stunning, not that Sanura thought she wouldn't be, being the sister of such a handsome man as Assefa. Despite them being twins, however, Najja and Assefa looked nothing alike. Sure, they shared the same tall frame, dark eyes, and skin color as their father but that was where the physical similarity ended.

Everything about Najja Berber was lean, from her long, manicured fingers to her slender neck, shoulders, arms, and waist. Short black hair with natural spirals accented a face made for movies and magazines.

Their mother must've been quite the beauty if Najja resembled the deceased Berber female.

"A menace, huh? Your manners are abominable, brother, no matter the compliment that preceded the insult." Najja caught Sanura's eyes over Assefa's right shoulder, glinting with amusement and mischief. "You must be a saint of a witch, Sanura, to willingly take on this Berber male, who thinks himself charismatic yet insults a woman he claims to love."

Assefa pressed a kiss to Najja's forehead, then stood.

"Sanura, this is my troublemaker of a sister, Najja Berber, who has even less tact than my father. Don't let her sweet smile and dulcet voice fool you, though, I'm convinced she's more Mngwa than wind witch."

Sanura couldn't help it, she gaped at Assefa. Where had her conservative special agent gone? Even wrapped in his father's arms, the stoic, cool Assefa remained. But there, in the presence of his sister, was the man she only saw when they were alone and Assefa completely at ease.

A small part of Sanura was jealous, but a larger part of her was relieved Assefa had Najja in his gilded cage with him. Without her friendship, humor and love, Sanura shuddered to think what kind of man Assefa would've grown into.

When Jahi Berber pointed one authoritative finger at a tall, familiar figure standing in the doorway where Najja had exited, she knew exactly how Assefa could've turned out. Because, no matter how charming and deliberately provoking Jahi Berber could be, the man couldn't conceal his true nature. He may not be as ruthless and heartless as his own father, but he also wasn't as reformed as he wanted his son to believe. Secrets, he reeked of them.

"Why are you here?"

"Not so charming now, are you, Father? He's my guest."

"An uninvited guest. Did you think to ask your sister if she wanted him here?"

"Despite what you and Najja believe, the two of you don't own the country. Citizens can come and go as they please. This is Omar's home as much as it is yours. His father still lives here. Can a man not come home to visit his own father? Or do you think to deny Omar that basic right?"

Omar entered the general supreme's office fully, blatantly ignoring the glowering man's hard gaze. Instead of answering Jahi's question or retreating under the weight of the ruler's frosty disapproval, he walked to a silent Najja and bent to her side.

"We haven't finished our conversation."

"I've said all I needed to say."

"That still leaves half of a conversation between us because I have a whole hell of a lot to say. And you're going to listen."

Wait. What? Had the world turned on its axis? Meek, polite Omar had just dismissed General Supreme Berber while also demanding an audience with the Secretary of State.

When Sanura's eyes shifted to Assefa's, it was to find him smiling at her. She couldn't help but wonder who'd won the bet, Assefa or Zareb because Sanura had figured out Omar's secret.

CHAPTER TEN

Razi stood in front of the general supreme's closed office door. He could hear nothing within, his grandfather smart enough to have the room soundproofed. Yet he didn't have to hear to know who was in there with his father, Assefa and his American witch.

Did the general supreme really think Razi had the slightest interest in dragging himself out of his witch's bed and to his father's office to greet his little brother? He'd bet his millions that Najja was in there, on time and fawning all over Assefa the way she always did, the way too many in the country did.

Razi glanced over his shoulder and to the man standing twenty feet behind him, back against the wall, posture deceptively relaxed. His eyes traveled to the open suit jacket, pushed back to reveal the butt of the black gun at the medja's side. The men's eyes met, and there was no friendship or warmth between them. There never had been.

If given proper provocation, Zareb Osei would shoot Razi dead without any regret. And if given the opportunity, provocation or not, Razi would do the same to Zareb, a bullet between the eyes or in the back.

They understood that much about each other, which was why neither had yet killed the other. The day was still early, who knew what the next twelve hours would bring?

Razi nodded, then smiled at Zareb, a small baring of fangs the were-cat would interpret as the threat that it was. Pushing back his suit jacket to reveal even more of his gun, Zareb nodded and smiled in return. Oh, yes, they understood each other very well.

Having decided to forego the family reunion and find his bed for a few hours of sleep, Razi nearly growled when the door in front of him opened.

"Nice of you to finally join us. You're late. I asked you to be here by eight."

"I had an early meeting and it ran over. I apologize, General Supreme."

"I'm not the one who deserves your apology." He gestured with his chin to Assefa, who stood to the general supreme's right. "Your brother has had a long flight and would like to rest and freshen up. It would've been nice if you'd showed him and Sanura the courtesy of being here on time."

As usual, the general supreme's voice echoed with disappointment when he spoke of Razi in relation to Assefa.

"Good to see you, Razi. You're looking well." Assefa extended his right hand, which he took in a firm grip. "This is Dr. Sanura Williams. Sanura, this tall gentleman is my brother Razi."

To her credit, the woman beside Assefa didn't so much as pause, grimace, or gape when he offered her his right hand to shake, scarred as it was. His left arm was half gone, his black shirt sleeve rolled up to the mangled stump.

"Nice to meet you, Sanura. Please accept my most humble apology for my lateness." Raising her hand to his lips, Razi kissed the back, tempted to open his mouth and take a lick of her soft, smooth skin.

What would Assefa do if he tasted his woman, a woman who smelled unlike any witch he'd ever met.

He held her hand longer than was polite, nostrils flared, jaguar confused yet intrigued. So was the man.

Najja sped past them all, a flustered Omar Wek right behind her.

Where in the hell had he come from? Razi thought he'd seen the last of the coward a couple of years ago.

By the time Razi refocused on the woman too damn sexy and beautiful for Assefa, she'd reclaimed her hand and Assefa didn't look pleased with him.

Razi grinned. "I look forward to seeing more of you, Sanura. Maybe we can walk and talk and get to know each other better. There's a topiary garden on the grounds I'd love to show you. While we're there, I can tell you the story of how I lost my arm. Unless," his brown eyes locked on Assefa's, "my little brother already regaled you with that family story. If that's the case, I have plenty of others that may interest a woman as attractive as you."

Even though he knew it was coming, the fist to his jaw sent him back but not down.

"Pulling your punches, little brother, or has living in America made you soft?" He swallowed the blood in his mouth, unwilling to give Assefa the satisfaction of knowing he'd drawn first blood.

It was nice to know he could still push Assefa's buttons, though, get around that prided self-control of his.

"You haven't changed. I don't even know why I hoped you had." Assefa stepped around Sanura and right into his face, the shorter man staring up at him with the same anger and disappointment he saw in the general supreme's eyes. "But you won't use Sanura as a tool to hurt and punish me for your failings as a man and were-cat. Sekhmet help you, brother, if you ever touch Sanura again, the way you just did, I won't stop with one pulled punch."

Yeah, they understood each other, too. Brothers.

"Father, Sanura didn't sleep well on the plane. She needs to rest."

Assefa handed the witch off to his medja, who'd come up to stand beside Razi. Together, they walked down the hall and toward the elevators, the same direction Najja and Omar had gone, which left the Berber men alone. Between the kiss to Sanura's delicate hand and the punch to Razi's jaw, the general supreme's guards had disappeared, no one, after the last time, wanted to be anywhere near the fighting brothers.

"Is she always so quiet and polite? Docile and manageable? I wouldn't have thought it of a fire witch." Razi's sneer didn't begin to capture how he felt about his brother. "Maybe she's not a fire witch at all, definitely not the fire witch of legend. But she does smell delicious and so very lickable that I'd like to have a taste."

"Shut your mouth, Razi."

"Why, Father, Assefa's a grown man? From what Najja told us, he's now an alpha of a witch council. But I think his flameless fire witch got him the job."

"I said shut your mouth."

Razi laughed, stepping away from Assefa, whose eyes glowed Mngwa gold. Yes, Razi recalled the last time those eyes had settled on him.

"I'm only playing with Assefa, Father. Can no one in this family take a joke? You're going to have a great sixtieth birthday, now that Assefa is home. He's the son who makes you the happiest, proudest, and now he's come home for your birthday." Razi laughed again, loud and with all the bitterness he felt. "He's also brought you another daughter to spoil. All women like to have gifts lavished on them, isn't that right, little brother? Even a witch who doesn't smell like a witch at all."

"Be warned, brother. When it comes to Sanura, I won't tolerate your malicious tongue and deceitful actions."

"Or you'll finish what you started six years ago?"

Assefa's golden Mngwa eyes bored into him until they returned to their normal dark-brown. Now that his little witch was gone, the man had regained control.

Interesting. This visit would prove to be even more satisfying than Razi had thought, now that he knew how much Assefa cared for his American girlfriend.

"Sanura and I will see you at dinner, Father."

"Seven sharp."

"I remember."

Razi and the general supreme said nothing as Assefa made his way down the hall and onto an elevator.

"That was mean and unnecessary."

Mean, yes. Unnecessary, no.

"Sanura Williams may not be the fire witch of legend I thought Assefa would bring home, but I like her and you'll show her the proper respect due her as a mate to a Berber."

Proper respect? As if the general supreme knew the first thing about treating a mate with proper respect.

"Of course, Father. As I said, your sixtieth birthday will be one to remember. I'll make sure of it."

"Thank you."

"You're welcome. After all, what are sons for?"

As expected, when Assefa arrived at his bedchamber, Zareb stood in front of the door, the perfect image of a medja on duty.

"Thank you. How's Sanura?"

"I'm not sure. She didn't say a word the entire way here. She's almost as good as you are about concealing her thoughts. You know, Assefa, I used to think that whatever Sanura uses to hide her witch scent from predators only did that and changed her hair and eye color. But after today, I think it does more. It never occurred to me before, but I think it also does something to witches. Did you see how Chayna looked at her, almost through Sanura, as if she didn't count at all? A witch should be able to spot another witch, especially a level five witch like Chayna."

Assefa agreed. He knew Sanura wore her moonstone, but he also knew she had a habit of modifying a spell if she thought it ineffective for a particular situation. He assumed, based on the unusual reaction from Chanya, that she'd upgraded the spell of her moonstone before leaving home.

"I think my witch is working very hard to not upset the delicate witch power balance here by bringing unnecessary attention to herself."

"Is that a wise tactic? I mean, the local witches will just view Sanura as prey?"

"The important point is that they won't think her a threat, especially water witches looking for a way to impress the general supreme and elevate their status by challenging the fire witch of legend."

"Watch your back."

"Razi doesn't frighten me."

"I know he doesn't, but I don't trust him, especially around a woman like Sanura."

Unfortunately, neither did Assefa. He had no desire to harm his brother again, but Razi would do well to heed his warning.

"What do you mean by 'a woman like Sanura'?"

"Do you really want to know because I like my jaw the way it is?"

"I won't hit you." His friend didn't seem convinced. "I give you my word."

"Fine, but don't say I didn't warn you. With or without her moonstone, Sanura's smell makes a were-cat want to protect her, worship her, spoil her, or fuck her. In your case, it's all four." Zareb raised his hands, palms up, in front of him. "Don't hit the messenger."

He had no intention of attacking Zareb. He'd done enough of that for one day. Besides, Zareb only voiced what Assefa had come to understand about Sanura these past months. It was the reason why the Witch Council of Elders wanted her as their next high priestess. The fire witch exuded untapped divinity, garnering witch allies through her kind nature and honest spirit. And she commanded were-cat's attention, even when she didn't wish it.

"I think we should take her home."

Assefa did as well. But why did Zareb?

"As adorable as she is, Sanura's power as the fire witch of legend is not at all pretty. When she saw us sparring, not knowing it was me and thinking my tiger was trying to hurt your Mngwa," Zareb shook his head, true fear entering his eyes, "I've never been so afraid of death than I was at that moment, surrounded by her hellfire."

"She wouldn't have hurt you."

"Yeah, she would've. To save you, your Mngwa, her fire spirit would do anything. That's what I believe, and that's what I saw in Sanura's eyes that day."

"She would never hurt you."

"Not now she wouldn't. I trust her with my life. She's as loyal as they come and as fierce. But Sanura also has a soft heart, which doesn't match her inner fire spirit. I think we should protect the balance she's developed and take her home before the scales tip into a direction no one will like."

Assefa couldn't deny Zareb's cautious stance, not after witnessing Razi's fascination with Sanura and her quiet but cold response to the were-cat. However, Sanura was far too self-possessed to harm Razi because he got too close or discomforted her. But three dead siren sisters and a cursed Paul Chambers were testaments to what happened when someone threatened Assefa and those Sanura loved.

"Stay vigilant, my friend."

"Always."

Zareb stepped aside so Assefa could enter his suite.

"Go home, see your parents, and get some rest. Dinner is at seven if you wish to join us."

"Seeing my parents sounds like a good idea. Mom has called me three times since we landed. She wants to see you, too, by the way, and meet Sanura." Zareb sighed. "Don't take this the wrong way, but I really don't want Mom to meet Sanura. She'll just remind her that I haven't settled down yet."

"Or found your mate."

Zareb's eyes flashed with anger then hurt. "Yeah, that too."

Assefa closed the door on a brooding Zareb. One of these days, his friend would have to come to terms with whatever in the hell kept putting that frown on his face and dent in his heart and armor.

CHAPTER ELEVEN

Except for the gorgeous, half-dressed woman in his bed, silver, high heel sandals on the floor, dress draped over the back of a chair, Assefa's bedroom looked the way it had several years ago. When Assefa turned eighteen, his father hired an interior decorator to redecorate his room, proclaiming Assefa no longer a boy and whose bedroom should reflect his new status as a man. Gone were his glass display of fútbol trophies and pictures of great soccer players like Pele, Diego Maradona, and Ziedine Zidane.

Light blue gave way to grim, growling grays, marking his unorthodox transition from child to man. Bigger big, taller and wide bookshelves, and a new desk did not alter Assefa's reality; his room had become both a sanctuary and a prison.

For years, Assefa's bedroom was the one place he could hide from his brother's taunts and threats. As an older brother, Razi used his large size and big mouth to dominate him. For his part, Assefa tried to stay below the radar, avoiding his violent brother as much as possible.

Yet when puberty kicked in, a subtle shift started to occur. Assefa's Mngwa began to speak to him, told the scared thirteen-year-old to defend himself against bullies, including his brother. He did, swinging wildly one day and landing, breaking his brother's nose. It was one of many days in which Assefa caught Razi stealing. Normally, Razi would shove him up against a wall, pushing and punching him until he promised to keep his mouth shut. On this day, Assefa's Mngwa had roared and attacked, defending himself and forcing Assefa to do the same.

By the age of eighteen, Assefa had gone through three growth spurts, added muscle mass and nursed a serious chip on his shoulder. He was angry all the time, his body changing rapidly, faster than was normal for a were-cat. Back then, Assefa had no idea what to do with so much unchecked power. Razi had thought his taller height and three-year age difference entitled him to push his "stupid little brother" around.

The day Assefa envisioned his Mngwa ripping Razi's throat out, tasting blood sliding down his throat and feeling elongated claws tearing flesh from bone, was the day Assefa began locking himself in his room at night.

On that fateful night, six years ago, no locked door protected Razi from Assefa's beast, his irrepressible wrath.

Undressing down to his boxers and undershirt, Assefa joined Sanura under the throw cover she'd pulled over herself. Snuggling in behind her, he sighed with contentment and relief when she turned in his arms and kissed him.

He wanted to turn the short kiss into much more, to get lost, no matter how temporarily, in the heat that always burned between them.

"How much do you want to go home, right now?"

"A lot."

That settled it then. "I understand. I'll just call—"

"I'm not returning home, Assefa, and neither are you. I won't have you missing your father and uncle's birthday because of me."

"Not because of you, and they'll understand."

"They won't. You're looking for an excuse to run, and I'm not going to give you one."

"I'm not—"

"You are." Sanura's soft hand came to rest on his cheek. "We're staying, beloved."

"We don't have to stay in the presidential compound. I can get us a suite at the best hotel in Khartoum."

Sanura's hand fell away, and she stared up at him, her eyes full of love and resignation.

"It's after us, and we can't run any longer."

"What's after us?"

"The prophecy, the gods, fate. I don't know for sure. It's stalking us, in my dreams and even here. It's everywhere we go, watching, waiting, and testing us."

He'd felt it too, but Assefa didn't want to frighten or worry Sanura by mentioning it without also having a plan of action.

"Since I made you my mate, my preternatural senses have heightened to an unnatural degree. I mean, they were always beyond the norm, but never like this."

Assefa sat up, wondering where this conversation was leading. "I take it, since arriving here, you've sensed something that no one else has because they don't have your level of preternatural sensitivity?"

"Your brother has cruel, vengeful eyes. I thought they would be like yours, after having met your father. But they aren't. Razi has Jahi's height, but he looks far more like Najja than you do."

"Najja and Razi resemble our mother."

Sanura nodded as if she'd already deduced the same.

"Bad things will happen while we're here."

"Even more reason for us to get out of here." She shook her head, adamant. "Why not?"

"Because the Day of Serpents isn't about a single day."

Sanura sat up, the throw cover falling to her waist and revealing an attractive red lace bra.

"At least I don't believe it is. It's about us, who we are as individuals and who we are as a team. I hide from my fire spirit and her power while you run from pain you don't know how to deal with other than through blood and violence."

For long seconds, Assefa said nothing, uncomfortable with how accurately Sanura had summed up his greatest weakness in one sentence.

"There's something vile here. I can sense it. Before I met Najja, I thought she could too."

"Why would you think Najja could sense anything on your level? I told you, she's a level sixth wind witch, which is impressive but not fire witch of legend impressive."

"That's just it. Najja shouldn't be a level six witch, not with you as her twin brother. She should be at least a level eight. But she really is a level six witch."

"Sweetheart, I've never felt stupid in my life, but I don't understand what you're talking about."

"There's so much I have to tell you and that you need to know, but none of it is what I want to share with you."

"I don't like the sound of that."

Sanura hugged him. "Tell me what happened between you and Razi. I assume it has something to do with Najja being bound to a wheelchair."

"I shouldn't still be surprised by your ability to make correct leaps in logic from the evidence before you."

Yet he had won his bet with Zareb, who thought it would take Sanura seeing Najja and Omar together twice before figuring out they were estranged mates. Assefa knew it would take only one time. Omar had always been horrible at keeping his feelings for Najja under the surface when they were in the same room.

"Tell me the story, and I'll hold you through the telling."

Until this moment, Assefa hadn't realized how much he needed to share the most awful event in his life with Sanura. And he felt so damn weak for loving how she straddled his hips, arms tight around his neck, and head on his shoulder. With Sanura wrapped around him like this, he would never run away from anything else, least of all her.

"I felt my sister die. Miles away, I felt Najja die. She slipped away into a shadowy void of nothingness."

He'd crashed to the floor, shivering in grief and physical pain. Tears had come, and he'd thought they would never end.

"I couldn't breathe. No air but so much pain. Our bond had been severed, and I felt it like a gunshot to my heart. I thought I would die along with her. I wanted to die. Three minutes. Najja flatlined for three interminable minutes before paramedics revived her."

Her hold on him tightened, and Assefa felt tears on his shoulder.

"When I reached the hospital, I knew. As soon as I saw his guilty face, I knew Razi was to blame."

He'd shifted in an instant and was tearing down the hallway, headed straight for his brother.

"We fought right there, Mngwa versus black jaguar."

The fight had been awful, blood and fur everywhere, screams all around them. Neither had cared about anything or anyone, nothing except killing the other.

"My father, uncle, Omar, and Zareb managed to pry me off Razi. His left front leg was severed at the knee, chewed beyond medicine or magic."

He'd maimed his brother. In the heat of the moment, Assefa hadn't cared. A part of him still didn't. He couldn't stay there after that. For a year, he tried. Everyone pretended as if Razi hadn't caused an accident that nearly claimed his sister's life and that Assefa hadn't tried to murder his brother.

Sanura now knew the ugly history between siblings.

"I suppose I'm the real Bloody Berber."

A soothing kiss to his neck. "Don't make me smack you, Assefa."

"Don't make you what? That's what you have to say after hearing the story of how I tried to kill my brother?"

Sanura scooted off his lap, which wasn't at all what he wanted her to do.

"Oh please, if you wanted to kill Razi he'd be dead."

"Maybe you didn't hear me. I ripped my brother's damn arm off and almost claimed the other. No witch could heal all his scars, although High Priestess Leila was able to help Razi regain full movement in his right arm. He was in rehab for months, struggling to relearn how to walk while in his jaguar form. He's developed what I can only think of as a phantom limb when he shifts. He manages quite well now, all things considered. But my anger and beast changed his life forever."

"I can see and hear how much that day traumatized you."

Assefa bristled at the word *traumatized*. He didn't like the sound of it, as if he were an emotionally disturbed mental patient.

"Listen, I'm not minimizing the fight you had with your brother and how hurting him made you feel and the impact it had, and still has, on your relationship." Sanura's hand came to his cheek again, stroking in that wonderfully soothing way of hers. "But you didn't try to kill your brother. Remember, I've seen you spar and fight. I've seen you spare a man when all Greg Chambers wanted to do was kill you."

"What does any of that have to do with what I did to my brother?"

"It has everything to do with it. If you were truly intent on killing Razi, no one could've stopped you. No. One. You're too strong, too stubborn, and too tactical in battle to allow anyone to stand between you and your prey. All Razi's wounds were to the lower parts of his body, places that incapacitate a were-cat but won't kill one."

She slapped Assefa when he gaped at her, to his face and with the palm of her hand, soft and with no intent to do harm. He comprehended her point. That was Sanura's way of knocking a bit of sense into him.

"I heard what you said."

She smacked the other cheek. "I know you heard me. But did you listen? Do you understand that, despite your pain and anger, you knew you fought your brother? A brother you may not like but a brother you love, no matter his shortcomings. Because if you ever refer to yourself as Bloody Berber again, we will fight, Assefa. Fire versus fangs."

Hard. Final.

No one, not even Najja, had laid out the confrontation between brothers the way Sanura had done. He'd fled home thinking himself a monster, for what kind of man would seek to murder his own flesh and blood?

Assefa still carried the weight of that painful day, despite the years between then and now.

"Is that what you really believe? You didn't know me back then, Sanura. I had far less control over my Mngwa than I do now."

"Think about what you just said. You know the truth. It's inside of you. It's always been there, but fear and guilt prevented you from seeing and accepting the truth. Yes, to fight your brother the way you did had to have been the twenty-two-year-old Assefa's worst nightmare."

Sanura straddled his waist again, her hands grasping his cheeks, lifting and holding his head up. "It's a lot to accept, I know. Do you really think Razi tried to kill Najja?"

"I don't know."

"Does Najja?"

"She doesn't remember the incident. But she thinks it was probably an accident, the way he said."

"But you think she only tells herself that because it makes it easier to accept her paralysis than to believe her older brother wanted her dead."

That's precisely what he thought. In the end, however, only Razi knew the truth. Not even Omar, who'd been with Najja and Razi minutes before the accident, knew what happened.

Omar's guilt, for not being there to prevent what happened to Najja, was far greater than Assefa's.

"Are you sure you want to marry into my family?"

She frowned. "I'm going to assume you meant that as a joke."

They knew he hadn't. But his witch, on this day of family drama, had little patience for his childhood insecurities and adult fears.

Her hands lowered from his cheeks to his shoulders. "I want to marry you." Sanura pulled on the gold chain around his neck until she slid it from underneath his shirt. On it hung the gold wedding band that once belonged to Sanura's father. She'd gifted him with the priceless ring as a promise of her intent to make Assefa her husband and full mate.

She twirled the ring in her hand, looking at him then back at the ring. "Don't take this off while we're here."

"So serious."

"I am. Don't take it off, Assefa. Our lack of a full mate bond means I can't protect you the way I want and need to."

"I'll be fine. Don't worry."

"I won't worry if you keep wearing this the way you have been. Trust me, if someone harms you, my fire spirit won't stop with a maiming to avenge you. Do you understand? By wearing my father's ring with the special spell it now holds, you'll be protecting more than just yourself."

"Sweetheart, I…"

Sanura shook her head, an unspeakable sadness having entered her eyes. "I'm tired, Assefa, so tired, but I'm afraid to sleep. Afraid to close my eyes and have the fire witch of legend come to me again, tainting my mind with her vengeance and heartache. And I'm terrified of learning what made her that way, what drove her over the edge of sanity and morality."

She tried to slip off him, but Assefa refused to let her go. How awful were those dreams of hers? How often did she have them?

"I'll hold you while you sleep."

"I need to tell you about Najja."

"Is she in harm or immediate danger?"

"Not in the way that you mean."

"Good. Will waiting a few hours change anything?"

"No."

"Then you have time to take a nice long nap with your familiar."

"You're going to shift?"

"Will you sleep better if I did? If my Mngwa curls around you while you slept, would that help?"

Sanura not only loved the Mngwa, but the big cat helped soothe her fire spirit. Perhaps he could also drive away her nightmares, if only for a few hours.

"I would like to see him, feel his warmth and strength."

That's all Assefa needed to hear. Handing Sanura the throw cover, he helped her off the bed, then stripped off his undershirt and boxers. A second later, the cat of legend stood before Sanura, nuzzling at her hand with his muzzle.

Obligingly, she scratched the beast's ears before leaning down and hugging him.

The Mngwa purred, and his witch whispered her love for him in his ear.

In the end, the Mngwa reclined on the floor with Sanura atop him, the throw cover forgotten, hands twined in his gray-and-black fur and face buried against the side of his neck.

Asleep.

CHAPTER TWELVE

"Are you sure you don't want Assefa or Omar in here with you?"

"What is it about me, Sanura, that gives you the impression that I require my brother and mate to have a simple conversation?"

Why must Assefa's family be so emotionally high maintenance? Under normal circumstances, Sanura wouldn't mind. But everything about this building clawed at her senses and left her raw.

"Pick one."

"What do you mean?"

Five minutes ago, Assefa had escorted Sanura to his sister's office. They'd run into a frustrated Omar, Najja's slammed office door echoing his dismissal.

"She's as obstinate as ever. Drives me crazy."

He'd appeared as if he wanted to storm back into his mate's office. But whatever calm part of Omar that hadn't drained away since reuniting with Najja, must've reasserted itself because the six-foot-seven lion shifter growled a goodbye before stalking down the hall and vanishing around the corner.

Now, Sanura sat in an elegant office and across from the wind witch, who sat behind her L-shape executive rail desk. The wide space behind the desk was perfect for maneuvering in a wheelchair from one end of the workstation to the other.

Sanura felt like running outside and away from the malignant spirits that kept triggering her overwrought senses. She couldn't do that, though. For now, she had to deal with an agitated wind witch. Najja may have inherited the Berber eyes, but she ran hot and cold, not cool like the Berber men.

"You determine how this conversation will go. Pick an emotion, anger, humor, nonchalance, which is one of your brother's favorite defaults by the way."

A grin split her beautiful face, replacing the unappealing frown put there by Omar and whatever argument she'd had with him before tossing the poor were-cat out of her office. Whether she'd also thrown him out of her life, permanently, Sanura didn't know. What she did know was that Omar, if he wanted Najja back, would have to do less talking and more showing.

"Berbers do nonchalance quite well, and you're not at all what I expected." Najja's elbows came to her desk, her Berber eyes keen. Sanura didn't flinch under the witch's open scrutiny. "What did you do?"

The thought of lying to Najja or even pretending to misunderstand her question never entered Sanura's mind. Beyond those being insulting tactics and below both women's intelligence, Sanura couldn't fault Najja her forthrightness and curiosity.

Sanura lifted her right arm, around which a gold Greek key cuff bracelet with a moonstone on each end glimmered.

Najja held a hand over her eyes as if she were shielding them from the blinding sun, smiling all the while. "My brother has no shame. A lot of money and excellent taste in clothes and jewelry but not an ounce of shame.

I bet he has no idea how you use all those expensive pieces of jewelry he, no doubt, showers on you. Be sure to visit my bedchamber before you return home, Sanura, and I'll show you my jewelry armoires. They're filled with," Najja raised her naked wrists and fingers, "outrageously expensive rings, necklaces, broaches, and gods only know what else that I'll never wear. I have only two ears, one neck, and ten fingers. Yet my father, uncle, and brother insist. So I accept because the pitiful look they give me when I don't is enough to make a wind witch want to create a downburst and blow them all the hell away."

Yeah, probably the same look Assefa gave Sanura when she told him to not buy her a piano, a combination of shock and hurt, then mulish rejection. Sanura didn't miss the singular brother, though, not that Razi struck her as the type of were-cat to purchase anything for a woman without the expectation of receiving something from her in return.

"I only tinker with the jewelry and do nothing to lower their value with my magical workings."

"You view casting a spell that alters the projection of your aura signature as 'tinkering'?" Najja rolled around her desk, stopping her wheelchair in front of but to the left of Sanura's chair. "So how much did you want to laugh when Chanya scanned you with those judgmental eyes of hers and turned up her nose because she thought you were an irrelevant level one earth witch?"

Sanura let her smirk serve as answer enough. Irrelevant, that's how too many high-level witches thought of their lower magic level sisters. It's why Rachel rarely recognized her worth as an earth witch. It's also why Sanura chose to mimic her friend's aura signature because there was damn sure nothing irrelevant or weak about Rachel Foster.

But, yes, Sanura found humor in her choice of a disguise.

Najja's hand reached over, a finger grazing the bracelet and one of the moonstones. "I sense nothing from this. If I didn't already know you were a fire witch, I would've never guessed the truth. That's some sophisticated spellcasting." Najja withdrew her hand, voice, and eyes serious, when she asked, "Do you know your power level?"

That was the equivalent of asking a woman if she knew her age. Of course, she did, but who were you to ask? Not even Assefa had ever asked, but there this near-stranger sat, guileless in her bold query.

"I know in many witch circles it's rude to not only ask but to find out for yourself by using your second sight. Unlike Chanya, I never use my second sight to invade another witch's privacy. But surely you must know why I asked."

She did, and couldn't blame the other woman, no matter how much she shrank from the truth hidden within.

"When Assefa called and arranged this meeting between the two of us, he told me what you suspected. He asked if I would grant you permission to examine my aura with your second sight."

Actually, Sanura wanted to do more than probe her aura, which Najja was smart enough to figure out.

"I know my power level. I'm also capable of casting the spell without the use of my familiar. I understand your skepticism. We may love the same man, but we aren't yet friends and you have no reason to trust me or my magical ability. Even if I told you my power level, that's just raw power, Najja. That knowledge would tell you nothing about the quality of my spellcasting or how I treat recipients of my spells."

"Good answer. Now tell me why you aren't wearing the engagement ring I helped Assefa procure for you."

The woman didn't have a subtle bone in her body, at least not when it came to her family. Sanura had neither seen the ring nor knew of Najja's involvement in its purchase. She did have faith, however, that what Sanura had planned for Assefa's birthday would convince him he could propose to her.

Sanura pushed to her feet. Standing in front of Najja, she removed the cuff bracelet, then lifted the white point-collar linen shirt she'd donned with matching pants and white strap sandals after she'd woken from her nap and showered. From her bellybutton, she plucked a circular-shaped whitish-pink moonstone.

Dark-brown hair turned red-gold, and brown eyes shone green. She stood there, permitting Najja to take her in, upturned eyes wide, as the wind witch shifted from her normal sight to her second sight.

"This is me, no spells, no illusions, and misdirection, but Sanura Wasola Williams, fire witch and the woman who loves your brother. I give you this willingly and with infinite faith because I trust Assefa, and he trusts you."

She knelt to Najja's level, her hands coming up to find and hold the wind witch's hands.

"You don't have a right to every aspect of his heart and our relationship no more than Assefa has a right to yours. He should've mentioned he was bringing your estranged mate home with him. I won't apologize for Assefa because he's capable of doing that himself. But know, I won't bleed for you, your father, or anyone else to gain approval or admittance into the Berber family."

They stayed like that for several tense seconds. The women silent and assessing.

"But you'd bleed for him, wouldn't you?"

"Until my dying breath and beyond. Assefa's my soul."

"And you're his fire witch of legend."

Rising, Sanura reclaimed her seat. "No, I'm his destiny."

A destiny that would be the death of Assefa Berber, something terrified and forlorn inside her cried.

"Even without your moonstones and the use of my second sight, I still can't read all of you, although I can tell from your aura that you're a fire witch. So why do you waste your time altering your aura signature if not even a level six witch can read you accurately?"

Sanura waited for what Najja said to catch up with her, which didn't take long.

"Oh hell." She slapped her forehead with the palm of her hand. "Your true power level cannot be read because you don't register on a witch's spectrum of sight, even by a witch who is beyond the one to five power level range."

It took a second for it to happen. But there it was, the look she'd seen on the faces of the Witch Council of Elders when she turned thirteen, and they could no longer sense her magic level. High Priestess Katherine had dropped to her knees before Sanura and wept, a prayer slipping from her about Ma'at and old and new gods.

Since that day, she'd taken to wearing her moonstone all the time, never wanting another witch to look at her with eyes of reverence and fear.

"You really are the fire witch of legend."

"Unfortunately." While Najja continued to stare and process all she'd learned about Sanura, she took the time to slip her bracelet back on and reinsert the moonstone in her bellybutton.

"Will it hurt?"

Sanura didn't think Najja meant the deep scan of her aura but the life-threatening spell that could come later, depending on the result of the scan and how Najja wanted to proceed once knowing the truth.

"I don't need to be in physical contact to use my second sight. If you wouldn't mind, however, skin-to-skin contact would give me a better reading."

Sanura could also use Omar's mate bond connection to Najja as a bridge between the witches but knew better than to offer that as an option. Besides, with the fractured state of their relationship, it probably wouldn't work especially since Omar would have to touch Najja, which would likely lead to another argument between the two.

"It won't hurt, but you'll feel a bit of heat."

"'A bit of heat?' You're the fire witch of legend. What does that even mean to you?"

Sanura swatted away the pang of hurt she felt at Najja's blatant fear. A justified emotion, but one that would leave Najja with one other option.

"If you don't mind traveling, I could introduce you to the Witch Council of Elders."

"Your priestesses? These are the same women who made Assefa their alpha?"

"Yes, water, fire, earth, and wind. Four bonded priestesses, one deep scan with no touching required."

"I offended you. That wasn't my intention."

The words were sincere enough as was the relief in Najja's eyes to have an option that didn't involve Sanura laying hands on her.

"Not offended. You don't know me." Sanura glanced down at her hands, unable to see them as tools of pain and death the way Najja obviously did. Yet they were.

She stood then shook her head when Najja opened her mouth on what was probably a false apology. She couldn't fault the wind witch her caution, not after what she'd already suffered, likely at the hands of her older brother.

"You'll like my mother and her sisters. But be careful of Priestess Barbara. She's on the hunt for a wind witch to replace her on the Council. One minute she'll blow you an innocent kiss and the next you're the leader of hundreds of wind witches and Barbara retired on a beach sipping a Sky Juice and crushing on a hard-bodied Bahamian were-cat."

Najja chuckled, but still appeared as if she wanted to offer her hollow apology. Yet she said nothing when Sanura walked away from her and toward Najja's office door.

Doorknob in hand, Sanura turned to see Najja back behind her desk.

"What if you're right about me, Sanura?"

"Do you want me to be right?"

"I don't know. It would change so much but nothing at all."

Sanura wondered if she meant her relationship with Omar, then decided it didn't matter because Najja was wrong. If Sanura were right, it would change everything for the wind witch.

CHAPTER THIRTEEN

No-one met with General Supreme Jahi Berber without being summoned. Yet there Tracey Kemraha sat in his office, head bowed to hide her glee. She'd borrowed on her mother's good name and reputation to get where she was, next to Assefa, her soon-to-be mate, and husband.

Mistress Kemraha, Tracey's mother, wouldn't approve of what she'd done or how far she'd go to secure her place in Assefa's life. He'd gotten away from her once, she wouldn't let him get away again.

"I'm sure you remember Miss Kemraha, son. If I'm not mistaken, the two of you dated before you left to join Ulan in Virginia."

Tracey lifted her head, wanting to see Assefa. She hadn't dared when he'd arrived a few minutes ago, but she did now, unable to resist. Gods, he'd grown even larger and more handsome. She was happy to see him, although he didn't look at all pleased to see her.

No matter, that would soon change.

"Good to see you again, Tracey. How's Mistress Kemraha?"

"She's well. I'll let Mom know you asked after her. Perhaps you'll make time to stop by to see your former teacher. Mom would love that, and so would I. It's good to see you, Assefa. I've missed you."

His expression didn't change. He merely watched her with eyes she'd never been able to read. But something percolated behind those dark irises of his, something that hadn't been there when she'd last had him in her spider's web.

"What's this meeting about, Father?"

"Miss Kemraha had a package delivered a couple of days ago. After being checked by security, my secretary placed the package on my desk, but I didn't open it until yesterday evening. Take a look."

The general supreme pointed to a white envelope on his desk and in front of where Assefa perched on the edge of his chair. From where she sat, she could read her own neat script on the front of the package.

Assefa picked up the envelope, dug his hand inside, and pulled out the folded piece of paper.

He read.

She ducked her head, grinning, enjoying how well her plan was proceeding.

"It's a lie." Low. Arctic.

"That's what I also thought at first. Take out what else is in the envelope, Assefa, and explain yourself."

Crumbling her letter in his hand, he grabbed the envelope again and shook. A small object fell into Assefa's lap. He picked it up, examined it, then turned to Tracey. "Where in the hell did you find this?"

Lowering her eyes again as if ashamed and hurt, she let the tense moment stretch, not wanting to appear too eager to push her claim.

"Our last night together, you gave it to me." Raising her eyes, Tracey let a laugh tear she'd been holding fall. Lower lip quivered for effect.

"I didn't give you my family ring."

"Then how did she get it?"

"I don't know."

"That's our family crest on that ring, son. The ring I commissioned for your twenty-first birthday. The same as I did for Razi, as my father did for your uncle and me, and so on. From father to son to mate. That's how it works for Berber males when we claim our mate." The general supreme nodded at the ring fisted in Assefa's hand. "That would explain why I didn't see your ring on Sanura's hand yesterday. You'd already gifted it to another woman."

Cold, black eyes shifted to Tracey, no trace of the boy she'd once known. Before her sat a seasoned man with a ferocious inner cat warning her to retreat.

Squaring her shoulders, Tracey refused to back down. No matter the threat in his posture and the glint of betrayal in his eyes, Tracey held fast, knowing in the end he would thank her for freeing him from a nothing level one earth witch.

Really, what was Assefa thinking? She'd hoped when the general supreme told his secretary to ask Assefa to meet him in his office, that he'd bring his American witch with him, so she could see the woman for herself. According to Chayna, the earth witch was quite pretty but possessed an embarrassingly low magic level.

Gods, someone was making this too easy for her. The general supreme could not have been pleased with Assefa's choice of mate, when he realized his son returned, not with the famed fire witch of legend but with a level one earth witch.

"Why are you doing this? I didn't give you my family ring. I have no idea how you got it, but I didn't give it to you. And I damn sure never claimed you as my mate."

"I never said you claimed me as your mate." Unable to hold Assefa's gaze, she focused on his father. "We engaged in the first part of the handfasting ritual. But his Mngwa wasn't drawn to my water spirit. We knew then that we weren't biological mates. But we were in love."

Risking his cat's wrath but betting on the man to keep his cool, Tracey turned back to face Assefa. "You did love me once, and I loved you. Still love you. You gave me that ring in your hand, said you would speak with my mother and your father. Said I was your chosen mate and that you wanted to be with me even though everyone expected you to mate with the fire witch of legend."

Tracey conjured up a few more tears, howling on the inside at Assefa's banked anger. She remembered now. Assefa didn't argue with women. Easy, so damn easy. He would be hers. Once he was, she would cast a mindwipe spell and erase all memories of his weak, little witch.

"Then your sister had that terrible accident, and you shut down. You stayed by her side as a good brother should. But things weren't the same with you after that day. You wouldn't talk to me about it, although you swore you still wanted us to be together. Then, one day, you up and left."

Had she spun just the right amount of fact with fiction for the general supreme to doubt his son's word over hers? Probably not. But convincing Jahi Berber she spoke nothing but the truth wasn't the purpose of this meeting. Her goal was to cast a repressive light on the general supreme's honor.

He had no true honor, of course. The man was the son of a lying, murdering dictator. But General Supreme Jahi Berber was supposed to be everything his ancestors were not: a man of truth, fairness, and morality. What was more dishonorable than a son who pledged himself to one witch then leaves her for five years, only to return with another witch on his arm?

Would a fair and equitable leader excuse the bad behavior of his favorite son or would he enforce the rules of their people and compel Assefa to honor his promise to the witch he'd abandoned?

Abandoned. Yes, she liked the sound of that. The word struck the perfect chord of sympathy and outrage.

"I never knew you could lie so well. Or act the role of the abandoned lover with such sweet, innocent conviction." Two big hands came together and clapped. "Bravo. If you weren't trying to ruin my relationship with Sanura, I would give your performance a standing ovation."

She thought the chair he sat in would tip over, so quickly did Assefa get to his feet.

"Believe what you want, Father, but I made Tracey no promises. We dated. We had sex. We broke up. I left home. End of story."

"What about your ring? I can't ignore the fact that she had it in her possession. No more than I can dismiss the fact that you have no idea how she came to have your ring. Do you have any idea how this will appear to the cabinet members and to the public if I take no action?"

"Politics always comes first with you, Father. Your image. The Berber name. What about the truth? When does that ever factor into your decisions?"

"I haven't made a decision."

"Yes, you have. The moment you read her letter of lies and saw my ring, your decision was made. Nothing I've said here matters when measured against opinion polls."

"We don't need another Berber scandal."

"So don't give them one. No one will force me to take Tracey as my mate. I don't give a damn what our custom dictates for me to do."

"What about Sanura? If you walk away from this, if you don't do your duty as a Berber and as a Sudanese, Sanura will be marked as *fasha*."

Yes, she would be labeled as a demon-witch who bespelled were-cats, stealing their affections from their one true love and then devouring the soul of the heartbroken witch. Tracey had made sure of it, thanks to her silent partner. The cunning bastard.

"Don't you ever use that word in relation to Sanura again. She's not a *fasha,* and I won't have you or anyone else calling her that. She's my mate."

This time, when Assefa moved, he did knock the chair over, the sound of crashing wood not nearly as loud as the sound of Tracey's impending win.

Still seated, the general supreme appeared no less annoyed and angry at the situation as his son. But he comprehended the full scope of the dangerous path before Assefa's earth witch if he didn't relent.

He stood, fingertips on his desk, eyes glued to Assefa. "When it comes to the internal affairs of the covens unless a witch law contradicts national policy, I cannot interfere. With this claim from Tracey, based on witch law and the evidence she's brought before me, I have no choice but to issue an edict for the union if you refuse to do your duty willingly."

Tracey watched as the general supreme strolled from behind his desk and toward an infuriated Assefa. They spoke in low tones, but not so low Tracey couldn't hear Assefa's angry baritone voice.

She glanced at the new text on her cell phone.

We have her. Is she fasha?

Sanura Williams was most definitely *fasha*. She'd stolen Assefa's heart from Tracey as surely as Tracey had stolen Assefa's family ring from him. However, when she'd concocted this plan, Tracey hadn't factored in the possibility of Assefa having fallen prey to the American witch. Yet he had and, from the defiant snarls coming from him, the were-cat had no intention of submitting to his father.

Yes, she is.

Assefa belonged to her. She would take back what was hers, one way or another.

Orders, High Priestess?

Lifting her head from her cell phone, Tracey observed father and son, opposite sides of the same arrogant Berber coin. But where one led a life of integrity, the other hid in its shadow.

Assefa would not relent. Well, he would, if provided the right incentive.

She either disavows all claims to Assefa Berber or she dies.

Assefa wanted to smash his fist into something, hard and repeatedly. Tracey Kemraha would do nicely if he believed in hitting women, which he didn't. That fact likely explained the smug way she kept looking from him and to the phone in her hand.

But it didn't begin to explain why a woman Assefa had known since childhood would craft an elaborate lie to ensnare him into a loveless union. They'd had a short affair, pretty much sex, and a few dates. Sure, she'd hinted at more, the same way her eyes got big and hopeful every time Tracey saw a dress or necklace she "had to have."

Assefa had bought the gifts, although he never remembered pulling out his credit card and paying for them. Yet there they were, every expensive item on his monthly credit card statement.

Pretty with pricey taste, that was Tracey. Assefa had known, even as a young man, that she wasn't the witch for him. But he kept going back, lured to her bed. Except that one time, the last time.

That had been six years ago, and Assefa hadn't given Tracey Kemraha a second thought after that day. Apparently, she couldn't say the same about him. This insane plot of hers wouldn't work. Except, from the intractable set of Jahi's jaw, it already had.

"Do you think I want to do this, son? Do you not think I can see through that girl's lies and manipulations? But she has your damn family ring, Assefa, and you have no explanation as to how it came to be in her possession. I haven't seen you wear it for six years. And that's because she's had it this entire time."

The last night they were together, Assefa had awoken, stared down at Tracey and wondered why in the hell he was in her bed. Because Mistress Kemraha had served as governess to the Berber twins, for a while Assefa, Najja, and Tracey had become friends.

While Assefa always thought Tracey good-looking, he'd never been attracted to her until one day he found himself asking her out and buying her a charm bracelet. From there, their relationship was pretty much a blur. Until a dream had awakened him. A dream that turned into a nightmare when he felt his sister die.

"No one will believe she stole your ring, and you know why."

Yes, Assefa knew why. Once on, only a Berber could remove the magic-laced ring, boiled in the blood of his father's jaguar and sanctified in the Temple of Sekhmet.

Assefa hadn't thought of his family ring in six long years. That was until he'd met Sanura. He'd wanted to gift his fire witch with the symbol of his birthright as a handfasting present. But he couldn't find the elusive ring anywhere. Now he knew why.

"I won't mate myself to Tracey. I'm Sanura's."

"What good is your devotion to her if your pride and stubbornness put the young witch in harm's way? You may not like it, but your Dr. Williams became *fasha* the moment Tracey drudged up your ring from wherever she's been hiding it. And don't you doubt a minute that she hasn't already spun this tale to her coven."

Shit. Assefa snatched out his cell from his pants pocket.

"What's wrong? Who are you calling?"

He dialed. Waited. Dialed again. Nothing, just more ringing then her voicemail.

"She's not answering."

Assefa hoped he could catch Sanura before she left the compound grounds.

Too confident. Assefa wondered why Tracey seemed so damn sure of herself. And who in the hell did she keep texting?

"Sanura's not answering her phone. She said she needed to get away from the building for a while, to get a bit of fresh air and to exercise."

"Who's with her? Please tell me you weren't so foolish as to send that sweet young lady onto the streets of Khartoum by herself."

"I'm not an idiot, Father." He dialed his best friend. "She went jogging with Zareb and Omar."

The were-cat didn't answer, either. Assefa dialed again.

Someone picked up on the other end, but all Assefa heard was splashing and then a growled, "What the fuck is going on?"

"That's my question? Where are you?"

Assefa heard roaring in the background. Omar's lion.

Dammit.

"Come get your witch before—"

"Before what?"

Assefa ran for the office door, gripping the handle so hard it broke in his hand.

"She's drenched and hurt, and they keep calling her *fasha*."

A sprint down the hall.

"Who hurt her?"

"The water witches."

Elevator too slow. Down the stairs.

"How many?"

More roaring, pained and enraged.

Faster.

"Shit, I think all of them."

Faster. Faster.

"What do you mean?"

Ground level. Finally.

"All of them, Assefa. The whole fucking Northern Khartoum coven of water witches are here."

Assefa darted past the lobby, no sign of Chanya.

Shit.

"How hurt is she?"

"Wrong question. She's hot. Scary fucking hot."

Assefa took off down the street.

CHAPTER FOURTEEN

From the shadows, Razi saw his brother barrel down the hall, lightning-fast and determined. A few minutes later, he watched Tracey Kemraha stroll from the general supreme's office, a self-satisfied smile on her face.

He stepped from the shadows just enough, so she'd know he was there. Not breaking her stride, the witch retrieved an item from her purse and tossed it over her shoulder.

Razi caught it and then blended back into the shadows. He waited. It didn't take long for the text to arrive.

Two drops a day for the next two or three days should do it. We're now even and free of each other.

Razi held the small vile of liquid in his hand, colorless, odorless and tasteless. Perfect.

The water witch was a piece of work as dangerous and untrustworthy as they came.

He smiled. Witches were so damn predictable as were the media.

Razi could hear the second television helicopter now, its whirling blades taking it in the direction where Assefa had no doubt run off to.

An anonymous tip, that's all it had taken.

Razi knocked on his father's door, opening it a second later when a gruff voice bellowed, "Come in."

"What's going on? I saw Assefa take off down the hall. And why was Mistress Kemraha's daughter here?"

Before his father could answer, the adjoining door swung open. Uncle Ulan and Najja wore matching frowns. Great. All the Berbers, except Assefa, were present and accounted for, Ulan having arrived bright and early this morning to celebrate his birthday with his twin.

"Brother, do you have any idea what's going on outside?" Ulan, with the gait of a man who feared no one, sauntered into the general supreme's office, followed by Najja.

"It's all over the news." Najja tossed her cell phone to the general supreme while Ulan found the remote to the television and turned it on.

Jahi's eyes shifted from the small cell phone screen to the larger television screen mounted on the wall across the room. Mouth open, he sat in his desk chair, dark eyes transfixed on the scene playing out for all of Sudan to see.

They watched, stunned, as Dr. Sanura Williams, Assefa Berber's American witch, *fasha*, as the growing, angry crowd called her, took a brutal beating.

Gods, yes, witches were so predictable and the worst predators of them all.

Fifteen Minutes Earlier

Sanura had to admit, for all that she disapproved of the forced removal of thousands of full-humans from the Sudan, there was something affirming about being in a place where no preternatural had to hide their true selves.

Which, considering Sanura still wore her moonstone in her bellybutton and her cuff bracelet, made her observation less than true for her. But there she was, jogging down the street, Zareb next to her in human form and Omar to her left in lion form. No one had batted an eye when they saw the huge lion trotting beside her.

Normal. For the people of this nation, it was all so wonderfully normal. Sanura, for the first time since landing in this country, saw the appeal, appreciated this small slice of freedom the Berbers had carved out for preternaturals.

Jogging had been a good idea. With each step she took away from the House of Berber and the spirits within, the better she felt and the less her skin crawled and inner spirit hissed. And while she would rather have Assefa enjoying the outing with her, Zareb and Omar were great company. They'd done this before, not in public, of course, but on Assefa's big estate. If nothing else, living with six were-cats guaranteed Sanura always had someone to exercise and spar with, although Zareb tended to do more flirting than actual exercise.

Except for today. Today, the man ran at her side, not as a friend, but as a medja. As they approached a group of women at the end of the street, the lion shifting closer to her, Sanura suspected Omar was there in the same capacity as Zareb.

They stopped a few feet from the women, none of whom Sanura knew. Ten, there were ten of them, just standing there, silent and watchful.

At noon, Khartoum was as busy as any metropolis, people out and about, on foot and in cars. The scene was no different than full-humans taking in a hot summer day in New York City, boisterous and moving fast.

As if a switch had been flipped, all movement around them slowed, then stopped, even the cars.

Dead silence.

Omar growled and shoved his large body between Sanura and the group of women blocking their path. A group that had just doubled in size.

"Um, Zareb, what's going on?"

"I have no idea, but I'm not going to stay here to find out."

Grabbing her hand, he pulled her backward and away from the group of women.

A water ball smacked Sanura in the face, snapping her head to the side with the strength of the magic and propulsion.

Another came. And another, until the sky rained water balls, aimed at Sanura.

Zareb pushed her to the ground, shielding Sanura as best he could with his body.

Omar snapped and growled at anyone who got too close, his sharp fangs and threatening lion enough to keep the water witches at a distance.

A chant began above her.

"Fasha. Fasha. Fasha."

What were they talking about? She knew that word. She knew but couldn't think, couldn't—

Zareb jerked away from her. A torrent of water smashed into him, forcing the were-cat into the street. His body slammed into the side of a stopped car, streams of hard water endless and bone-breaking.

A yelp sounded behind her. Twisting, she scrambled to reach Omar, but it was too late. The water witches had him drawn and quartered. The golden legs of his lion were taut. Rope of water binds that cut deep had the proud lion growling his fury and pain.

"Fasha. Fasha. Fasha."

Sanura struggled to her feet, only to have a blast of icy water shards spiral into her back, slicing shirt and skin.

Down she went. The ground a slowly forming lake of water witch power.

"Release Master Berber from your spell, *fasha*."

Hair plastered to her head, Sanura forced her eyes up to the woman who stood over her.

Chanya, the receptionist.

"I said release Master Berber from your demon spell."

The woman spoke in fast Wolof, spittle flying from her mouth as she repeated the sentence over and again.

But when she opened her mouth for the fifth time, Sanura knew it was for a water spell.

She lunged, grabbing Chanya by her knees and driving her backward and down into the water.

Splash. Slam.

Chanya's head smacked against the hard concrete, eyes going wide with pain, anger, and surprise.

A succession of quick punches to the face had the woman spitting up blood, nose broken, and lip split and bleeding.

Sanura didn't know why in the hell these water witches decided to attack her, but she'd be damned if she permitted—

A deluge of water lifted Sanura off Chanya. Stabbing slices of water found vulnerable flesh and cut, making it rain blood.

Omar stilled howled his pain, and Sanura feared those goddamn water witches just might tear the lion apart.

And Zareb, where was he?

She needed to protect them, couldn't let these women hurt her friends.

Gritting her teeth against the onslaught of water that threatened to drown her, Sanura closed her eyes and listened. Through the cacophony of curses and threats to "kill the demon-witch," Sanura could barely focus, much less locate Zareb with her witch-level hearing.

The pounding of water rapids grew around her, beating at Sanura's body and tearing flesh.

Her inner spirit raged in her cell. Fire wings snapped. Sharp beak screeched. Lethal talons clawed against Sanura's fraying self-control.

"Stay inside, beast," she screamed. She couldn't lose control, not now, not when Omar and Zareb were in danger and her rational mind all that stood between them and dozens of witches who would, she promised her beast, answer to her fire spirit.

Grasping for the mate bond link she shared with Assefa, Sanura pushed past the stabbing pain of endless water assaults, body sliced, bones broken, and head hammering.

On a ragged scream of agony, she collapsed to the ground completely but held onto the link. Using that tether of strength that was her bond to Assefa's Mngwa, she searched for and found the aura signature of the two she sought.

In her soul, she could sense the echo of her Mngwa's magic within the Bengal tiger and lion. Assefa's magic, the men's brotherhood and bond to their alpha.

It would do. Hell, yes, it would damn sure do.

On a screamed command that had her swallowing, then throwing up water, she pushed out her spell. Forced her way through the sheets of cold water beating down on her and to the hot air of freedom on the other side, Sanura's fire magic exploded out of her and toward twin points of were-cat light.

Fire witch magic crunched in the air, pungent and intense. She could feel the barriers forming, strong with the heat of her magic.

Thicker. Thicker.

Sanura had to make sure, had to guarantee none of those soon-to-be flambéed witches could hurt Zareb and Omar. So she pushed outward again, testing what she'd done and finding nothing but solid, protective heat.

Good. Her friends were safe. She appreciated their effort on her behalf.

On broken legs that shouldn't hold her but did, Sanura pushed to her feet.

Time to roast these bitches.

"Those goddamn water witches. They're going to kill her."

Ulan had no idea why his brother was so upset. Sure, a battle between witches, a mere quarter mile from the presidential compound, wasn't exactly the kind of pre-birthday festivity Ulan had in mind when he arrived home.

But Jahi had dispatched a platoon of cheetah shifters to the location, on orders to, "Arrest every one of those fucking water witches, beginning with Tracey Kemraha."

On the general supreme's orders, they'd headed out, assault rifles in hand.

Ulan smirked. They wouldn't get there in time. Well, probably in just enough time to drag off to jail what remained of the very stupid coven after Sanura got finished with them.

"Calm down, brother."

"Calm down? Calm down? Do you see what's going on? Am I the only person in this heartless family who gives a damn about what happens to Assefa's witch? They're trying to murder the poor girl and on nationwide television."

Okay, the water witches did seem intent on doing Sanura bloody, permanent harm, which Ulan didn't understand. And yes, Razi appeared as if he couldn't give a damn, which was par for the course for the jaguar. Najja, whose eyes never left the television since the moment the image of her mate popped up on the screen, growling and fighting a losing battle against so many witches, sat frozen. Her long fingers gripped the arms of her chair, body leaned forward and tense, as if she could will her legs to stand, so she could fight by her mate's side.

Berbers were far from heartless, and Sanura was no helpless witch.

"Give her time. She'll pull it together. They just took Sanura by surprise. She'll be fine."

Jahi tore his eyes from the one-sided fight scene, Sanura's beleaguered body taking a serious pummeling.

"Tell me what I don't know, Ulan. Because, from here, instead of a wedding, I'll be traveling to the States for a funeral. I don't want to face that girl's mother and explain to her how I failed to protect her daughter in my own damn country."

That wouldn't go over well with Makena. The fire witch likely to set Jahi ablaze where he stood. But none of that would happen. Jahi just needed to calm down.

"Did you see that?" His brother jumped to his feet. "Sanura tackled Chanya to the ground."

They watched Sanura dismantle the receptionist's face, one well-delivered blow after another. No wild punches. No wasted energy. No telegraphed shots. Just quick, hard jabs from the mounted position.

Impressive, the woman kept surprising Ulan. Apparently, she'd also shocked Chanya and her sisters, who'd just retaliated.

Najja's right hand came up to her mouth, covering it in shock when over forty water witches attacked Sanura at once.

So much water. Too much. Too goddamn much.

Ulan became worried. He could no longer see Sanura behind the walls of thundering water. He'd been enjoying the battle so much, confident in Sanura's fire magic that he never once considered that those bitches could kill her.

For Sekhmet sake, what was taking Assefa and those soldiers so long to reach Sanura? And why wasn't she fighting back?

"Fight back," he yelled at the screen. "Come on, girl, fight the hell back."

"She can't fight back, Uncle Ulan." Razi pushed from the chair where he'd been lounging, nonchalant and as cold as any snake of prey. "Everyone knows Assefa brought home a witch who's so powerless that she doesn't even smell like a witch."

Ulan stared at his nephew and then his brother, who appeared just as clueless. But when his gaze fell to Najja, he knew he wasn't the only one in the room who knew the truth.

"You're both blind fools. Sanura wears a scent disguise charm. The best spellcasting I've ever seen, even tricked my jaguar senses, when we first met." He turned back to the television, watched and then smiled with relief. "Yes, that's my girl."

Out of nowhere, a forcefield blazed to life, behind Sanura, bright red and exploding with fire witch power. Omar no longer howled in pain, no longer a prisoner of those water witches, who, if they survived Sanura's wrath, would have an angry wind witch to contend with when they were brought in for attempted murder and assault.

He couldn't see Zareb, but Ulan assumed Sanura had conjured a forcefield for him as well. Paul Chambers had learned the hard way what it meant to be on the wrong side of a protective Sanura Williams.

Gods, he adored her, especially when Sanura's eyes told him she would murder Ulan in his sleep if he hurt her mother.

"Brother, that tempest is the best birthday present you'll ever receive."

He shoved Jahi until the stunned man got the hint and retook his seat.

"S-she told me she was a fire witch. But I thought…"

Ulan laughed and slapped Jahi's shoulder. "Yes, a fire witch, brother. The most powerful fire witch in five centuries."

"Bullshit," Razi snarled. "That sweet-smelling witch couldn't be the fire witch of legend."

Razi's face contorts into livid realization and then utter disbelief when Sanura's heat pushed back the onslaught of water.

Hell, yes, his girl was on her feet, hell angel mad and gloriously beautiful in her fury.

A camera zoomed in on Sanura, and Ulan thanked the gods she'd never looked at him like that.

No brown.

No green.

Just red. Her eyes. Damn, her eyes seethed crimson fire.

Water witches went in for the kill, and all hell broke loose.

CHAPTER FIFTEEN

"What are your orders, Master Berber?"

Assefa glared up at the towering wall of water and swore foully. Ten minutes. Ten goddamn minutes of running at full speed around the perimeter, only to be brought up short each time.

"The water witches have about a five-mile radius cordoned off," Staff Sergeant Durka said, voicing what his platoon and Assefa damn well knew.

The entire coven of Khartoum's water witches, Zareb had said, Tracey's coven.

Damn the witch. It had to be at least two hundred water witches in there, maintaining the impenetrable wall. How many of them were attacking Sanura, thinking her *fasha* and a danger to them all?

Assefa didn't want to think what Sanura was going through in there, didn't want to contemplate what she would do if pushed too far. He'd already sensed her pain.

So much pain it had his Mngwa howling with the need to protect his witch.

One of the soldiers pointed his gun at the barricade of water. "I know one way to get those witches to bring this wall down."

Before Assefa could reach the young, stupid soldier, he aimed and fired.

Bullets sprayed.

Staff Sergeant Durka barked a cease-fire, but it was too late. The soldier's bullets hit the wall of water, ricocheted and found homes in unsuspecting bodies.

Soldiers.

Bystanders.

Assefa.

He dropped to his knees, the bullet to his side sending white-hot pain through him.

"You fucking idiot," he heard Durka yell. "We need medics. Call it in. Now!"

"Gods, I'm so sorry. So sorry."

Durka got in the man's face, his big hand taking a fistful of the younger man's black BDU shirt. "I don't have time for your tears, soldier. I gave you an order. Now get your shit together and call this in."

"Y-yes, sir. Yes, sir."

A sturdy arm helped Assefa to his feet. "Are you okay, Master Berber?"

He breathed as deep as he dared. The bullet hadn't gone too far. He could probably reach it.

"Give me your knife."

"My what?"

"Just give it to me."

After a beat, the sergeant seemed to figure out why Assefa wanted his blade and yanked it from the sheath at his ankle.

Tearing off his dress shirt, the right side stained with his blood, Assefa examined the entry wound. He had to get the bullet out before his were-cat healing kicked in and the hole closed with the bullet still inside.

He took the offered knife, the sound of sirens a shrill cry behind him. "Go take care of the bystanders. They need you more than I do."

"But the General Supreme—"

"I won't die, Durka. I'm not your priority here."

When the sergeant made to argue again, Assefa stabbed the blade into his side. The man winced as if he were the one with a six-inch knife stuck in him. But he got the message.

Assefa could take care of his damn self. But fuck, the combination of bullet and knife had him tightening his jaw and swallowing a scream of pain.

He used the knife to locate the bullet, after thirty excruciating seconds of rooting around inside, poking at things that were never meant to feel the sharp point of a blade. But he found it and dug the crushed steel from his side, unsure why the bullet hadn't gone deeper.

Shirt fisted against his bloody side, covering the gaping wound, Assefa didn't notice the low hum of fire witch magic coming from the necklace around his neck. Sanura's promise ring dangled as he reached into his pants pocket and pulled out his cell phone.

"Assefa," Najja breathed on the other end of the line. "Where are you? Why haven't you gotten to Sanura yet? They're trying to kill her. But gods, I think she's going to kill them first."

"Listen." He coughed, spitting up blood. "Stop talking and listen. I need your help."

That four-letter word was all it took, his sister suddenly calm. "What do you need me to do?"

Everywhere she looked, Sanura saw water. She sensed the witches drawing from the underground waterlines running throughout the city. And beyond.

Felt tremors as they drew the water upward, breaking through concrete, ripping trees from roots, and unsettling the foundation of buildings.

Casting off the shredded remnants of her tank top and her sodden running shoes, Sanura stood in the middle of a fountain of whizzing water in only her sports bra and leggings.

The razor-sharp water drew nearer, spiraling up and over her head. Sanura was no longer able to see the bright sun or news helicopters and their greedy lenses.

Cold, deadly water closed in, and Sanura screamed when it sliced through her, ragged and raw.

Somewhere, amidst her shrieks of pained anger, she began to laugh, maniacal and with thoughts of charred bodies floating in watery graves.

As her blood fell, oozing from bone-deep lacerations, it caught fire, latched onto streams of water and followed the water back to the summoning witch.

Water, blood, fire.

Fire. Fire.

Sanura stepped from her prison of water, now stained red with blood-fire.

"Heat," she commanded.

Explosion. Screams.

"Heat."

More explosions. Even more screams.

"Fasha," the water witches yelled, followed by, "Kill the demon-witch."

They tried, casting spell after spell. Cursing Sanura each time they encountered her ever-growing forcefield of blistering heat, their water spells dissolving on contact.

"Where is your high priestess?" Her fire spirit wanted her, whoever the woman was because these many witches were not acting without the approval of their high priestess. "Tell me."

The ground in front of Sanura rumbled, another waterline broken. A funnel of water rose above her, formed the body of a Frilled Shark and went in for the kill. The body bent and lunged forward like a snake, its huge fossil-like teeth sharp and biting into Sanura's field.

The water beast broke through, opened its jaws and swallowed Sanura whole.

Heat.

The silent command surged out of her, and with it came her wind and lightning magic, carrying her spell on the sweltering air.

"Where is she?" *Lightning.* "Where?" *Lightning.* "Where?" *Burn in hell.*

Sanura smothered the water witches in her flames, shoving the heat down their throats, through their eyes, and up their nostrils.

They screamed.

But not all the fire belonged to Sanura, nor were all the deaths caused by her heat.

There were more than water witches on the decimated street with Sanura. They chanted, too, but not *fasha*.

"We got here as fast as we could. My gods, Assefa, what happened to you?"

Najja's and Ulan's eyes gaped at the blood-stained shirt he pressed against the gunshot wound.

"Later." Assefa jerked his thumb in the direction of the wall of water. "Can you get me in there?"

"What?"

"I need to know if you can break through that mountain of water and get me inside, so I can get to Sanura. It sounds like a war is going on in there."

Najja handed Ulan the headwrap she removed from her head. Dropping the ruined shirt, Assefa raised his arms so his uncle could wrap the print material around his waist, covering the hole and staunching the bleeding.

"That's because it is a war. There's more than water witches inside there with Sanura. Once she removed her shirt, revealing her mate mark and then her fire magic, the others knew."

"Gods, don't tell me."

Assefa lifted his eyes to the wall again. "Water versus fire."

"Once they realized who Sanura was and that she wasn't *fasha*, the fire witches inside of the cordoned-off area began to fight by her side as did the earth and wind witches. But they're outnumbered by the water witches. Can you hear it, brother? Can you hear how they chant for her? The worship in their voices? The song of pride in their magic?"

He could.

"Fire witch of legend. Fire witch of legend."

Assefa could also hear death and feel Sanura's soul being ripped in two.

"I need you to get me in there."

He didn't know the last time his sister had used her magic. For a while after the accident, she stopped practicing magic. Still, even with a daily magic practitioner, what he requested was no small task.

Assefa could see the doubt and fear in Najja's eyes, but also her stubborn Berber pride. He wanted to kiss and hug her, to tell Najja her disability didn't define her as a woman or as a witch. That she was, quite frankly, the glue that held the Berber men together.

"I wouldn't let her touch me." Najja stretched her hand out to Assefa, who took it, helping his sister to her feet, knowing what she needed him to do. "She sacrificed herself until she could protect Omar and Zareb, and I didn't trust Sanura enough to examine me."

Assefa lifted Najja into his arms and began walking.

Ulan followed.

"It's all right."

"It isn't. I owe her an apology." Najja's hand, palm out, glided across the wall as Assefa walked.

This scheme of his was taking too long. But it couldn't be rushed.

"Jahi ordered an airborne unit to the scene, but they're at least ten minutes out." Ulan moved up to walk beside Assefa, his dark eyes tracking Najja's hand. "They're dying in there."

"I know."

And there wasn't a damn thing he could do about it. Assefa refused to think of this as anything other than a rescue, not a recovery mission.

"Here."

The men stopped.

"Are you sure?"

"I'm sure, Assefa. Put me down."

Lowering Najja to her feet, Assefa held her around her waist while the palm of her hands went to the wall.

"It's weaker here. I think I can break through."

"You get ready, nephew. I got Najja."

Ulan switched places with Assefa, freeing him to dash through whatever space in the water wall Najja would make for him. He hoped it would be big enough.

"No soft, gentle breeze. No ripples without crests. Wind, wind, widespread and wild. Wind, wind, violent and strong. Come to me. Come to me." Najja slammed the palms of her hands against the wall, chanting. "No light flags extended. No whitecaps on waves. Wind, wind, widespread and wild. Wind, wind, violent and strong. Come to me. Come to me."

For a long while, nothing happened. But she didn't stop, didn't once lose her focus or remove her hands from the wall in defeat.

She stayed. She fought. She apologized to Sanura each time she recited her spell, although Assefa knew Sanura hadn't blamed Najja for her fear and wouldn't want an apology.

His sister offered it anyway. In the only way Berbers knew how, by showing up and doing what they did best.

Fight and win.

"Duck," Najja yelled.

They did.

A microburst came out of nowhere, speed over one hundred miles per hour and barreled right into the spot where Najja had concentrated her spell.

The wall rocked. The microburst had tunneled through and left a gaping hole in its wake.

Assefa didn't need his uncle to say, "Go get our girl," because he was already charging through the opening, a blur of Mngwa speed.

Thick, stifling air greeted him. Hot, so lung-burning hot, Assefa could barely breathe.

He ran toward the epicenter of the heat, jumping over obliterated pavement and dodging exposed water lines, passing destroyed buildings and maneuvering around burning cars and scorched people.

Skidding to a halt, Assefa caught the scent of burning gardenias, but he still didn't see his witch.

Until he did.

For long seconds, he gawked, unable to reconcile the woman he'd seen just an hour ago, lacing her running shoes and happy at the prospect of seeing more of Khartoum with the brutalized figure in front of him.

By the gods, her body was nothing short of a horrific landscape of bruises, abrasions and puncture wounds. Broken bones pushed against moist skin and blood, wet and sticky, clung to her unyielding frame.

A single tear tracked down Assefa's face as he walked toward Sanura, who floated several feet off the ground, eyes closed, hair whipping in a wind that only touched her.

All around her were witches, on their knees and faces upturned, a prayer to "Oya's chosen one" spilling from their lips.

Sanura opened her mouth and uttered one word: "Lightning."

Assefa craned his head skyward. Dozens of jagged, splintery spikes of whitish-red lightning appeared. They broke off, forming eight groups of spiky armors. Like an Armadillo Lizard, standing against a threat, each group of lightning formed a tight circle, the mouth of the lightning grasping its tail and presenting a tough, jagged surface of spikes.

"Heed your mistress and destroy my enemies."

Sanura's whispered command sent the lightning spikes outward, spiraling down and straight into the building-high water wall, detonating on impact. The reverberation of magic sent the water witches flying backward, impaled by the spikes of burning lightning and landing in defeated sewers of water.

Assefa's eyes slid away from the carnage, from a death battle that should've never been, and back to his Sanura.

Climbing over the prostrated witches, Assefa reached up and claimed his mate. Cradling Sanura against him, he walked away from the wretched scene of lies and heat. Tracey's lies. Sanura's heat.

When his skin began to burn from the wildfire heat coming from his mate, Assefa held Sanura even tighter, a tear escaping and falling to her forehead.

"I have you now, sweetheart. Stay strong, Sanura. I have you."

CHAPTER SIXTEEN

"You need to shift."

Assefa stalked away from his father and back to the closed bathroom door of his bedchamber.

"Son, look at you. You need to shift."

Pressing his forehead to the bathroom door, Assefa contemplated barging in on the fire witch healer.

A soft hand touched the center of his back, and it was then Assefa felt the chill of the air-conditioned room, temperature set to maximum. Turning, he looked down into the concerned eyes of his sister.

"You have second-degree burns and a gun wound. Listen to Father, you need to shift so your Mngwa's healing magic can take care of your injuries."

Najja was right. But how could he shift now when Sanura needed him the most? He'd wear her burns if only he could hold her again and take away Sanura's pain with the power of his love and regret.

But he couldn't.

"I should've never brought her here."

Assefa glanced around his bedchamber. His father and uncle wore matching scowls, Ulan's red tie balled around his knuckles as if preparing to take down a foe with his bare hands. Jahi's glasses were broken, thrown against a wall when Assefa returned to the presidential compound, an unconscious and battered Sanura in his arms. He'd cursed, the likes Assefa hadn't heard since Najja's debilitating accident.

Omar crouched in the west corner, where he'd been since running back to the compound and dressing before seeking out Sanura. He'd rushed into Assefa's bedchamber, not bothering to knock, his eyes bright with worry, anger, and guilt.

"How is she?" Omar had asked of the room, but his eyes had settled on his mate. "I'm fine," he whispered to Najja, answering her unasked question. "Thanks to Sanura."

Assefa had turned away from Omar then. Of all the times to call Sanura by her first name, it was when the witch couldn't hear and appreciate the respect and friendship in the lion's voice.

Omar and Zareb were freed from Sanura's forcefield when she passed out from her injuries. Zareb caught up to Assefa three blocks from ground zero. They'd waved down Staff Sergeant Durka, but Assefa refused their assistance to help him secure Sanura in the back of the military vehicle.

He had no idea how her fire spirit would react if unfamiliar hands touched Sanura. As it was, his touch seemed barely tolerable and the contact had cost him a layer of skin.

They rode back to the compound in silence, Zareb sitting as close to Sanura as he dared, eyes never leaving her water-shredded face.

"She should've killed all of them. Sanura should've set every one of those fucking water witches on fire." Reaching out, Zareb had found one of Sanura's limp curls and twined it around his finger, uncaring how even that small contact with her burned. "She didn't, though, because of me and Omar and because of the other people who were in the wrong place at the wrong time."

Their eyes had met then, as they did now, and Zareb nodded. He'd warned Assefa, advised him to take Sanura home. But he'd permitted her to talk him out of it, allowed his witch to convince him that running was an option he could no longer afford to take.

He should've run. If he had, if he'd given in to that character weakness, Sanura would be safe instead of submerged in a bathtub full of icy water, her body temperature frighteningly high.

"Son, no one knew this would happen. Tracey will pay. Ten lion squads are hunting for her as we speak."

"What about her coven?"

The ones that weren't dead, of course, and dozens of them were. But not all by Sanura's hand, he would wager, because those bystanders had turned on the water witches, including the were-cats. They'd rallied behind the fire witch of legend. Even now, hundreds of witches and were-cats sat vigil by the compound gates, more appearing by the hour.

Sanura wouldn't want this, the awe, the hero and god worship. Yet it touched Assefa, after the ugliness done to Sanura, to see so many Sudanese, lit candles of life waving in the air and prayers for a woman none of them knew.

Still, Sudan, thus far, held few happy memories for his fire witch. He doubted if Sanura would want to return, which saddened him.

The door to the bathroom opened. All talking ceased, and eyes shifted to the middle-aged woman.

High Priestess Leila closed the door behind her, blotting her face with the black-and-white headwrap that once adorned her head. The diminutive priestess glanced from one anxious face to the next before settling on Assefa.

"Her fire spirit won't let me near her."

"But you're high priestess of the fire witch coven." Jahi frowned. "That's why I asked you here. Sanura's too hot for anyone else to get near her. Assefa's dumped pounds of ice in the tub with her, and they melt within minutes."

"I understand, General Supreme." The petite woman, dressed in a black stone lace floral skirt set, laid a warm, sympathetic hand on Assefa's arm. "Your mate's inner spirit is guarding her. It's angry and afraid that her witch won't survive her injuries. The problem is that the fire spirit doesn't understand that by protecting Sanura so fiercely, she's also standing in the way of Sanura getting medical attention."

"Does that mean that the fire spirit is in control and not Sanura?" Assefa asked.

"Not exactly. I used my second sight on the fire witch of legend. There's something else inside of her, but I couldn't determine what it was. Whatever it is, it's also protecting her. Combined, I can't breach the protective spell they've woven around her." She lowered her hand. "She'll die without medical or magical intervention."

Ulan swore. "We need to get Makena here, right now. I knew I should've called her. She'll know what to do."

Assefa disagreed. "Makena's more than twelve hours away. She'll need time to book a flight, which will only add to the time it'll take her to get here to help Sanura."

From Leila's slumped shoulders and mournful eyes, Assefa didn't think Sanura had fourteen hours.

"Goddammit, Assefa. You know what Sanura means to her mother. What they mean to each other. We must do something. We can't just stand here, looking at that closed bathroom door and let Sanura die."

"She won't die, uncle, don't say that," Najja blurted, her fear thickening her voice and filling her eyes with unshed tears. "We just have to think of another plan." She rolled closer to Assefa. "Who else, brother? Can you think of anyone who can help Sanura?"

For a minute, Assefa didn't register his sister's questions. As her mate, his Mngwa should've been able to reach Sanura, to calm her fire spirit. Maybe, if it were only the fire spirit he had to barter with, his Mngwa could've done so with relative ease. But it wasn't only Sanura's overprotective fire spirit that guarded her, but her father's jaguar spirit.

It was that spirit, Assefa suspected, that kept his Mngwa out. The fire spirit may have stood between Sanura and other witches, but it was Sam's jaguar spirit that barred the Mngwa.

He'd failed to protect his mate from the water witches. And now her father's cat spirit felt the need to do what he hadn't, which made Assefa feel awful.

"Did you hear me, brother? What are our options? Is there anyone else we can call, something we can do that we haven't already tried?"

Sanura once told him how her father had prayed to Sàngó, the god of fire, thunder and lightning, the night of Sanura's birth, wanting the god to bless his daughter. During the meeting between mortal and god, the newborn Sanura, while held by Sàngó, became deathly ill. She'd almost died. A post-birth and fatigued Makena was barely able to calm her own fire spirit enough to save her daughter. Yet there had been one other fire witch present in the Williams' household, and it was she who helped Makena save Sanura.

Could she do it again now that Sanura's fire spirit was stronger and mature?

"Sanura's grandmother, High Priestess Wasola Toure, lives in Nigeria. That's less than three hours away by air."

As soon as the words were out of his mouth, the bedchamber became a hive of Berber activity, Jahi contacting the President of the Federal Republic of Nigeria, Ulan phoning the airfield, and Najja arranging for a guest room to be prepared for the Toures.

He would take care of placing the call to Sanura's grandmother. Assefa hoped to meet the matriarch under different circumstances, like his and Sanura's wedding.

Assefa found Sanura's cell phone on his nightstand. Wasola Toure was listed simply as Ìyáñlá—grandmother.

He called

Tracey closed and locked the motel room door behind her. Rushing to the thick, brown window curtains, she yanked them shut, hoping no one saw her enter the room. She'd bespelled the motel manager, manipulating him into giving her a room. He wouldn't remember Tracey, despite the news playing on the small television he'd been watching when she'd scurried into the motel lobby.

Her face and name were everywhere, including on the television the were-cat was watching. When Tracey stood on the opposite side of the check-in desk, sunglasses on and hair pulled back in a ponytail, the older man's eyes lifted, stared and then snapped back to the television screen. He did a double-take between the television and Tracey, and his uncertainty was all the time she needed to cast her spell.

Gods, what was she going to do? How did this happen? How had her plan gone to complete shit? Sanura Williams was supposed to be a level one earth witch, not the fire witch of legend.

Tracey sank onto the lumpy motel room bed. She couldn't go home or to any of her coven sisters. By now, they all would know she'd lied about the American witch being *fasha* and a danger to Assefa.

She only had the clothes on her back and her bank and credit cards. And was terrified of using either. Couldn't those cards be tracked? Weren't ATM machines equipped with tiny surveillance cameras?

He would know. Gods, the general supreme would know where to find her if she tried to use her cards to get the hell out of Khartoum. But she had to go somewhere farther than this motel.

Kicking off her shoes, Tracey scooted back onto the bed, her back going to the mattress, her eyes to the white ceiling.

He would send soldiers after her, she feared. They would track her down and drag her back to the presidential compound. She shuddered at the thought. Would the general supreme have her interrogated? Tortured then killed?

Would he give her to the fire witch of legend? Would the woman burn her alive for what she'd done?

Tracey closed her eyes, fear dredging up a memory.

Once leaving the presidential compound, elated with how well she'd executed her plan as well as the sheer luck of Chanya spotting Sanura Williams leave the protective gates of the House of Berber, Tracey had decided to slip through the water barricade to witness the death of Assefa's witch.

And what a beautiful barricade her sisters had conjured, Chanya able to galvanize hundreds of water witches at the last minute. They'd come, eager to serve their new high priestess and ready to battle a demon-witch who'd gotten her claws into Assefa Berber, Sudan's favorite son.

Yet the scene wasn't at all what she'd expected. In the beginning, yes, but not when the supposed earth witch formed two forcefields.

Fire magic fields. They'd glowed ruby red with potency, unlike anything she'd seen a fire witch create.

Then the fire witch emerged from a multi-witch attack, not unscathed but far from defeated. Impossible. Shit, that should've been impossible. Dozens of witches, layered witch magic, coven magic, yet there Sanura Williams had stood, eyes scarlet and demanding the whereabouts of the coven's high priestess.

Murder was in her voice. Flames of retribution in her hands.

She'd run, back through the water barrier and ducking behind a car when Assefa, Najja, and Ulan came into view. Luckily, they hadn't seen her and neither had the soldiers and first responders.

Tracey had no idea what happened to the people bleeding on the ground, and she didn't care. The bustle to tend to the wounded served as a perfect distraction, allowing Tracey to slip away unseen.

But they would be coming for her. She had to flee, had to somehow make it across the Sudanese-Egyptian border. Once in Egypt and surrounded by full-humans, she'd be safe. The general supreme wouldn't dare send witches or were-cats after her there, not with the risk of exposing themselves to full-humans.

If she could only make it to Egypt, she'd be safe.

Tracey closed her eyes and sighed. She could do this. She just needed to think and be patient. The goddess was with her. She'd always been with her. Mami Wata wouldn't abandon her faithful water witch now, not when she needed her the most.

Laughter erupted around her, jolting Tracey into a seated position. It came again, raucous and with a timbre of malevolence.

Such a disappointment, mortal. The mangy beast was in your thrall, but you let him slip away.

"The spell broke. I don't know how, my Goddess. I tried to lure him back to me, but once the spell broke, I couldn't get it back."

She'd explained this before to the water goddess, begged her forgiveness, which she'd given, conditionally.

Excuses. I granted you much. Power. A coven. A second chance. Even an ally, selfish and cynical, but a perfect partner. Yet you failed me again. What am I to do with such a useless water witch?

She shivered, her mind scrambling for the right appeasing words.

"My coven hurt the witch. They attacked her with all they had. No one, not even the fire witch of legend, can survive that much damage to the body. If she isn't already dead, she soon will be."

Tracey got to her knees, hands clasped as if in prayer, eyes darting around the room. She saw no one else, just her reflection in the mirror, which didn't mean Tracey was alone.

"That's a bonus, right? I didn't know Sanura Williams was the fire witch of legend. But I got her for you. I stopped her when all you asked me to do was keep Assefa from his American witch and to prevent their bonding."

Surely the water goddess would appreciate all that Tracey sacrificed to redeem herself. She'd risked everything and betrayed many, all for Mami Wata's blessing and the promise of a lifetime with Assefa and power beyond her imagining.

Tracey fell, the sturdy weight of the mattress disappearing from under her. Improbably, liquid rose to surround the witch, the room transformed into an aquarium of dank water.

She banged against the glass, breath held, eyes stinging but seeing nothing as she pressed her face to the glass. Staring up, Tracey glimpsed a low light coming from the top of the aquarium.

She began to swim, fast and hard.

When she finally reached the top, lungs burning from holding her breath so long, she saw a face. The woman smiled, thick wavy hair blotting out the meager light, a huge hissing snake around her neck.

Tracey wanted to call out to the woman, to the goddess she'd only ever heard in her mind. But she couldn't, didn't dare risk drowning, so she reached up, fingers searching for the edge of the aquarium.

Mami Wata reared back, smiled again, beautiful yet vicious. Out came dozens of electric eels on a waterfall that flowed from Mami Watas's gaping mouth and into the aquarium with Tracey.

Elongated, cylindrical body. Seven feet in length. Forty-five pounds. Dark-gray brown and no scales.

Desperate, Tracey attempted to lift herself from the aquarium, fingers slippery, the edge narrow and wet.

The first electric shock lasted only a couple of seconds. As did the second, third, and fourth. By the fifth, Tracey could no longer hold onto the edge, her attempt at freedom slipping away as each finger relinquished its death grip.

She fell into the pool of despair. Thousands of volts coursed through her body, excruciating shocks that heated her skin and sent currents straight to her brain, passing through.

Again. And again.

When will mortals learn? Never bargain with a god. But you have served Mami Wata well. Sleep now, Tracey Kemraha, and may Apep welcome you to Duat and Ammit devour your pitiful soul.

CHAPTER SEVENTEEN

The Fire Phoenix added another layer of burning sticks to her nest. At the bottom of the twenty feet deep and thirty feet wide nest, her witch slept, curled in a ball and dreaming fitfully. Such a tiny thing, her Sanura. Yet her heart and will were strong and trials too many.

Sanura needed to rest, to find peace in a world determined to tear her down, body and soul. The Fire Phoenix, red eyes glowing with rage each time they discovered a new wound on her witch, blew spirit fire around the nest, keeping out all who would do Sanura harm.

Glancing up from her protective ward, the Fire Phoenix caught the familiar black coat of the jaguar, his spots visible to only a keen eye such as hers. He reclined on a large branch several feet above her, keeping watch as she finished building the nest for their witch.

They would protect Sanura. No one would be allowed to harm her ever again. If anyone else tried, she would burn them to dust.

"Sanura will be safe here with us."

The jaguar crept closer, graceful as he descended and stopping one branch above the nest. "How long has it been since we brought Sanura here? Since she drifted off into a nightmarish slumber?"

"She dreams, but even I cannot see what torments her mind."

"Why not?"

"Because we're two fractured spirits."

"And that truth brings you pain?" The jaguar jumped onto the branch with the Fire Phoenix, his landing silent.

"You do not belong here, cat spirit."

"Yet here I am. With my daughter."

"You take the place of the Mngwa."

"I stepped into the void he has yet to fill. The boy needs to grow up more."

"Or perhaps it's the father who needs to let go and allow Assefa to be the man to Sanura he already is."

A disembodied head with snapping flames for hair floated from the top of the deciduous tree and down toward the Fire Phoenix and jaguar, not stopping until she hovered in front of them.

The Fire Phoenix extended her beak and touched the flames of hair. The heat felt familiar, familial.

"Who are you, fire spirit?"

The mouth in the head smiled and nodded at the cat spirit. "He knows. I was saddened by Sam's death, by the sacrifice he thought he needed to make to save his daughter." The uninvited spirit's scarlet eyes fell to the nest and the sleeping witch within, sparking with fury when she took in Sanura's ravaged body.

"You see what Mami Wata and her water witches have done to our Sanura?" the jaguar asked.

"Yes, my friend, I see. And the sight pains and angers."

"Then we agree." The jaguar lowered his long tail into the nest and caressed Sanura's face, a tender and loving gesture from the ferocious cat.

"About protecting her, yes." The fire spirit glided closer to the cat. "But you're not protecting Sanura by encasing her inside your ward and by blocking Assefa's Mngwa. Look at her. Both of you, look at your witch. She's dying."

"You can't have her, Wasola." The jaguar spirit swatted at the fire spirit with his claw, the deadly nails sliding through the ethereal head.

"Let her go, Jaguar. If you don't, Sanura will die." She nodded to the sleeping witch. "The damage you see to her soul-body here is nothing compared to what she actually looks like in the physical plane. Sanura's barely recognizable. Her body is broken, skin a tapestry of sliced wounds, carved deep and oozing blood fire."

The cat spirit growled but didn't offer another pointless attack or counterargument. Instead, he dropped his tail into the nest again, wrapped it around Sanura's boneless form and lifted her into the air.

Bringing her close, he sniffed her, and reddish-yellow eyes became moist.

"She's all I have left. I don't want to let my precious witch go."

"She's also all Makena has left. If Sanura dies, her mother's heart will shatter into a million fire witch pieces of inconsolable grief."

Held tears fell and the jaguar's tail tightened around his dying heart. "I don't wish for my mate to suffer any more than she already has."

"Then give Sanura to me." The fire spirit lifted her head to the Fire Phoenix. "And you, mighty firebird, will you allow me to take your witch knowing I love her as much as you do and will do all in my power to protect and heal her?"

"She doesn't love me."

"There you are wrong, young firebird. Sanura loves you more than you know. You're her, and she's you. And I am grandmother to you both."

The fire spirit floated upward, her observant eyes traveling over the Fire Phoenix's large body. "You were just a baby bird when I last felt your spirit, crying and raging out of control. Makena's fire spirit soothed you then, will you allow me to soothe you now, granddaughter?"

Neck, shoulders, arms, torso and more formed from the head, growing into a lithe, tall woman made of sizzling flames and fire magic. Arms found the Fire Phoenix's massive neck and hugged.

"She does love you, young firebird." The fire spirit grazed a white feather at the base of her neck that belonged to the Fire Phoenix but wasn't hers. "Sanura loves you, but she doesn't yet understand."

Neither did the Fire Phoenix.

Another caress over the white feather that shouldn't be, but was.

"Let me take her. Please."

Sanura moaned, shifted on the bed and then moaned again. Gods, her body. She felt, hell, she didn't know. Lethargic. Hot. Wet.

Fisting her hands in the cool sheets at her sides, Sanura bent her knees, her feet finding the mattress and pushing her hips upward. A weight settled on her hips and pulled her forward.

She didn't fight the sensation, her body boneless, aching and wanting, needing… release.

Back bowed, thighs wide, Sanura keened. Dry mouth opened on a gulping cry of pleasure. She didn't want it to stop, didn't want to part her lids to discover it was just another torturous nightmare meant to send her over the edge.

A long, thick tongue delved deep, over and again, fucking her from one orgasm and straight into the next. Keeping Sanura in an extended state of carnal bliss, her eyes shut tight, nails bit into palms, thighs quivered and sex soaked.

Assefa kept going, his tongue in her relentless, the thumb stroking her clit into oversensitive hardness just as persistent.

Sanura fell apart, her entire body trembling with orgasmic shocks that began at her curled toes and traveled all the way to her ringing ears.

And still he didn't stop, just kept pleasuring her with his tongue, large hands on her thighs and holding them open for him.

She whimpered, maybe even blacked out for a second or two, then Sanura was coming again.

By the time Assefa lifted his head from between her legs, face drenched, grin wicked and self-satisfied, Sanura couldn't move, could barely, in fact, breathe.

Crawling up her body, Assefa settled his muscular form between her legs, pushing into Sanura with a gentle hardness that brought tears to her eyes.

Then he was fucking her again. Not making love, but long, grinding thrusts that rocked the bed and demanded a physical response.

Sanura gave in, slamming her hips upward and meeting Assefa hard thrust for hard thrust. Grabbing his face between her hands, Sanura kissed him, long and deep, mimicking what he was doing to her body.

Pleasure, not pain.

He knew, gods, Assefa always knew which hunger of hers to feed. And he was just as ravenous, eating greedily from her mouth while filling her. His gyrating hips were in constant motion and hands everywhere.

"Yes, Assefa. God, yes."

He swallowed her moans and stole her breath.

"Don't you ever scare me like that again." The bed banged against the bedroom wall. Assefa's eyes glowed Mngwa gold as he lifted himself above Sanura, wrapped her legs around his neck, knees to her chest, and proceeded to fuck her Hard.

Cracked wall and falling paint chips were evidence of Assefa's temporary loss of control.

When she collapsed, it was onto Assefa's sweaty chest and into his protective arms, breaths ragged and body sated. For several minutes, neither spoke. They simply held each other and basked in the afterglow of their coupling.

Sanura felt emotionally raw from her battle with the water witches and had no interest in learning the why of the attack or how many witches she'd killed. The awful thought had Sanura dragging the covers off the floor and over their naked bodies. The air conditioner, she'd just noticed, set to Christmas in the North Pole.

"Your grandparents are here."

Sanura figured as much. Only Makena or Wasola would've been able to heal Sanura after the amount of damage her body had sustained.

Sanura shot up. "Oh gods, they aren't next door, are they?"

Assefa laughed, encouraging Sanura to retake her place on his chest and in his arms.

She did.

"No, sweetheart, Najja arranged for the Toures to be placed next to her bedchamber, which is around the corner." Assefa reached up with a fist and banged on the wall above the headboard. "Razi is next door, but he hasn't been around much since the attack."

"What time is it?"

"Probably about nine."

She didn't have to ask whether it was day or night, the morning light answer enough.

"What day?"

"The fifteenth."

Hell, she'd convalesced for nearly a day.

"It's Ulan and Jahi's birthday."

Assefa kissed the top of her head, his arms tightening around her. "They've been waiting for you to wake up. Everyone has. I think my father is an official fire witch of legend fanboy, and my uncle wants to adopt you." A single finger went to her chin and lifted until she met his eyes. "I'm taking you home the morning after their birthday dinner. No arguments. I don't care if it's running, we're going home."

Sanura didn't argue. Not because she knew it would be pointless when Assefa got like this, but it was the day of their scheduled departure anyway, which he should've recalled. Her poor mate, what had he gone through when she'd been out of it.

She kissed him and straddled his waist to take Assefa inside. He was still hard and Sanura still sopping wet. This time, they made love, slow and passionate and infinitely more sensual for all that went unsaid.

Sanura hadn't died. Assefa wasn't to blame. And they had hours yet before dinner.

CHAPTER EIGHTEEN

"I'm sorry, Manute. I don't know what to tell you, that's just how Rachel is. I know, I know, but…"

Sanura kicked off her sandals and sat on the edge of the bed, cell phone up to her ear, head and eyes cast to the floor. Eventually, she swung her legs onto the bed, laid down and let Manute ramble on.

From his spot at his desk, laptop open, Assefa pretended not to listen to Sanura's phone calls and watch her for signs of… he didn't know what. But she hadn't been herself since waking for the second time.

He'd waited until she'd showered and dressed before telling her about Tracey, her claim, his ring and the aftermath of her attack. He avoided mentioning being shot and his second-degree burns.

"So, your crazy, jealous girlfriend tried to kill me? Do I have the story right?"

"Ex-girlfriend. Tracey's my ex-girlfriend." Sanura had summed it up perfectly, although the relaying of the details seemed far more complex when he told it and without the edge of vengeance as had been in Sanura's tone.

"Where is she now?"

Oh, but that question had come out as nothing short of lethal intent. Luckily for Tracey, the witch was already dead.

"Omar found her dead in a motel room."

For his own reasons, Omar had gone hunting for Tracey despite squads of lions already scouring the city for the water witch. Yet he'd slipped from Assefa's bedchamber after arrangements were made to fly Sanura's grandparents from Nigeria and to the Sudan. A single call from the general supreme to the Nigeria's president had helped expedite the Toures' last-minute travel plans.

Two hours later, Omar had returned with news of a dead Tracey. "At first, I thought she was asleep until I got closer. She was on the bed, eyes open and glassy. Her face was frozen in a pained death pose, and her body, bed, and floor were soaked."

He'd left her there, untouched and alone, but called Zareb, who'd informed Jahi and Ulan. An autopsy would be performed later today, Tracey's mother having already confirmed her daughter's identity last night.

Assefa hated the pain Mistress Kemraha now felt, having buried her American-born mate a decade ago. He took comfort, however, in being able to tell the Toures that the woman responsible for their granddaughter's attack was no longer a threat.

They'd nodded. Mr. Toure had shaken Omar's hand. The tall were-cat had to lean down to accept a grateful hug from High Priestess Wasola. She'd kissed both of Omar's cheeks, whispered her thanks and then complimented the were-cat on his "superior lion tracking skills."

Embarrassed, he'd slinked away, and Wasola squared her shoulders, turned and went into the bathroom to see Sanura.

Assefa glanced at what used to be his bathroom door. Worthless now, three basketball-size holes burned through but no longer sizzling. If the family resemblance weren't enough to let Assefa know Wasola was related to Makena and Sanura, her calm exterior then quick temper certainly would have been.

Odafe had patted him on the back, smiling at Assefa with wise eyes. "That's why I stayed out here. I love them dearly, but my wife, daughter, and granddaughter require a man above the norm, who has the patience of a saint and quick reflexes." The older man settled onto the chaise lounge and closed his eyes. "Welcome to the family, Assefa. Take a seat. Wasola's going to be a while if her Yoruba curses and fire-balls were any indications of Sanura's injuries."

Quick reflexes. Assefa laughed, which had Sanura looking at him from her spot on the bed. The eighty-two-year-old man still had it, ducking even before Assefa did to avoid his wife's fireballs, which landed across the room, stopped by a wall that now bore burn marks.

Sanura no longer spoke to Manute but Rashad, having already had a lengthy conversation with Dahad. Assefa wished Zareb hadn't called them, but he was thankful he'd refrained from making similar calls to Makena and Mike.

Sanura would tell her friends and family after they returned home.

"Why would you tell your preternatural friends that you live with the fire witch of legend?"

"Because it makes the were-cats envious, and they're already afraid of Assefa's Mngwa, so they treat me like a king."

She sighed. "Rashad, you can't go around telling your friends who I am."

"I'm building you an army."

"I don't need an army, especially an army of college students."

Rashad, uncharacteristically, went quiet for a long while before he said, "My dreams say differently, so I'm building you an army. Every goddess needs an army. And I'm going to give you yours."

What had Zareb said about Sanura and were-cats? *With or without her moonstone, Sanura's smell makes a were-cat want to protect her, worship her, spoil her, or fuck her.*

He'd seen the truth in so many little ways since meeting Sanura. Zareb was right, but he was also wrong. It wasn't about Sanura's smell, at least not just that. It also wasn't only about the effect she had on were-cats but preternaturals in general.

She wasn't a siren, nothing so banal as that. But thousands of Sudanese, different preternaturals, not just fire witches and were-cats, had flocked to the presidential compound and refused to leave until they saw the fire witch of legend.

Even a press conference from the general supreme hadn't sent the people back to their homes. It wasn't until had Jahi pleaded with a healed Sanura that she'd submitted to a short interview, televised nationwide, that the crowd finally dispersed.

General Supreme Jahi Berber pleaded with no one. He told. He commanded. He ordered. He rarely asked. And never begged.

"Rashad, I'm fine. You don't have to worry about me."

Rashad talked more, and Sanura pretended to listen, responding at appropriate times but barely maintaining her side of the conversation. Eventually, she began to drift off to sleep and Assefa rescued the falling phone from her hand.

"What do you think about—"

"She's asleep."

Assefa covered Sanura with a throw cover before claiming the chaise lounge to watch over her.

"Assefa, good. Tell me how Sanura's really doing. She sounded tired."

She was. No matter how long she slept, Sanura never awakened fully rested. She no longer wanted to share the details of her nightmares with him, which didn't stop Assefa from asking or worrying. He didn't know how to help her or whether Sanura even wanted his help.

"The battle took a lot out of her. Her injuries were severe. We need to be patient, and Sanura will be back to her old self in no time."

"Who are you trying to convince, Alpha, you or me?"

"Smart man."

"Yup, that's why you're paying my tuition. Makes you feel all useful and shit, doesn't it? Like you aren't just paying for me to attend parties, get into fights, and eat peaches."

Eat peaches, where did Rashad come up with these euphemisms? Assefa felt a headache coming.

"Listen, I like it when Sanura laughs and smiles. She's brought sunshine into our home, and I want it to stay that way."

Assefa agreed, but where was young Rashad going with this?

"I know you're kind of conservative about certain things, but hear me out before you say no."

"Go on before I hang up and join my witch in bed."

"Okay, okay. I was thinking you could send Sanura a dick pic."

"A what?"

"Damn, you didn't have to growl as if I offered to send her a picture of mine. It's not like Sanura hasn't already seen your general and two colonels."

"I'm not sending my mate a picture of my dick."

"Look, it's easy and girls love it. But here's the thing, you can't just whip it out and take a pic. You gotta put some thought into it, set the stage."

"Rashad—"

"You want to put on a really good show. You know, some muscled thigh and ripped ab action to go with the dick. The combo is what sells, Assefa, trust me. And make sure the grass on the field is mowed. No witch wants to wade through overgrowth to get to the good part."

"Rashad, I really don't think—"

"Don't rely on the light from your cell phone's camera either. From my experience, natural lighting works the best. Finally, you want that monster to be a thick, ready-for-action pole. Like a stripper pole, but better because she can swing on yours and then it can fuck her."

Assefa hung up. Unbelievable. What in the hell made Rashad think Assefa would...? He looked from his cell phone and to Sanura, then to his pants.

What the hell. His witch did love to look at his dick. If nothing else, it may just shock Sanura back to life. Give her something to make fun of Assefa about.

Unbuttoning his shirt and pulling down his pants, Assefa took himself in hand. Closing his eyes, he thought about this morning and how Sanura had tasted when he awoke her with his mouth. Then how she felt when he sank into her, her legs going around his waist and pulling him closer and deeper.

He stroked, recalling it all. Her moans in his ear. Her nails down his back. Her teeth against his shoulder. Her nipples in his mouth.

Finding the camera on his phone, Assefa took a burst of rapid-fire photos. At five in the afternoon, plenty of natural light streamed through the pyramid's windows. He had no grass on his field, which Sanura loved.

After putting himself to rights, Assefa, ever so meticulous, scanned each photo for the perfect shot. They all looked the same. Assefa had to admit, his dick did look impressive.

Hitting the share icon, Assefa scrolled until he found—

"What are you doing?" Sanura watched him from the bed, eyes open and questioning.

Without looking, Assefa hit the contact name, then sent the picture. Quickly, he stuffed his phone into his pants pocket.

"Checking emails." He rose. "Want me to join you?"

"Yes."

Taking off his shoes, Assefa climbed into bed with Sanura, spooning behind her and pulling her close. Wrapped snuggly around his witch, Assefa closed his eyes, knowing they only had about an hour before they would have to dress and join the others for Jahi and Ulan's cele-bratory birthday dinner.

He began to fall off to sleep when Sanura asked, "What were you really doing on that chaise lounge. You're hard as a rock?"

Sanura walked between her grandparents as they followed Assefa down the long hall and toward the family dining room. As much as she'd like to return to Assefa's bedchamber and fall back asleep, Sanura had no interest in seeing more of the fire witch of legend's sad and violent memories. At this rate, if Sanura wanted to get a good night's sleep, she would have to use an anti-dream spell, which she didn't wish to do. Mind spells were tricky and dangerous. And there was a slight possibil-ity Sanura could either not wake up or her mind forever trapped in a nightmare. She wouldn't risk it, which meant she'd have to learn how to deal with the dreams or find a way to banish the fire witch of legend from her mind.

"I was unaware Makena had begun seeing someone."

Her grandfather spoke low and in Yoruba, which told Sanura he was talking about Ulan and didn't want Assefa to know. It was rude, but Sanura knew better than to correct her grandfather.

"They're just friends."

"I got the impression they were a bit more. He was in the limousine that picked us up from the airport."

"Mom and Ulan aren't more. He just wishes they were."

Sanura slid her arm in the crook of her grandfather's, happy to see him despite the circumstances of their reunion. Six one, clean-shaven, and a firewoman mate mark on his left forearm that "danced" when he flexed it, Odafe Tour, in his navy-blue suit and gray shirt cut quite a handsome image.

"I'm not sure about that Ulan fellow, but it's time for Makena to start thinking about what she's going to do with the rest of her life and how long she plans to mourn Sam and shut herself off from other men."

"Don't start, Odafe." Wasola took hold of Sanura's other hand, twining their fingers together as they walked. "Makena will choose another mate in her own time, if at all. Besides, if you pressure her, Makena will only dig her heels in even more."

"Stubborn fire witches," Odafe mumbled, and Assefa chuckled. "Understood that, did you, young man? Well, I guess you know some Yoruba after all."

"A very little, sir."

"Well, let me teach you a few key phrases if you're going to survive in this family of women."

Odafe released Sanura's arm and moved up to speak with Assefa, leaving Sanura and her grandmother to walk behind them.

"I know I already said it, but thank you for coming."

Sanura kissed Wasola's cheek, the white-haired woman a mere inch shorter than her. She looked lovely in a navy wrap dress the same shade as Odafe's suit, double notched collar, front and back pleating and a belt looped at her tiny waist. And while Sanura's and Makena's hair

grew like weeds, Wasola always kept her hair cut ruthlessly short, preferring to "brush and go."

"You're welcome. You never need to thank me for loving you."

"I know, but still." She squeezed Wasola's hand. "Please tell me
what happened when I was unconscious."

The women's pace slowed as they talked, so engrossed were they in
their conversation they hadn't realized they'd reached the dining room.

"A white feather? What do you think it means?"

"I'm not sure. I'm not even certain whether the feather was a rare
albino feather or a feather that shouldn't have been a part of your Fire
Phoenix at all. But it was there, out of place but not quite, if you know
what I mean."

Out of place but not quite. That explained how it felt to be the fire
witch of legend. But a white feather on a red fire spirit? That made no
sense.

Sanura fell quiet, her mind replaying the jaguar spirit's memory of
the night of her birth and Sam's conversation with Sàngó. What had the
thunder god told Sam when her father had asked him to bless Sanura?

Sanura knew the dream-memory by heart, but her tired brain wasn't
cooperating.

"What's wrong? Why are you frowning?"

Assefa stood before her, his eyes since she'd survived her deathbed,
shadowed with emotions he tried to hide. In many ways, they'd come
far in their relationship, in other ways, not at all.

Sanura didn't have the energy to get into why Assefa wasn't to
blame for the actions of his psycho ex-girlfriend, who, Sanura was convinced after hearing his story, had bespelled Assefa into her bed and her
hands into his wallet.

Powerful, unscrupulous witches didn't hesitate to use their magic to
get what they wanted from unmated were-cats who had no witch to protect him from the manipulative spells of another witch. As mighty as
Assefa's Mngwa may be, Assefa, the man, was no less susceptible to
potions and spells as any other were-cat.

"I'm fine."

"You keep saying that, but it's untrue."

"Well, they say if you tell a lie often enough it becomes the truth."

"Don't do that."

"What? Lie?"

He grabbed her hand and pulled Sanura away from the entrance to the dining room and into the room across the hall.

"Don't act like everything is fine to spare my feelings. Don't pretend that you haven't spent most of your waking hours thinking about the witches you were forced to kill. And stop looking at me as if my death date is written on my damn forehead. You were the one who nearly died, Sanura, not me."

Assefa may be a genius, but he didn't understand a damn thing. She chose to kill those water witches. Sanura, not her fire spirit. She'd decided they deserved to die, so she sent them to hell. She'd judged and found them wanting, death their rightful punishment.

Sanura had done all of that, her responsibility undeniable.

How could she confess her sins when Sanura knew she would make the same decision? She had no right to claim those souls, although she felt as if she did.

Those water witches weren't innocent, weren't pawns or even victims of Tracey Kemraha's schemes. They'd earned their fate, her mind and magic told her. But her heart ached at her foul deeds, hemorrhaged to the point of grief and physical weakness.

And she didn't want to think, much less talk about Assefa dying.

Sanura kissed him on the lips, and quick. "I love you and will do anything to protect you."

The ever flirtatious Zareb approached before Assefa could respond.

"There the two of you are. The general supreme sent me to find the two of you."

Dark-brown eyes sparkled when they took in Sanura, green eyes and red-gold hair. No moonstone. During the battle with the water witches, she'd lost the cuff bracelet as well as her treasured moonstone.

To her surprise, Zareb enveloped Sanura in a big bear hug. She hadn't seen him since he'd tried to protect her, his body no match for the pounds of water leveled against him.

Sanura returned the hug, grateful for Zareb's loyalty and friendship. Words of gratitude weren't exchanged. None were needed.

Stepping back, Sanura took in the tall man, noting for the first time what hung around his waist.

"Um, Zareb, that's a really big sword you got there."

He looked from Sanura to Assefa and then back to Sanura before bursting into laughter.

"Why, yes, fire witch of legend, I do have a big sword. Better to—"

"You better not finish that sentence or I'll castrate you with your ceremonial sword."

Zareb ignored Assefa's threat but didn't finish his sentence. He did pluck the tip of Sanura's nose with a, "You're adorable. The things you say, Dr. Williams."

Gods, they were back to that stupid word.

Sanura pushed past the men, making a strategic retreat while Assefa glared at Zareb.

By the time she made it across the hall and to the dining room, Assefa was right behind her, handsome in his dark-gray.

She kissed him again, then joined the dinner party, hoping this evening would be better than her afternoon of a day ago.

CHAPTER NINETEEN

Razi sat at the hand-carved wooden table, upheld by four jaguar-shaped legs. He lifted his glass of wine, toasting the statue of the goddess Sekhmet located in the west corner of the spacious dining room. Depicted as a human with the face of a lioness, atop her head rested a solar disk and uraeus while she held an ankh of life in her right hand and a was, a symbol of power and dominion, in her left. Made of granite, the statue represented the wealth, power and history of the great ancient nation of Sudan.

Swallowing the savory white wine, Razi's eyes slid to the people around the table. The general supreme sat at the head of the long table and Ulan at the other end. Instead of being seated to the right of his father as the eldest son in the family should, Assefa sat there with his witch to his right.

To the left of the general supreme was Najja, and next to her sat the goddamn medja as if he belonged at the Berber table, a servant from a were-cat family Razi's ancestor should've eliminated completely when he secured this land for the Berbers. Worse, Najja's mate claimed the spot to the right of Ulan, the executive chef's bookworm son whose kingly lion's mane was wasted on a man who had no balls or bite.

Yet, he had been the one to discover Tracey's body in a motel in a run-down part of the city. Dead, thankfully. After their plan had gone south, Sanura Williams no low-level witch ripe for plucking and squashing, Razi worried what Tracey would reveal once in custody.

Like Omar and the squads of lions, Razi had gone hunting for the most wanted water witch in Sudan's history. He'd hoped he would find her before his father's soldiers did, certain the weak woman wouldn't hold up against the general supreme's methods of information extraction.

Razi toasted the statue of Sekhmet again, preferring an inanimate object to dinner conversation with grandparents. They'd come and saved the fire witch. Yet, no one could save Tracey. For that, Razi was grateful. Still, he'd been looking forward to raking his claws across the witch's face, drawing blood and gurgled gags while watching her die.

Razi would've enjoyed that very much. But Tracey was gone, and Sanura was there smiling at his father and speaking Wolof as if she were born with the language on her tongue.

The goddamn fire witch of legend. Assefa found her, the lucky, entitled bastard. His good fortune would end tonight.

"It's my great privilege to have my family here to celebrate a milestone. And I welcome Sanura, Wasola, and Odafe to the small but mighty Berber family."

The general supreme grinned, happier than Razi had seen him in months, English flawless and used to accommodate the Toures. Since when did the general supreme care about the feelings of someone else to the point of altering his behavior? He'd never given a damn about Razi's thoughts or feelings, not even when he was a teenager, crying and demanding answers about his mother.

A cough from the general supreme had him clearing his throat and taking a sip of wine before finishing his thought. "Even my wayward brother managed to fit me and our birthday into his busy schedule."

"I see you still have a way with words, brother." Ulan reached down beside him and pulled up a shirt size box. He placed the gift, with black wrapping paper and a red ribbon, on the table in front of his place setting. "On this day, there's nowhere in the world I would rather be. I even remembered to bring you a gift."

"We haven't exchanged gifts in years. Is it expensive?"

"Of course."

"Is it inappropriate to open in front of ladies?"

"Without a doubt."

Jahi smiled, eyeing the box with much interest. "Wait." He nodded at Sanura, who stared down at her lap, preoccupied with whatever was on her cell phone. "Is it better than Assefa's present?"

"Nothing's better than the fire witch of legend as a gift."

Sanura's head snapped up. "You two do realize that I'm in the room and that I'm also a person, right?"

"Yes, that's what makes you such an adorable present. Tell my brother what you did to Paul Chambers."

Irritation flickered in the bold, green eyes that all but skewered Ulan where he sat, his teasing grin deliberately provoking.

"Telling is so boring, Ulan. We could put on a demonstration for your family. I'll be me, and you can be Paul. We can begin with the binding spell I used to contain him. Will that work for you?" She set the cell phone face-down on the table and whispered to Assefa, "We'll talk about this text message later." Those same exasperated eyes traveled first to Ulan, then to Jahi, and finally to Zareb. "From this day forward, none of you will refer to me as adorable. I'm not a bunny or gerbil, or even a puppy or kitten. Fire witches are not adorable, we're—"

"Hot-tempered," Jahi coughed out.

"Volatile," Ulan added.

"Spicy." Zareb eyed Assefa before mouthing to Sanura, "Sexy."

Assefa shook his head, as annoyingly calm as ever.

"Fire witches are two parts sweet and one part sour, the perfect Daiquiri—classic, delicious, and deceptively potent."

All the men around the table stared at Odafe Toure, who shrugged and accepted a kiss to his cheek from his mate.

Zareb whooped and clapped. "Old school charm. I love it." He pointed to Omar and Assefa. "The two of you could learn something from Mr. Toure."

"Be quiet, special agent, grown men are speaking." Grinning, Ulan handed Zareb the wrapped gift, who then stood and placed it on the small gift table, next to which was propped his ceremonial medja sword and shield. "As you can see, brother, my future step-daughter isn't at all loving. But she did get me this wonderful tie for my birthday."

Everyone watched as Ulan dug into his suit pocket and pulled out a folded silk tie. Unfurling it, he held it aloft in his right hand, his left pointing to the red faces on the tie.

While Najja threw her head back and laughed, everyone else turned their gaze on an unrepentant Sanura.

"Oh, come on. I can't be the only one who thinks Ulan dresses like the devil."

"And now he has a tie to match." Najja guffawed. "Gods, Uncle Ulan, there are six red-faced horned devils on that white tie. And they're smiling, knowing purgatory awaits the next damned soul. Finally, another woman in this family of testosterone and fur."

"I didn't give you that tie by the way." Sanura narrowed her eyes at Ulan. "The last time I saw the gift box the tie was in was when I placed it on Assefa's desk in his bedroom."

"The box had my name on it, so I took a little peek. You can't blame a were-cat for his curiosity."

"Curiosity killed the cat, Ulan. I don't suppose you also peeked at your real gift." Sanura nodded in the direction of the gift table. "It's over there. Be warned, opening it may be dangerous to your health."

Unbelievably, Ulan Berber, Chief of the Preternatural Division of the FBI and hard as steel jaguar, roared with laughter. "You see, everyone. Sanura threatens me with her eyes, and I'm afraid to fall asleep at night lest I awaken with her in my bedroom, a curse spilling from her sweet lips. No, I don't want to end up like Paul Chambers, so I'll wear a bomb suit when I open my present."

Sanura rolled her eyes and slouched in her chair. "One little curse, Ulan. You saw me cast one little curse, and you won't let it go." She sprang forward. "By the way, don't forget to tell everyone you were in Chambers' home to put a bullet in the man. Probably through his wretched heart or despicable brain."

"All right, that's it. It's my birthday, and I want to hear the story about this Paul Chambers."

"So do I."

"Et tu, Omar?"

"I apologize, Sanura, but Paul Chambers is a terrible man, so I find myself wanting to know how you cursed him."

"Wait, you called me by my first name." Green eyes shifted to Najja. "I don't know if you broke or fixed him."

"I didn't do either, and you're deflecting. Tell us the curse story."

Sanura turned to Assefa. "Are you planning on just sitting there while your family and friends gang up on me?"

"Sanura, I haven't been home in nearly a year. But there's one thing I can tell you, the Berbers have never talked this much at any meal we've shared together. And you haven't been this playfully animated since arriving. So, no, I'm going to sit here and continue to enjoy myself."

"Fine, I'll tell the story. My way." When she finished, Sanura smirked at Ulan and crossed her arms over her chest.

"You spiteful little fire witch." Ulan took a sip from his glass of wine, genuine affection in the eyes that watched Sanura. "What was that, a Songhay language?"

"It was," the high priestess answered. "By the time Sanura was ten, she spoke English, Yoruba, French, and Spanish. Not all with the same level of fluency, mind you. Whenever she traveled to Trinidad with Sam, her father would show off how well his daughter could speak the many different languages of his island home. Except for Caribbean Hindustani, she never did learn that Indo-Aryan language."

Talking ceased as the servers delivered the first of three courses, sliding the dining room doors closed after they finished.

Najja picked up the thread of the previous conversation as if they'd been no break. "Sanura, you're a polyglot. What's your IQ?"

"Why does every conversation we have include you asking me a question that requires a numerical answer? First my magic level and now my IQ. At this rate, Najja, we'll never become friends."

"This is what I heard. My IQ is higher than Assefa's, but I don't want him to know because it'll bruise his Berber ego. By the way, all Berber men have annoyingly high IQs, but it's the Berber women who are their intellectual safeguards. We keep them grounded and challenged, which is why my uncle has taken such pleasure in toying with you tonight and why, I guarantee, a week or two after you've returned home you'll find an obscenely expensive gift from my father waiting for you."

For the first time this evening, Najja focused her attention on Razi, who hadn't uttered a word during dinner. He hated how his sister looked at him as if she could see all that he attempted to conceal.

"It's also why Razi has nothing to say tonight. He doesn't care for strong, intelligent women. He prefers them malleable and needy or perhaps made of granite, like Sekhmet over there, unable to contradict him but also incapable of gifting him with her heart."

Claws, Najja Berber had them, sharp and deadly.

He wondered if she knew, if her memory had returned with the arrival of her mate. The sad yet angry glint in her eyes, Razi just thought she may have. No matter. This family farce would be over soon.

Two coughs had Jahi reaching for his wine, finishing it off in a long swallow.

Razi smirked. That was all of it, Tracey's empty vial in his pants pocket.

As the night drew on, laughter, childhood stories and tales of America, Razi felt torn. A part of him wanted to make an excuse to leave the family to their fate but a larger more devilish part of him wanted to see their faces when his friends arrived.

He would stay, at least for the opening ceremony.

His father had earned this gift a thousand times over as did Assefa. For the rest of them, well, there was no room for the old in the new Berber regime.

Another hour passed, and Jahi's coughing that had started out as a small inconvenient hiccup had grown into an uncontrollable battery of phlegm-induced rages. Sweat covered him in a thick sheen, and those gathered wore matching worried faces.

Assefa pushed from the table and went to the general supreme. "I don't know what's going on, Father, but your coughing has gotten worse. You look feverish and ready to pass out."

Najja rolled to the general supreme's side, her hand going up to touch his forehead. "You're sticky but cold. And your irises are blown as if you've taken a narcotic. What kind of doctor are you again, Sanura?"

"Unfortunately, not the kind that Jahi needs."

"Zareb," Assefa began, "please call Dr. Taban and have him meet us at the hospital."

The good son that he was, Assefa removed the general supreme's dashiki, leaving him in a sweaty undershirt as Razi continued to eat his dinner. He may have no use for Omar, but his father was one fine cook. After the dust settled, he just may keep Chef Wek. Then again, the old man may be too heartbroken over the death of his son to prepare a decent meal for the new general supreme.

"Come on, Father, let's get you into your limo." Assefa settled one of the general supreme's arms around his shoulders and lifted. Ulan, who'd found his way to his brother's side a minute after Najja, took hold of the general supreme's other arm, helping Assefa get him out of his chair and away from the table.

"I'm fine. I can walk." His head lolled forward, perspiration dripping from him. "Okay, perhaps I could use a bit of assistance."

They began walking toward the closed dining room doors, Assefa and Ulan bearing most of the general supreme's weight. Yet as Assefa reached for the door handle, a gust of wind pushed back his hand.

Razi glared at Najja, but Najja's eyes were on Sanura as were Assefa's.

"Ìyáñlá, do you sense what I do?"

Wasola stood, her slim, tall frame facing the closed doors, a hum of fire witch magic emanating from her. "A second before you cast that small wind spell."

Wind spell? Razi hadn't heard the witch recite a spell, which all witches had to if they wanted Mother Earth to respond to their sorceress' call for obedience.

"And you Najja? Can you feel the spell that now encircles this room?"

"Barely, but yes. Brother, you may want to get Father away from that door. I'm not sure what will happen if you come into contact with the barrier."

"I don't sense anything. But I trust the three witches in this room."

Omar and Zareb yanked off their suit jackets as did Odafe. Ulan and Assefa were gentle as they helped the shivering, coughing were-cat to the floor.

Razi ate the last bite of his creme carmela dessert—milk, sugar, butter, vanilla, and candied berries—perfect. Yes, Executive Chef Wek had outdone himself for the general supreme's final meal. Razi approved.

"Sanura," Assefa said, "tell me what you see with your second sight."

Razi expected the witch to scan the door or even walls. Instead, she looked over her shoulder and directly at him, one eye green, the other red.

"A blood sacrifice is required when dealing with the dead. How much blood did you offer up, Razi? What's the going price for the life of your father?"

"You see my blood in the spell, witch?" He pushed from the table. "You think you know me, know him?" An accusatory finger pointed to the man Razi no longer thought of as his father. "He's the worst Berber of them all. His smiles are his lies. His laughter and gifts hollow and strategic."

A clawed hand swiped at dessert plates and wine glasses, sending the antique dishes flying across the room and smashing against the wall.

"Jahi lies and Ulan covers them up. You have no idea how apt that devil tie of yours was, Sanura. Your only mistake was not getting one for that lying, cruel bastard on the floor."

Assefa stood from where he'd been kneeling at the dying man's side. "Tell me what you've done."

"You know what I've done." Razi made a show of lifting his right arm and looking at the gold watch on his wrist. "Tracey was a stupid, money-and-Assefa-hungry bitch, but the witch knew her poisons. Your father has less than thirty minutes, give or take."

Assefa went to grab for Razi, but Jahi's ragged order of, "Don't, son," stopped him.

But it didn't stop Ulan, who'd closed the distance between them in a blur of speed.

A fist to Razi's stomach sent him crashing to one knee.

"You spoiled, ungrateful brat." Ulan jerked Razi up by his severed arm, only to send him back to the floor again with two more hard, angry fists to the face. "You're responsible for this? You dare try to take the life of your general supreme, your father?"

Surging to his feet, Razi spat a mouthful of blood onto his Ulan's spotless leather shoes.

"No, Uncle," he blocked Ulan's fist with his good arm, "I dare to take the lives of this entire worthless family and claim Sudan as mine."

Lights flickered, then all went dark.

But Razi heard them. His gift for the former general supreme.

Clippity-clop.

Clippity-clop.

Clippity clop.

CHAPTER TWENTY

Blistering wind Assefa knew wasn't Sanura's or Najja's, swept through the room, a howling tornado uprooting people and furniture.

Zareb, Ulan, and Omar smashed into different walls. Najja went flying out of her wheelchair and dropped to the floor with a hard thud.

Assefa covered his father's body with his, digging into the wood floor with his Mngwa's claws to keep him rooted and Jahi safe.

Assefa searched for Sanura and the Toures in the dark room. But he needn't have looked far because Sanura stood in front of her grandparents, her wind grappling with the tornado.

Hair whipped.

And hooves neared.

Clippity-clop.

Clippity-clop.

Through the walls and from the darkness emerged a pack of snarling beasts, charging at the group.

Assefa had to do something. Had to protect his family, but there was no time, the beasts were nearly upon them.

Crash.

The dining room shook seismic waves that had Assefa clenching his jaw and digging his claws in even deeper.

Not one but three forcefields surrounded the small group, two fire, and one wind.

"Is everyone okay?" Sanura glanced over her shoulder and to the crowd huddled behind her. Her forcefield, the strongest of the three, red with power and purpose. "Najja, that's one hell of a field. Thanks for the assist."

Dragging herself to her chair, Najja waved off the help of her mate. And managed, with too much pride and stubbornness, to pull herself into her wheelchair, breaths heavy when she was done.

Assefa took in what Razi's malicious soul and red blood had summoned.

Leucrotas.

The wolf-lion hybrids were cloven-hooved animals the size of a male donkey, which made them as tall as Assefa's Mngwa but not as wide. Yet there were twenty of them, and Leucrotas were strong, intelligent and vicious in battle. They had the haunches of a horse, the tail, chest, and neck of a lion and the head of a wolf. Their mouth could open as far back as their ears. And where teeth should be were ridges of bone, capable of crushing anything or so the tales told. The Leucrotas could also imitate the sound of a human voice, serving the beasts well when hunting humans.

They shouldn't be there, not these mythical creatures of Ethiopian lore. Yet twenty stood before them, and Razi had disappeared like the traitorous snake he turned out to be.

Assefa didn't want to waste time dwelling on his brother's betrayal. There would be time enough for that pain later.

The largest of the Leucrota stepped forward. Probably the leader, based on his size and the deferential way the other Leucrota looked to him. His large snout tested the strength of the barrier, then yanked it back when Sanura's fire forcefield, the outer layer, crackled in warning.

"We've been summoned by General Supreme Razi Berber." The Leucrota's voice grated, sounding like regurgitated carcasses. "We've been summoned to kill you all, starting with the weak were-cat on the floor." The twenty Leucrotas moved to surround them, a military formation that preceded their attack.

They charged again, on all sides of the fields.

Crash.

The fields held, the strength of them forcing the Leucrotas back and sending some to their knees in surprise and pain.

The leader snarled. "That protective shield won't hold for long. My pack will rip through it as easily as we'll crush your insignificant bodies. You only delay the inevitable." He walked a few feet away, surveying the members of his pack for injuries.

"He's right." Sanura's eyes lowered to a deathly still Jahi. "We can't hold this circle indefinitely. Razi said thirty minutes. It's less than that now."

"You witches are strong enough to hold the circle until help arrives."

"What help, Uncle?" Najja asked. "Besides the fact that none of Father's guards know we're in trouble, there's still the issue of the spell around this room. That means we're on our own."

Tentatively, Zareb laid a hand on the first forcefield—blue-and-white, Najja's field. "I've never seen overlapping forcefields before. I'm sure they'll hold."

"For a while," Assefa said, "but the Leucrotas are strong, magical creatures. I have no idea of their upper power level. If someone does, now's the time to speak up." No one spoke. Assefa used his handkerchief to wipe the sweat from his father's face and neck. "Sanura and Najja are correct, we may have time but Father doesn't."

Ulan, who'd said nothing since his fight with Razi, his focus more on his sick and dying twin than the imminent threat on the other side of the fields stood. "Options, people, we need them. Now."

"Divide and conquer," the high priestess spoke from beside Sanura, her gaze unwavering and still on the pacing Leucrotas. "Only Sanura and Assefa can manage the spell required."

He had no idea what spell Wasola had in mind, but Sanura offered an explanation without anyone having to ask.

"We have a better chance of maintaining the integrity of the forcefields if we didn't have to contend with all of the Leucrotas. Twenty of them will be able to breach the circle in less than ten minutes. They'll have to work damn hard, but I believe they can do it."

"I get that, sweetheart. Tell me what I'm missing from Wasola's plan."

"We can send half of the Leucrotas to another part of the city."

"If you're thinking along those lines, why not transport them to the same hell dimension you sent the Raven Mocker to?"

"Because, Assefa, no matter how violent the beasts before us may be, they have souls. I can't send soul bound creatures to a hell dimension. And I can't let them loose on an unsuspecting dimension either."

"The two of you can do that? Shit." Zareb's hand rose to his waist, belatedly remembering he'd left his sidearm at home in exchange for his sword and shield.

Assefa didn't have his gun either, and neither did Ulan. Although it would likely take more than a normal round of bullets to take down the Leucrotas. If he had his gun, he'd sure like to find out.

"Cat and fire witch of legend magic, I assume," Ulan said. "So, if you can't send them to another dimension, Sanura, how will sending half of the Leucrotas to another part of Khartoum to wreak havoc there be a better choice?"

"It's a better choice because she intends to send me with them." Assefa pushed to his feet, knowing how his mate's mind worked and the faith she had in him as a warrior cat.

"I'm going with you." Zareb already had his sword in his hand.

"And Najja," Sanura suggested. "The two of you will need a witch on your side."

"But Najja's—"

His sister bristled at her mate's objection. "What, Omar, a helpless crippled?"

"I didn't say that."

"No, you've never said. You just walked away when things got tough."

"It wasn't like that. It's never been like that."

"Son," Ulan interjected, "save the drama for when the two of you are alone, and it's not an emergency. I don't like my niece going up against those Leucrotas either. She can call me a sexist bastard all she wants later. But right now, we need all hands on deck and that means Najja. That also means you. Isn't that right, Sanura?"

"Yes. We're outnumbered, and we have a man down. Listen, Omar, I can send you with your mate if that's what you want. But I need Ulan to help me with Jahi, which makes him unavailable to fight when this field breaks. Trust me, with how hard they're attacking it, the fields will eventually cave. And no disrespect to my grandfather and his spotted jaguar, but he's fifty years your senior and no match for ten Leucrotas."

Assefa knelt, back to Najja, and she climbed on. "Staying or leaving, Omar? The choice is yours but make it now. My father doesn't have much time."

Assefa hated everything about this moment. Hated the strength of Najja's arms around his neck contrasted with limp legs he held around his waist. Hated, because of him, that Sanura would have to fight another enemy after barely surviving the last. Hated the still, silent form of his father behind him, breaths slow and soft. And hated the broken heart in Omar's eyes for a mate he wanted to protect but had no idea how to reach. A mate who would never rely on his strength until she learned to accept her frailty. And Assefa did not mean Najja's paralysis.

"You have my mate, and I have yours. If Sanura says she needs my lion, I'll stay and fight by her side."

"Good man. Thank you, Omar."

On Assefa's back the way she was, Najja could do little when Omar pressed his lips to her forehead. "I will chase your wind to the end of the Earth, Najja. I love you. Be safe."

Unsurprisingly, Najja said nothing, just tightened her arms around his neck as the Leucrotas continued to slam into the forcefields, their wolf heads like battering rams.

As if guided by the same invisible hand, the twins stared down at their father. He looked awful, face wet, eyes cloudy, body slack.

"Don't worry, I'll take care of him." The reassurance was meant for the twins, but it was Assefa's shoulder Sanura reached out and squeezed, eyes light-red with determination.

Ram. Ram. Ram.

"Where will you send us?" Najja asked.

Sanura looked to Assefa for the answer. "The last time we spoke, you said part of the Grimba Forest had been razed to build a new hospital. This time of night, it should be deserted. We'll make our stand there."

Ram. Ram. Ram.

"That's fine. Give me your hand, Assefa. Zareb, you take my other one. Najja's already connected to Assefa, which completes our magic circle."

Ram. Ram. Ram.

"Shut them out, sweetheart, and focus. Focus on our aligned aura, and I'll envision where I want you to send us."

Sanura closed her eyes. Assefa saw what she saw, felt what she felt. Fire, wind, and lightning; the fire witch of legend's three elemental powers hovered in the dark spaces between their individual hearts and their combined love. Sanura called the elements to her. "Be my eyes and see what I cannot. Be my arms and carry them where I cannot. Be my heart and protect them when I cannot. This I ask of you. This I know you will do."

In her mind's eye, Assefa saw Sanura form the image of the Leucrotas. Sanura extended her magic outward, slipping through the three fields but leaving them intact.

She paralyzed half of the Leucrotas, sending electrical currents through their tough hides and making them shriek their pain.

His witch, mean and strategic when she had to be, did what she could to give his team a fighting chance.

The rest was up to Assefa, Najja, and Zareb.

Ram. Ram. Ram.

They disappeared.

Ram. Ram. Ram.

"You did it. They're gone. Sekhmet be with them." Ulan removed his red tie, tossed it on the floor and then pulled Sanura's gift from his pants pocket. He tied it loosely around his wrist, the red devils smiling.

Ram. Ram. Ram.

"To defeat those bastards, you'll need a devil, Sanura. I'm that devil."

No, she needed a Berber. But a devil Berber would do.

Ram. Ram. Ram.

"I promised my alpha I'd protect you, so if you have a plan, Sanura, I'd like to hear it before the Leucrotas tear the fields down around us. Do you want me to shift?"

Before he'd finished the question, Omar had stripped out of his dress shirt and kicked off his shoes, lion claws peeking out from his fingertips.

"Young man," Odafe started, "while my jaguar is roaring with the need to get out and fight those hybrid beasts, we can't go on the offensive until Sanura's had an opportunity to help Jahi. He's her priority, which means we have to tell our cats to be patient."

Odafe's words had the desired effect, Omar anxious to end this, but not so foolish as to risk shifting and presenting his lion as an open challenge to the Leucrotas.

"Omar, when the time comes to fight, don't hold back. None of us can afford to hold back."

He would know what she meant. During the Sankofa alpha challenge, when Assefa's clan of legend fought Paul Chambers' pride of lions, Omar, at first, hadn't given the battle his all. And the other day, when the water witches had attacked them, he'd waited too long to defend himself.

"I need your lion all in. Do you understand?"

He stripped down to his boxers, frame tall, dark, muscular and taut all over. He was primed and ready to shift at Sanura's command.

"Good man," she said, repeating Assefa's words to Omar.

Ram. Ram. Ram.

"Do you still run in jaguar form every day, babañlá?"

Sanura didn't want her eighty-two-year-old grandfather to fight, but she feared she couldn't stop Odafe and that they would likely need the extra fangs and claws.

"Every day. Now stop worrying about me and tend to your mate's father."

Right.

"Ìyáñlá, I need you to maintain the integrity of the fire fields, shoring up the damage from the attacks. Give me as much time as you can."

Wasola nodded, serious and beautifully fierce. The witch was a descendant of the first fire witch of legend, she would do what needed doing.

"And me, Sanura?"

"I need you to help me perform a magical surgery on your brother." She knelt beside Jahi, no trace of the virile, charming man she'd met two days ago. "Jahi isn't my familiar, which means I can't connect with his aura without force. I can do it, but I don't want to cause him more pain."

"You want to use my familial bond as a bridge to my twin. Makes sense. Have you done this before?"

"With my friend's husband."

Ulan settled his brother's sweaty head in his lap, his eyes wet with tears. Seeing the formidable man weep sent the force of what could happen in these next few minutes to Sanura's solar plexus. The reality was a hard blow that left her breathless.

Every member of the Berber family could die tonight. She'd done what she could for Assefa and Najja, but ten Leucrotas wouldn't fall easily.

The Mngwa would fight, to the death, as would Zareb and Najja.

They would all return or none.

Silk draped around her neck, and warm lips touched her cheek. "Don't worry. I have faith in you. Take care of my brother, then be the devil and vanquish our enemies. That's what makes you adorable to me, not your magic and might but the heart that burns and bleeds because it cares so much about others. You protect, but you also judge and punish the wicked. And you have this Berber male's most humble respect, trust, and unwavering affection, even though you refuse to call me Uncle Ulan. It's fine, though, it gives us something to argue about when this is done."

Ulan kissed Sanura's cheek again, and she wished she didn't like this arrogant man so much. But she did, which made what she had to do even more stressful.

"Thank you."

Ram. Ram. Ram.

"I'm about to test the truth of your words right now. Don't fight my magic keep, when you feel its touch. I need you to also maintain physical contact with your brother. If you do those two things, I'll take care of everything else."

Placing her hand under Jahi's soaked undershirt and to his chilled chest, Sanura relaxed into her second sight. His heart beat far too slow, and she saw why.

The dispersion of poison was visible. How could it not when it coursed through every organ of his body? They were all beginning to shut down. This amount of damage couldn't have occurred this evening. Days, at least two, maybe three.

Sanura pulled her fire magic through Ulan similar to the way she used her familiar. But she had to be careful. Ulan wasn't made to handle her level of power. Only her Mngwa could hold and manipulate her magical energy in a manner that would have optimal effect. But there were no better options, and Jahi's cat spirit was waning faster than the man's infected organs.

Ram. Ram. Ram.

She needed to cleanse each organ of the toxin so Sanura started with the most vital one, the brain. Ulan's jaguar chi was strong, and his cat purred in supplication when her fire magic caressed his head. Ulan trusted her, and so did his cat spirit. The heart came next, followed by the kidneys and liver. Sanura transferred Ulan's healthy chi into his brother, hoping to suffocate the toxin into submission.

A good start, but not enough. The pancreas, stomach, small and large intestines, and lungs still needed cleansing. But she had to stop.

Ulan coughed, spitting up blood. His eyes were weary, face haggard. "Why did you stop?"

"You're struggling to breathe, and you're exhausted. I'm taking too much of your chi."

"I don't care. Finish what you started."

"I won't exchange one Berber life for another."

"My decision. Do it."

Crack. Crack.

"You hear that? The fields are weakening. We don't have much more time. Finish it."

"Even if I took all your cat's chi and gave it to Jahi, it wouldn't be enough. I didn't know for sure until I saw the extent of the poison's damage. I won't kill you to only have Jahi still die."

Ram. Crack. Ram.

"Then what?"

Ram. Ram. Crack.

She needed to think. Dammit, she needed to think, but the hooves were so loud, the sound of bone colliding with hard fire thunderous and distracting.

"What else can we do?"

Ulan.

"Sanura, the field is cracking."

Omar

Ram. Ram. Ram.

"Too many fissures coming too fast. I don't know how much longer I can keep repairing them."

Wasola.

"They've redoubled their efforts, and my jaguar wants out. Give the order."

Odafe.

They all called her name, their fear, and anxiety in their strained voices. Omar, Ulan, Wasola, Odafe, even Jahi, whose dark eyes had opened.

Assefa's eyes.

They stared up at Sanura with such trust that she wanted to scream.

Instead, a tear dropped when Jahi murmured, "It's all right. I know you tried your best. My son chose well."

No, no, no. This was not happening.

Ram. Ram. Ram.

When you die, Samuel Williams, the balance of the long life you would have lived will transfer to your daughter. Inside of her, an echo of your jaguar spirit will slumber until the time it is claimed by her mate, the cat of legend. Then it will be he who will step into the void left by the father. He who will protect the child of fire. He who will fight by her side. A Mngwa with the added might and magic of a powerful jaguar. This, Samuel Williams, is my blessing to you. So I have spoken. So it will be done.

Ram. Ram. Ram.

I cannot bless this child. If I do, she will reek of my magic and interference. That I cannot have, Samuel Williams.

Crack. Crack. Crack.

I saw a white feather on your Fire Phoenix. I didn't get a close look, but it was there, out of place but a part of your firebird.

Ram. Ram. Ram.

I cannot bless this child. If I do, she will reek of my magic and interference.

"Sàngó, you lying son of a bitch."

Ulan coughed up more blood, ignoring Sanura's stream of curses. "If you won't take more chi from me, what are we going to do?" Ulan's voice sounded every bit as tense as Sanura felt.

For better or for worse, she knew what she had to do.

"A sacrifice"

Ram. Ram. Ram.

"I don't understand."

Ulan didn't have to.

Her father had died so that Sanura could live. He'd trusted a god who'd used Sam's love for his daughter and fear for her future to get what he wanted. Sanura had no idea what the white feather meant, but she comprehended one thing.

She had the power to save Assefa's father, to guarantee that Samuel Williams' sacrifice wouldn't be in vain.

Ram. Ram. Ram.

"Lift Jahi's head and open his mouth, Ulan, as if you're going to give him CPR."

He did as she requested, holding Jahi's mouth open.

When Sanura lowered her head toward Jahi's, a spell entered her mind. For weeks, she'd searched for an incantation that would allow Sanura to transfer the jaguar spirit from her and into Makena. She'd found nothing. But there, now, with this man's life in the balance, the right spell came to her.

It was then, as she recited the spell, that she knew that Sanura finally understood her reticence to part with her father's jaguar spirit hadn't been about holding onto the old and the fear of embracing the new.

Whether she knew it then or not, this decision was made the moment she met Special Agent Assefa Berber, gorgeous chocolate eyes and an amazing aura signature.

"A father's sacrifice." The spell touched Jahi's lips. "A father's love." Sanura blew, sending her spell and magic across Jahi's dry lips, onto his tongue, and down his throat. "A daughter's grief. A daughter's love." More blowing. Red wisps of fire magic spiraled out of Sanura's mouth and into Jahi's, her lips an inch away from his.

"On this day of your birth, you dangle at a crossroads, clinging to the Principles of Ma'at. Truth, justice, law, morality, balance, and order. It's with my imperfect heart, but with a depth of love for a man above all men, that I gift to you my father's jaguar spirit. Be worthy, Jahi Berber, be worthy."

He began to wheeze as Sanura breathed life into the were-cat, filling him with Sam's magnificent cat spirit.

She cried tears of loss and joy.

She cried because the cat spirit didn't want to leave her but knew he had to go.

And she cried because when her magic reached Jahi's soul when it offered a route out of the grim darkness of despair, it dimmed with regret and sorrow. For a son he'd failed. For a son he'd lost.

She blew once more and felt the remaining essence of her father's cat spirit slip from her.

Ram. Ram. Ram.

It was done. The rest was up to Jahi.

Omar and Odafe shifted.

The forcefields shattered.

And the Leucrotas attacked.

CHAPTER TWENTY-ONE

Hot air and the scent of trees hit Assefa, a second before his body dropped to the dirt. On his hands and knees, Najja on his back, barely, he scanned his surroundings. Acres of upturned earth and no one else in sight except for Zareb, face-down beside him and hand gripped around the hilt of the medja's sword.

"I never want to do that again." Zareb got to his feet, taking in what would be their battlefield. "They aren't here. Do you think Sanura got her spell wrong and the Leucrotas are all back at the presidential compound?"

He'd never known his witch to get a spell wrong.

"Best guess, time lapse."

Zareb lifted Najja from Assefa's back, which made getting to his feet easier.

"You mean Sanura purposefully sent us first? I swore I saw the Leucrotas disappear when we did."

So had Assefa.

"We've only done this once before, so I don't know how it all works. Sanura is smart and intentional with her magic. But I don't think we have much time. Whatever time she gave us was for shifting. Let's not squander her gift."

Clippity-clop.

Clippity-clop.

"Ah, brother, do you hear that?"

They were close. Not much time.

Clippity-clop.

Clippity-clop.

Not bothering with undressing, Assefa shifted, knowing Zareb wouldn't have time to do the same. His sword would have to do, a family heirloom he wore to honor the general supreme on his birthday. A family heirloom that soon would be coated in Leucrota blood.

Clippity-clop.

Clippity-clop.

Zareb arranged Najja on the back of the Mngwa, her hands going up to fist his fur, holding on tight.

They'd done this many times, trained this way as teens. But never like this, Najja unable to grip the Mngwa's waist with her legs.

"I won't fall off." Her hands dug deeper into his fur, holding him as firmly as she could. "I won't be a liability in this battle, so stop worrying."

The Mngwa did worry, and even the best jockeys sometimes fell from their mount. But Najja a liability? Never.

Clippity-clop.

Clippity-clop.

Zareb took cover behind a mound of dirt, a mere twenty seconds before the howling Leucrotas arrived.

They crashed to the ground, a hard, rough landing the Mngwa knew to be deliberate. Shrieks of pain followed Sanura's electric shock still doing damage.

Not waiting for the wolf-lion hybrids to recoup, the Mngwa went on the offensive.

Najja held onto his thick gray-and-black mane as the Mngwa ran full speed at two of the Leucrotas. He could hear her casting above him.

Perfect, a temporary blinding spell. Thirty seconds, he remembered from their training. It wasn't much time.

He pounced, knocking both down with his bulky frame and pinning them with his lethal claws. Raising a massive paw, he slashed their throats in two smooth motions, catching fur, arteries, and ligaments.

They weren't dead, though. The strong Leucrotas fought, wide mouths snapping, throats a gaping wound spurting blood.

A microburst stormed through the air, right for the thrashing Leu-crotas, guided by the wind witch. Into gaping holes and out through exploding heads, splattered brains everywhere.

Berber females were vicious in battle, which the two Leucrotas just learned.

"Three more to your flank."

The Mngwa turned. Najja cast another binding spell, catching one of the rampaging beasts. The Mngwa's next target. He flew at the bound Leucrota using his quick speed to dodge the other two.

Slam.

Broken ribs.

Crunch. Squish.

Ripped jugular.

Another microburst. Slicing wind cleaved exposed belly, a horse's hide no match for Najja's magic.

Blood. Wail. Death.

Three down.

He ran, pursued by three Leucrotas who had no chance of catching the Mngwa. The cat of legend was too fast. But he needed them right behind him, near enough to distract them with the seeming possibility of overtaking him. He approached a twenty-foot-high mound of dirt, and the beasts followed. Nearing the hill, the Mngwa used his strength and agility to clear it.

Najja toppled forward but maintained her seat.

Unable to perform the same feat as the Mngwa, the Leucrotas, in single file, ran around the mound.

Mistake.

From his crouched position behind the high mountain of dirt, Zareb sliced at the rear legs of each passing Leucrota.

Slash. Slash. Thump.

Slash. Slash. Thump.

Slash. Slash. Thump.

Breathing hard, Zareb loomed over the downed beasts of prey, his sword dripping with green blood. One by one, Zareb raised and lowered his muscular arms, dress shirt and pants sprayed with blood, decapitated heads at his feet.

"Four more, brother."

Najja's heavy breaths tickled his ear. He wondered how much her magic use had tired her and what she had left in her reserve. His sister didn't have the added strength of Omar's lion to fuel her wind magic. What Najja did have, though, was doggedness and the desire to see the Leucrotas dead.

Four growling Leucrotas bolted around the mound. Zareb flattened himself to the ground and pushed up against one of the dead hybrids. They didn't see him, which was good. Without the element of surprise on his side, Zareb and his sword wouldn't stand a chance against the Leucrotas.

Their wolf heads snarled, as the horse part, haunches and legs propelled them forward. Sweat glistened and rippled muscles bulged.

Najja cast one binding spell after another, but they only slowed them down. The creatures were resilient, breaking the binds and hardly losing their stride.

"I'm spreading my magic too wide and diluting its effectiveness. Hold steady."

He felt one of Najja's hands release him. No, what in the hell was she doing?

The Mngwa trotted backward, his golden eyes trained on the approaching Leucrotas. With Najja unable to grip him with her legs and now holding on with a single hand, he feared running too swiftly or cutting too sharply.

She leaned forward onto his neck. Her right hand shot out and in the direction of the closest Leucrota. "Let you feel the pain of a hundred arrows upon your hide."

The Mngwa saw nothing but heard everything.

The lashing of wind.

The stabbing of flesh.

The moaning of agony.

And the fall of defeat. The mark of a hundred Sudanese Broadhead Liberty arrow blades were tattooed in the di-brown horsehide.

Najja slumped against him, exhausted.

The last three Leucrotas took no time surrounding the twins. One ran at the Mngwa head on, causing him to pivot to his left and directly into another Leucrota. The second Leucrota rammed the Mngwa on the side.

Down went the wind witch, slamming to the hard ground.

"Wind rise and protect." The spell poured out on a scared, desperate scream. Blue-and-white wind witch power glowed in the dark night, shielding its mistress in a forcefield made for one.

Satisfied his sister was safe, the Mngwa rounded on the closest Leucrota and grabbed him by the scruff of his lion's neck. Clamping down with his long fangs, he sank deep, gnawing and ripping and swallowing blood.

The remaining two Leucrotas went in for the kill. Their wide mouths did indeed extend to their ears. One fastened onto a leg, the other the Mngwa's flank. Those bone-crushing ridges had his inner man screaming in agony.

But the Mngwa held fast to his prey. He didn't stop ripping and tearing at the unnatural creature until it stopped twitching and the Mngwa's maw was soaked red with his win.

Out of the sweltering darkness came Zareb, sword in hand. He leaped onto the back of the Leucrota, who had the Mngwa's leg in a vice. Down came his sword into the neck of the Leucrota. "Die, you ugly piece of hybrid shit." Leaning his two-hundred-plus pounds on the hilt of the blade, Zareb drove the sword even deeper. So deep, the beast opened its mouth and wailed.

Freed, the Mngwa charged instead of stumbling backward. He sank his teeth into the wounded Leucrota, crushing his windpipe the same way the remaining Leucrota was crushing his back.

Snap. The Leucrotas neck.

He released the dead Leucrota, and then he nodded his head in Najja's direction. She needed the medja more than he did. Zareb, bloody sword in hand, eyes on the Leucrota working to bring the Mngwa to his knees, didn't move. The Mngwa growled. Zareb knew what in the hell he wanted him to do.

Swearing, Zareb began kicking off shoes and shedding clothes. In a few minutes, he'd be a Bengal tiger and an exhausted Najja would be on his back. If the medja knew what was good for him, he'd take the witch back to the presidential compound and leave the Mngwa to deal with the Leucrota.

With nothing but strength and grit, the Mngwa ran away from Najja and Zareb. He pulled the Leucrota along as every bone in his back was squeezed and twisted, his left front leg broken and bleeding.

Two hundred excruciating yards later, the Mngwa's leg gave way, sending him to the ground and loosening the Leucrota's grip. Scrambling as best he could with a broken back, the Mngwa managed to free himself from the bone-crushing ridges.

The Leucrota reared up on his cloven hooves and brought them smashing down onto his side.

Crack.

His legs.

Crack.

His shoulder.

The Mngwa couldn't move, could only snarl and snap each time the Leucrota's mouth neared his face or throat. When the beast brought his cloven hooves down on his eyes, blinding the Mngwa, the Leucrota managed to brace its massive jaw ridges around the cat of legend's neck.

Sekhmet must've been bored or in a vicious mood when she created the Leucrota, for they served no greater purpose than this, hunting and killing.

The Mngwa struggled to breathe. Each breath cut short by the Leucrota's ever-tightening hold. He didn't want to die. Yet, he had nothing left to defend himself.

If the Leucrota didn't break his neck first, the Mngwa would die of strangulation.

The jaw ridges constricted even more and the Mngwa felt something inside his neck crack and pop.

This was it then? The end of the cat of legend? Taken out by a wolf-lion hybrid with the strength and tenacity of a blood-summoned demon?

Tighter.

Tighter.

Pain. So much pain. And no air.

No. Air.

The gold necklace around the Mngwa's neck, in the mouth of the Leucrota, began to heat and vibrate.

Warm and angry.

Love and wrath.

Magic. Fire witch of legend magic.

Healing him. Strengthening him. Protecting him.

The Leucrota's grip around his mouth slackened. The beast's mouth glowed a bright red, and the vibrating necklace pulsed with ferocity.

Not the necklace, but the ring. Sanura's promise ring.

When you shift, the necklace will adjust to your size. It's aligned to your Mngwa's chi. A magical kiss from my fire spirit.

The ring vibrated in time with the Mngwa's recovery, ramping up the violent pulsating waves the stronger the cat became.

The high-pitched noise from the ring split the night air. The Leucrota opened its mouth as it burst into flames.

The healed Mngwa shrugged the beast off him. Getting to his feet, he watched as the Leucrota's once deadly maw burned and melted under a fire witch's protective curse. And what a curse it was. Sanura's fire engulfed the entirety of the beast, but it didn't die. It just burned and burned.

The ring around his neck glowed. A magical kiss indeed.

The Mngwa turned away and saw Najja atop the Bengal tiger, Zareb's sword in her hand. They ran toward him. He should've known better than to think they would leave him.

The Mngwa snarled at the Bengal tiger as he ran past him and toward the presidential compound.

A second later, he heard the thudding footsteps of his friend behind him and felt the cool wind of his sister's magic.

He hoped his father still lived and that everyone was safe.

The Mngwa ran faster.

Sanura looked up to see the ten Leucrotas converging on them. Omar's huge lion tackled the nearest Leucrota, ripping and slashing with his heavy paws. Wasola cast a confusion spell, and two of the beasts started tearing at each other with their extraordinary jaws. Odafe attacked another Leucrota, smartly staying behind the creature and away from its dangerous mouth.

Ulan worked to ward off one Leucrota, having picked up Zareb's abandoned shield. He stood in front of his brother, who'd passed out a second before the fields gave way. But Ulan, weak of chi and in human form, held no real chance against the mightier force.

Holding the half-body length shield in front of him, he swung and connected with the Leucrota's wide mouth. The attack snapped the Leucrota's head to the side but nothing more. The beast reared up on its horse's haunches, prepared to bring its considerable weight down on Ulan's head.

Sanura knocked the monster away from the were-cat with a strong wind spell. It flew across the room, crashing into the Leucrota Odafe's jaguar still fought and sending them both into the back wall.

Odafe's spotted jaguar sprinted to Omar's side, helping him bring down the donkey-size Leucrota he fought. The two cats wasted no time finishing the beast off before double teaming another Leucrota.

The six remaining Leucrotas stood in a semi-circle, the leader of the pack in the middle. The leader's gray eyes were on Sanura and the hands that had sent a member of his pack flying.

Smart beast. But not smart enough. Watching her for a tell would yield nothing.

Unharmed but breathing hard, the spotted jaguar nudged Wasola behind him and closer to where Ulan stood near Jahi. The golden lion, snout and mouth bloody, positioned himself next to Sanura.

"Now, Ìyáñlá!"

Up her grandmother's forcefield went. Not around herself, Jahi, or even her only grandchild.

The remaining six Leucrotas howled at their unexpected captivity.

Sanura intended to make them holler for a different reason.

Encircling her grandmother's field with her own, Sanura walked up to the sizzling forcefield, sank her hands into the fire and closed them into fists.

The forcefield began to move inward. The space inside shrank and the beasts huddled closer together. Their bodies jostled as they fought for freedom and air, knocking into the blazing-hot field and singeing body parts.

Sanura squeezed her fists tighter.

The Leucrotas burned, bellowed, and burst into flames.

She watched them as they burned and screamed and clawed at the forcefield.

She watched them, eyes red, heart remorseless, and judgment final.

"Be gone beasts. Back to where you came from. Let my fire show you the way."

The floor under the burning Leucrotas opened. In the wolf-lion hybrids fell, red-hot and doomed to burn until their punishment outweighed their crimes against humanity.

They would burn for a very long time.

CHAPTER TWENTY-TWO

Cold. Darkness.

"No!" Sanura screamed. "Get away from me. Get away."

"Wake up."

Dark, freezing water was everywhere. It slapped against her shivering body, head barely above the water, legs, and arms leaden weights pulling her under.

"Wake up, sweetheart, it's just a dream."

Under the water, she went. Legs twitched and arms flailed. She sank, breath held, lungs burning, and eyes wide open. But gods, she wished they weren't because, *no, no, no*, she saw orange-and-black scales gliding through the water and straight for her.

Sanura wanted to scream, wanted to swim away and back toward the surface where there was air to breathe and the possibility of safety. But her body wouldn't cooperate.

Closer the slithering scales drew. Mouth opened. Fangs extended from gums, sharp and long. It grabbed her, hard, strong and determined.

"Wake up. Wake the hell up."

Heart racing, lungs blazing and head thumping, Sanura opened her eyes. Unfocused, she struggled to make out the large form in front of her.

"Are you all right?"

She knew that voice.

"Assefa."

"It's me. I'm here."

Slumping in his embrace, Sanura wept. What in the hell was wrong with her? Why wouldn't her nightmares go away if only for a single night?

Tired. Sanura was so damn tired.

"I want to go home."

Not that it would matter. Her dreams hadn't begun in the Sudan but in the home she shared with Assefa.

"Zareb will take you later today. I'm sorry, I wish I could go with you. But I'll return as soon as I can."

Assefa retrieved the comforter from the floor and covered them. She curled in a tight ball, the way she did when she was five, praying she wouldn't die in her sleep when the snakes came for her. Back then, she'd screamed for her father, needing him to save her.

He would come running and Sanura would jump into his arms and cry like a baby. She was no less afraid of water and snakes as a woman of twenty-nine than she'd been as a girl of five.

She wouldn't be able to go back to sleep, no matter how good Assefa's warm body felt wrapped around her. Sanura would miss this, Assefa's strength and reassuring presence, so she soaked it in now. Come tomorrow, she'd be in their bed alone while Assefa would be a half-world away. For a couple of days, maybe a week or more while Jahi's body acclimated to the presence of another jaguar spirit.

Assefa and Ulan needed to be with their family while Sanura had to return home to begin the new school year. She couldn't stay, and Assefa wasn't ready to leave. Apparently, neither was Omar, who made his intention to stay and fight for his mate quite clear. Which left Zareb, who'd offered to fly with Sanura back to Virginia. She didn't require an escort, but she would appreciate the company.

"Do you want to talk about the nightmare?"

"No."

"The battle with the water witches or Leucrotas?"

"No."

"The gift you gave my father?"

"Not that either."

He sighed. "You aren't supposed to be the one to shut down. That's my role."

"I'm not. I'm just…" Sanura sat up. "I feel out of balance. No equilibrium. You want to know what I'm thinking, how I'm feeling? I'll tell you."

Assefa's hand came to her thigh and began to rub but all she felt was cold.

"Right now, my mind is so messed up. My magic wants out. Not just my fire spirit, but the magic itself. I see and feel everything. Every bad thing, Assefa. Chanya. The water witches. Razi and the Leucrotas. Soldiers at the airfield. Compound employees. The guy who served us dessert yesterday. I see right into them. I see, and I know. And I wish I knew nothing at all because my magic screams at me to judge and punish them. But my mind knows, and I have no idea how it does, that it's not their time for judgment and that I have to wait."

The gentle thigh massage halted, and Assefa pushed himself up and against the headboard. "Wait until when?"

She didn't want to say, but Sanura made herself give voice to what she knew in her heart to be true. "Until they die." Although dying seemed to have a meaning beyond the death of the body, such as death of the soul or spirit. She didn't really know. And she damn sure didn't understand.

"Perhaps you're finally ascending."

"Yeah, ascending into a crazy woman who teaches psychology online to college freshman. Just what every parent wants, their eighteen-year-old's mind molded by a lunatic."

She laughed, humorless and a bit hysterical.

Assefa reached for her, but she jumped from the bed.

He followed.

"I make up spells and they work. There's no way I should've been able to do what I did with your father." Sanura pointed to the necklace around Assefa's neck. "The protection spell in that ring didn't come from a book. The punishment spell I cast on the Leucrotas literally popped into my mind. I cast it with absolute certainty that it would work. The floor opened and sucked them inside. When it was over, it closed. Perfect. Not a single crack."

"I don't have an explanation. I wish I did."

So did she.

"Something's wrong with me."

It hurt like hell to admit that to him, but it was true.

"Nothing's wrong with—"

"There is, and this trip proved it. Everything that could've gone wrong has gone wrong."

"We're still here. We fought and we survived, Sanura. We knew Mami Wata and her water witch of legend would come after us again, and they have."

"I think it's more than that." Sanura took hold of Assefa's hand and placed it on her chest, over her heart. "I don't know what's going to happen to us, but I fear my heart and sanity won't survive your loss."

"Nothing's going to happen to me."

"You don't know that. You almost died yesterday. And I nearly died the day before that. We don't know what will happen."

The hand on her chest rose and found the nape of her neck and pulled Sanura forward. They hugged, Assefa's bare chest and arms a familiar feel that had Sanura sinking into his body and wishing they could stay like this until all the bad shit in their lives went far away.

"We're not going to lose ourselves to this prophecy or lose each other. I won't pretend to know what the future holds for us, but we love each other and that counts for a hell of a lot."

They did love each other. For the first time, however, Sanura was beginning to think their love, their visceral need to protect and defend the othe, would bring nothing but blood and death.

People would die because of their love. In truth, people already had—the Livingstons, Joanna Blackwell, Detective Salazar, and more.

The question was how many other lives Sanura and Assefa were willing to sacrifice for their bond of the heart? So yeah, their love counted for a hell of a lot. A hell of a lot of death because of their morbid destiny.

"Take a shower with me?"

"Later. I think we should perform the spirit fire ritual before you leave."

Sanura didn't want to, not in her current frame of mind. Yet this was the first time had Assefa requested the ritual. She could refuse him, use fatigue as an excuse to avoid looking inward and reflecting on the divine principles of Ma'at.

She'd slain, cursed, assaulted, behaved with violence, all within the course of a couple of days. Would Ma'at forgive Sanura's sins, view her actions as excusable? Justifiable? No, Sanura had no interest in the spirit fire ritual.

Still, how could she deny her mate? Sanura could not, so she removed her nightgown and reclined on her Mngwa.

He purred.

And she began the opening lines of the ritual.

"How long has she been in there?"

"About twenty minutes." Assefa looked from his father's closed bedroom door and to his sister. "Father wanted to see Sanura in private before she left for the airfield."

"Why in private?"

"I don't know. Maybe he wants to apologize for Razi, Tracey, and the water witches."

Najja reached out and grasped his left hand. "This has been an awful visit for you, brother, and an even worse first impression of our family and country for Sanura. Do you think she'll ever want to come back and visit us?"

He didn't think so. At least not with the way she felt now.

"In time, I hope she will."

"Any news from Ulan about Razi?"

"No, our brother is still missing. Apparently, Razi is quite skilled at hiding and eluding soldiers and an angry uncle."

Najja tugged Assefa's hand until he dropped to the floor beside her. He pressed his back against the wall outside of his father's bedchamber. "I would've never thought Razi capable of plotting our deaths."

"Why do you think he hates Father so much? Hates us?"

"I wish I knew. I believe Father knows. It's clear there's a lot between the two of them we know nothing about."

"Do you think that's what he's talking to Sanura about?"

"Sanura is an excellent psychologist, but I doubt even she could part Father from his secrets. More than likely, he's trying to convince her to accept whatever overpriced gift he's going to have sent to her once Sanura gets home."

"He gained a daughter but lost a son in one night." Najja kissed the palm of his hand. "It hurts, you know? Razi's cruelty and betrayal, it hurts."

It did, so very much.

"For all that he's done and deserves to be caught and held accountable for his crimes, I can't help but ache for him. He didn't used to be like that. Do you remember, Assefa? Razi used to be a great big brother. Sad, like us, after Mother passed away, but a sweet and loving boy. Then something happened, and he changed."

Assefa remembered. What he didn't know was the catalyst for Razi's shift in attitude and behavior. He'd bet every dollar he had in the bank that his father knew.

"When Father's feeling better, we need to have a serious conversation about Razi." Assefa shifted to his knees, arranging himself in front of his sister. "And you need to settle things with Omar." Najja dropped his hand. "Five years is a long time to be separated from your mate. I've never asked what happened, and I'm not asking now. But the two of you can't go on like this."

"I know."

"Sanura told me she extended an invitation to our home. I've been trying to get you there for years."

"It's also Omar's home. I wasn't ready to deal with him and our issues."

"Are you ready now?"

"I don't know."

"What about what Sanura told you? Are you at least willing to travel to the States to have the Witch Council of Elders examine you?"

He wondered, after six years of paralysis, if Najja feared the truth and what it would mean. If Sanura were right and, when it came to such things she always was, a dangerous enemy lurked in the shadows. An enemy who'd targeted the daughter of the House of Berber.

"Sanura could examine me before she leaves."

"She could, but she won't."

Assefa may not know what was going on with Sanura's magic or even the current state of her mind because she damn sure wasn't fully present during the spirit fire ritual, but, at her core, Sanura was a psychologist. As a psychologist, she would know how important it was for Najja to initiate any change she wanted to see in her life and within herself.

The window of opportunity on Sanura's initial offer had closed with Najja's refusal. Sanura wouldn't touch her until Najja was emotionally ready to handle the results of the probe.

"When you're ready to visit, Omar will make arrangements and Sanura will set up a meeting between you and her priestesses."

"I'm capable of making my own arrangements."

"True, but you're smart enough to know that's not my point. Until or unless you decide to break your handfasting bond, Omar is your mate. Either treat him like it or let him go so you can both move on. This in-between isn't good for either of you."

When Najja said nothing, just stared down at the hands folded in her lap, Assefa reclaimed the spot against the wall. For several minutes, they sat there in silence.

"I have a parting gift for Sanura." Najja handed Assefa a small white box she pulled from a side pocket of her chair. "Open it."

He did and smiled.

Rainbow teardrop earrings with green moonstones in the center sparkled from the gift box.

"Her last one was whitish-pink but the jeweler didn't have a moonstone close to that color, so I opted for green. Love, grounding and healing, an important blend of birth month energy for the fire witch of legend."

"It's beautiful. The moonstone is the same shade of green as Sanura's eyes. How did you have this made so quickly?"

"I have my ways."

"She'll love it. Thank you."

"She lost the ones she brought here, which, in a way, is our fault. Sanura shouldn't have to return home without the protection of a scent disguise charm. With the long flight, she'll have plenty of time to cast the requisite spell."

Zareb, in tiger form, had been the one to go back to the battle scene in search of Sanura's cuff bracelet and the moonstone she kept in her bellybutton. He'd scoured the area but hadn't found them, not that Assefa thought he would. Zareb had been angry about Sanura's injuries and wanted to "do something for her." He'd gone but had returned empty-handed.

"Now who's the one giving expensive gifts?" Assefa joked.

"Sanura's a good woman. I'm glad you found each other. I also think she's more than Oya's chosen one."

Assefa now thought the same. He just didn't know how much more. One fact was clear, while Sanura may not have *ascended* on her birthday, she was now *ascending*.

"She gave Father the most incredible gift. How much do you think that cost her emotionally?"

Assefa had no idea. He'd been stunned to learn of her sacrifice. What did it mean for their partial mate bond? Would Sanura set a date for the final part of the handfasting ceremony or would she continue to put it off? They had a lot to discuss. Unfortunately, it would have to wait until he returned home.

"Sanura told me that Father needed the jaguar spirit more than she did and more than I did."

That had been right before they'd gotten into the shower together. She'd added nothing more.

"She did it for you."

Assefa handed the gift box back to his sister.

"Not just me. For all of us."

"I think you're right. For all that she's extraordinarily powerful, Sanura cares deeply and is so very adorable."

Assefa laughed. "You better not let her hear you say that."

The door opened and Assefa stood.

Sanura glanced from Assefa to Najja and then back to Assefa. "What did I interrupt?"

"How many zeroes is on that check my father gave you?"

"Another number question, Najja, really?"

"What I heard was the check has enough zeroes to buy a small island."

Sanura shook her head and then opened her hand. Pieces of torn paper littered her palm.

Najja chuckled. "That's a first, and you're a keeper. No one turns down Berber money, especially not a check from the General Supreme of the Republic of the Sudan."

"She's as stubborn as you," Jahi croaked from his bedchamber. "And I'm thoroughly offended by her polite but stern rejection. But I did manage to wedel the Paul Chambers curse story out of her." He coughed, then laughed. "In English, this time. And it was priceless. Absolutely priceless. Gods, such an adorable fire witch of legend. The best birthday present ever."

CHAPTER TWENTY-THREE

Twenty-One Years Earlier
Baltimore, Maryland

"Settle down, my wiggling water witch, and allow me to finish your bedtime story."

"But I've heard this one before." With a resigned sigh and pout when Sharon only stared at her granddaughter with endless patience, Christie flopped onto the bed. "I already know the ending of this story."

Sharon helped tuck her granddaughter in, careful to keep her voice low. She didn't want Christine to hear her. Her daughter didn't like Sharon "filling Christie's head with myths and monsters."

"The ending to the story isn't yet written. I told you before, honey, you'll determine how the story ends."

"I don't get it. I'm not in the story."

"You're very much in the story."

To be on the safe side, Sharon went to the bedroom door. From the sound of things, Christine was downstairs doing dishes, the television on low in the background. A twinge of guilt rose within Sharon when she thought about Christine alone on another Saturday night.

She didn't date or even go out. Christine had no friends and seemed uninterested in making any. All she did was work and take care of her daughter. And while her child made Christine happy, nothing else in her life did. Heartbroken. Disconsolate. She missed Andre almost as much as she despised him for leaving her alone to raise their daughter, who, even three years later, cried whenever she saw a tiger on television or at the zoo.

It had taken Christine a year to come to terms with what the police suspected very early on. They'd found no blood in Andre's car or any other evidence that he'd been robbed, hurt, or kidnapped. All the staff, who'd seen him that last night, had said the same thing. They saw him leave, alone. He'd also made no withdrawals from their shared bank accounts, which proved to be a near insurmountable fact that kept Christine from believing that her mate had left his family behind with only the clothes on his back.

She didn't want to believe or accept that the man she'd given her heart and faith to wasn't the man she'd thought him to be. As weeks had turned into months, and the missing person's report all but forgotten by the police, Christine's desperate hope turned into bitter anger and then depressed acceptance.

Despite the questionable state of her daughter's heart and mind, Sharon had made the best decision for her family, and she wouldn't start second-guessing herself now. After Andre's disappearance, she'd talked Christine into moving from Arizona to Maryland. By this time next year, Sharon would have enough money to help Christine pay to send Christie to Sankofa Preparatory School. Not that Christine knew anything about the private witch/were-cat school yet or why a public school education wouldn't do for the water witch of legend. Something else Christine didn't need to know right now.

Secrets. Sharon had many of them. None of which Christine would understand. Not yet, anyway. In time, she would, especially once she realized how powerful her daughter would be. She'd seen the potential herself, the goddess sharing images with her of the fire witch of legend when the girl was a chubby five-year-old with a head full of thick, wavy hair and a toothy grin.

The night of Andre's death, Sharon prayed to the goddess. During that prayer, she'd received the first of what would be many images of the little girl over the years. That first-time Sharon had witnessed the immature but powerful might of the young fire witch.

The girl had literally slept on a sofa in an office that raged with fire, her sleep and breathing unaffected. Then she'd awoken, unafraid. Her little hand had reached out and toyed with the flames that lapped at the end of the sofa. Holding her hand over the fire, the flames had licked at her skin but didn't burn the child. Amazed, Sharon watched on as the flames curled around the fire witch's hand, doing a good imitation of a purring cat.

When she'd swung her legs over the side of the sofa and jumped down, the hissing of the flames quieted when she whispered, "You messed up Daddy's office. He's gonna be mad. Go away."

The flames receded as the girl, still groggy from sleep, made her way across the ruined office and to the closed door. Before she reached it, however, it burst open. On the other side stood a tall, dark man with even darker worried eyes. In a matter of seconds, he'd shifted into a large black jaguar, ran toward the little girl, grabbed her by the back of her pants and then bolted from the burning office.

No other image she'd seen of the fire witch of legend since that night compared to the first. At five and untrained, the fire witch of legend, in her most innocent state, was the culmination of generations of perfect fire witch magic in one privileged family. A divine matriarchy that, with each generation, the sole fire witch born to that time, grew stronger until the fire witch of legend was born. She was the apex fire witch with a genetic legacy of greatness.

Mami Wata hadn't tried to murder the child that night, although much of the apartment building had gone up in flames. The goddess had a different purpose. Sharon grasped her point the minute the child communed with her element and the fire responded with absolute obedience. If Sharon played willing puppet to Mami Wata's puppet master, her granddaughter would be granted power on par with the fire witch of legend but without the slow process of divine magical matriarchy.

Now that she'd convinced her family to move to Maryland and closer to the fire witch of legend, Mami Wata expected more of Sharon. With more responsibilities came greater power.

A level three water witch. She smiled as she closed the door and made her way back to her granddaughter's side. Yes, level three, and she would continue to receive the goddess's blessings if she did her bidding. Which, Sharon knew, was the real reason Mami Wata graced her with a higher witch level. Level one and two witches couldn't cast dream spells, not even when the dreamer's mind was that of a child.

Level four and, of course, level five witches excelled at high-level spells like dream manipulation. But Sharon was learning. She'd managed a short nightmare two days ago. She'd try again tonight. The fire witch of legend was a deep sleeper and a sweet, trusting girl, which made slipping into her dreams a relatively easy task.

Yet Sharon couldn't be incautious. Sanura's young fire spirit also lurked within, protecting the girl as best she could. But she only needed to touch the girl's mind for a second to create a nightmare that would have young Sanura shaking and screaming and begging the snakes to, "Get away."

Tonight, she'd attempt a longer touch as well as water to go with the snakes. The combination should scare the hell out of the eight-year-old, make her fear the water witch of legend and the Day of Serpents. Psychological warfare at its best. By the time Sanura Williams reached her twenty-ninth year, half the battle would've been won, her mind warped from years of mental terror and Sharon's granddaughter's win a foregone conclusion.

Despite her complaints about hearing the same story over and again, the little rascal's blue eyes sparkled with interest when Sharon sat on the side of her bed and began to speak.

"The oceans of Earth are unique in this solar system because no other planet has liquid water. Seventy-one percent of the Earth's surface is made up of water, and the oceans contain about ninety-seven percent of its water supply."

"That's almost all of it. Is that where we water witches get our power?"

"Yes. We need water to cast our spells. The more water around us, the stronger our magic."

"I like to swim. The water feels good on my skin. Cool. But I'm too young to cast spells. One day, will you teach me?"

Sharon would do more than teach her. She would show Christie how to use her water magic to destroy the fire witch of legend and all who would stand between her and absolute victory.

"Yes, now listen, so I can finish before your mother comes in to kiss you goodnight. Life on Earth originated in the seas, and the oceans continue to be home to an incredibly diverse web of life. It is the goddess Yemaya, the Yoruba Orisha, who's considered the mother of the living ocean. As all life was thought to have begun in the sea, all life is held to have begun with Yemaya.

After millennia, Yemaya was lonely and yearned for someone to love other than the cold, unfeeling creatures of the sea. She rose above the oceans of the world and pulled from their rhythmic essences, swirling the liquid molecules and drawing from the waxing and waning of the moon to create a child in her image.

"She named her daughter Mami Wata and endowed her with power over the oceans and water spirits. She was considered beautiful with unnaturally long hair. Mami Wata has been known to take many non-human forms, such as a mermaid or serpent. It's the serpent that is most associated with the deity."

At the mention of snakes, Christie's eyes went wide as they always did and then began to search her room for the slithering reptiles. Ignoring her, Sharon pushed on, knowing Christine would soon appear with a smile on her face for her daughter and an age-appropriate story for the eight-year-old.

Those who worshipped Mami Wata included water witches, mainly those in Africa. But this wasn't enough for Mami Wata. She wanted people of the world to worship only her. This displeased the other gods, especially Ma'at, the upholder of the principles of truth, balance, and order.

Ma'at confronted Yemaya about Mami Wata, wanting her to restore balance to the god and human realms.

Cowing to Ma'at, Yemaya floated above the oceans, but she did not seek their assistance. She looked around the massive Earth and reached for the volcanoes, sitting deep in the planet's crust. She then turned her gaze above the volcanoes and latched onto the atmospheric discharges that produced electricity. Finally, she closed her eyes and captured the flow of gases moving southwest over the Niger River Basin.

"'Come forth daughter of fire, daughter of thunder, daughter of wind. Come forth and claim your equal place in the world beside your sister. Come forth and be known as Oya.'"

"Is that when the war between Mami Wata and Oya started?"

"Years later. Sisters fight. But only one can be victorious."

"I don't have a sister."

Sharon kissed her granddaughter's forehead. "You don't need a sister, honey. Friends are better. Sisters betray but friends trust."

"I'd like to have both."

There went her twinge of guilt again. Two weeks after Andre went missing, Christine had learned she was pregnant. A fall down the steps in her home had ended the unexpected pregnancy. Christine swore she'd seen a large snake on the steps, a moment before her bare feet tripped over it, sending her face-first down the stairs. The animal control professional Christine hired hadn't found a snake, or evidence of one, in the house or the backyard but Sharon knew the truth.

She'd heard her daughter fall, saw her unconscious body at the bottom of the stairs and watched as the snake shifted into a man, smiled down at Sharon and then disappeared.

Christine was to have no more children, none that could potentially divide Sharon's time from the water witch of legend and her devotion to Mami Wata. She understood, although Sharon now feared for Christine's safety if at some point the goddess deemed her, like Andre and the baby, as impediments to her plan.

"What's wrong, Grandma?"

Sharon swiped at the tears that had fallen. "Nothing, honey, just tired. It's been a long day. I suppose you won't get to hear the rest of the story. Maybe tomorrow."

Christine would be upstairs soon. While she was in with her daughter, Sharon would retreat to her room. It had rained all day and straight into the night. Tonight would be perfect for a dream about drowning and snakes. If she were lucky, she'd work the spell so well that she'd make the nightmare last double her usual time. If not, well, there was always tomorrow and the days and weeks after that.

Sharon had time.

And Sanura Williams was too young to stop the nightmares that would always be there when she fell asleep.

CHAPTER TWENTY-FOUR

Alexandria, Virginia

"And you didn't think it important for me to know until now?"

"I didn't want to worry you."

"Worry me? Worry me? For Oya's sake, Sanura, you almost died. And you've been back from Khartoum for two weeks."

Sanura refilled Makena's glass of wine, hoping to calm the fire witch. Not that plying her mother with alcohol was the best course of action when she had to drive home.

In retrospect, she should've driven to Baltimore. But Makena had insisted on making the trek to Alexandria. They sat in Assefa's refurbished living room. In an uncharacteristic fit of anger and grief, Assefa had taken Mngwa claws to his sofa and loveseat, after learning of the massacre of over a dozen African immigrants by a Baltimore City Police Detective Assefa liked and respected.

Makena sipped from her wine glass but appeared no less furious.

"I'll also have a word with my parents as soon as I get home. One of them should've called me." Makena crossed her legs in a gesture that seemed anything but relaxed. Dark-brown eyes that greeted Sanura with such warmth when she'd arrived on her doorstep, now examined her from head to toe. With her second sight, no less.

"I'm fine, Mom."

Sanura moved down one sofa cushion, putting her next to her mother. Claiming Makena's hand, Sanura waited for her mother to acknowledge the truth.

"I see no lasting effects from the attack." A tight, long hug preceded sniffles and suppressed tears. "I won't allow anyone to take you from me. Do you hear me, Sanura? I forbid you from dying."

"Yes, I hear you, Mom. But I'm pretty sure that even a judge can't forbid something like that."

Sanura tried to inflect humor into her voice, hating the fear and concern in her mother's.

"You know what I mean."

"Actually, I don't."

The women separated; Makena's eyes wet. "You've always been a sweet and kind girl. The first to help and the last to blame, which is why you're such a good psychologist and professor. You care about people you don't know and will likely never meet. When your friends and family hurt, so do you. You're empathetic and far more attuned to the feelings of others than is probably healthy for you."

"Okay, thanks, I think. What does that have to do with anything?"

"Sometimes, sweetie, you have to be proactive instead of reactive. There's nothing wrong with throwing the first punch when you're up against the likes of Mami Wata's dangerous followers."

On the flight home, Zareb had made the same point. Sanura had never heard anyone string together English and Wolof curses to create a third language the way Zareb had. The man had a gift, his diatribe leaving Sanura exhausted.

She'd fallen asleep soon afterward. Not a peaceful rest, unfortunately, but she did manage not to scream herself awake.

"I need you to fight."

"I have been."

"No, you've been surviving, reacting to the unscrupulous acts of others. Look at you. When was the last time you had a good night's sleep?"

Grabbing her glass of wine, Sanura drank. Not deeply, just long enough to give herself time to prepare for another outburst from Makena.

"I haven't been sleeping well." Placing the glass back on the living room table in front of the sofa where they sat, she added, "It's been a few weeks. The dreams come and go. Well, now they mostly come and stay."

Makena closed her eyes, leaned against the soft cushion behind her, and exhaled slowly.

When her mother got like this, her fire spirit close to the surface, Sanura knew to stay still and to shut up. She downed the rest of her wine, wondering where Omar kept the hard stuff.

"Dreams or nightmares?" Makena asked, her eyes still shut, voice deceptively composed.

"Nightmares."

"For weeks? You've been having nightmares for weeks and this is the first I've heard of it?"

Okay, voice not so composed anymore.

"I can take care of the nightmares on my own. I don't need to run to you to help me get through the night. I'm too old for that."

Makena's eyes popped open, fire spirit red mixed with human brown. "How's being an adult working out for you? Have you managed to put a stop to the dream spell yet or did you hope the perpetrator would grow tired of torturing your mind and go away?"

Sometimes, she disliked how simplistic Makena made serious issues appear as if Sanura were being dramatic or a glutton for punishment. Today, it just pissed her off.

"I'm not a child."

"Then stop acting like one. Do you not remember how awful your nightmares were when you were a child?" Makena shifted to her side, facing Sanura. "You would awake in a sweat, eyes blazing red, skin hot to the touch and your throat hoarse from screaming. Gods, Sanura, for months, Sam and I had no idea how to help you."

Sanura didn't recall it all. The haunted look on Makena's face told the tale of a mother's helpless anxiety.

"At first, we didn't think much of your nightmares. We thought they were normal. You didn't even remember them. Over time, the nightmares occurred more often, some weeks nearly every day."

Night terrors. Her dreams as a child were night terrors, not night-mares. No one called them that back then, lumping bad dreams children had into the category of nightmares. But night terrors in children were different. Night terrors happened during the first two or three hours of sleep. The transition between deep non-REM sleep to lighter REM sleep was when night terrors usually occurred.

Children often awoke suddenly, thrashing about, crying, screaming and breathing fast. All the symptoms Makena had described of the child Sanura frightened awake by whatever horror plagued her dream state.

"One night, I decided to watch you sleep. Nothing happened that first night, so I continued staying in your bedroom for hours. You went two weeks without a nightmare. Then you had one." Makena shook her head, anger flaring again. "I could feel the presence of the witch when she entered your room and then your mind. Her magic, weak though it was, was enough to arouse your central nervous system while you slept, causing you to see and feel only Oya knows what."

"I thought you were being dramatic when you mentioned a dream spell. I mean, sure, I assumed the water witch of legend or Mami Wata had cast a dream spell on me these past few weeks. But you're saying the same was done to me when I was a kid?"

What kind of cold-blooded witch would do that to a child?

"That's when I began protecting our home with wards and stopped you from sleeping over at friends' homes. I couldn't risk the witch find-ing you there and assaulting your mind. When you were with me in our home, I could protect you when you slept."

"Wait, what did you do when you sensed the water witch in my room?"

"I used my magic to shield you from her intrusion."

"What does that mean?"

"It means I used my fire spirit to slip into your mind, found the water witch's magic, corralled it and then forced her from your mind."

"Then what?"

"Did you know that a dream spell is one of the rare spells that a witch casts that can reverberate back to her body?"

"Yes. Gods, Mom, what did you do?"

Oh, but that was a wicked smile that crossed Makena's face.

"I had no way of tracing the spell back to the spellcaster. But I did have a part of her mind and magic trapped in my field. I did what any mother would do."

Sanura doubted that.

"There used to be a small medical facility for the criminally insane in Howard County. I drove there a day after I caught the water witch's dream magic and placed it into the mind of one of the patients. I was told those patients dreamed a lot, reliving their vile actions that had placed them in the facility instead of prison."

She was beginning to understand her mother's ruthless twist on the water witch's dream spell. "The caster of the dream spell can see the dream of the mind where her magic resides."

"Yes, but the water witch who tortured you didn't stay long enough to witness what her cruel touch did to you. If she had, my fire spirit would've sensed her presence when it first started. The coward ran away and left you to deal with the fallout of her villainy."

"You trapped a part of her in the mind of, I assume, a serial killer?"

"Precisely, the kind of killer who hated women and enjoyed cutting them into little pieces after committing the most horrendous acts against them."

"That's sick."

"What the killer did or what I did?"

"Both. I can't believe you did that."

"She never returned. That's all I wanted. She never even tried to breach the ward. Mercenary, sweetie. What I did to her was awful but no less than what she deserved. I had to make a point, which she got. The ward was a contingency plan in the event Mami Wata sent another water witch after you. I can't protect you from all harm, I know that. But when I can, I will, with every magical fiber in my bones."

Sanura didn't know what to say. Makena Williams wasn't an inherently violent or malicious woman. What she'd done, however, was both. She didn't regret it, either.

"One day, sweetie, when you have a child of your own, you'll understand the depth of a mother's love and need to protect. You'll surprise, maybe even terrify, yourself with what you'll do for your child. We're witches, not saints."

Witches, not saints. All too well, Sanura knew the truth of the simple but complex statement.

"Stop being afraid."

"What do you think I'm afraid of?"

"You need to answer that for yourself." Makena stood. "Show me your new car. That's why I'm here."

"You're changing the subject, and I could've sent you a pic of the car if you wanted to see it so badly."

"You said you were planning on returning it because it was too expensive."

Sanura had meant it until Rashad had spent the past weekend at home and had whined until she'd taken him for a spin. The car drove like a dream and the leather seats were pure butter.

Sanura escorted Makena to the multi-car garage.

"If I knew how to whistle, I would." She touched the shiny hood of the car. "My gods, a black jaguar convertible and it's gorgeous. I'm uncertain, but I don't think this beauty has been released to the public yet. It's on exclusive order." Makena clapped. "Jahi Berber has outdone himself in the gratitude department. He's also made it nearly impossible for you to return his gift." Makena walked around to the back of the car and Sanura followed. "He even got you vanity plates."

She'd noticed the Heritage-style plate. Virginia's state bird, the Cardinal, was perched on a branch of a Dogwood, the state tree. In the center of the license plate were six letters: ADORFW. The man was unbelievable.

"What do the letters stand for?"

She'd never met anyone like Jahi Berber. The were-cat thought he could buy anything and anyone, which was probably true in most cases. He also thought himself above reproach. Yet there was a vulnerable charm to the man when it came to his children. He loved them with the same protective passion that Makena had for Sanura. She found that she couldn't fault Jahi for erecting psychological blinders to the ruthless nature of his eldest son. She would never accept money from him, but she found herself questioning the merit of not allowing Jahi to demonstrate his genuine gratitude for the woman who'd saved his life.

"ADORFW. It means adorable fire witch."

Makena didn't bother to hide her smile. "I've told you for years, but you never believed me."

"I'm not adorable."

"Well, not today. Today, you're grumpy due to lack of sleep, which, by the way, is doing terrible things to your eyes. Anyway, Sanura, Lex Luthor should've gone with red, but he wants you to know how much he appreciates your gift. A black jaguar for a black jaguar. He's not subtle, but the were-cat does have exquisite taste."

No one in the Berber family had the slightest ounce of tact, and Sanura hoped this was the first and last time Makena referred to Jahi Berber as Lex Luthor.

Sanura had told Makena everything that happened in the Sudan, including giving Jahi Sam's jaguar spirit. She'd made only one comment. "A man needs his father."

Assefa did need his father, which was why Sanura hadn't worried this past week when Assefa hadn't called. They'd spoken the day she'd returned to Virginia and several times since then. This past week, however, he'd neither called nor returned Sanura's calls. She didn't want to worry and had tried not to read more into his lack of communication than there probably was. Still, it wasn't like Assefa to go days without reaching out to her.

"Go get the key so you can take me for a ride."

"I'm not even sure if the tags and registration are legal. MVA doesn't work this fast."

"He probably had someone killed, promoted or fired to expedite the purchase, registration, and delivery of the car." Makena shoved Sanura toward the back door. "Go get the key to the Jag. I have a lot of hair, and I want it to blow in the wind."

"We're not Thelma and Louise."

"Of course not. A '66 Thunderbird has nothing on a twenty-first-century Jaguar. And really, Sanura, we make a much better duo than Sarandon and Davis."

"No driving off a cliff together?"

"Are you feeling suicidal?"

"Nope."

"Homicidal?"

"Maybe a little."

"Toward Mami Wata, her followers, and the water witch of legend?"

"Yes."

Makena's smile was pure fire witch wickedness. "Good. Now get your key. I want to see what this baby can do."

CHAPTER TWENTY-FIVE

One Week Earlier
Khartoum, Sudan

"You're looking better today."

Jahi sat propped up in his luxury steel style gold bed, black duvet pulled to his waist. His white, silk pajama top was a bright contrast to his skin color and the surrounding bed linen.

"I feel much improved." He touched his chest. "It's a strange sensation to have another mans were-cat inside of me."

He'd wondered how his father felt about that, but Assefa assumed it too personal to ask. The Berbers didn't do that level of personal, although he tried with Sanura. She didn't deserve an emotionally walled-off mate, so he worked to not give her one.

"I don't have the jaguar's thoughts. I think he's keeping them from me, but he seems content if not happy."

"He probably misses Sanura." Assefa grabbed a chair from his father's desk, placed it beside his bed and sat. "The spirit was with her for almost four years. As much as it's an adjustment for you, it's also an adjustment for him."

"I know." Jahi touched his chest again. "He was meant for you, correct?"

"Yes. Sanura told you the story of her father's sacrifice?"

"The morning before she left for home. I don't think she relayed the entire story, but enough so I'd understand."

"Understand what?"

Jahi's eyes fell from Assefa's, his voice suddenly low and tone oddly reflective. "That all gifts aren't free and that this one comes with a price."

"Sanura told you there was a price for saving your life?"

That didn't sound like his witch. Jahi must've misunderstood what Sanura had told him.

"Not a price. I chose that word poorly. She told me she hoped I was 'worthy' of her father's jaguar spirit. Sanura touched me here." Jahi lifted his hand once more to his chest. The area over his heart. "I felt heat where her hand met my shirt. Not painful or even uncomfortable, but her heat felt like it reached me on the cellular level, her eyes blood-red as she scanned my soul."

Assefa leaned forward as Jahi described his encounter with the fire witch of legend.

"It wasn't the first time I felt her magic. When I was dying from the poison, sweaty, cold and weak on the dining room floor, Sanura was there using her magic to fight for my life and for the life of my cat spirit." Stark brown eyes lifted. "I've never known shame in my life, son, although I probably should've long before my sixtieth year. But when I gazed into Sanura's fire eyes, her warm hand over my beating heart, that organ overflowed with shame. And it hurt worse than the poison."

Tears fell from Jahi. Was the world coming to an end? General Supreme Jahi Berber didn't cry. If he did, he certainly didn't do it in front of anyone, least of all another male. Yet there he sat, tears of… shame? running down his cheeks.

Seeing Jahi like this, Assefa was forced to admit as he reached for his father's right hand and held it, frightened him. Berbers didn't cry. Except, of course, they did. He'd cried when his mother died, when he felt his sister die, and when he feared Sanura would die from her battle wounds.

"Layer by layer, her heated magic peeled away decades of false-hoods and self-delusions. She told me, 'Your heart needs to be lighter. You yet still have time. Begin with the truth and maintain that path. If you do, when your time comes, all will be forgiven.'"

Jahi swiped at the tears, but they still fell.

OF DECEPTION AND DIVINITY · 207

Nothing his father said made sense. Or rather, nothing Sanura had told Jahi made sense.

"It was as if she were in a trance. The voice was hers, but the message" —Jahi accepted the tissue Assefa handed him and wiped the last of the tears from his eyes and face— "sounded odd on her modern lips but also right in its ancient feel. I know that doesn't make any sense, but you would understand if you'd been here."

Assefa needed to get back to his witch. If he required any more evidence that Sanura had begun her ascension, which he didn't, this would be it. She'd already received wind and lightning magic from Oya, which she used with more proficiency each time she cast a wind or lightning spell. What Assefa had yet to determine was if the other changes in Sanura were an unknown extension of being Oya's chosen champion or whether her unusual behavior and new abilities had nothing to do with Oya. If that were the case, then no one, not even Sanura, could know what would happen next with her, which put Assefa on edge.

"Listen, son, there's something you need to know."

Assefa didn't like the sound of that.

"Since you're here, I'll tell you now. I was hoping to only say it once, but your sister is tied up in meetings all day, taking care of many of my duties while I've been convalescing. I'll have the same discussion with her later if she isn't too tired or annoyed from another argument with Omar." A hand came up to rub across Jahi's forehead. "Their fractured relationship is something else I'll have to atone for, although I have no idea how. By the end of today, I may have turned all of my children against me."

Assefa pushed away from the chair and got to his feet. He couldn't remain seated after a statement like that.

"Did Sanura tell you to atone?"

"All but, yes."

"Then you might as well begin."

Assefa paced Jahi's large bedroom as he spoke. The story, over twenty years old, was one Assefa thought he'd never hear.

When Jahi finished, face anguished, eyes on an enraged Assefa, he noticed for the first time the bloody state of his knuckles.

Over a dozen fist-sized holes riddled his father's back wall.

"No wonder my brother hates me."

His fist connected with another wall, over and again until a guard came running into the bedroom, gun up and prepared to take down a threat to the general supreme. When he glimpsed a golden-eyed Assefa, he took his cue from Jahi, who waved away his concern and retreated.

"I'm sorry."

"You're sorry? That means nothing to me."

"She filled Razi's head with lies."

"And you lied to all of us."

"I couldn't tell you the truth."

Assefa roared. Windows in the room cracked, and he roared again.

"Son, please." Jahi struggled to his feet, stronger than the day before but still weak. "This is what I didn't want. I knew the truth would wound you. Her decision wasn't your fault. I only wanted to protect my children. That's why I lied."

Assefa backed away from his father when he made to touch him. He didn't want his sympathy, his worthless pity.

"You should've told me. Maybe not when I was a child, but when I became a man."

Jahi moved closer, his hand once more reaching for Assefa's trembling shoulder.

He shrugged him away.

"What do you expect me to do with this information now?"

"It's the truth you deserved years ago. I owed it to you and to your sister."

"It would've been better if you said nothing."

"No, you deserved—"

"What? Confirmation that I'm an animal? How does that knowledge help me? What can I do with it but know that I can never have what I want?"

"This doesn't have to change anything between you and Sanura."

Assefa turned away from his father. He pulled out his cell phone, scrolled to his list of contacts and found Sanura's phone number. Her picture appeared on the screen. It wasn't one where she was smiling for the camera, but a picture he'd taken when she'd been asleep in their bed. Quiet and beautiful and heartwarmingly his.

But not anymore.

"It changes everything. She'll stay because she loves me because Sanura's loyal and thinks we can have the type of marriage her parents had."

"You can."

"We can't," he yelled. "I heard every word you said. Every ugly, depressing truth. I won't put her through that. I won't endanger Sanura's life because I want her so desperately." He looked at his father's expensively decorated room. "How can we have so much but so little of true value?"

"We have each other. That's worth everything."

Assefa backed away, shaking his head.

"No, son, don't go. Not like this. I can't lose you, too."

"I didn't care about the dangers of the prophecy as long as I had Sanura in my life. I wasn't afraid, even of dying. I only wanted to protect my witch." Assefa grabbed the handle to the door, his hand gripping it too hard as he yanked the door open. "I'll still protect Sanura. But from a distance. I can't be with her, not as her familiar and not as her mate."

Assefa fell to his hands and knees. His body quaked with loss and heartache.

Before he knew it, he'd shifted and was racing through the halls, down the steps and out into the rainy summer day.

To save Sanura from him, Assefa had to give her up.

Atlanta, Georgia

She observed Assefa, eyes as enchanting as a Blue poppy in early summer. Half-naked, she and the bedsheets smelled of sex. Blonde hair,
long and streaked purple, covered small breasts. The tan sheets hid her
hips and legs but not the small bulge of her stomach.

"You like what you see?"

No, he didn't.

Sheets were tossed to the side, revealing the rest of her. Assefa assumed she wore something on her lower half. He was wrong.

Parting her thighs and raising her knees, she took herself in hand,
cupping and playing, blue eyes on him all the while.

"She's beautiful, isn't she? Young and supple. Men like girls like
her. They give me whatever I want, especially if I let them touch me
here."

Fingers slipped inside as she continued to speak, her innocent eyes
incongruent with her worldly actions and callous spirit.

When he raised his gun, she stopped. And began to cry.

Assefa didn't lower his weapon but neither did he shoot.

"You would kill me?" A shaky hand rose to her stomach, thin fingers
spread over the small bump he'd noticed earlier. "Kill my daughter? Do
you have no heart in that rigid were-cat body of yours?"

He waited to see if the fraud would shift into her true form. She
didn't. She maintained the charade, wearing the gentle image of the last
person she'd murdered. Another full-human, based on the briefing he'd
received from Ulan's assistant director.

Emily Gardner, age nineteen, Emory University sophomore. Her
roommate reported her missing a week ago. Before that, it was Hannah
Campbell, Samantha Roberts, Ashley Bailey, Brianna Stewart and ten
other students from colleges and universities in metropolitan Atlanta.

There were likely others, deaths that hadn't been flagged by the Preternatural Division of the FBI, especially since Ulan thought Assefa,
during the Baltimore serial killer case, had dispatched with all the adzes.

Yet there one sat, not in her bat-humanoid form, but as a young woman who would never see her twentieth year. The body of the real Emily Gardner was found forty-eight hours ago, drained of blood like the others.

The adze had used the past few months to move from preying on witches, for their life-extending blood to hunting full-humans. This adze no longer hid, but mimicked the form of her victims, so she could live among them while also preying on them.

Assefa released his gun's safety.

The adze charged. White skin, blue eyes, and blonde hair rolled back as fangs, leathery skin and red eyes surged forward.

He fired twice, stopping the transformation and the threat.

She thumped to the floor, most of her body still that of a naked Emily Gardner. But the adze's face, well, that gruesome mess was splattered on the hotel room floor.

From across the room, another shot rang out.

"I had to make sure."

Zareb holstered his weapon. A bullet straight into the adze's stomach. Yes, Zareb had to make sure the baby didn't survive her mother's death. He'd killed it, like the monster it was, the beast it would grow to be.

The sight sickened him. As did the thought that he, in a twisted way, was like the unborn adze, unnatural and destined for a life of violence and blood.

"I'll take care of clean up and disposal. You go to the car and call Sanura. She's called me a half dozen times this week and I don't know what to say to her, so I haven't answered."

Neither had Assefa. She'd called him far more than six times, leaving voice mails and text messages. He hadn't found the right words to explain his absence and distance. Assefa feared he never would.

"Two missions in two weeks. And we haven't been home once since leaving Khartoum." Zareb began stripping the bed and throwing the sheets over the unmoving adze. "I don't know what's going on with you, but you've been shit for company. You don't talk and you hardly eat. And anytime I mention Sanura, you get that look." He raised his finger and pointed it at Assefa. "You don't break up with a woman like Sanura. She's your soulmate. You're like a fucking zombie without her. And not the fun kind of zombie, but the rotting kind that smells like shit and has flies buzzing around them."

Assefa pulled two pairs of medical gloves from his pants pocket and handed a pair to Zareb, which he pulled on. "You don't understand." Assefa bent to help Zareb wrap the sheets around the corpse.

"I don't understand because you haven't told me a damn thing. You know what, it doesn't matter. I get it. Your father told you some raw shit that makes you think you can't be with your witch. Maybe you're right. But you're wrong for not calling her, for leaving Sanura hanging while she worries about you, which you know she is."

Retrieving towels from the bathroom to clear away the blood, Assefa couldn't ignore the guilt burning a hole in his chest. Zareb was right. Beyond cowardice, Assefa had no excuse for not facing Sanura and the decision he'd made. He tossed the towels onto the floor and began to scrub away the blood and brain matter.

An hour later, a bagged corpse in the trunk of their car and Zareb finishing up in the hotel room, Assefa sat in the driver's seat, cell phone in hand.

He'd missed three calls from Sanura, his Thursday tally. There'd been two yesterday, three the day before that and one on Monday.

Sanura deserved better than this treatment. The weak part of him thought that by not speaking with Sanura he could spare himself the pain of breaking up with her.

Stupid.

Spineless.

He called, and she picked up on the second ring.

"Gods, Assefa, I've been worried sick. How are you? Where are you? I called your father and sister, and they said you left Khartoum two weeks ago."

Her sentences ran together in a breathless barrage of relief and concern.

For a minute, he just listened to Sanura's voice. He hated to hear the anxiety he'd created but also couldn't help the sad smile that rose to his lips. He'd missed her, even the undercurrent of anger she couldn't mask.

"I apologize. I should've called before now. I don't have a good excuse, so I won't bother offering you one."

"Just tell me you're all right. I can always kill you for worrying me when you get home."

Assefa wasn't all right, and he had no intention of returning home until Mami Wata and her water witch were no longer a threat to Sanura.

"We need to talk."

"Okay, but I don't like the way you sound."

He heard rustling of fabric in the background but couldn't tell what Sanura was doing, maybe changing into nightclothes or getting into bed. Assefa knew her nightly routine, school work, shower, read and then sleep. When he was there with her, they'd make love before she showered and sometimes again in the morning.

Assefa had no idea how to do this. There was no good way to tell Sanura something that would hurt her as much as it already pained him. Every time Assefa considered flying back to his witch, his father's confession reared up and took another chunk out of Assefa's heart and hope.

"Um, listen, Sanura. We only have a partial mate bond, which means you aren't bound to me."

"Our partial mate bond doesn't mean I'm not bound to you. We're more to each other than a claiming bite. That's not the way I think, and you know that. Where are you going with this?"

"My point is that with only a partial mate bond between us, the dissolution spell will be easy for you to cast."

She didn't speak immediately, but he heard her sharp intake of breath when he'd finished his sentence.

"Why would I dissolve our mate bond?"

Slow. Measured. Livid.

"So you can be free of me, my Mngwa, and my dysfunctional family."

"I'll ask again, why would I dissolve our mate bond?"

No good answer, other than the truth, which Assefa refused to give. Sanura thought she could solve everyone's problem even when it wasn't hers to resolve. She couldn't fix this.

Even through two layers, Assefa could feel Sanura's promise ring against his chest. She hadn't rescinded her pledge to fight for them. But there he was, breaking his vow in the worst way possible.

"Cast the dissolution spell. You don't need me there for you to break the one-way bond."

Heated silence stretched between them.

"Come home."

"I can't."

"Please, Assefa, come home, so we can speak face-to-face."

Assefa clutched the phone, hating the desperate plea in Sanura's tone and the pain in her voice.

"Don't do this."

He didn't want to.

"I thought I could give you more, give you everything you deserve and want, but I was fooling myself. I can no longer be your mate and familiar. I'm sorry, Sanura, I really am."

She went quiet again, and what was left of Assefa's heart shattered.

When she finally spoke, however, it was with a steel he hadn't expected.

"I don't accept a damn thing you just said. If you were here, I'd throw a fireball at your arrogant, fool head. You don't get to decide this on your own, especially without an explanation. And you damn sure have no right to order me to dissolve our mate bond because some shit is going on with you that you can't handle emotionally. You're running again, and I won't allow you to fuck up our relationship because you have your head up your Berber ass."

"Sanura I—"

"Do you have any fucking idea how tired I am? I need to sleep, but I don't want to deal with the fire witch of legend. But I will because she's pissing me the hell off, just like you are right now. I'm snarling and cursing like one of those reality show women I dislike because they come off as shrews and bitches, and I hate that kind of skewed representation of females."

"But Sanura—"

"I really want to call you to me in a thunderbolt, so I can smack you. We're not even married yet and I want to strangle you with my bare hands. That doesn't bode well for your life expectancy, Assefa, or my chance of staying out of prison on a homicide charge."

The fire witch went on, describing in astonishing detail what she would do to him if he didn't return home, so they could talk. Then she hung up on him.

Stunned, Assefa still held the cell phone in his hand and up to his ear when Zareb opened the car door and slid into the passenger seat.

"I hear nothing on the other end. Why are you holding the phone?"

Good question. He pressed End and dropped the phone in the car drink holder.

"How did it go with Sanura? Were you stupid enough to break up with her?"

"I tried."

"What did she say?"

He shook his head and then started the car. "The witch that everyone thinks is adorable threatened to kill me, then hung up before I could say anything else."

"Did she use curse words before giving you a virtual middle finger?"

"More than I've heard her say before and none ever directed at me." She'd also called him an elephant's ass in Wolof.

Zareb grinned. "Good for her. Sanura's too smart to put up with your Berber bullshit, which makes her the perfect mate for you."

"This doesn't change anything. Sanura's refusal will only make this harder on her when she realizes that I'm not changing my mind." Assefa drove out of the hotel parking lot, rain pouring, the sky and his mood dark. "I'm not going home, no matter how mad it'll make her."

Undoing the first three buttons of his shirt, Assefa pulled Sanura's necklace over his head. He knew one way to convince her of his seriousness. After this, she would dissolve their partial mate bond.

She would be free of him, although Assefa would forever carry the pain of losing his soulmate.

CHAPTER TWENTY-SIX

Realm of the Gods

"Will you not allow me to go to her?"

Compelling her green dragon flower eyes away from the wall-sized scrying glass and her fire witch, Oya turned them to the tribunal of gods behind her. On the gold-and-white dais stood Ra. The sun god, hands behind his back, chest bare and body sculpted to inhuman perfection, wore nothing but a white shendyt pleated at the front. His hair, a brown-and-white mix of thin, tapered falcon's feathers grew away from his prominent forehead and down to his lean waist.

An actual falcon, his companion whenever Ra chose to wear this god form, perched on Ra's chair. It was a solid gold structure trimmed with the image of a sun boat, which represented Ra's nightly travel through the underworld and the primordial waters of Nun. Underneath the boat was an image of the primordial serpent, Apep, who sought to stop Ra's journey. Standing inside the sun boat and in front of Ra was the god's ever-protective Ma'at, Apep's counterpoint.

The King of Gods watched the same scene in the scrying glass as the others.

Oya didn't want to see more. She'd witnessed this slow, malicious torture for too long. Yet the others, enthralled, continued to take in the fire witch's nightmarish torment.

To the left of Ra's high-back throne chair sat Sekhmet, his daughter and the creator of were-cats. A yellowish-red lioness sat at the warrior goddess's naked feet, her rounded head in Sekhmet's lap. She wore an ankle-length, tight-fitting two-strap sheath dress, the upper edge just above her breasts.

Seated in the third chair on the dais to Ra's right was Yemaya. Her wavy black-blue hair flowed down her back and over her ocean blue dress, which mimicked tidal bulges as the moon moved through its phases. As comfortable and entitled as she appeared in the chair, that position of power didn't belong to Yemaya but to Ma'at.

Unsurprisingly, next to Ma'at's throne chair, a quiet, furry reminder of the unbalanced scales of *ma'at* and *isfet*, stood Anubis. The god of the afterlife and the patron god of lost souls and the helpless wore the animal form of a jackal-dog hybrid, black, long legs, pointy ears, and curved canine teeth.

Oya didn't need the visual reminder, the silent condemnation of his diminished role as the Guardian of the Scales and the protector of graves and cemeteries. She knew what her centuries-old war with Mami Wata had cost him, the funeral rites he could no longer perform.

"This is her journey, Oya, and you must allow the child to traverse it without interference from you."

Ra's words fell hollow on her ears. As always, he did what best served his purpose at the moment, no matter his previous decrees.

"I do not wish to interfere. At least no more than Mami Wata has been permitted to do so."

Even now, Mami Wata wasn't in Ra's temple, her absence noteworthy but unnoted by the others in attendance.

"She and Apep have never been held to the same restrictions you have placed on me." Oya stepped toward Ra, her purple dress swaying with her movement. "Sekhmet and Yemaya are supposed to oversee our actions, yet they permit Mami Wata to go where I cannot."

Large black eyes rimmed in yellow lowered to Oya, Ra's voice a warm breeze over her cool skin. "Without Mami Wata's and Apep's schemes, she will never ascend. Without their heartless calculations, Sanura Williams is nothing more than an overpowered fire witch. Without *isfet*, your child of fire cannot know or understand *ma'at*."

Ra stepped from the dais, hands still clasped behind his back. When he reached Oya, he laid a hand on her shoulder and motioned her around to the scrying glass. From their perch in the godly realm, where the fate of mortals intersected with the might and hubris of the gods, they watched Sanura twist and turn as she slept.

"She is in pain."

"No, she is growing, learning, becoming. Where you see a child in need of mothering, I see a struggle for birth, for actualization. This is the closest any of your fire witches have come to ascending. If you meddle now, the child of fire will flounder then fail."

Sanura screamed as she awoke from her nightmare. Alone and with no mate to comfort her, Sanura pushed back the duvet and stumbled out of bed, her eyes filled with unshed tears. She stomped around her bedchamber, hands clenched into fists and voice angry as she swore at an invisible enemy, the fire witch of legend who came before her.

Hair long and wild, it smoldered gold fire around her shoulders. Steady hands formed two fireballs, which crackled as Sanura flexed her fingers. She hurled the fireballs around the room, catching them when they returned.

With each throw, the fireballs increased in velocity. They flew around the room at a speed that should've had them spiraling out of control and burning whatever they collided into. Yet they returned to Sanura each time, the room and all within unscathed.

"Do you see how that simple act has calmed her?" Ra asked. "The repetition, the focus, even her frustration to stay in control, it is all an internal battle."

The warm sand of the temple floor clung to Oya's bare feet. The walls were made of limestone blocks and were covered with depictions of deities the world and time over: Mesopotamian, Inuit, Chinese, Germanic, Orisha, Māori. So many images and even more beliefs, all held together by intertwined threads of faith and fear.

The last of Oya's daughters reclined on her back and the rumpled bedsheets. The fireballs hovered above her, waiting for Sanura's command. With closed eyes and an open palm, Sanura snapped her fingers and the fireballs burst into a shower of fire rain that descended in reddish-orange droplets onto Oya's last hope for salvation.

Sanura curled onto her side, hand going to the ring that hung on a gold chain around her neck.

Oya thought she would weep for the loss of her mate, for the heart that ached for a man hundreds of miles away but even further than that in mind and soul. Instead, she slid from the bed and went to her closet.

"She is the one we have waited to be born," Sekhmet said from the dais. "Have more faith in your chosen mortal, Oya."

She did. If Sanura failed, however, there wouldn't be another fire witch of legend.

"Daughter, Sanura's bloodline is strong." Oya shifted to see Yemaya glide toward her. "The young one is not at her apex, but with her beast and their bond she will ascend to her fullest potential."

True, but the were-cat was lost, unable to divine the truth of self through the miasma of rejection and lies.

"My Mngwa will persevere, worry not."

Persevere? The last Mngwa found only death at the vengeful hands of Mami Wata. Still, this incarnation of the cat of legend had much heart and fortitude, despite the current confused state of his mind.

Ra touched her shoulder again. "We have no more white feathers. *Isfet* has infected the mortal realm, and Apep is poised to claim the realm for himself. He seeks to rule, to bring about darkness, storms night and death. Neither Mami Wata nor Apep grasp the full extent of what will happen to the mortals, to us all, if Sanura and Assefa succumb to *isfet* or lose to the water witch of legend and Mami Wata's horrific creatures."

Ra was to blame. He could've stopped the war between Oya and Mami Wata, could've intervened long before he did, thus sparing the mortal realm countless deaths and the foul stench of restless souls. Centuries passed, religious wars raged and Ra soaked it all in, the prayers, the offerings, the worship.

Until he lost her. Four white feathers were all Ra had left of her. Now, only one white feather remained, delivered to the fire witch of legend, by Sàngó, on the day of Sanura's birth.

"Mami Wata is not the only one who has interfered in the battle between water and fire," Ra said as if that fact absolved him of culpability.

Oya had only sought to minimize her sister's malicious schemes, such as the breaking of Assefa's bespellment by Tracey Kemraha and the manipulation of the water witch of legend's mate bond. At the thought of that well-made countermove, Oya grinned to herself. Mami Wata had yet to discover the truth. When she did, she wouldn't be pleased.

Still, in comparison to Mami Wata and Apep, Oya had done little to aid her fire witch in the battle to come.

"All mortals are not driven by greed and power. Love, Oya, it is their unquestionable weakness as well as their greatest strength."

Ra spoke of mortal love. But it was his immortal guilt that had driven the vicious battles between fire and water witches.

With a wave of his imperial hand, a golden chair appeared in front of Oya. "Sit Orisha of fire, winds, and lightning. Let us watch and wait."

"For Sanura's death?"

"Yes, but also her rebirth, her ascension to—"

Sanura screamed. All eyes returned to the scrying glass. No, not Sanura but the fire witch of legend.

Chicago, Illinois

"This would be a great view of Lake Michigan if I weren't looking at it through sheets of rain." Zareb continued to stare out of the window, despite his near-constant grumbling about the torrential downpour.

Assefa sat at the oversized desk in a comfortable chair, but he could do without the lemon color. Which is the word the bellman used when Assefa had arched an unpleased eyebrow when the man brought his luggage in, and he'd growled, "Great, three hundred seventy-five dollars a night and I get to sit in yellow chairs."

The bureau wouldn't reimburse him for the luxury room, and Assefa hadn't needed to book him and Zareb into this upscale Chicago hotel. But it was near Lake Michigan, their target location, and Assefa was feeling surly and self-indulgent. If he couldn't have his witch to soothe his rough edges, he'd settle for a king-sized bed with a high thread count.

Zareb turned away from the window and claimed the single black leather chair in the room. "The snakes could be coming from any number of rivers and streams. We can't stop this."

They were the only were-cat partners in the Preternatural Division of the FBI. All others were witch/were-cat pairings. Most cases it didn't matter. Others, like this one, the lack of magic diversity did.

"We'll observe, do what we can, write a report and then stay here until Ulan sends a witch to join us or another team to take over the case."

"How's Sanura?" Zareb pointed to the cell phone on the desk in front of Assefa. "I was in the bathroom when you called Dahad and missed his daily report."

If Sanura knew Assefa called Dahad to check on her, instead of coming home and seeing after her well-being himself, she'd be mad as hell. Since their last phone call two weeks ago, Sanura hadn't called him.

She'd also stopped calling Zareb, which left Assefa with no other recourse but to have Dahad or Manute spy on Sanura. Since Manute was having witch issues of his own with Rachel, that left Dahad. The older man's lecture still rung his ears. But he'd agreed.

"He said Sanura's tired all the time. Dahad's taken to driving her to the university on the days she must go in. Luckily, that's not most days, and she can work from her office."

"Sounds like Sanura's still having nightmares."

Every cell in his body ached with the need to reach out and call Sanura. The distance he'd put between them left Assefa unhappy and guilty.

Zareb propped his forearms on his thighs and faced Assefa. "Now that I know the truth, I get why you stepped away from Sanura. But I still think you can make it work."

"She'll want to try. And I'll give in because, when it comes to her, I'd do almost anything to make Sanura happy."

"Being with your mate also makes you happy."

"Which is why I have to stay away from her. If I return home, I won't have the strength to walk away from Sanura again. I'm not that strong."

"This is the thing. One of these days when you call Dahad, it'll be to learn that Sanura's finally had enough and moved out. It's been a month. How much longer do you think she'll wait before pride and hurt has her packing her bags? Have you thought about that? Have you thought what it would mean for Sanura to move on?"

Zareb scooted to the edge of the black chair, his dark-brown eyes serious. "I mean really move on? Not just out of your home but onto another guy? Not right away because she's not that kind of woman. In a year, maybe two, she'll fall for someone else. Perhaps one of those Sankofa were-cats who worships the ground she walks on. Maybe a full-human. I don't know. But Sanura's beautiful, funny, and smart. And, if we're going to keep it real between us, if she weren't your mate and you my best friend, I would do all in my power to make her mine."

Leave it to Zareb to voice every one of Assefa's unspoken fears. He didn't think he could handle anything Zareb said, although they all would happen, eventually, if Assefa continued on his path.

"She could die. I can't ignore that possibility."

"Then don't have kids. Not every couple does. There's also adoption. Between the Witch Council of Elders and your father's connections, I'm sure the two of you could find a little witch or were-cat who needs a good home and loving parents."

"I considered all of that. But mistakes happen. Birth control isn't one hundred percent. Despite our best efforts, Sanura could still become pregnant."

While Assefa had no doubt Sanura was as pro-choice as she was anti-war, he didn't think she would abort their child, even if it would save her life. She'd love and want to have their child.

He would too.

"I don't want to find myself in the horrible predicament where I'd have to choose between my unborn child and my mate. I'd always choose Sanura, but it would destroy a part of me if I had to make that decision knowing my fear ended my child's chance at life." Assefa stood. "I'd rather see Sanura with another man than put us through that possible future."

"Either way, she won't be able to have children. You're her biological mate. Even if she marries another guy, he won't be able to get her pregnant. You're the only one who can give her a child." Zareb also stood, his big hand going to Assefa's shoulder and pulling him in for a one-arm hug. "It's fucked up. I wish I had an easy answer to give you, my friend. But there's no easy answer. It's all a risk. But it's Sanura's gamble to take. Respect her enough to allow Sanura to make her own choice."

Zareb stepped away, and Assefa slumped onto the bed, the pillowtop mattress featherbed, down duvet and goose-down pillows not enough to turn his mood from stormy to placid.

"I'll call the chief and see what he wants us to do about Lake Michigan. You call High Priestess Anna Spencer. I'll meet you in the lobby in thirty?"

Assefa nodded then Zareb left. He was a good friend, always had been. Zareb was also one of the few people who wasn't afraid to tell Assefa the truth and to challenge his decisions and actions. Yet Zareb hadn't found his soulmate. The were-cat didn't know the overpowering need to protect the witch of his heart, even at the expense of his own. If he did, Zareb would understand Assefa's decision had nothing to do with a lack of respect for his witch but a profound love that left him breathless and weak.

Assefa called Anna, glad when she picked up, and he didn't have to leave a message and wait for her to return his call. Time was of at a premium, if the increase in rain around the world was a barometer of things to come.

"Hi, Assefa." The high priestess sounded surprised to hear from him, which made sense since he'd never called the woman at home before. She obviously had caller ID, which provided her a few seconds to wonder why the Council's Alpha would phone her at midnight. "Are you calling me about the rain?"

"No, but how long has it been raining there?"

"About three days. It starts and stops, but each time it resumes it lasts longer and rains harder. We've had to cancel all Sankofa's outside activities. Is this it? The beginning of the Day of Serpents?"

The fear in the older woman's voice was expected. She should be afraid. They should all be afraid.

"I believe so. That's why I've called. I'm hoping you can help me find the water witch of legend."

"If I knew that, the Sankofa fire witches would've already killed the woman. Probably not before the water witches took care of her. I have no idea who she may be. I don't even know where to begin to narrow the list of possible candidates."

Assefa had an idea where to begin, although it was still a longshot.

Earth births water. The sun births fire. But the moon, in its crescent state, brings forth the beast, giving away half of itself to make the beast whole to birth the man.

Assefa remembered the beginning of the children's story of the fire witch, water witch, and cat of legend. The water witch was born first, then the fire witch, and finally the Mngwa. Assefa had never interpreted it as a birth order. This past month, however, as he wracked his brain to craft a plan that could save his witch, Assefa recalled the children's tale. He'd also remembered everything Sanura told him about her father's sacrifice the day of her birth, seeing a possible link between the two.

Sam had not only asked Sàngó to bless his daughter but whether the cat of legend had been born.

It is not yet his time. But soon the Mngwa will come forth, completing the trinity.

The sentence hadn't resonated with Assefa until two days ago when he was in bed, unable to sleep because his mind was on Sanura. The children's story and the thunder god's answer were a perfect match.

Water witch. Fire Witch. Mngwa.

Sanura's birthday was in June. His in September. Which meant the water witch of legend's birthday had to be between January and May, maybe even June, but before Sanura's birthday. She would have turned twenty-nine this year, like Sanura and like Assefa in a couple of weeks.

It wasn't much. But it was a start. During another restless night, a second thought came to him, which was why he called Anna for help. From Assefa's experience, Mami Wata's strategies involved psychological attacks as much as they did physical ones by her water creatures. She seemed to enjoy bringing her enemies emotional pain before killing them. So why wouldn't her selection of a water witch be any different? He didn't think that it would.

"I need a list of all the water witches born the same year as Sanura but before her June birthday. Any water witch, in the last twenty-nine or so years, who've had any contact with your network or the Sankofa schools."

"You think the water witch of legend is one of us?"

He didn't know. At the Oshun ceremony, Assefa had met dozens of water witches, none of whom seemed a threat to Sanura. The Sankofa witches, regardless of their element, were sisters. They loved each other, and they seemed to care for their fire witch of legend. He hadn't met them all, though. If nothing else, Assefa needed to rule out the Sankofa witches.

He'd also placed a similar call to his sister and Wasola. Both women knew high priestesses they could tap for information. After what happened with Sanura, Najja would have no trouble getting the Sudanese water witches to cooperate. It was impossible to create an exhaustive list, but Assefa didn't think one would be required.

"Mami Wata is shrewd, and we can't be too cautious. Reach out to the other witch networks. Ask them for help. I'm sure they'll give it."

"They will. I just hate the idea that the water witch of legend could be so close. My mother tried to initiate a policy to deny admittance of new water witches into the Sankofa schools and our community after Sanura's birth. It was terrible racial profiling, but she did it anyway. I disagreed with her stance. It was cruel and unjust. Maybe she was also right. In her own way."

Perhaps the former high priestess had been.

"It'll take a few days, but I'll search Mom's old files to see if I can find the water witch applicants she was able to convince the Council to reject. The birthdays may not match, but I'll cross-reference everything based on your search criteria. There's probably a good deal more rejections than I know. Before her death, she became obsessed with weeding out Mami Wata sympathizers within our network. After she passed and before the Council named me as high priestess, I believe they went back and extended offers to those water witch families Mom rejected. I should ask Priestess Barbara. She was on the Council back then."

"Thank you. You have my email. Please send me the list once it's compiled."

"I will. Be safe, Assefa, and take care of our Sanura."

She hung up, and Assefa needed to change out of his suit. He and Zareb were going snake hunting in Lake Michigan.

CHAPTER TWENTY-SEVEN

Alexandria, Virginia

Swinging the doors to her closet open, Sanura pushed aside clothing. In the back of the closet was a pink footlocker Sanura's had since college. The trunk had served her well over the years. Since moving in with Assefa, she'd used it to store her casting materials, athames, candles, salts, pendants, grimoires, oils and other magical supplies.

Having gathered what she required, Sanura dropped the items on her bed before going to her drawer and pulling out a tank top and shorts. After dressing, Sanura used her ritual broom to clean her chosen area of the bedroom of negativity. She'd selected Assefa's side of the room for her magical working. If he had a problem with what she was about to do and where she was about to do it, then he could damn well be there to voice his objection.

Since he wasn't, Sanura had no problem unleashing her anger at her mate by wrecking his side of the room. Petty, but she couldn't give a damn.

Once clearing the energy field, Sanura did it again. She wanted nothing in the space onto which the soul could latch. Satisfied, Sanura walked in a counterclockwise direction as she poured the salt, creating a large ritual circle.

Retrieving her ritual knife from the bed, Sanura sliced the palm of her right hand. Beginning three feet from the circle of salt, Sanura walked around the outside of the circle, allowing her blood to drip down her palm and over her fingers. The blood formed a second circle of protection. Her hand stung where it bled, but she ignored the pain as she opened and closed her hand, forcing out more blood onto the bedroom floor.

After the second circle was set, she used her left hand to gather up and place four red candles in the space between the salt and blood circles. At each cardinal point, Sanura set a candle. Red, birth, and death but also protection and healing.

At the north quadrant, Sanura lit the candle. "I summon you, living earth, as I light this candle. I summon you, Isis. Bring power and strength to my spell." She moved to the east. "I summon you, breathing air, as I light this candle. I summon you, Isis. Bring power and strength to my spell."

Sanura recalled the last time she'd set this kind of magic circle. It had been the night of the handfasting ritual with Assefa. That night had been full of fear but also possibility. They'd come far since then, individually and as a couple. But they had further to go. She wouldn't give up on them, despite Assefa's temporary lapse in faith.

At the south quadrant, she lit the candle and incanted, "I summon you, warming fire, as I light this candle. I summon you, Isis. Bring power and strength to my spell." Finally, she walked to the west quadrant. "I summon you, chilling water, as I light this candle. I summon you, Isis. Bring power and strength to my spell."

She examined her work. Sanura had never done anything like this before, even though she'd memorized the summoning spell weeks ago. She'd hoped it wouldn't come to this but knew that it would.

A quick stop to the bathroom to cleanse and bandage her hand, Sanura was back in the bedroom, standing several feet away from the magical circle. This was it then, time to face her nightmare.

She knelt and recited the summoning spell.

"Born into fire yet cast into darkness, I call to thee. Born into fire yet cast into war, I plead to thee. Born into fire yet cast into sorrow, I summon thee."

Standing, Sanura repeated the chant forty-two times. At the end of each recitation, she ended the chant with one of Ma'at's divine principles.

"...I have not worked evil."

"... I have not placed myself on a pedestal."

"... I have not polluted the water."

"Born into fire yet cast into violence, I call to thee. I summon thee. Come, sister." Sanura formed a fireball in the palm of her hand, blew on it and then whispered, "Come fire witch of legend. I demand your presence."

Using wind magic, Sanura shoved the fireball into the center of the salt circle.

Wind merged with fire and exploded. Howling flames and furious shrieks followed. In the center of the roaring storm of chaos was a fully formed and contained fire witch of legend.

Green eyes bled to scarlet when she saw Sanura. Enraged, she dove for her, only to slam into the protective barrier of Sanura's salt and blood circles.

She tried over and again, hurling her body against the invisible field, her anger growing with each failed attempt.

Salt crackled and blood sizzled, keeping the soul of the fire witch of legend within the containment field.

Still, the wild woman fought, cursing in a language Sanura didn't know, her brown, lithe form naked and red-gold hair in a plume of billowing smoke.

Exhausted from watching her predecessor wage a pointless battle, Sanura sat on the floor in front of the circle and waited.

"Release me, you pathetic layer of volcanic ash," she screamed.

Sanura ignored her as if she'd gone through all the trouble of summoning and capturing the fire witch just to turn around and let her go because she asked. Not even nicely, which was what Sanura had come to expect of the dead witch. She was a nasty piece of work, but Sanura didn't think the woman had started off that way.

She practiced patience. It was Saturday, Assefa was off doing whatever bullheaded were-cats did, and Mr. Siddig and Manute knew not to come knocking when they heard strange noises coming from her bedchamber.

Sanura must've fallen asleep because the next thing she heard was the witch yell, "Wake up, you despicable child. How dare you summon and cage me then have the temerity to fall asleep while I'm in the middle of cursing you and your unborn children."

Sleeping on the floor didn't feel good without her Mngwa to serve as a big, fluffy pillow. Sanura rolled from where she'd been sleeping on her side and to a cross-legged position.

"It's your fault that I'm so tired." As if to prove her point, Sanura yawned. "I haven't slept well in weeks, not since you began invading my dreams. Which, by the way, I don't appreciate."

The fire witch slumped to the floor, mirroring Sanura's cross-legged position. Considering she wore nothing below the waist, Sanura made sure to keep her eyes north of the border.

"What do you want from me, child?"

"To know why you've decided to haunt my dreams."

"Because I can. Because I'm evil and that's what evil creatures do. Because you're my only connection to a life I loved and lost. Because I hate you for your youth and innocence and utter ignorance. Because your mate still lives while mine is long since dead."

Okay, that was a hell of a lot of reasons, most of which Sanura had no interest in exploring.

"Tell me about your mate."

"My what?"

The question had taken the fire witch of legend by surprise. Good.

"Your mate, the man you loved and lost. Tell me about him. What was his name? In fact, what's your name?"

She blinked at Sanura. "You summoned me here to kill me."

"I never said that."

"B-but, you have me in this cage of salt and blood. Why else if not to kill me for terrorizing your sleeping mind?"

"I have no desire to kill you, but I do have a vested interest in you not murdering me."

"Perhaps not so ignorant after all. Well, you still are. You're just not a fool, for I would slay you, now that I'm corporeal and you're so very close."

"Good to know. So, tell me your name, and the name of your mate."

Sanura crawled to the bed, making sure to not break the circle. After grabbing a pillow, she made her way to the wall closest to the fire witch, propped the pillow against it and then leaned her back into the pillow. This felt better, but Sanura still wasn't comfortable. Perhaps she should've gotten two pillows, one for her back and the other for her to sit on.

"Done, child? First, you fall asleep, now you squirm and frown as if you have crickets in your pants."

"You sound like my mother. And I only need one of those. By the way, before you start judging, you may want to first close your legs."

The fire witch of legend glanced down at herself, then shrugged. "There's no shame in the nude form. I suppose times have changed, but I see no point for me to do so. I am, after all, quite dead."

Technically, the witch was undead, which explained how she could both travel into Sanura's dream and be summoned and contained in a magic circle, body as solid as Sanura's.

"You aren't nearly as entertaining awake as you are asleep. As such, I will humor you and answer your odd questions. My name is Shanumi and my mate's name was Abubaker."

Sanura's head clunked against the wall. The same initials as Sanura and Assefa. That was taking the prophecy and fire witch and cat of legend too damn far. It bordered on weird and was creepy as hell.

"Tell me about him. How did you meet? When did you know you first loved Abubaker?"

After another hesitation and grumbled curses about "intrusive and impertinent children," Shanumi began to speak. Sanura closed her eyes and listened to her love story. Like most true stories, it was full of tears and smiles, laughter and anger, joy and heartbreak. In other words,

Shanumi and Abubaker were quite human, she shy and awkward, and he proud and overprotective.

"He had the most glorious smile, brighter and more beautiful than my fire. But it's his laughter I most miss, even more than the feel of his hands on my skin." Shanumi ran a single finger from her throat, between her breasts, and over a thigh. Not sensually, probably not even consciously, but with sad remembrance.

Once she began speaking of her mate, Sanura didn't have to ask any other leading questions. As she'd done countless times in her therapy sessions, Sanura's opening questions were unthreatening and intended to give her patients an opportunity to share whatever they felt comfortable divulging.

Slow at first, for some. While others relished the opportunity to have someone to listen for understanding and assume good intentions. Once the proverbial dam broke, Shanumi volunteered information freely, sharing details of her childhood, her rapid magic growth and fear of possessing too much power.

"It's unnatural to grant a witch godlike powers. It does things to the mind and to the spirit. Such powers make one think themselves invincible, capable of defeating any foe. That level of power also causes one to forget what they most value and why they breathe. Not for war and certainly not for vengeance."

"Then what?" Sanura scooted closer, curious as to Shanumi's answer.

"For peace and justice, child. Those are the only reasons witches like us should ever cast a single spell. But I forgot, young fire witch. I forgot, and my Abubaker paid for my trespass against the gods. You saw. I made sure you saw."

The first night in the House of Berber, she'd dreamed and Shanumi was there. But not as she'd been in her previous dreams, mocking, murderous and mean. That night, she'd shared the worst day of her life.

The vivid images of fire, water, and death had Sanura collapsing to her knees along with Shanumi when her Mngwa fell in battle. So quick had Mami Wata's magic been the were-cat had no chance of dodging her attack, his death instantaneous.

The depth of Shanumi's grief had produced a visceral reaction in Sanura. Tears had fallen and chest had ached for the woman's loss.

"He shouldn't have been there, even though he was born for that purpose. Abubaker was always willing to protect me, even when it put him in danger. I should've gone into battle without him, left Abubaker home with our daughter. But he'd insisted and I relented."

"What about the water witch of legend's mate? I didn't see him in any of the final battle scenes you showed me."

"That were-cat elevated the power of my enemy, although he was no Mngwa. Yet his cat strength made the water witch more powerful and dangerous. Understand this, young fire witch, the battle you'll wage is not about the water witch. That was my mistake. I was once as ignorant and naïve as you. Since my physical death, I've had nothing but time to think."

Sanura stood when Shanumi did. Sanura moved as close as she dared to the barrier. Shanumi had been Sanura's age when she died. They were of the same height, build, and coloring. Their eyes gleamed the same shade of green and their hair the same red-gold.

Yet the centuries were etched across Shanumi's soul, although not on her beautiful and youthful face. Like Ulan and Jahi, they could've been fraternal twins.

"The gods lie. They deceive and we fight. After so long, I still don't know the full truth. But I do know the purpose of the Mngwa."

After listening to the story of Shanumi and Abubaker and seeing all the ways their emotional relationship mirrored Sanura and Assefa's, she thought she knew the purpose of the Mngwa as well.

"The Mngwa is the fire witch of legend's fail-safe. We're passionate and destructive to the point of blinding violence. We're the only earth witches who can create our element from nothing but will, skill, and magic. When enraged, no other element can stop us, not even our elemental opposite, water."

Shanumi took another step toward the salt circle. At this distance, she had to feel the sizzle of the protective spell, warning her to proceed at her peril.

"The Mngwa can cool our fiery heart and tempestuous fire spirit. He maintains his reason when all we feel is heat. His patience and strength grounds us. And his love reminds us of our humanity. Without him, we are primal power whose heart bleeds crude fire." Shanumi pressed her palm to the invisible barrier and power crackled. "Without us, he is bitter ice, his soul emotionless."

Sanura raised her hand and laid it against the invisible dome of the barrier, right where Shanumi's hand rested. Through centuries and fire magic, they touched.

The circle of protective magic dissolved, leaving two fire witches of legend staring at each other.

"You're proof that my and Abubaker's daughter lived, that I didn't lose everything on that wretched day of snakes, fire, and water. Tell me, Sanura, why did you summon me?"

Their fingers laced, and Sanura had never felt so close to anyone. Not Sam. Not Makena. Not even Assefa.

They weren't the same women. Yet, the kinship was there, the symmetry that coursed through Sanura when they touched.

"I want to set your soul free."

"Because two fire witches of legend shouldn't exist at the same time?"

"No, sister, because you've suffered enough. It's time you go to ash, to be reborn and start life anew."

"You offer me salvation?" Heat began to pulse where their hands were locked together. "You offer me an honorable death despite my sins?"

"I offer you freedom because of the sins committed against you and your mate. Only you can grant yourself forgiveness. That isn't for me to give. But if you want it, if it matters, then I forgive you. Peace and justice, Shanumi, like you said. I offer you peace and justice. Will you accept?"

Before Sanura could blink, a naked fire witch held her in her arms, sobs wracking her body.

Sanura returned the unexpected embrace, her eyes filling with tears.

When she'd cast the spell, Sanura gave herself a twenty percent chance of success. The witch who cried in her arms was not the same woman who'd haunted her dreams and tried to kill her when summoned. Yet she was the same emotionally-crippled and guilt-ridden witch.

"Will it hurt?"

"No, sister. You've suffered enough."

Shanumi stepped away from Sanura and back into the salt circle. Going to her knees, green, watery eyes stared up at Sanura.

"Find your Mngwa."

"I will."

"Protect him."

"Of course."

"And let him protect you."

"Yes. Now close your eyes, Shanumi, and allow me to set you free."

The fire witch did as she was asked but not before casting a spell of her own. "I bless you, Sanura Wasola Williams. I bless you with my fire spirit. When you need her, she will be there. When you need her, she will break the primordial silence to reach you. Be safe. Be truthful. But most of all, be in harmony. These things I wish for thee. This blessing I bestow on thee. Never forget, what you possess makes you more powerful than the gods."

Tears flowed and Sanura let them. This could be her. At the end of the Day of Serpents, if it ended badly, Sanura could very well turn into the most awful version of Shanumi. She'd rather die first. But death, as she now knew, didn't free one from centuries of regret.

"You were born from flames of peace but died in chaos." Sanura created a fireball the size of the magic circle several feet above

Shanumi. "From fire, you will go. Into your final death, it will take you." The fireball dropped, igniting Shanumi in the scorching heat of a resurrected sun. "I unbind you from eternal restlessness. Be free and find your mate in the Field of Reeds."

The fire witch of legend burned. With a smile on her face, the emancipated soul turned to ash.

CHAPTER TWENTY-EIGHT

Baltimore, Maryland
Sankofa Preparatory School

"You burned a person to death? That's hardcore."

Sanura shoved Rachel, and the earth witch stumbled backward with all the drama of a stunt double, laughing.

"I mean, who does that other than sociopaths?"

"Shut up, Rach, before I release the rain over you and let it ruin those cute shoes of yours."

Rachel craned her head to observe Cynthia's magical handiwork.

They were in the quad of Sankofa Preparatory School in front of the Tree of Ma'at. All around them rain poured, but above the three friends was a protective arc of water witch power. Better than an umbrella, Cynthia used her magic to disperse the water to other areas while keeping them dry so Sanura could perform the funeral rites.

"That's freaky, by the way. I didn't want to say anything earlier, Cyn, because, yeah, I like my new shoes dry instead of waterlogged. Same cranky dog but new water tricks. What else do you have in your magician's hat?"

"Remind me again why you asked Rachel to join us."

Sanura yanked Rachel from the earth path, one of four element paths that led to the Tree of Ma'at, and beside her when it looked as if Cynthia would make good on her threat. Cynthia, as usual, had less tolerance for Rachel's sarcasm than Sanura. The last thing she needed was a wet and irritated Rachel Foster.

One ill-tempered friend was enough.

"Because we're friends and I need Rachel's help. What's wrong, Cyn? You seem a little tired, agitated."

"I am. Everyone is tense, students and parents, even the faculty." She pointed to the gray sky and endless rain. "They think this is a prelude to the Day of Serpents. A dozen or more of the residential students have gone home with their parents. And they only just arrived for the new school year three weeks ago. But their parents are frightened and don't want them away from home if the worst happens."

The worst would likely happen, though there or somewhere else, Sanura didn't know.

"I understand the angst and uncertainty. The students are scared and the faculty want to know what they can do. They've all but created a hunting party for the water witch of legend."

"What does that mean?"

"It means every time I walk into the teacher's lounge, all talking stops. I think they're trying to give me plausible deniability in the event they do something illegal and get themselves arrested."

"Killing a person is against the law," Rachel needlessly reminded them. "Unless you're the fire witch of legend. In that case, you can burn an undead witch to a crisp and then sweep up her remains and store them in a plastic baggie. How much are you planning on selling that fire witch of legend cannabis for? Or are you going to roll and smoke it yourself? Like a game power-up for when you face the water witch of legend." Rachel laughed as Sanura and Cynthia stared. "Oh wait, it could be like medicinal marijuana. That way, if you're caught in possession of it, you won't go to jail."

Instead of getting angry, Sanura grabbed Rachel into a tight hug and draped her tall frame over the much shorter woman. Sanura's right hand held an urn with Shanumi's remains, not a plastic baggie as Rachel had so ridiculously stated.

"You weigh a ton. Get your Amazon butt off me."

"I love you and your smart mouth." She kissed Rachel's cheek, knowing how much her friend despised this level of open, physical affection. "You and Cyn are my best friends, sisters I never want to do without."

Rachel wedged her hands between them and shoved against Sanura's stomach. "Gods, you're like a boa constrictor. Get off, so we can bury the evidence of your crime. I can't do my thing with your big behind all over me."

Sanura kissed her cheek again before releasing her, not offended when Rachel made a show of laying down wrinkles from her dress shirt and wiping Sanura's lipstick from her cheek.

She cut her eye at Cynthia. "Don't you even think about doing the same."

"I neither love you nor have any interest in kissing a tree whisperer. Now stop acting like a jerk and ask the damn question of the tree. We don't have all day, and I can't hold back the rain forever."

Rachel turned away from a grumpy Cynthia and to the soaring Tree of Ma'at. The tree was planted by members of the first Witch Council of Elders as a reminder of the importance of harmony and truth within oneself and in one's community and family. At Sankofa Preparatory School, witches diverged when their courses became element-specific in the ninth grade. Yet, by the time they finished twelfth grade, the witches met at the Tree of Ma'at—unified and balanced.

The four-element paths were both real and symbolic.

South, fire witches.

North, wind witches.

West, earth witches

East, water witches.

Between the pounding rain and Rachel's low voice, Sanura couldn't hear anything the earth witch said to the tree. But she did hear Rachel when she said, "That urn better be biodegradable."

"I know the rules of the earth witches. Ask the tree about engraving Shanumi's name in its bark."

"You want to use fire on the tree?"

"You must think I'm an idiot. No, I want you to do it with your magic."

Rachel turned back to the tree, whispering something. This time, the odd conversation lasted two minutes.

"Why both?"

Sanura knew what Rachel was asking her. And while she had no idea if any of this would help Shanumi find peace, Sanura wanted to at least give the woman a proper burial.

"For Shanumi's soul to move on and travel to the Field of Reeds, her body needs to be buried and her name must be written down some-where." Sanura patted the trunk of the tree. "I couldn't think of a better place to lay to rest the fire witch of legend than here. It seemed fitting."

"Go ahead then, Sanura. Place the urn in the hole."

"What hol—"

The ground shifted and a hole appeared at the base of the tree and in front of Sanura. Kneeling, Sanura placed the sand-crafted urn inside the hole. It was a perfect fit.

With Rachel's hand on the tree, the hole closed, enveloping the ashes of Shanumi. A second later, her name appeared on the spot where Rachel's hand had been. Sanura didn't know what she expected, maybe one of those tree carvings that some people did with a pocketknife, something like Shanumi heart Abubaker. But it wasn't that at all. Shan-umi's name had become such a part of the tree that it would go unnoticed by the casual observer. It was, quite literally, in the bark of the tree. The vines had formed letters to spell out the dead woman's name.

"Thank you, Rach, that's lovely."

The level one earth witch possessed an understated power of magic. It was beautiful in its unpretentious execution.

"Yeah, nice work. It's about time you put that big mouth to good use. Speaking of putting your mouth to good use, how was your date with Manute?"

Rachel glowered.

Cynthia laughed.

And Sanura hugged them both. She couldn't wait to introduce her friends to Najja. They needed a wind witch to balance them out. Najja and Rachel would either be like oil and water or two insufferable pains in the ass.

"Will you recite a prayer for Shanumi?" Sanura pulled back from her friends, her question directed at Cynthia.

"Why me?"

"Because you're a water witch, and she was the fire witch of legend."

"According to you, Shanumi killed the last water witch she saw."

"True, but that was then and this is now. I think it'll help if a water witch prays over her remains and blesses her departed spirit. Will you help me lay my ancestor to rest, Cyn?" Sanura held out her hand to her friend.

Sanura had a prayer prepared if Cynthia refused, although she hoped she wouldn't. For once, Rachel remained silent, not interjecting an inappropriate joke into a serious moment. This mattered to Sanura. Fire and water witches weren't meant to be enemies, in life or in death.

Yes, Shanumi, in her grief and fury, had killed the water witch of legend. But the water witch, from what Sanura had witnessed, tried to do the same to Shanumi. Neither were without sin. But Shanumi had known regret and, in the end, sought repentance. Who better than to pray over her lost and found soul than a water witch whose best friend was a fire witch?

"You can't solve everyone's problem, Sanura. When will you get that through your stubborn head?"

"Never." Her hand remained steady, Sanura undeterred by Cynthia's soft words of challenge.

Cynthia stared down at the hand between them and then closed her own around it. She linked her other hand with Rachel's before beginning a prayer for the deceased.

It was one Sanura didn't know. Cynthia spoke with sincerity and without awkwardness, despite her initial hesitation. Yet it wasn't until tears fell from the water witch that Sanura realized she had heard this prayer before. It was the same one she'd written for her mother's funeral, but her teenage grief had been too much for her to recite her parting words to her mother. Makena had joined Cynthia at the altar, held one of her trembling hands, and read the prayer of mourning to those gathered.

This time, it wasn't Sanura who hugged her friend but Rachel, who'd also been at the funeral.

"She heard you, Cyn." Rachel, not one to normally cry, teared up. "She heard you. She knows the truth of your heart. Mothers always do."

Sanura couldn't have asked for a better prayer for Shanumi, Cynthia voicing a prayer that the fire witch's own daughter might have given if she'd been old enough to wish her mother eternal rest.

Without them realizing, the rain had stopped and the sun peeked out from behind the clouds.

Chicago, Illinois
O'Hare International Airport

This was it then? The Day of Serpents? Shit, Zareb had grown up hearing the children's story of the Mngwa of myth and his powerful mate of a fire witch. Assefa and Sanura were much more than what any fable had depicted them as being. They were real people with hearts and minds and feelings.

Zareb said nothing when Assefa pulled out his cell phone, eyes glued to the little screen. He knew what the man was doing, scrolling through pictures he had of Sanura in his Gallery. It was an awful form of torture as much as it was a testament to how much Assefa loved, missed and needed his fire witch.

Assefa spent the last two weeks following weather patterns and international news reports. There was a disturbing link between sightings of strange water creatures and hammering rain over the nearest land-mass. He'd compiled a report of his findings and submitted them to his uncle. After a lengthy phone conference with the chief, Assefa and Za-reb were to join three other agents from the division, two shifters, and one witch. Their first stop was the Congolese province of Tanganyika where villagers reported to have seen a Ninki Nanka, a large reptilian creature of West African legend.

Zareb and Assefa sat at gate twelve of Terminal 5, waiting for their plane to arrive. Flags of countries of the world hung above them, a vis-ual clue that this terminal was for international flights only.

"Call her."

Without looking up from his cell phone, Assefa said one word. "No."

"You know our team won't be able to defeat Mami Wata's creatures without the combined might of the cat and fire witch of legend. You can't protect Sanura from this." Zareb moved to the seat next to Assefa, then risked covering the screen of his phone with his big hand. "This is why she was born, what Sanura was made to do."

"I know, now move your hand or lose five fingers."

Zareb withdrew his hand but not his point. "We need Sanura's help, her magic, and her strength. She wouldn't want you facing the water beasts without her. I'm your shield, so I go where you go. But even I know this is madness. Our division is spread thin, agents deployed all over. But it's not enough. Reports keep coming in from the smallest village to the largest metropolis. Snakes are everywhere, and people are scared."

"Don't you think I know? I feel the weight of the prophecy with each raindrop and unexplained sighting and death. But I also know Sanura and I are in no position to make a collective difference. Our bond isn't what it was, thanks to me. And do you really think Sanura will do noth-ing because I'm not with her? She'll fight, and I'll fight. We just won't do it as a mated pair."

"That's the whole damn point of the cat and fire witch of legend. You know, two good guys are better than one psychotic bitch of a goddess."

Zareb tried to keep his voice down but all he wanted to do was yell. This was bullshit. Of all the times for Assefa to think with his heart instead of his overly logical brain. He would punch him if Zareb thought starting a fight would bring the were-cat to his senses.

"You could fix this with one phone call and a bit of groveling and ass-kissing. Sanura loves you, she won't make you work too hard. Besides, I'm pretty sure you're not officially broken up. Although you did return her father's wedding ring, which was a stupid move and one you'll pay for." Zareb lowered his voice and leaned closer to Assefa. "I can tell you, from personal experience, make up sex is phenomenal. So, you know, after Sanura kicks your ass for leaving her, she'll kiss it all better and punish you in a totally different way."

Assefa stood, his face stony. "No more talk of Sanura. I've heard enough from you, Dahad and Manute. I'm serious, Zareb. Don't mention her name to me again. The plane is boarding, let's go."

Yeah, he'd heard the announcement as well as Assefa's order. He hadn't been himself since his father's big reveal. What a shortsighted asshole. The general supreme should've had the good sense to wait until all this prophecy and Day of Serpents business was over before dropping his secret on Assefa. How in the hell did he think the were-cat would react? Assefa hadn't needed this extra shit to deal with so close to the biggest battle of his life.

"Bathroom. I'll catch up." Zareb jogged away.

Assefa's attention had shifted to his cell phone, long legs already on the move toward the line of boarders.

He hoped Assefa was only pulling up his eBoarding Pass and not another pic of Sanura. If this was what love did to a were-cat then Zareb would pass.

Once Zareb was out of sight and hearing range, he yanked out his cell phone and made a single call.

Alexandria, Virginia

"What are you doing here, Mike?"

Sanura's gaze roamed the faces of the men standing before her. She stood at the bottom of the steps, her rolling suitcase beside her. Her godfather, Mr. Siddig, and Manute were in the foyer and blocking her exit.

Her eyes settled on a green duffle bag by the front door. "Mom or Mr. Siddig, which one called you?"

Mike's bushy unibrow rose. "Both."

"Are you here to loan me your old army bag? I think I got it covered in the suitcase department, so you can go home."

"Oh, for the love of Betty Friedan, now is not the time for your feminist crap. Since you won't accept the were-cats help, Dahad will drive us to the airport, and then he and Manute will move into Sankofa until whatever in the hell is going on is over."

That had been Sanura's directive to the two men. After speaking with Zareb, she'd called her department chair to let her know she'd be taking family sick leave. The call proved pointless since most Maryland schools were under a Code Red, which meant they were closed except for emergency personnel.

She didn't give a damn what was going on between her and Assefa. He couldn't defeat the goddess's water beasts without his witch no more than she could beat Mami Wata without her cat.

"Are you sure, Sanura?" Manute, beard full and hair as wild as ever, moved to take her suitcase. "I know you said you want us to put the safety of the students of Sankofa before you, but if you and Assefa fall we all die."

Manute was right. But they would be more helpful there than where she was going.

"The Council needs all available witches and were-cats. Since Assefa is also the Council's Alpha, that means you, Mr. Siddig and Rashad, whenever he gets here."

"You really think Mami Wata will target the school?" Dahad asked, probably thinking about the way the water goddess had targeted his chosen mate, Joanna Blackwell, to hurt Assefa by causing his friends' pain.

"I can't be certain, but I think she will. So does the Council and the were-cat alphas. It's all arranged, Sankofa will not be a casualty in this war."

Manute and Mr. Siddig seemed convinced, though not happy at leaving their alpha's mate in the hands of a single dwarf.

They hugged and kissed Sanura before leaving the house, Manute carrying her suitcase and Mr. Siddig hitting the key fob to the black limo parked in front of the house.

Mike snatched up his faded duffel bag. "Come on, Sanura, Assefa and his team have a thirty-six-hour head start. In this rain, Dahad can't drive but so fast. The last thing I want is to help another Williams woman bury her mate."

That wouldn't happen. She'd accept Assefa's stubborn desire to break-up with her, but she'd be damned if she accepted his death.

Sanura pulled her godfather into a grateful embrace. "Thank you, Mike. I love you very much."

"Don't get all mushy on me. Save that for Assefa. Get your purse, and let's get our asses on the road."

CHAPTER TWENTY-NINE

Democratic Republic of the Congo

The ancient giant trees of the Congolese rainforest towered two hundred feet above the team, darkening the forest floor with their shadows. Sporadic streams of light fought through the emergent layer of the forest giving life to the reptiles and insects living in the canopy below. Exotic fruits and flowers indigenous to the region emphasized the beauty and complexity of the area.

The forest floor, where Assefa's team hiked, was like a curtain drawn room in the middle of the day. If the curtain was pulled back, the bright light of the high sun would kiss them with its reassuring rays. But the curtain of the canopy of trees couldn't be pushed aside to reveal the midday sun to the heat exhausted agents.

Assefa's uncle had put together a decent mix of land shifters and water shifters. While the special agent hoped he could keep the fight on land, the probability the mythical alligator would retreat to the safety of the river was uncomfortably high.

"How much farther before we reach the Congo River?"

At least Zareb had asked him something other than why they couldn't track the Ninki Nanka in cat form. It would make moving through the thick brush easier, but it would also mean leaving behind too much of their gear they wouldn't be able to carry while in cat form. He and Zareb were also the only two whose beast was big enough to carry the sole witch on the team. Special Agent Janet Bell had made it clear she wouldn't ride on either of their backs, which left hiking in human form.

Assefa bent and posed Zareb's question, in Lingala, to the agogue guide. The four-foot human-like biped lived in one of the villages on the outskirts of the Congo River Basin, renting out his services to pre-ternaturals who sought escape from full-human society.

The agogue pushed his long, woolly hair out of his face, looked up at Assefa with his small canines and rounded forehead and mumbled an answer. Assefa turned to the group. "It'll be another hour before we reach the river. Let's take a ten-minute break."

The team made the most of the short respite, drinking water and fi-nalizing plans. After the team had landed in the country, Assefa received a call from Ulan. The Ninki Nanka was on the move. Last re-ports had it traveling from Lake Tanganyika toward the Congo River, bringing with it heavy precipitation and thunderclouds. The special agents no longer had to charter a second plane to travel to the eastern region of the Congo once they reached Kinshasa for the large alligator was on its way to the country's urban capital. Assefa intended to halt its progress, the lives of over ten million people at stake if his team failed.

An hour and a half later, the group reached the clearing of the rain-forest and before them was the largest river in Western Central Africa, over twenty-nine hundred miles long, seven hundred fifty feet deep. From where Assefa stood on the bank, he could see Livingston Falls and its rapid movement of water over the horizon.

The trail they'd been following ended at the water's edge. No sign of the Ninki Nanka.

With a nod of his head and a wave of his hand, the agogue scurried away. The guide's service would no longer be needed. Assefa had al-ready paid the man, and he'd delivered them where they needed to be. The agogue was smart to flee to whatever secure place he could find.

"This was a waste of time." Agent Yutimo Sataa, an Alaskan native and Yupik, the largest of the Native groups in Alaska, squinted out at the river before turning his brown eyes and wet face to Assefa. "We walked miles through that damn forest tracking that thing for nothing. For all the good it did us, we could've chartered a plane if we were going to end up here with our dicks in our hands."

As an afterthought, Special Agent Sataa seemed to remember the water witch, who said nothing but appeared no less annoyed than Sataa by the absence of the Ninki Nanka they were tasked with finding and killing.

"True," Special Agent Demetrio de Gama said, "but then we wouldn't know whether it was hiding in the thicket. At least now we know it's most likely in front of us instead of behind. I prefer to have it that way instead of the other way around."

"But—"

"Be quiet, Sataa." A hushed order. Slowly, Assefa began to back away from the river's edge, gesturing for the others to do the same. "It's here," he whispered.

The team retreated, all eyes on the dark river. Even with Assefa's enhanced sight, between the storm-darkened sky and driving rain, his vision wasn't as keen as normal.

Like Special Agent Sataa, he saw nothing, but Assefa was positive he'd heard movement in the river. Something big.

He and Zareb wasted no time stripping off soaked clothes and shifting.

Five Hundred Miles Away

Sanura and Mike made their way through the N'Djili International Airport in Kinshasa. "Zareb's text said they had a last-minute change of plans and were rerouting to the Congo River Basin."

Pushing her way through the crowd, Sanura managed to locate her suitcase and haul it off the conveyer belt. A few minutes later, Mike had his duffle bag, and they were on the move through the packed airport. She wondered if the mass of people leaving were trying to flee what they couldn't understand with their eyes or mind but felt with their heart.

Disorder.

Danger.

Death.

"That's a hell of a lot of area to cover, Sanura. We'll need to charter a plane if we hope to catch up with them." Mike used his duffle bag to shove people out of his way.

Sanura stopped when a familiar flutter of magic went through her, a sharp pulse she hadn't felt in six weeks. Her mate bond. Not as strong as it should be. The jolt had awakened her fire spirit, whose wings began to flap against the cage Sanura kept her locked in.

That would soon have to change. Sanura and her Fire Phoenix could no longer go on like this. She needed to fix their broken relationship. But first, she needed to get to her mate.

Catching Mike's arm and pulling him with her, so they wouldn't get separated, Sanura found the nearest wall and leaned against it. Closing her eyes, she took three fortifying breaths.

"What's wrong? I hope you aren't planning on fainting on me. I thought you were made of sterner stuff than that."

"It's Assefa. He's changed into his Mngwa."

"You can feel that? Never mind. What does it mean?"

Sanura opened her eyes. "It means the battle has already begun. We won't make it in time."

"Can you locate him?" Making sure she had her suitcase, Mike took hold of Sanura's wrist and pulled her behind him as he got them moving again, cursing for people to, "Get the hell out of our way."

"I can track his aura signature."

"Good. I'll get us a ride and you'll be our GPS."

The rain fell from the sky in heavy, thick globules, pooling at their feet. Mud slicked tracks led from the river to the shore like a beacon to a horrible crime scene. Special Agent Janet Bell's bloody, crushed body laid half in and half out of the giant alligator's mouth. Her eyes were open, aware, mouth twisted in a scream compressed in her midsection by the jaws of the beast.

The Mngwa and Bengal tiger tore into the twenty-foot, eleven-hundred-pound monster of scales and teeth. Each took a forefoot in their jaws, pulling, biting, and scratching at the creature. Nothing. Special Agent Sataa, in wolf form, joined them, grabbing the long, rigid tail and trying to break through the armor-plated spiked skin.

But nothing they did stopped or damaged the Ninki Nanka enough to incapacitate the animal.

Or to save Bell.

Her scream finally penetrated her throat, raspy and garbled with blood. Her distorted retching cry of agony and impending death saturated the sweltering September air. The monster tossed the upper torso of her body into the brush, then swallowed what was left of the special agent.

The water witch hadn't stood a chance against the Ninki Nanka, the alligator's thick hide enough to withstand every one of her water attacks. The gator was swift, and morbid fear had made Bell's spellcasting slow. Too slow to prevent the creature's jaws from seizing her in a move so fast no one could prevent the attack.

Agent de Gama jumped on the back of the alligator, shooting it with his handgun. The bullets pierced the armor but didn't slow the beast down. It reared up, throwing the agent into the river and shaking itself free from the grasp of the Mngwa, tiger, and wolf.

The Mngwa's saber teeth had damaged the left foot of the beast, but that only served to anger it even more. It charged the Mngwa, but the cat of legend wasn't easy prey.

It missed him.

Alligators were fast land animals, running upward of 11mph, quite capable of overtaking a full-human but far too slow to catch the swifter and more agile Mngwa.

The three shifters circled the Ninki Nanka, waiting for the right opening to strike. The giant gator snapped at the trio, claiming the shore as his. It rushed the smallest of the hunters, the gray wolf, chasing Sataa to the river's edge. As the wolf backed up, cautious and with reticence, the body of the nearly pure white wolf began to disappear, his waist covered in fresh river water.

The alligator went in for the kill but the Mngwa attacked first, unwilling to lose another agent to this monster.

The Mngwa pounced on the Ninki Nanka's neck, gouging the two layers of eyelids to reach the delicate orbs while the Bengal tiger clamped his sharp teeth around the gator's tail and pulled with considerable strength.

The Mngwa tried to keep track of the wolf as he fought Mami Wata's deadly creature. But the canine disappeared into the murky water where de Gama had yet to reappear.

And still, it rained. The muddy and wet terrain perfect for the gator but not for the were-cats.

But they didn't stop fighting, no matter how hard the rain beat against their bodies or how strong the gator defended itself.

One hundred fifty miles away, a rented seaplane sped through the late day sky, pummeled by rain and guided by Sanura's fire spirit and her mate bond to Assefa's Mngwa.

"He's struggling, Mike. We need to move faster."

"We're moving as fast as we can, considering this tidal wave of rain. Why don't you just pump him with some of that witch magic of yours and help a cat out."

"I've tried, but he's blocking me."

"Try again. I'm sure Assefa wouldn't block you on purpose." He leaned over Sanura, who sat next to the window, to glare at the rising river below.

"I've tried. Many times." She was worried and angry.

"Talk to me. Tell me what's going on." Mike had to yell over the raging rain to be heard, even though he sat right next to her.

"We're out of balance." Sanura hadn't realized how much until she'd reached for her mate bond and found an emotional wall instead of Assefa's warm, loving magic. "Our bond is fractured, and until it's repaired our connection is limited."

"Fuck, Sanura, how limited?"

Very limited, but it didn't matter. This plane had to move faster.

She stood.

"What are you doing? Sit down before you fall and break your fool neck."

The plane tumbled through the rough sky, but the pilot, some native guy Mike either bribed or threatened to fly in weather conditions only the two of them would be caught in a plane in, was one hell of a pilot.

But the plane, on its own, could only go so fast. She'd been using her wind magic to help it along, increasing the knots, so she'd reach Assefa and Zareb as quickly as possible.

Yet she'd held back, afraid to push the seaplane too much.

Holding onto the back of the chair in front of her, Sanura focused on the howling wind outside and the air touching the plane as it flew through the roaring rain.

Sanura knew little about wind magic. She'd never been one to wing her spells, knowing how dangerous it was to cast without full knowledge and proper preparation. Yet every wind spell she'd cast, to date, had started off as a fire spell. Where she'd normally see fire in her mind and feel the reassuring warmth of it on her skin, she thought of the gaseous mixture in the atmosphere, oxygen and carbon dioxide, among other gases that made up the air and then the horizontal motion of the air that created winds.

The perceptible movement of the air, wind, ran up and down her spine as she held onto the chair and began to cast. This time, Sanura held nothing back. Her nails dug into the cotton material; her wind magic stronger than it had ever been.

Lightning crackled, illuminating the path for the pilot, who at this point only steered the plane, Sanura's winds doing more than the engine alone ever could.

The Mngwa would see this beast dead. He'd done all he could to blind it, was sure the Ninki Nanka could see nothing out of its right eye.

Good.

The monster opened its mouth, trying to get the Mngwa away from its remaining good eye. The Mngwa continued his attack, so did the Bengal tiger, even when the Ninki Nanka ran into the river taking the shifters with it.

They should've stopped, should've let the prey retreat to the river without them. That wouldn't have been a good option, though. The Ninki Nanka could've decided to lick its wounds and retreat, only to reappear later to wreak havoc somewhere else.

No one wanted that, least of all the Mngwa. But this, by the gods, this had been Assefa's worst case scenario. In the water, the cats were as defenseless as a couple of baby deer. They thrashed about, weighed down by their heavy fur while the beast glided effortlessly through the water, circling them. They used the time to change back into their human forms, which did wonders for their maneuverability but nothing for their defense.

In fact, the alligator seemed even more interested in the new prey. It set a course straight for them. They swam against the roiling river to reach the shore. The water felt heavy, compounded by the relentless rain. Arms and legs tired, Assefa turned and could see the beast's right eye hanging from the socket. And damn if it didn't appear as if it was looking right at him.

The giant alligator opened its large mouth, showing two rows of gleaming sharp teeth. Assefa flinched at the terrible sight, knowing death was but a chomp away but not ready to die.

A torpedo-shaped body sped between Assefa and Zareb and the Ninki Nanka. A thick layer of blubber pushed the special agents back and away.

He'd never worked with Special Agent de Gama before, but he'd known the encantado shifter could transform into a dolphin, which was why Ulan handpicked the man for this mission. There were few water shifters and even fewer drawn to law enforcement. But there the encantado was, shielding his teammates with his dolphin form and giving them a chance to swim to safety.

Behind the alligator was Sataa, transformed into his orca form. The agent was a rare double shifter Ulan had flown to Alaska to recruit for the division. Sometimes, like today, land shifters weren't enough even when one of the shifters was the cat of legend.

Assefa and Zareb made their way to the grimy shore and out of the river. Dragging on wet and dirty clothes, they could do nothing but wait for their teammates or the monster to surface.

A warm, forceful wind came out of nowhere. Raising his hand over his eyes to shield them from the rain, Assefa lifted his head to the sky and saw a yellow plane with a red hull coming their way. A second later, he sensed familiar wind magic in the air, guiding the plane in the direction of land.

Within minutes, an amphibious aircraft landed about forty feet to the west of his and Zareb's location. Out of the plane jumped Sanura and Mike, water and mud splashing over their hiking boots and pants when they landed.

"You called her."

"Damn right, although I didn't expect the detective." Zareb waved at the approaching witch and dwarf. "An amphibian seaplane. Your mate wins for the best entrance by a heroine in an action-horror movie. We could really use her help."

"I know."

He had always known. But knowing and admitting the truth wasn't the same. As much as he'd missed Sanura, he wasn't happy to see her, not there, not with the killer Ninki Nanka on the loose and the scent of a dead witch's blood still in the putrid air.

Their eyes met but neither spoke. Sanura looked mad and so was Assefa. Not at his stubborn witch, whose eyes burned through him, but with this entire dangerous situation they found themselves.

He opened his mouth to say something, to ease the awkward moment, but he heard howling and splashing coming from the river. They ran to the shore's edge in time to see blood bubble to the surface.

"Sataa and de Gama are down there." He wanted to rush into the river but knew, in cat or human form, there was nothing he could do for either special agent.

"Okay, Sanura, you and Assefa are together. Do your thing and destroy that son of a bitch down there." Zareb's words came out as a rushed, desperate plea, which Assefa understood.

Sanura's eyes moved from Zareb to Assefa to Mike and then to the bloody river water.

"You don't have time to explain it to him, Sanura," Mike said, snapping his fingers to get her attention as she continued to fixate on the gloomy water. "Just do what you can."

"How many agents are alive down there?"

Assefa didn't know if Sanura's question was directed at him or Zareb, but he answered. "Two. Maybe one. Hell, maybe none."

Sanura nodded, eyes still on the river and the unidentified blood. "Move away from the edge."

The men did as told, retreating, but not too far. Assefa didn't like this, Sanura so close to the river's edge. The Ninki Nanka was quite capable of dashing from the water and snatching Sanura up and dragging her back into the river with him. That kind of attack was when the alligator was the fastest, victims dying of drowning before being eaten by the predator.

Assefa inched closer to Sanura, prepared to shift the second he caught a glimpse of Special Agent Bell's killer.

He couldn't see what she was doing, probably using her second sight, which made the most sense.

"I assume the giant alligator is the enemy and not the orca?"

"The orca is Special Agent Yutimo Sataa," Assefa said.

Sanura hadn't mentioned the dolphin, which could only mean one thing.

Damn, another dead agent.

"Can you kill the Ninki Nanka without hurting Sataa?"

"I don't think I can't start fire in water, Assefa. On top, probably, although I've never tried. I'm going to have to pull that thing to the surface with a binding spell. Can you kill it then?"

"You get it up here and hold it down. We'll take care of the rest."

Assefa watched as Mike marched to the seaplane and yanked a duffle bag out, which he hoisted onto his shoulder.

Dropping the bag beside Assefa, Mike slid the zipper down, revealing the contents.

Zareb whistled. "How in the hell did you get that through customs, Detective?"

Mike pointed to Sanura. "She didn't like using her magic to manipulate the minds of full-humans. It goes against what she believes in and how Sankofa witches are trained to use their magic."

Yet Sanura had done it anyway, and Assefa knew why.

He braced himself, waiting to feel the familiar heat of his witch's fire magic course through him. Sanura didn't have to be there, didn't need to be there, yet she was. He would lend her his Mngwa's strength for her binding spell.

As he watched her by the edge and waited for her magic to reach out to his cat spirit, nothing happened.

"Come to me, creature of land and water. Come to me and serve Mami Wata no more. Come to me, beast of scales and spikes. Come to me and bid the water goddess farewell."

Sanura repeated the incantation thirty times before Assefa saw the head of the Ninki Nanka break the surface of the water. With each recitation, she dragged the beast farther onto the shore.

At one point, she wiped her nose with the back of her hand and Assefa swore he smelled Sanura's blood.

Her nose bled from overexertion, which wasn't right. Why wasn't Sanura using their bond to bolster her binding spell? The creature weighed well over two tons. And it no doubt fought her for control, which was why it took her so long and dozens of recitations to get the alligator to the marshy field.

Was Sanura so upset with him that she would rather use brute strength to battle the water creature than rely on her familiar? It seemed so because she hadn't tapped into their bond once.

Like all her binding spells, they were invisible to the naked eye. Up close, the way Assefa was now, the Ninki Nanka strangely still, he could see just how enormous the creature Mami Wata had unleashed onto the world was. Its one good eye watched Assefa, the dangling one lost somewhere between the river and the shore.

It tried to open its mouth and snap at him but whatever kind of binding spell Sanura held it in allowed for minimal movement. One thing was for certain, if it got free, it would try to devour them all.

"Use a wind spell to lift and flip it over on its back." Assefa held a flexible whip-like sword ancient dwarfs used to extend their reach in battle. A priceless artifact, care of one crazy dwarf with a duffle bag full of illegal and rare weapons.

Assefa's eyes swept over Sanura's tall, wet form, hair matted to her head, pants and shirt clinging to her every curve, leaving little to the imagination. He closed the distance between them in five long strides.

He wanted to kiss her, wanted to wrap Sanura in his arms and bury his face in her neck and breathe in her sweet smell, which had Assefa stiffening his spine. Instead of reaching for Sanura, however, Assefa tightened his grip on the sword. "Flip the monster over, so we can put it out of its misery." Even with one eye remaining, caught in Sanura's binding spell as it was, Assefa could tell the beast's mind wasn't its own. "We can't permit it to live to only have Mami Wata control it again."

She scowled at Assefa, clearly unpleased with him, and he winced on the inside. His request had come out as an order and his voice had taken on the cold, impersonal tone he used when dealing with people he had no intention of letting get too close to him.

He'd sounded like his grandfather, which meant he'd spoken to Sanura as if she meant nothing more to him than an agent under his command.

Sanura said nothing, but her eyes held both hurt and a promise to kick his ass later.

The fire witch raised her hands, moved them in a circular motion and began to pull gases from the air. She continued this movement, stirring her arms harder and faster, increasing the flow of gases. Sanura directed the churning air currents over the Ninki Nanka until the wind spell exploded in a loud, violent gust of wind that tossed the witch and the men to the ground but also lifted and flipped the beast onto its back. This position left the Ninki Nanka's more vulnerable underbelly open for attack.

Assefa, Zareb, and Mike rushed to their feet, modern and ancient weapons of war in their hands. Between the dozens of bullet and sword wounds and the sheer size of the twenty-foot, eleven-hundred-pound Ninki Nanka, it took long minutes to bring the beast to its brutal end.

It made no sound, didn't wail or cry out when they hacked and shot it to pieces. Didn't squirm in Sanura's binding spell. Didn't do anything other than succumb to its bloody judgement, Sanura shaking her head when it was done.

With exhausted effort, Sanura set the creature on fire. And kept burning it, despite the lashing rain, until it was unrecognizable. Then she retreated to the seaplane while the men pushed what they could of the Ninki Nanka into the Congo River.

By the time they crammed into the seaplane, including Special Agent Sataa, Sanura was asleep in a chair. And the pilot's eyes were wide with shock and fear.

Damn, Sanura would have to wipe his mind before they let the full-human go on his way.

Assefa found a blanket in the back of the plane and covered his witch before sitting in the chair farthest from her.

"Here." Zareb handed Assefa his cell phone, still in the plastic bag where he'd put it for safekeeping.

"Even wet and muddy, she's still the most beautiful woman I've ever seen." Assefa removed his phone from the bag and snapped several pictures of his life-saving witch.

He loved her. Six weeks hadn't changed his heart. But it had altered something fundamental between them. As he watched over Sanura as she slept, he knew what.

Their mate bond was no more.

CHAPTER THIRTY

The rain that had battered the Democratic Republic of the Congo for the past two weeks, escalating in intensity the last few hours, was now nothing more than an evaporating drizzle. Likewise, the seven bordering countries were also experiencing the first hour of a rain-free deluge.

Exhausted, wet, and dirty, Sanura and Mike, and what was left of Assefa's team, made their way to Kinshasa's Hotel Lumumba. Assefa checked them in, making sure to pay for two standard rooms with no extra accessories his uncle would complain about when he got the bill. With his personal credit card, he paid for Sanura's room.

"Zareb, you bunk with Sataa. Mike and I will have a room three doors down from the two of you." Assefa handed Sanura her hotel room key card. She hadn't spoken a word to him since awaking and casting a mindwipe spell on the pilot. She still appeared tired but mostly she stared at him with mute disappointment. "Sanura will be two floors up from us."

"Come on, Berber, why do I have to bunk with anyone? Why can't we all have our own room like our lovely savior?" Sataa winked at Sanura, unfazed by the way she looked at but through him.

"We're on the bureau's dime, and the chief will pay for only three rooms."

He was in a wretched mood, having lost two fine agents whose mates he' have to notify when he returned stateside. If he weren't mistaken, Special Agent Bell had a little girl who'd just started kindergarten. The team had needed a water witch on their side and Bell had been available. The agents knew the risk they took every time they went out on a case. Bell and de Gama were no exceptions. Still, the Ninki Nanka hadn't been the normal preternatural rogue the division tracked down and dispatched.

The special agents hadn't been prepared for the enemy. For that, Assefa blamed himself.

"Okay, then you bunk with Zareb and I'll stay with the pretty Sanura."

When Sataa made to walk up to Sanura, Zareb stepped in front of the smaller man. "I wouldn't do that if I were you."

"Come on. This beautiful woman saved my life, the least I can do is show her a bit of gratitude." He tried to get around Zareb, but the were-cat blocked his every move. "Really, Osei? Get out of my way, man, I just want to thank the woman face-to-face." He reached around Zareb and toward Sanura. "How about you and me go upstairs and—"

Assefa hauled the special agent by his collar, away from his witch. Harmless, Sataa's flirting was harmless and Sanura could take care of herself. But he didn't like the way the shifter looked at Sanura, hated, even more, the way Sanura refused to look at Assefa.

He shook Sataa, hard and with a low growl of warning. "For the remainder of the time we're here, I don't want you looking at or talking to her."

"I was just—"

"I know. But don't. Not her. Not ever. Do you understand me?"

"Yeah, yeah. Damn, Berber. Let me go already. I get it."

"Apologize."

"Okay, yeah, whatever you say. Sorry, Sanura. I meant nothing by it. Too much time around men and beasts and I forget my manners."

Sanura, as expected, said nothing. But she did allow Mike to steer her toward the bank of elevators, his duffle bag slung over a shoulder and Sanura's suitcase in his other hand.

He'd overreacted to Sataa's innocent flirting. Assefa still held the man in a violent grip and people were beginning to stare. Well, they'd stared the moment the bedraggled group ambled into the hotel.

Assefa released the special agent.

"I've never known you to lose your cool, Berber." Sataa nodded in the direction of where Sanura and Mike had gone. "You should've told me the fire witch who saved our asses was your mate instead of letting a man make a fool of himself in front of a taken woman."

"You shouldn't talk to any woman like that."

"Fair enough, but still. You're mean when you're jealous." Special Agent Sataa found his backpack and shrugged it on. "For the record, I don't think she likes you very much. You may want to watch your back, bro."

Assefa walked away from the other agent, snatching his own backpack off the floor and heading to the elevators. Zareb followed, and so did Sataa.

Less than five minutes later, he and Mike were in their hotel room.

"When are you going to stop acting like an ass and go see Sanura?" Mike sat on the end of one of the two double beds in the room, untying his filthy boots and letting them fall to the hardwood floor.

Other than the beds, the room consisted of a fridge and mini bar, a closet for two, a television with cable, and free Wi-Fi. The room overlooked the outside pool, full of people, probably grateful to escape confinement after too many days of unrepentant rain. The room was comfortable enough, done in neutral shades of whites and browns with an occasional blue thrown in to add flavor to the otherwise conservative decor.

It would do, but the annoyed detective glaring at him wouldn't.

"I'm not in the mood, so leave it alone."

He grabbed a few items from his pack, including a toiletry bag, and went into the bathroom.

Forty minutes later, he emerged from the bathroom showered and shaved.

"Why are you bunking with the detective instead of your mate?"

Zared stood in the middle of Assefa's hotel room wearing fresh clothes and a scowl.

"Why in the hell are you in my room instead of your own?"

Mike stood beside Zareb. This was an ambush, and he'd walked right into it.

"Sataa talks too damn much." Zareb found the remote to the television and turned it on.

"I didn't come all this way to help Sanura save your furry ass for you two not to make up."

Stalking past Mike, Assefa moved to his backpack, which he left on the floor beside his bed. Bending, he shoved the toiletry bag inside, his dirty clothes fisted in his hand, boxers on but not much else.

Both men watched him.

Ignoring them, he shoved his dirty clothes into a dresser drawer, making a mental note to have them laundered tomorrow. He then proceeded to unpack his bag and hang up his clothes after pulling on a pair of jeans, a short sleeve fitness shirt, socks, and athletic shoes.

"Neither one of you understand. And I'm not in the mood to argue with either of you. Go back to your room, Zareb, and leave me alone."

Zareb muted the television. "I understand that your mate bond must be messed all the hell up because I watched Sanura struggle to pull that big ass Ninki Nanka from the river all by herself. I understand that she's pissed as hell at you, and I understand that you're afraid of both having her and of losing her." Zareb closed the short distance between them, his hand going to Assefa's shoulder. "And I understand that unless you two make up and bring balance back to your bond, that we're all doomed. Today proved that."

Bond. What bond? They'd only ever had a partial one, which Assefa doubted still existed.

"Sex? We're talking about sex?" Mike laughed. "Is that all it'll take to get you and Sanura in fighting order, to stop that Mami whatever chick from drowning the whole damn world?" Mike laughed harder.

"I'm glad you find this so funny." Assefa slammed the closet door shut.

"Actually, it's the saddest damn thing I've ever heard. Look," Mike said, dropping all humor from his voice, "I used to have a wife before I moved to Baltimore. I joined the army, and when I returned she was gone. No note. No kiss my tiny dwarf ass. Nothing. Just gone. The last

I heard, she was living in some dwarf commune in Maine." He laughed again, without humor and with much pain. "Can you believe that? A fucking commune in clam chowder eating Maine."

Assefa realized three things. One, Sanura hadn't told her godfather what happened between them. Two, Mike thought Sanura was to blame for the wedge in their relationship. Three, he knew little about Michael McKutchen's personal life beyond his love for Sanura and Makena Williams.

"She flew halfway around the world to be here with you. Sanura was going to do it by herself. I hate the thought of that."

So did Assefa. He'd already felt guilty, and Mike's words made him feel even worse.

"Thank you for getting her here safely."

"Like I told you before, kid, Sanura was my goddaughter long before she became your mate. I'll always be there for her, even when she thinks she doesn't need any help. That's one thing the two of you have in common." Mike ran a hand through his salt-and-pepper hair. "I didn't believe in all that witch/were-cat prophecy business. And I still don't believe in all those gods that you all talk about. But that mammoth gator was real. If that's the tip of the iceberg, what in the hell is next?"

Sliding his keycard into his back pocket, Assefa moved to the bedroom door. He couldn't put this off any longer.

Zareb unmuted the television and sat his big body on Assefa's bed. "I never thought I would have to tell a were-cat this but go have sex with your mate."

Assefa left the room. He needed to see Sanura, but didn't know what he would say so he roamed the hotel until he found himself an hour later standing in front of room 1012.

He knocked.

Dressed in a black, sleeveless nightgown that fell to her ankles, Sanura sat, cross-legged, in the middle of her queen-size bed. The lights in the room were off except for the nightstand lamp to her right. Sanura should be asleep. But her mind kept replaying images of a bloody dolphin and of half a woman's body carried into the Congo River by Assefa.

He'd prayed over the dead agent's body before releasing her into the water. She'd watched it all from the plane. The robotic way Assefa moved about the battlefield, using the river as a disposal site for so much death and carnage. When he'd fed the river the body of the witch, Sanura nearly leapt to her feet in protest. The woman's family would want a burial. They deserved the chance to say goodbye to their loved one.

Sanura hadn't known the agent and could barely stomach seeing her partially eaten body. Did anyone other than them need to witness what had been done to her, to know how she'd died and how frightened and in pain she must've been in before death finally claimed her? If she were Sanura's sister or friend, would she want to know how the witch spent the final minutes and seconds of her life?

She wouldn't. Gods, she wouldn't want to know. No one who loved the deceased would, which Assefa understood. So, he'd given her the best burial he could've, casting the water witch into the element of her birth.

Sanura hadn't needed Zareb to tell her Special Agent Bell had been a water witch, which he did, among other details of their battle against the Ninki Nanka, on the cab ride to the hotel. If Bell been an earth or wind witch, Assefa would've buried her. A fire witch would've received the same fate as the dead Ninki Nanka. But Assefa hadn't asked her to burn any other bodies, which left only the river and the water witch.

She replayed it all, including the cold, distant look in Assefa's eyes when they'd come face-to-face. Sanura had never seen anyone look so vulnerable and strong at the same time. Shanumi had come close, in that fragile moment when she realized Sanura intended to set her soul free, afraid yet hopeful.

The cut to her palm from when she'd cast the blood circle had healed the second her hand touched the fire witch of legend's undead flesh. She ran a finger over where the cut used to be, hoping her predecessor's soul was at rest. More, she prayed Shanumi and Abubaker would find each other in the Field of Reeds. Overdue as it may be, the couple deserved their happily-ever-after.

Sanura flopped onto her back, thinking of her mate and their future. She was so mad at Assefa. For all that she'd threatened to harm him, Sanura could never hurt Assefa.

She knew he was already in pain because Assefa would never abandon her unless he thought he had a very good reason. For Assefa Berber, only one reason would be serious enough to take him from her. The special agent, like Abubaker, was overprotective. It grated as much as his care warmed her.

When a knock sounded at her door, Sanura was neither surprised nor relieved. So, this was it then? She pushed from the bed, found her robe and slipped it on. Sanura planned for this moment. But if Assefa refused, she wouldn't fight him any longer. If he were intent on them not being together, she would respect his wish no matter how much heartache it would bring her.

Sanura opened the door.

Dark-brown eyes, she adored, stared at her. Assefa's gaze, so intense, held Sanura for his silent examination.

After showering and washing her hair, she'd arranged the long hair into a series of double-strand twists, which hung past her shoulders in coiled waves.

There was longing and hunger in his eyes, but also indecision and concern.

Sanura tucked a twist behind her ear, feeling nervous and exposed. She stepped aside. "Are you planning on coming in or did you only come here to stare at me?"

Assefa blinked as if he hadn't realized how long he'd been standing there looking at her while saying nothing at all.

"I would love to come in. Thanks."

Assefa took over holding the door, which meant he wanted her to move deeper into the room, so he could close and lock the door after them. She obliged him. They would get to his compulsive need to stand between Sanura and every perceived threat, whether real or imagined.

"This is a nice room."

An understatement. It was a suite, expensively decorated and large enough for four adults. No way had Assefa's division approved the booking of this suite. But Assefa's sentence was as close as he would come to admitting that he'd upgraded whatever room was intended for Special Agent Bell to the one given to Sanura.

"It is. Thank you."

His eyes scanned the spacious living area. He'd come to her. She figured he'd eventually get around to speaking his mind. In the meantime, she had no intention of standing in a dark room while she had a perfectly good bed waiting for her.

She left him to his brooding.

Three minutes later, Assefa stuck his head into her bedroom. She sat in the center of the bed as she had before, the lamp still on.

"I think I broke our bond." Assefa walked into her room and stopped at the foot of the bed.

"Isn't that what you wanted?"

"No. Yes. No. Dammit, I know I asked you to perform the dissolution spell but it wasn't what I really wanted. I would never want that."

"But you asked anyway. You stayed away for almost two months."

"I know. I had to stay away, Sanura. I know none of this makes any sense. I also know that I've handled everything badly. But I have my reasons."

"What reasons?"

"We don't celebrate Mother's Day in the Sudan. Americans turn everything into a moneymaking opportunity. I always thought it a pointless, capitalistic holiday." Assefa sat on the edge of the bed, his big body seeming to take up so much room. "Then I met your mother. I hadn't had one in so long. Makena treats me like I was born to her. I love her hugs and sweet kisses and the way she cooks my favorite dishes when I visit. I found myself wanting an excuse to buy her something, anything to let her know how much she means to me."

Sanura began to reach for Assefa, but he was so lost in his emotions that she feared if she interrupted he wouldn't begin again.

"I missed the holiday this year. But I bought Makena twenty-nine Mother's Day gifts, one for each year of your birth. They're in my closet, wrapped and waiting. Jewelry mainly but also gift cards and crystal tableware." He shrugged. "I don't remember them all, and she'll probably think me crazy for giving her twenty-nine gifts when I haven't even known her for one year."

Makena wouldn't. She'd think Assefa sweet and in need of a mother's love and care.

Nothing he'd said explained the distance Assefa had put between them.

"I don't know how to do this."

"Then let me help." When she reached for Assefa this time, she didn't stop. Her hand found his and she squeezed. "Our bond isn't broken. I know it may feel that way to you, but it's still intact, though weaker than I'd like."

Sanura grabbed two pillows, then jumped from the bed. She placed both on the floor, in front of the sofa and five feet across from each other. Sitting on a pillow, she glanced up to see Assefa remove his shoes.

"I assume you want me to sit on the other pillow."

"Yes. I'd like us to perform a realignment ritual."

"I never heard of it."

"The spell will grant me access to your heart and your mind. Once inside, there will be nothing you'll be able to hide from me, including the secret that's kept you away from home. If you want me to fix our bond, you'll have to let me in. You'll have to trust me more than you're afraid of me knowing the truth."

"This has nothing to do with trust."

"It doesn't?"

"Not in the way that you mean. I trust you to love me despite how much of a coward and ass I've been this past month and a half. I trust you to try to see the good in a story where there are only minuses. I trust that you'll try to solve an unfixable problem. And I trust that what I say to you will remain between us."

Assefa found her right hand and brought it to his face, holding her palm to his cheek. "You have no idea how much I've missed you, how hard it's been to stay away from you and home. You're my home, sweetheart. I would never leave you unless I thought it was in your best interest." Sliding her hand from his face, Assefa kissed her palm before placing Sanura's hand back in her lap. "We don't need to perform a ritual. I'll tell you what's on my heart. I'll explain what's kept me from you and why we can't be together."

Assefa was right, no matter what he told her, Sanura would do her damnedest to find a solution. Because them not being together wasn't an option she was willing to entertain or to accept.

CHAPTER THIRTY-ONE

He wanted to kiss her. Assefa desired nothing more than to push Sanura onto her back, crawl on top of her, and kiss his witch until she moaned and ached for him and her warmth and curves made him forget the impossibility of a shared future.

She watched Assefa not with the eyes of a trained psychologist but with the heart of a woman who loved to the point of angry, concerned patience. Sanura wore the evidence around her neck. When she'd opened the door to her suite, Assefa had seen the gold necklace with the ring around her neck.

In a callous attempt to push Sanura away, Assefa had returned her promise gift, thinking she'd take one look at it and know she'd made a mistake in taking him as lover and mate. Yet there she was, silent in her resilience and defiance.

Sanura had a level of emotional intelligence Assefa didn't possess. The gap, while always there, was easy to overlook and ignore when cast against Assefa's general intelligence and physical prowess as a man and Mngwa. But a man must be more than his IQ, might, and skill in battle.

Running away. Shutting down. Sanura's diagnosis since the day they'd met, offered with both a smile and a frown but never as an impossibility for personal growth.

"My mother's not dead." He hadn't meant to say it like that, to blurt it out without preamble. "All this time I thought she was dead, but my mother's alive and well."

"Um, wait, I'm confused."

"So was I."

"But..." She stared at him, trying to process what he'd just told her. "You said she died when you were five. If she didn't die, where in the hell has she been? Why didn't she contact her children? Why did your father lie?"

With each question, Sanura's voice lowered and her annoyance rose. Such a good woman, so quick to anger on his behalf.

"That's what your father told you after I left? That your mother is still alive?"

"He said he gave her an ultimatum."

Sanura slid closer to Assefa, their knees touching. "What kind of ultimatum?"

"I told you my memories of my mother are sketchy. I remember her reading me and Najja bedtime stories, hugging us goodnight but not much else."

"That makes sense. Most people don't remember too many details from their childhood prior to elementary school."

"According to my father, Mother had no interest in doing much of anything with us. She doted on Razi, giving him all her affection and time. With me and Najja, Father had to force her to spend time with us. When she did, he made sure she was supervised by our nanny."

"I'm still confused. None of this makes any sense."

That's because he'd left out one huge detail. Gods, Assefa didn't want to tell her. Even Zareb hadn't been able to conceal his shock, although the man had rallied quickly, schooling his features and hiding them behind genuine concern for Assefa's wellbeing.

"My sister was born before me. We were always told we were born a few minutes apart, but that's not true."

Assefa had never been one to take a circuitous route to anything, least of all the truth. Still, he found the words stuck in his throat and the urge to shut down, once more, unacceptably high.

"The truth is that, after Najja came, Mother went into distress. Her heart rate increased, she began to bleed and the doctor was forced to take me."

"Take you? You mean your mother had to have a C-section?"

"Apparently, the doctor feared for Mother's life as well as mine. But I was fine. She almost died. She probably would've if the doctor hadn't also been a level four witch. Magic and medicine saved the life of Nyanath Berber."

Sanura said nothing, waiting with clinical patience for him to fill in the gaps of his story.

"I was... I wasn't born like every other were-cat."

"What does that mean?"

Assefa cleared his throat and then just got it over with. "I was born as a Mngwa cub. Fur, paws, and gold eyes. That's how I looked when the doctor cut me from my mother."

While Assefa knew she heard him, there was no change in Sanura's body language. She continued to stare at him as if frozen by the knowledge that Assefa had come into this world as beast instead of a baby. An animal whose birth nearly killed his mother.

Without uttering a word, Sanura pushed to her feet and paced the bedroom.

Assefa remained seated on the pillow, unsure what to do now that Sanura knew the truth other than to tell the rest of the pathetic story.

"According to Father, Mother thought she was cursed because of how I was born. She thought the gods were displeased with her and viewed my birth as an omen of blood, violence, and death. After she recuperated, Mom refused to hold me. And, by extension, Najja. That's when Father hired us a live-in nanny. I think the memories I have of my mother may actually be of the nanny, but I'm not certain."

Sanura paced, not once looking at Assefa. She also didn't interrupt, so he kept going.

"At some point, Father began to fear for my and Najja's safety. He didn't go into detail, and I didn't want to know. By the time we were five, she'd gotten worse in her negligence, all but ignoring us in favor of Razi. Father told her to either be a proper mother to us or leave. She left."

General Supreme Jahi Berber had chosen the physical and emotional safety of his children over that of his mate bond. Assefa had no idea what that decision had cost his father. When he'd told the story of Nyanath, there'd been sadness and regret in his voice. He wondered if Jahi still loved his mate and ever wondered what his life would've been like if Assefa hadn't been born at all or been born normal.

Assefa would never know because he feared the answer too much to ever ask.

"Unbeknownst to Father, when Razi was thirteen, Mother began writing to him."

That had Sanura stopping and staring down at him. "What did she say in her letters?"

"I don't know. I don't think Father saw the letters. But Razi confronted him. Father told Razi everything. Well, probably not everything. This is the thing, Sanura, I was a cub for a month before I shifted into the form of a normal baby. During that time, my father kept me hidden in my nursery. Only the doctor and attending nurses saw me. They fed me and Najja and made sure we were cared for. The only other people who knew the truth were Uncle Ulan and his mate."

"Let me guess. Once you shifted into a 'real boy,' your father had a highly skilled witch, who knew nothing of your unique birth, wipe the minds of all who did except Ulan and his mate because Jahi trusts his brother with his secrets and lies."

Secrets and lies. Yes, the same words Razi had used before he unleashed the Leucrotas to kill his family.

Assefa got to his feet, feeling the need to stretch and move and release the tension in his body.

"I also suppose your mother cultivated a relationship with her oldest son while feeding Razi a cauldron full of lies about why she left and how your little cat of legend self nearly ended her life. Probably blamed Jahi for most, if not all of it. Don't get me wrong, your father isn't a saint. But when he loves, it's with his entire heart. He gave his mate her five years." Sanura closed the distance between them, close but not touching. "Do you understand how long that is for a man to watch the woman he loves treat two of their children with disdain, disgust, and fear?"

She stepped away, renewing her pacing.

He wondered about those three words: disdain, disgust, and fear.

His father hadn't described Nyanath's feelings about Assefa with those or similar words, but they'd been the unspoken emotions. Jahi's attempt to soften the truth was appreciated but not indecipherable in all that he did say. And Sanura had just laid it out there in a way that reminded Assefa how blunt the fire witch could be.

The way her mind worked still surprised him. She moved from thoughtful and kind to fierce and critical with a range of beliefs and actions in between. Assefa realized as she stopped in front of him again, that he had no idea what she would say or do.

"You know how all the tales about the mythical Mngwa includes how no one was ever able to capture one? How the Mngwa was such a stealthy predator that it killed and then disappeared without a trace?"

"Sure. What does any of that have to do with what I just told you? Do you have nothing to say about the fact that I was born as an animal? That my mother almost died and experienced years of postpartum depression because of me? That if we have a child and it's a boy, you could die in childbirth?"

"That story is one of the saddest and craziest I've ever heard. Since you want to leap forward, as if I wasn't going to get to all of that, I'll tell you what I think now."

She punched him in his stomach.

"What in the hell was that for?"

"I'm still mad at you. And don't even act as if that little punch hurt because I barely put any strength behind it and didn't use an ounce of magic. But I've been wanting to hit you since the moment I got off the plane and you glared at me in that detached way you know I despise."

She kissed him on his lips, short and sweet.

Damn.

Assefa's arms raised to twine around her waist, but Sanura stepped back before he could hold her to him and deepen the kiss.

"And I've been wanting to do that ever since you covered me with the blanket on the plane."

"I thought you were asleep."

"I nearly was. Did you take a picture of me?"

"Like I said, I thought you were asleep."

Sanura leaned in again and pressed another too short kiss to his lips. She knew he wanted more. Assefa always craved more of her. Yet she held back, mad as she said, but also a woman who loved her man.

The thought of her stalwart love and devotion, despite these past six weeks and his revealed secret, thrilled and frightened him.

"Even for a witch, Assefa, who has were-cats as family and friends, we don't expect to actually give birth to one."

Her finger ran over his bottom lip, caressing the skin with such tenderness and care Assefa couldn't prevent the shudder. He closed his eyes and soaked in her touch.

As Sanura stroked his lip, her own so close, he recalled all the times he'd wept for his mother. And all the times he held Najja when she did the same.

"She left because of me, but Razi and Najja suffered. I drove her away, and they were denied a mother's love."

He opened his eyes when he no longer felt Sanura's touch.

"That's not true." She bit his lower lip, achingly soft and erotic. "There's a lot I don't know and questions I will pose to your father after we finish this Mami Wata and prophecy business, but I know the feel of a mother's love. Come here."

She yanked his hand and pulled Assefa to the bed. Off came her black robe and Assefa closed his eyes again. Damn but his witch looked good in black silk, especially when the silk showed off her breasts and hips and thighs, and, hell, everything to mouth-watering fire witch perfection.

When he opened them again, Sanura sat propped against the head-board, her legs under the covers and the other side pulled back in invitation. This wasn't about sex, although his body screamed at him to skip the talking and get to the making up.

Yet his mind recoiled from the prospect of giving in to the needs and wants of his heart and body. He just couldn't shake the horror that could befall his Sanura.

He accepted her invitation anyway. Assefa folded his shirt and jeans and placed them on the sofa before grabbing the pillows from the floor and handing one to Sanura.

She patted her lap. "Come here. I want to touch you. I'm feeling possessive and angry, which isn't a good combination for me."

And Assefa was feeling needy and scared, which wasn't a good combination for him.

Crawling onto the bed, Assefa slipped under the covers wearing only his boxers. He'd missed sharing a bed with Sanura and felt the weight of their separation pull his body down as he reclined his head on the pillow she'd put on her lap. Turning onto his stomach, Assefa wrapped his arms around Sanura's waist, his face buried in the pillow that smelled of gardenias.

One hand stroked his shoulders while the other played with the tight curls on his head.

Assefa loved this. Loved Sanura, and the way she took care of him, even when he was often too proud to ask.

Six weeks.

He'd needed this, her, for six interminable weeks.

In the loving arms of his witch, Assefa wept, the height of his emotional meltdown.

Once again, Sanura said nothing. Her soothing, accepting touch was all Assefa ever needed, which made him cry harder. He couldn't lose her to Mami Wata, the water witch of legend, or childbirth. But he was no longer capable of pretending that he could give her up.

He hadn't.

He couldn't.

"I know you're afraid and so am I. Makena had two miscarriages before she delivered a healthy baby girl."

He hadn't known. Gods, two dead babies.

"My parents wanted a baby, wanted a child of their love and commitment to each other. And it took them three tries to finally get their wish. I don't know how they felt when my siblings died, although it's not hard to conclude they were devastated. But sadness and grief, even fear, can turn into faith and courage and pure stubborn effort. Their loss didn't define them or drive them apart. It made my parents better partners and stronger individuals. We aren't Makena and Sam, but can't we be just as stubborn in our will, not in spite of our fear but because of it?"

Assefa lifted onto his elbows. "You're still willing to fight for me, for us, after everything I've done?"

She wiped the tears from his cheeks and smiled. "You learned something that took you off your feet, made you question so much of what you thought to be true. You feel guilty, think it's your fault that your mother left, which it isn't by the way. Without any details to go on, I'm calling bullshit on her supposed postpartum depression. But we'll talk about that later. My point is that under stress people act in ways that aren't healthy, sensitive to others, or even smart. Do you remember how kind and patient you were with me when I rejected your claiming bite?"

Assefa sat up, facing Sanura. "You weren't ready, and I would never push you."

"I know you wouldn't, but rejection is still rejection. And mine hurt you. Sometimes, we'll hurt each other, Assefa. It happens in relationships. But at the end of the day, no matter how furious I am with you, I'll always fight for our love."

"I want so much, Sanura."

"So do I. What you told me is shocking. I'd be lying if I didn't admit that. Whatever form our children take, I will love them. But I know that's not your fear."

It wasn't.

"I want to build a life with you, Assefa, and that includes having and raising children. When we're ready, I'll want to try, no matter the possible consequence. This is what I think about you being born as a Mngwa cub. You said it wasn't normal. On the face of it, that would seem true. But I thought back to the myth of the Mngwa. Sekhmet created were-cats, giving what used to be warlocks the ability to turn into a big predatory cat. If you think about it, every cat a modern were-cat shifter can turn into exists. All except for the Mngwa. Even the Ninki Nanka and Leurcrotas, while abnormal, the animals they resemble actually exist in nature."

He knew Sanura was building to a point, but Assefa was too tired to track her train of thought. "I'm only partially following you."

"What I'm saying is that I think the way you were born was normal for a Mngwa. The reason why no hunter ever captured a Mngwa, never even found his den, was because Mngwas were the first were-cat shifters. You shifted within a month of your birth. That doesn't happen. But it does if you were created to have two equal and elegant forms, neither dominant to the other. You always told me you and your Mngwa were two but also one. I think that's literally true. But only for you. That's probably why your shift is near-instantaneous."

Assefa slid down the bed to lie on his back, eyes on the ceiling but mind thinking about Sanura's theory.

The first shifter? Could that be true? Was the Mngwa the prototype for were-cats? As crazy as it was, Sanura's theory made a lot of sense. It would explain much, particularly his intense relationship with his inner spirit.

"It's a lot to take in."

"I know, and I may not even be right. But if I am, there was nothing abnormal about your birth. As for the safety issue, newborn lions and tigers, for example, weigh only two or three pounds when they're born. The average human newborn weighs about seven and a half pounds. I can't imagine your little Mngwa self was the cause of whatever happened to your mother after she gave birth to Najja."

"You're only saying that to make me feel better."

"True, but that doesn't mean I'm not right."

Assefa moved back to the pillow on Sanura's lap. His arms, once more, going around her waist. "You're the stubbornest person I've ever met. Everything isn't solvable. One of these days, you'll have to accept that."

"I do."

No, she didn't. In a way, Assefa envied Sanura her compassionate approach to life, her empathy and drive.

"Do you know what time it is, Assefa?"

"Probably late. Why?"

"It's quarter after one. Do you know the day?"

"Sweetheart, I have no idea. That's how tired I am."

A hand came to his chin and lifted until he stared up at her. "It's your birthday, beloved. September twenty-fifth."

He grinned. Assefa had forgotten, but Sanura hadn't.

"I have two gifts for you. One I'll give you now. The other will have to wait until after we get some sleep."

"You bought me a gift?"

"No, I made you a gift. And Rachel's big mouth almost ruined it."

"What are you talking about?"

"When I thought of it, I assumed we'd be in our bedroom after a nice dinner at your favorite restaurant. Candles, wine, a sexy negligee." She gestured to the room with her hand. "I didn't envision this. But today's your birthday, and I've waited weeks to give you your present."

She made him a gift? And today was his twenty-ninth birthday. Sanura hadn't only come to the Sudan because he needed his fire witch to help him defeat the Ninki Nanka, she'd also come because no matter where he was or the state of their relationship, she wanted to spend Assefa's birthday with him.

He touched the ring that hung from the gold chain around her neck. Assefa should never have taken it off, never have returned it to Sanura. He wondered if she would consider gifting it to him again.

"May I have this back?"

"Not yet. I have something else to give you." Assefa made to roll off Sanura, so she could retrieve the gift, but she placed her hand on his shoulder. "I don't need to get up. I've memorized it, although I did create an instrumental track and uploaded it to my phone." She laughed, the sound tinged with nervousness. "I haven't done this in a long time, so I hope I don't sound too awful especially without the musical accompaniment."

He opened his mouth to speak but thought better of it. He would find out soon enough, so Assefa resettled himself on Sanura's lap. This time, however, he reclined on his back, his head on the pillow and eyes lifted to her. Whatever she was going to do, Assefa wanted to see her lovely face while she did it.

"It's entitled, *Seasons of Our Love*."

The moment Assefa connected the dots about Rachel almost spoiling Sanura's birthday surprise for him, their disagreement over who would buy Sanura a piano, and her failure to tell him she could sing, was the same moment she opened her mouth and—

By the gods, Sanura had the most beautiful contralto voice, low, full, and warm.

A griot speaks of you
You're his fantastical news
Daring, dangerous, and delectable
In surround sound, he tells the tale of the man, sensitive soul, and sweet lips.

You're as thoughtful as shade on a blistering summer's day
Protective as snow on a mountain in the chill of winter

He speaks and I listen
Enraptured and forever captured by the story of the man and the myth

Of his beast, as well as his heart
As well as his heart

An artist paints you
You're her mythical muse
Handsome, heady, and heroic
In full color, she sees the depth of the man
And his heart
His wonderful heart
His wonderful heart

Thoughtful as shade on a blistering summer's day
His heart, his heart
Thoughtful as shade on a blistering summer's day

Her brush never falters, painting against the canvas of my heart
My nostrils fill with the scent, chasing the liquid current of our
love
The air amplifies the sound of our joined hearts
Our joined hearts

You're as giving as raindrops in a garden of spring blossoms
You're as courageous as a bird taking flight on a windy autumn
night

These are the seasons of our love
Cyclical, changing, forever
These are the seasons of our love
Seasons of our love

These are the seasons of our love
Cyclical, changing, forever
These are the seasons of our love
Seasons of our love

He speaks and I listen
Enraptured and forever captured by the story of the man and the
myth
Of his beast, as well as his heart
As well as his heart

An artist paints you
You're her mythical muse
Handsome, heady, and heroic
In full color, she sees the depth of the man
And his heart
His wonderful heart
His wonderful heart

Before Sanura finished the last word of his birthday song, Assefa was kissing her, long and deep and with a passion rivaled only by the depth of his love for this woman.

"You wrote me a song."

And she'd sung it with such tenderness. Sanura's lyrics of love were sweet kisses to all the places he hurt.

"I'm not a songwriter, but I wanted to give you as special a birthday present as you gave me."

Assefa kissed her again, unable not to. According to her friends and mother, Sanura hadn't sang since her father's funeral over three years ago. But on this day, Assefa's birthday, she sang for him.

Assefa was touched on a level he could only express through his kisses because words of love and gratitude were inadequate.

"Will you sing it again?"

"It's your birthday. I'll sing your song as many times as you'd like."

She did.

When Assefa fell asleep, it was to the angelic voice of his witch.

CHAPTER THIRTY-TWO

Nineteen Years Earlier
Baltimore, Maryland
Sankofa Preparatory School

High Priestess Katherine Spencer was no fool. Did the pathetic excuse for a water witch, sitting across from her, think she wouldn't be able to see past her lies? Did she think the leader of the Witch Council of Elders, the most powerful network of witches in the United States, feebleminded or power poor? Or maybe the woman had told so many lies in her lifetime that she assumed everyone she met would swallow her deceptions if spoken with a sweet smile and peppered with compliments.

"I know my granddaughter will love it here. The grounds are beautiful, the students excel academically, and I've heard nothing but good things about Sankofa's courses on defensive and offensive spells."

"From whom?"

"Um, excuse me?"

Katherine rested an arm on her desk, leaned back in her chair, and smiled at the lying witch. "From whom did you hear such glowing reviews about Sankofa's instructors?"

"Well, around. Witches talk to one another. My daughter and I've found Baltimore witches to be friendly to newcomers."

Sankofa witches were friendly, but they weren't stupid and neither was Katherine. Her sisters knew better than to speak of the school and its unique classes to someone not a member of their network of witches and were-cats.

Katherine brightened her smile, revealing white teeth she wished were sharp enough to rip out the deceitful throat of Sharon Hays.

Perhaps if she hadn't brought her daughter along to the initial interview, the high priestess insisted on for all new applicants, Ms. Hays may have made it past Katherine's first round of scrutiny.

Yet she had brought her daughter with her, who, for all that Katherine could discern, seemed like a pleasant woman if not a particularly astute judge of character. Then again, Sharon Hays was Christine Walker's mother. The young woman trusted Sharon, probably had no reason not to. Still, Walker's utter naiveté only strengthened Katherine's position to not admit the woman's child.

The question, for which she had yet to answer, was what she would do about her speculation. She should examine the child's aura signature one more time before she kicked them off Sankofa property.

She'd never murdered a child before. To her surprise, the thought of ending the life of the cute little girl felt like an acidic boulder in her stomach. There were people, of course, were-cats whom she could call who would do the foul deed.

Ugly business, the defending of one's family and friends through brutality and bloodshed. If Sharon Hays thought she could smuggle the water witch of legend into the Sankofa community without a fight from the high priestess, well, she would soon learn that not all water witches served the despicable Mami Wata.

Ignoring the women, Katherine got to her feet and walked around her desk and to the wide window in her office. It faced the quad. On a nice summer's day and with Makena in court, Katherine knew where she'd find young Sanura.

A huge black jaguar trotted around the quad while Sanura ran after him, giggling when her father would slow enough for her to touch his tail before darting away again. By the Tree of Ma'at sat Sharon's granddaughter, knees tucked to her chin and eyes on the father and daughter.

Katherine had asked about the child's father. From the women's reactions, especially Christine's, who'd turned two shades of red, Katherine concluded the man wasn't in the picture. From the quick look of guilt that had crossed Sharon's face, Katherine assumed the were-cat was dead, which made sense.

Even without the ability to read auras the way high-level witches could, a were-cat's enhanced sense of smell would've detected the change in Sharon Hays's aura signature.

From her office and at her magic level, reading the child's aura from this distance proved a simple feat. The same. Damn, a part of Katherine wished she'd been wrong.

The girl at ten was already a level three water witch. Impossible. No normal witch at that age possessed so much power. No one, except for the fire witch of legend, that was. And while everyone at Sankofa expected it of Sanura Williams, Katherine did not of Christine C. Walker.

"Christie's a powerful little girl." Katherine twisted to face Sharon, her statement meant for her. "Too powerful to be the daughter of a level two water witch." Her blue eyes narrowed on the flushed face of Sharon Hays. "Did you really think I wouldn't scan your family's auras with my second sight? Did you think you could stroll in here and trick me into opening Sankofa's doors to a Mami Wata sympathizer?"

"I have no idea what you're talking about."

Sharon pushed to her feet, her blue eyes casting past Katherine and to the quad. Sam's jaguar lounged on his side while Sanura, ever friendly, knelt next to Christie, showing the child a fire trick Katherine had seen a dozen times.

"I was there for Sanura's birth. I saw her mother struggle to bring the child into this world. I promised, on that stormy night that I would do everything I could to protect her."

"I have no idea—"

"You may lie to your daughter, but I see through you. Christine is a level two witch. You're a level four, and Christie, as young as she is, is a level three. That doesn't happen in families."

Katherine's voice had risen, her anger undeniable.

"Mom isn't a level four water witch, High Priestess Katherine, and my daughter couldn't be more than a one at this point. I doubt if she's even that." Christine looked from Katherine to her mother. "Mom, what is the high priestess talking about?" Christine stood when Sharon didn't reply. "What is she talking about? We're both level two witches. Except for a few cousins, who are level ones, every woman in our family are level two witches. When it comes to power levels, we've never been that strong. There's no shame in that. It's just the way things are."

Sharon didn't answer her daughter, and Katherine doubted the older woman felt no shame about being born a low-level witch. Her eyes stayed fixed on the playing girls outside, chasing each other around the quad as the black jaguar watched on, vigilant and protective.

So was Katherine.

"You thought to worm your way into the Sankofa network. To find out how strong we are. To learn how far we'll go to protect our own, to fight for the life of the child who'll grow into a woman who'll protect us all." Katherine, seething inside and knowing the child outside had to die, closed the distance between herself and the blonde water witch. "I'll answer your unasked question. We'll kill to protect the fire witch of legend."

To her credit, Sharon Hays didn't flinch. She stared right back, steel in her steady gaze. That was until her daughter ran from the office.

"She now knows what you've done. You used her daughter, and you took advantage of her low magic level, knowing level two witches aren't adept at reading auras. Not that Christine would have reason to read her daughter's aura. Or yours, for that matter."

"You've made a monumental mistake."

"No, you have. I'm not afraid of you."

Sharon stepped back. "You should be."

"Threats will only make your death more painful. I'll spare the child the same bloody fate. She'll go peacefully in her sleep. A suffocation spell should suffice."

The slap came, quick and hard.

"You stay the fuck away from my granddaughter or so help me gods, I'll flood this entire school."

Katherine laughed, enjoying the sting of pain to her right cheek.

"You're a level four water witch to my five and an unnatural one at that." Katherine retook her seat behind her desk. "Run along, Sharon, and tell your gullible daughter more lies. But know this, whatever your plot, it ends now. As high priestess and protector of Sankofa, I'll see you and your granddaughter dead."

Sharon raised her hands and opened her mouth to cast a spell. But Katherine was quicker, her forcefield in place before the other witch spoke the first word of her spell.

She laughed. "As I said, you're an unnatural water witch. Too slow. Too inexperienced. And no match for me in a one-on-one battle. Not get the hell out of my office before I kill you here."

The vile woman went, back straight, retreating eyes threatening. If she could, Katherine knew Sharon would see her dead first, which meant she had to deal with Mami Wata's puppet as soon as possible.

She picked up her desk phone. Katherine knew who to call. The man was a bastard and all wrong for Anna and Greg, but he'd get the job done, quickly and quietly.

"What do you want?"

"Nice to speak to you too, Paul. I find myself in need of your particular services."

The lion shifter growled, and Katherine smiled. Paul Chambers would never be the Council's next alpha. That had been the reason he'd seduced her naïve daughter. Most days, she had no use for the loathsome were-cat. Today, however, Katherine had no problem using Paul's power-lust to get the were-cat to do her bidding.

Katherine glanced out her window again. Christie Walker was gone. But she'd see the little water witch again. Her threat against the child's life hadn't been an idle one. Now that Katherine knew the identity of the water witch of legend, she couldn't allow the girl to live, no matter how cold she became at the thought of killing a child.

Sanaura slept on her father's jaguar, which was curled next to the Tree of Ma'at, the leaves providing protection from the heat of the sun.

Safe.

Katherine Spencer would make sure Sanura stayed that way.

The morning sun cast a beam of glowing light through the east window, across the tranquil room and onto Sanura, who stirred, feeling Assefa's tepid breath on her neck and a strong arm draped across her midsection. She smiled, happier than she'd been in weeks. There were days while Assefa was away that Sanura feared they would never be like this again. She sometimes wondered if she should pack her things and move back in with Makena. For all intents and purposes, Assefa had broken up with her.

Yet she'd remained in his home, convinced they could work out whatever it was that plagued Assefa's mind and heart and made him think they could no longer be together. If Sanura thought Assefa truly wanted to end their relationship, she would've moved out. No matter how much she loved him, though, Sanura had been prepared to let Assefa go. She wouldn't hold onto a man who wanted to be free of her, regardless of his reason.

And he had a damn good reason. Assefa had been born as an animal. That truth, combined with the knowledge of his mother's rejection, had served to confirm what Assefa feared about himself his entire life. That he was more animal than man, more beast than human, more violent than kind, none of which were true.

Sanura didn't relish the idea of giving birth to an animal. It just wasn't done, no matter that taxonomists categorized humans as animals. But chimps didn't give birth to humans or vice versa. Apparently, some witches could give birth to a Mngwa cub.

The thought was a lot to wrap her mind around. She didn't think what happened to Assefa's mother would happen to her. Now that she knew of the possibility and potential risk, Sanura would make sure Makena and Wasola were with her when she gave birth. She would also have a long conversation with Jahi and, depending on the depth of the mindwipe, speak with the doctor and nurses who tended to Assefa and his mother.

Sanura believed, once Assefa laid aside his fears and thought about this rationally, he would see the issue wasn't an insurmountable one.

Assefa's hand twitched on her stomach, stilling Sanura's thoughts. He often moved in his sleep, caressing whatever part of her that happened to be in contact with his hand. This time it was her stomach, and Assefa began to trace circles on Sanura's taut belly. She could feel every sensation through her silk nightgown.

And it felt so good, his sleeping, hard form pressed against her back. Gods, had it only been six weeks since they last shared a bed since Sanura had him between her thighs and inside of her? Surely it must be longer because her body strummed with need from each of Assefa's unintentional touches.

She tried to ignore her building arousal, tried to drift back to sleep. But Sanura couldn't, not with Assefa's hand skating from arm to hip and then up to her breast.

Caressing.

Not unintentional touches then.

A kiss to her bare shoulder. A lick. A suck.

A hand wandered lower, inching up her nightgown and finding nothing but naked, hot skin underneath, Sanura foregoing panties after her shower.

He explored, rubbed, massaged.

Gods, she'd missed this, the way Assefa made her feel, sexy and desired and not at all self-conscious about her needs and wants.

His hand moved forward, over hip, and the heel rubbed. Up and down, up and down. He knew just what to do, how to build her arousal by stimulating the area so near to where she wanted him the most.

Needed him the most.

She shifted, and so did Assefa, bringing his magnificent erection flush against her bare ass.

Sanura moaned because she couldn't hold it in any longer.

Long, thick fingers slid down, exploring but not entering.

She bit her lip, wanting him to make her come already because she was so desperate for the release, but for him to also take his time, so she could savor this moment between them.

Two fingers slid inside, an easy entry, Sanura so damn wet and ready for him.

"I'm sorry."

Deep, sleepy, accented voice.

"I know."

"Do you forgive me?"

The question was followed by a third digit and exquisite thrusting of fingers and hips.

She moved against those big fingers of his, rocking forward, and then backward into his erection.

"Do you forgive me? Will you take me back?"

Assefa's fingers were in her as far as they could go, and the only barrier to him penetrating her anus were his boxers. If that didn't scream forgiveness, Sanura didn't know what would.

She understood, though. His mother had rejected him. His siblings had lost a parent and his father a mate, all because of one woman's inability to see past her own bullshit. And it all, in Assefa's mind, stemmed from him being born as a Mngwa instead of as a baby.

Now Sanura knew the truth. But the truth wasn't ugly, the way Assefa thought of it as. It was just another fact of life they would have to deal with as best they could.

Sanura couldn't speak, could barely think with his fingers driving in and out of her. Assefa's pace increased the louder she moaned and the harder she rocked her hips against him.

In one quick and unexpected move, Assefa shifted onto his back and lifted Sanura on top of him, her back to his chest and her head on his shoulder. Sanura's legs were open wide, straddling his legs, and the bottom of her feet were flat against the mattress.

His fingers were still inside of her. His other hand had come up to stroke her clit, and Assefa was kissing every part of her face he could reach.

"Tell me. Say it."

When she only moaned, and spread her legs wider, Assefa doubled his efforts, using his natural speed to flick her clit with his thumb, a human clitoral stimulator with no recharging required.

"Gods, Assefa."

Legs trembled, breath hitched, and hands found sheets and twisted.

"Not those words. You know what I want to hear. Tell me."

She did know. But it wasn't that she'd forgiven him or even that she would take him back. Both were a forgone conclusion when she'd invited Assefa into her bed last night and sang to him.

No, the arrogant man thought to use sex to convince Sanura to give him her promise ring back.

She would, but not today. Today, Sanura had something better planned for Assefa's birthday.

"Don't stop. Yes, there."

Going even faster, his fingers worked Sanura. Slick and determined, Assefa's strong digits wrenched everything from her as he thrust his hard dick between the cheeks of her ass.

When in the hell did he pull his boxers down to free that glorious penis of his? It didn't matter because it all had the combined effect of sending Sanura to another dimension.

She writhed and moaned and saw gold-flecked stars each time he pinched her clit. The pain-pleasure was body wracking and mind whirling. Her orgasm overtook her, Assefa relentless, thorough, and utterly wicked in his single-minded pursuit of her pleasure and submission.

Oh, gods. Damn.

"Say it."

"You can have the promise ring back." Low. Breathy.

"Good."

He flipped them over, Sanura on her back, Assefa over top of her.

Then he wasn't. He pulled her to the edge of the bed, and he went to the floor, on his knees, her legs over his shoulders.

Oh, gods.

He dove in, all lips and tongue and strong hands holding her legs wide open for him.

She swore the likes she'd never before when they made love. Then again, Assefa had never been this feral and aggressive in their oral play. Never used the tongue of his Mngwa as long and as deep as he did now, the shift of that one body part an easy transition for the were-cat.

And—*yes, yes, yes*—it was so deep, so wide, and—*fuck, yes*— ribbed for maximum oral pleasure.

Sex magic. Damn, Assefa was using sex magic, which meant two things. He'd torn down the wall he'd erected between them, and their partial mate bond was as solid as it had been before Sanura left the Sudan.

Bringing her down from her orgasmic high, Assefa kissed her thighs. Her knees. Her calves. Her toes.

Now was the time. She'd wanted to do this differently. Wanted to set the mood and tell him how much she loved and appreciated the man and the were-cat. Wanted to apologize for taking so long to get to this point.

Yet, with Assefa between her legs, mouth wet from their shared pleasure, and eyes full of trust and love, Sanura knew the time was now.

No candles or magic circle were required. Just them. Only ever them.

After taking off her nightgown and tossing it onto the floor, she moved to the center of the bed and Assefa followed, gloriously naked and stunningly dark. Muscles defined the topography of his spectacular body, breathtaking and sensual.

Large arms and legs caged her in, Assefa's remarkable form and posture predatory.

Her body went taut with desire, Sanura no longer surprised by the effect this male had on her. Or how turned on she became when Assefa did, in fact, exude more of his animalistic side.

"What's my other present?" He eyed the necklace around her neck. His husky, carnal voice had her nipples pebbling. "It isn't the promise ring, so tell me what it is."

As if doing a push-up, Assefa lowered himself and took one of Sanura's nipples into his mouth and sucked with such sweet intensity her back arched clear off the bed.

"Y-you know what it is."

Assefa pushed himself back up. "I'm afraid to hope."

Down again, her other nipple in his mouth, sucking loudly.

If he kept this up, she wouldn't be able to speak, much less give him his gift, which should come before any more intimacy.

Back up. His eyes were beginning to show the slightest shimmer of gold.

She touched his cheek, soft yet rugged under her hand. "The night of my birthday, I made you a promise. I told you I would fight for you, even if that meant fighting myself. I meant it then, and I haven't changed my mind. The pledge I made to you gave me the kick in the butt I needed to work on truly accepting my father's death."

"You gave Sam's jaguar spirit away."

"I didn't need it. I never needed it. I only thought I did. What I need, what I want is right here." Her other hand pressed to the area of his chest where his heart beat. "I've known since before we left for the Sudan what I wanted to give you for your birthday."

Down, his probing lips on her neck, kissing and licking.

Back up, his eyes less brown, more gold.

"I'm ready for you to claim me as your mate. In magic and in body."

Assefa's eyes went full-blown gold. And those exotic golden orbs of his stared down at Sanura with so much love, fear, and relief it made her want to weep.

"Are you sure?" His voice trembled, but his arms were steady, strong in how long he could hold his two-hundred-pound body over her. "After what I told you about my birth and my mother, I need for you to be sure. Because once we take this step, there's no going back for either of us. I'm yours and your mine."

She laughed, tilted her head, and kissed him. "Foolish, man, we've belonged to each other since the day we met."

"Because of the prophecy?"

"No, because it's our destiny to be together. Even the gods can't manufacture feelings."

"How do you know?"

"I just do. They can set us on a path, even manipulate the paths before us. But, in the end, we decide, we choose whom to love."

Down, a kiss to her lips, long and soft and so wonderful she wrapped her arms around his neck and deepened it.

Up, smiling, lips plump and so very carnal in all the ways they could give her pleasure.

"I can recite the final handfasting prayer for the bond. Would you like for me to bless our union?"

"I would like that very much."

Hungry eyes cast over her body, examining Sanura in a way Assefa hadn't done before.

The first two times Assefa had attempted to claim Sanura with his bite, he'd focused on her neck. This time, however, Assefa seemed to realize he had her entire body from which to choose.

She stayed still and quiet, giving him all the time he needed to make his decision. The neck was a common spot for a were-cat to bite his witch, but far from the only part of her he desired to sink his claiming fangs into.

Closing her eyes, Sanura reached for and found the cage she kept her fire spirit locked in. The bird perched on the limb of a huge, deciduous tree, eyes as red as the feathers of her body. They watched each other, Sanura's hand on the door of her fire spirit's cell.

Without hesitation, she destroyed the prison. Magic exploded around the fire spirit when the cage dissolved into the metaphysical plane of Sanura's mind.

"Will he join me now?"

"Yes, your Mngwa will come."

The bird lowered herself to the ground.

"Will you return? Can we be friends?"

Friends? Sanura would like that. She also needed to know what Sàngó had done to her fire spirit and why it was so difficult for them to find a balance.

"Yes, I'll return, and we'll talk. And I would be honored to be your friend."

Her fire spirit lowered her head, and Sanura petted her warm, soft feathery top. And saw, for the first time, the white feather she'd never known existed until Wasola told her.

Yes, Sanura would return. For now, she needed to finish the mate bond.

It was time the woman and the spirit, as one, accepted their mate. Sanura began the ritual language.

"Keep him safe, Fire Phoenix. He is, and forever will be, ours to love and to protect."

"He is our wind."

"Forceful and soothing."

"He is our earth."

"Spectacular and inspirational."

"He is our water."

"Dangerous and reflective."

"And he is our fire."

"Radiant and deadly."

Sanura's hand found the white feather on her fire spirit and touched it. It felt like all the other feathers, but Sanura knew it wasn't. Intuitively, she knew her hand had to be in contact with the feather while she recited the final words of the handfasting ritual.

"We accept his bond, his claiming bite. His heart, his soul, and his magic. We accept all of him. And give him all of us in return."

"Yes, my fire witch. We accept him, our divine mate."

Sanura wrapped her arms around the neck of her fire spirit, the bird smelling of gardenias, fire, and love. *"My heart to your spirit. My soul to your magic. My faith to our bond. Let us make peace, Fire Phoenix. Let us become one, with each other, with our mate."*

She closed her eyes as an eclipse of red wings lifted and covered Sanura, pulling her into the bird's chest, into which she disappeared.

Merged.

Sanura opened her eyes and then slammed them shut when toe curling magic surged up her thigh and straight to her pulsing sex.

Damn, she couldn't breathe. That wasn't true. Sanura knew she breathed because she heard herself screaming from an orgasm that had come out of nowhere. From an orgasm that had her keening for more. An orgasm so powerful it unleashed her fire magic, which sent another wave of carnal bliss through her enflamed body.

Assefa's tongue soothed the bite to her inner thigh, right before he bit her again, twin puncture wounds breaking skin and shredding the last of Sanura's self-control.

She was on fire. Everything inside of her burned with the sensual satisfaction of closing the circle of their bond. It felt like nothing she could've ever imagined.

Beyond physical decadence, spiritual gratification and mental satisfaction.

Beyond all of that was Assefa Berber, the man, and his claiming bite that had wrecked her.

CHAPTER THIRTY-THREE

The Mngwa spotted the tree before he did the flaming bird perched atop it. The tree went way up, reaching high into the cloudless sky. Jumping onto the lowest branch of the tree, which wasn't low at all, the Mngwa began to climb.

Halfway up, he glanced down and saw nothing but white sand for miles. Beautiful, but not as lovely as the fire spirit waiting for him.

He continued to climb, making slow but steady progress. She'd done this deliberately, a Fire Phoenix on her chosen throne of thick branches and a seemingly endless path to her nest.

The Mngwa was up for the challenge. Not that she'd made it particularly difficult for him. The cat of legend and trees were old friends. He could scale most any if the tree could hold his weight, which this one most certainly could.

Leaping from one branch to the next, he relished the small test of exertion, of the faith the spirit had in his skill and fortitude.

He craned his head upward, a playful growl forming when he glimpsed his prize, his mate.

She didn't stir as he crouched low and leaped over three branches to reach the one directly below hers. Long, sharp talons gripped the branch under the Fire Phoenix and wings as breathtaking as a red sunrise lifted into the air.

The Mngwa jumped onto the Fire Phoenix's abandoned branch as she flew, wingspan expansive and impressive. In the air, as on her branch, the spirit made no sound. Her flight pattern didn't take her far from the Mngwa, who looked on with awe and satisfaction.

The flight dance of the Fire Phoenix, the acceptance of his claiming while she displayed the might that had the cat climbing her towering tree to reach her heart.

Dipping low, the crimson bird pivoted and then shot straight upward, her head high, and wings at her side, riding the whistling winds of her heated magic home.

When she barreled downward, red eyes on him, the Mngwa knew she meant for them to play.

Good. He liked to play with a formidable partner.

"How fast are you, cat?" She taunted as the Mngwa began his descent, much faster than the climb to her forgotten perch.

"Fast enough, bird."

With a hard thud, the Mngwa landed on the sand. And took off in the direction of where his mate had flown.

His mate. Yes. Finally.

She swopped down, gliding her wings over his black-and-gray fur, then retreating to the safety of the air.

She did it again.

And again.

The Mngwa ran, full out, enjoying every minute of the game, of the dance of mated spirits.

"So slow, my mate. How will you ever catch me?"

"I already have."

The Fire Phoenix made another pass, low, as she'd done before, her right wing prepared to swipe the Mngwa on his muzzle as she glided by and back up and out of reach.

A second before she reached his muzzle, the cat sidestepped the teasing gesture and pounced when she lost her focus.

Down she went on her face and chest, sand all over her.

So was the Mngwa. His big body crouched overtop of her, the Fire Phoenix's back to him.

He licked her. Her head. Her feathers. Then plopped down beside his mate, spent and gloriously happy.

"You're beautiful."

She nudged him with her beak. *"So are you."*

"And fast."

She laughed. *"I'm a big, red bird of lore, I'm supposed to be fast."*

"True, but not faster than the cat of legend."

"Says you."

The Mngwa nuzzled the neck of his fire spirit, who watched him with the same fatigue and joy he felt. *"Yes, says me."* He pushed up on his legs. *"Now, let's go home."*

The Fire Phoenix also rose but didn't take to the air. Well, until she did with a, *"The first one home wins."*

Win? Win what?

It didn't matter because the damn bird was already heading back to their tree.

The Mngwa took off, his heart full, his paws swift and his soul complete.

How many times had he bitten his witch? Five? Seven? Assefa didn't know. What he did know was that he couldn't stop. Not once the combination of Sanura's blood and magic touched his fangs and then his tongue. Not when Sanura felt so warm and soft and inviting, her melodic cries of delight encouraging as hell.

Assefa bit her. And she came.

Then he bit her a second time. And she came again.

So he bit her a third time, blissed out of his mind on her blood and magic and the final merging of their hearts and souls.

When she screamed his name, he couldn't take it anymore. Assefa made his way up Sanura's body, nipping and licking every part of her, including each breast. Where he, once again, claimed her with his shallow fangs.

She smelled of sex and heat and desire, which had Assefa sinking his teeth in her neck and his dick into her waiting sex.

He stopped, closed his eyes, and reminded himself to breathe. Damn, how could being inside his witch feel better than every other time they'd made love? How could Sanura feel both familiar and new?

"Gods, Assefa, you feel so good but I need you to move, baby."

Yes, he needed to move, needed to slake his hunger on the bounty that was his witch. No, she was now his claimed mate.

In unison, they moved. Each other. The sheets. The bed.

Together, they moaned and screamed and sweated.

As one, they came, over and again, kissing and straining and never wanting to stop. So they didn't. Sanura and Assefa kept going, reaffirming their love and consummating their union.

They ignored the ringing of their cell phones, the knocks on the door and even the bangs on the wall from other hotel guests.

Loud, yes, Assefa knew they were loud, and he couldn't give a damn. He'd been patient, and his fear and pride had almost cost him the woman he loved. So, no, Assefa wouldn't be quiet, wouldn't stop making love to his mate until they were hoarse, boneless and thoroughly spent.

Hours later, they relaxed in Sanura's sunken tub, bubbles everywhere. About an hour ago, their growling stomachs had won out over other demands of the body. Now, having gorged themselves on practically everything on the room service menu, Sanura fed Assefa chocolate-covered strawberries from her mouth.

They tasted good, but not as delicious as Sanura, who straddled his hips, Assefa deep inside of her.

She kissed him as she rode him, water splashing up and over the tub.

Hands dug into hips, hard enough to leave bruises to match the love bites that decorated the landscape of Sanura's gorgeous, heaving body.

Assefa finally understood. He'd been lost, but not anymore. He wasn't her shield or even her safeguard, but Sanura's equal, her partner. She was his neter, his goddess, not to worship or even to serve, but to bring harmony and balance to her soul. Rashad had been correct when he referred to Sanura as a goddess, although Assefa didn't think the young man meant it in a literal sense.

"Sex with you shouldn't be this good."

He couldn't help it, Assefa laughed. "Is that a complaint, sweetheart?"

Sanura opened eyes blown fire-engine red and smiled down at him. "You know it wasn't."

He touched her belly, gliding his hand over the tattoo that never disappeared, the Mngwa guarding the child Assefa while he slept. Sanura's hands were already gripping his arms, the image of her Fire Phoenix emblazoned across his right arm.

"Our mate marks didn't change. How is that possible?"

She kissed him, and her gyrating hips had him moving against her, thoughts of mate marks and neter gods forgotten.

By the time they finished, there was more water out of the tub than in it. Thankfully, a fire spell was all it took to evaporate the water.

They sat in the living room of the suite at the circular wooden table, eating dinner and wearing nothing but bathrobes. Sanura had already eaten her body weight in vegetables, fish, and bread.

"Are you ready to go home?" he asked her.

Sanura pointed to the cell phone in his hand. "I assumed the text message from Zareb was about another one of Mami Wata's water creatures."

It was. A Grootslaang was terrorizing locals in Richtersveld, South Africa. Like the Ninki Nanka, the humongous snake shouldn't exist outside of a horror movie, which the prophecy was to full-humans and preternaturals.

"It's another diversion. Like all the other sightings, I think. Mami Wata has kept me and the division flying from one country and continent to another, chasing after her beasts."

"But we can't let them keep killing."

"I know, that's why we have to stop being baited and think."

"Think about what?"

"The identity of the water witch of legend. We need to find her."

Taking a long drink of cold water, Sanura placed the glass onto the table, her eyes no longer on his.

"What's wrong?"

"Nothing. I thought you wanted me to help you find a way to kill Mami Wata."

"I still do. But that doesn't mean we don't also need to put an end to her water witch servant."

"What if she's like me, Assefa? What if she isn't evil or bad but is forced to fight because she has no choice?"

"Then she'll tell me that when I find her. Trust me, Sanura, I will find the woman. And if she's as dangerous as her goddess, I'll end her to protect you and everyone else."

"I know you will, Special Agent Berber."

Assefa didn't know how to take her tone of voice or eyes that seemed far away.

"Secrets already, sweetheart? We've only been mated for a few hours."

He'd meant it as a joke, and Sanura did smile at him, if weakly.

"Not secrets, just thoughts I haven't worked out in my mind yet. A lot happened while you were away. I can tell you now or on the flight home."

Stretching, Sanura got to her feet.

"You bought a piano, didn't you?"

"Yup, a really cheap one for your outrageously expensive living room."

She wouldn't have dared. But the way Sanura sashayed from the living room and into the bedroom, she just may have.

He followed.

"How cheap?" He removed the hotel robe and joined Sanura in bed, her head going to his shoulder as soon as he settled beside her. "How cheap, Sanura?"

She covered her mouth and yawned. "I guess you'll have to see when you get home."

"Is this what I have to put up with now that we're full mates?"

"Pretty much."

"Okay, I can deal with that."

"You're smiling, aren't you? Elusive dimple and all?"

"Maybe." He was. Assefa damn sure was.

"By the way, I've been meaning to ask you something. I probably should've mentioned it before letting you bite me all the hell up."

"You loved it."

"Not the point. Anyway, why did you send my mother that picture?"

"What picture?"

"I had to get a new phone after the fight with the Leucrotas in your father's dining room. The phone was smashed to pieces. During dinner, Mom forwarded me the picture you sent her, saying something about you sending it to her by mistake."

"I didn't send your mother a picture."

At least Assefa didn't remember texting Makena. Wait.

Assefa shot up in bed. Shit.

"Remember now, Kinky Agent Berber? You sent my mother a dick pic. How you managed that, I'll never know. M and S. They aren't even close."

They were, and Assefa could never face Makena again.

"Wait, don't tell me."

He nodded. "You're in my contact's list as Mate and not Sanura. I was rushing and..." Assefa slumped down, feeling queasy. He'd sent a picture of his dick to his mate's mother. Damn him.

Sanura began to laugh—loudly.

Of course, the woman would. She enjoyed times like these.

"It's not funny."

"It's hilarious, and you should see yourself. So embarrassed." Still laughing, Sanura climbed on top of him. "You're adorable when you're mortified." A kiss to his lips. "So very adorable, in fact, it makes me want to take a picture and send it to my mother."

Her mocking laughter had Sanura falling off Assefa and onto her back, her entire body shaking.

So, this would be his life with Sanura as his mate. A woman who found humor in his disgrace. A woman who didn't let Assefa Berber, second son to the House of Berber, special agent, and cat of legend, take himself too seriously.

He smiled. Yes, this was his mate, and Assefa loved every sexy, playful inch of her. But she needed a spanking.

Assefa pounced.

Sanura screamed.

And the bed broke.

CHAPTER THIRTY-FOUR

Alexandria, Virginia

"This isn't necessary."

"Yes, it is. I want to see."

Tired from their long flight and wet from the incessant downpour that was their homecoming, Sanura wanted to go to her bedroom, strip out of her soaked clothes and soggy shoes and slip under the spray of a hot shower. But, no, instead she was being dragged behind a determined Assefa.

Her fault. She shouldn't have mentioned the piano. Knowing Assefa, it would've taken him days before he ventured into the living room and noticed the addition.

Sanura followed Assefa into the living room, a spacious area they rarely used except when they entertained. She stayed by the door while Assefa marched right up to Sanura's first material contribution to their home.

Preservation, protection and performance, she had to take all three into consideration when Sanura considered where to have the delivery men place her piano. Not near a window, direct sunlight, or a vent, any of those choices would diminish the condition and performance of the instrument.

She'd had the men, under the watchful eye of Mr. Siddig, her self-appointed bodyguard in Assefa's absence, to place the straight edge of the piano against the left inner wall. Its position would allow Sanura to look into the room while she played.

"It's exquisite." Assefa ran an admiring hand over the French Provincial Cherry finish. "A compact grand piano. What are the specs?"

She told him.

"Five music desk positions, nice. This isn't a cheap piano."

The piano cost more than the car she drove. Well, not the Jag Jahi had bought Sanura but her very nice yet reasonably priced mid-size car.

"Another birthday gift?"

"I bought it for me." Sanura joined Assefa next to her piano. "But, yes, it could also be considered a gift for you. I'll play, you'll listen and then give me a standing ovation while throwing roses at my feet."

"Roses, huh?"

"Yes, lots of them." She smiled.

"Play something."

"Now?"

"Why not now? I'm home. We're alone in the house, which is rare. Zareb's in the guest house, probably dead to the world so now is perfect."

"We're drenched. And I'm tired. I want a hot shower, dry clothes, a soft bed, and a nap. In that order."

"Is that all you want?" Assefa toed out of his dress shoes. Next came his shirt, pants, and socks. "Get undressed then play me a song. Are there any you know by heart? *Midnight Sonata*? *Rhapsody in Blue*? Although something by Duke Ellington or Catalina Berroa would be even better. Berroa was Trinidadian, like Sam, so you're probably familiar with her music. Or do you require sheet music?"

Who knew Special Agent Assefa Berber, when happy and excited, could babble?

When Sanura only gaped at him, Assefa began to remove her sodden clothes. Before she knew it, Sanura stood in the living room in only her panties and bra.

"I don't have any roses, so I'll have to toss something else at your feet." Large hands circled her waist and pulled Sanura against Assefa's damp, hard chest. "All I have are my boxers. Will they do, mate?"

"Umm—"

Sultry lips pressed to hers, a shower of slow, feather-light kisses, Assefa's tongue a shadow of temptation peeking out and playing.

Sanura opened her mouth, offering unrestricted access and Assefa accepted her invitation. A slow slide into her mouth, his tongue above hers, then around it when she reciprocated with blossoming interest.

Hmmm, Assefa knew how to kiss. Not too deep or too fast to begin, but slow and playful to start. Then faster, deeper and with more pressure, his hands caressing her hips, her back, her shoulders, her nape.

And then her face cradled so lovingly between his strong hands. Gods, what were they talking about? Roses and boxers?

No, her playing him a song on her piano, which she did. Well, sort of. They both sat at the bench, naked, and Sanura on Assefa's lap, her back to his chest and her front to the piano keys.

Music wafted through the living room but not from the grand piano.

If they kept this up, when Mami Wata's water creatures came for them, they'd be too exhausted to fight. But it was so difficult to think of that when Assefa touched her, needing to be close and revel in their new mate bond.

Sanura wanted it too, the physical expression of their love, the renewal of their faith in themselves and each other, and the agreement to not allow fear to come between them ever again.

By the time they'd finished, Assefa and Sanura were sprawled on the floor of their bedroom, not quite having made it to the bed before Assefa reached for Sanura again. Yet, she'd been the one to stop Assefa on the steps, pressing him against the wall and wrapping legs and arms around her strong special agent.

He'd come fast that time, but not so quickly that he hadn't made sure Sanura climaxed first.

"We smell like sex." Assefa rolled onto his stomach and stared down at Sanura, a self-satisfied grin on his face. "And us. I like our scent."

"Which tells me we need to shower and that we're officially sex addicts. I've lost count of how many times we've made love since you bit me."

A nip to her jaw and then a chaste kiss to her lips. "Don't think I've forgotten about my ring. I want it back." A kiss to the neck around which hung the gold necklace with her promise ring.

"I'm your mate now. I've fulfilled my promise," she teased him, then got to her feet. "I need a shower. You may like the smell of sex, but I don't."

He hopped up. "I'll join you."

"We'll just have sex again if you do."

"That's kind of the point of taking a shower together." He smacked her bare bottom. "While we're in there, you can return my ring. I'm serious, Sanura, I want it back."

She would return her gift. She'd meant to do just that before they checked out of the hotel in Kinshasa. But time had gotten away from them, and she'd forgotten. Then they were in a cab headed for the airport, praying flights wouldn't be cancelled due to inclement weather.

Now, she enjoyed the game they'd turned Assefa's request into. He didn't need to ask, yet he did. And she didn't have to keep putting it off, although she did.

He was home, after six weeks of being away, so Assefa was overdue for a bit of fire witch teasing.

Sanura was in the master bathroom when she heard Assefa yell, "Dammit, Sanura, there's a huge burn and blood circle on my side of our bed. And it smells like salt over here."

She peeked her head out of the bathroom. "I told you about Shanumi on the plane."

"You said you set the witch on fire so her soul would be free. You didn't say anything about setting the fire in our bedroom and on my side of the bed." Big arms came up to cross over an impressive chest. "You chose this spot purposefully. To get back at me."

"I told you I was mad at you. Did you think I was satisfied with empty threats over the phone?"

"This is not a healthy expression of your anger. Should I check the closet to make sure you haven't taken a fireball to my clothes?"

"I wouldn't do that. You're being ridiculous."

"I'm not being ridiculous, and this is vandalism. Malicious mischief is punishable under law, a fine or jail time. You need to make restitution."

She huffed. "To you?"

"Yes, to me. This entire part of the floor will have to be replaced, which you could've done while I was away."

He moved closer to Sanura, no real anger or heat in any of his words. She was sure by "restitution" Assefa meant sex.

"You didn't because you wanted me to see and know how deeply I hurt you."

"I was feeling petty that night. And tired of being haunted by my great, many times over, grandmother. I just wanted everything to stop, my fatigue, my heartache, the temptation to bring you to me in a lightning bolt. I didn't want to do that. I didn't want to transport you here against your will."

Assefa's hands clasped around hers. "You wanted me to come home when I was ready to be here with you, without fear, insecurities, or secrets between us."

"Yes, but I shouldn't have left that mess for you to find. It was always my intention to ask Manute to make the repairs."

"It's all right, sweetheart. I'm sorry."

"So am I." Sanura hugged him, feeling drained. "Tell me everything will be okay. Tell me we'll survive this. That you won't die and I won't turn out like Shanumi."

Assefa's embrace tightened, his hold and body strong and secure, rooting Sanura to him and the bond they shared.

"I won't let you fall, Sanura. And you'll take care of my soul and cat spirit, no matter what happens to my body."

"Don't say that." Tears formed, and she shivered from the false promise he wouldn't make and the very real likelihood that Assefa, like Abubaker, would die at Mami Wata's merciless hands.

If the goddess took him from her, Assefa wouldn't be there to keep Sanura from falling into a fiery abyss of blood and vengeance. She could already taste the wrath that would boil inside of her, nauseating and rotten.

Removing the gold necklace from her neck, Sanura placed it around Assefa's.

"May it protect you when I cannot. May it give you strength when I cannot." The necklace glowed red with each word of her spell, heated against Assefa's chest but not burning. "May it bring you to me when I cannot. I am your witch, and you are my familiar. You are bound to me as I am bound to you. This is my prayer, my sworn vow. No one will part us. Not in life. And never in death."

Thunder crackled, lightning raged and rain doused all, unforgiving and unrelenting.

Assefa pressed the button on the remote and turned on the television. Sitting up in bed, Sanura snuggled at his side, more asleep than awake. Assefa didn't have to hit but two buttons to find the station he sought. The National Doppler Map covered the entire screen, highlighting current precipitation in the United States, a color-coded scheme that represented light to heavy rain.

From there, various world satellites appeared, Caribbean, Africa, Europe, South America. Yellow, orange, and red were everywhere, moderate, heavy, and very heavy rain soaked the national and international landscape. No landmass or ocean was spared, the deluge of rainfall too much and unnatural.

"I wonder if this is what happened during Shanumi and Abubaker's time." Sanura pushed to a seated position and tucked a wet strand of hair behind her ear. "It hasn't let up in hours. In some places, days. It seems as if the water goddess intends to overflow her oceans and drown the world. I can't defend against that level of water, Assefa."

"I don't think you have to. It's all a show, I think."

"I don't get it. I've never understood what the gods gained from the battle between fire and water. Why make witches fight? And why allow Mami Wata and Oya to continue their feud when the destruction is so horrendous to full-humans and preternaturals?"

Assefa had wondered the same but never came up with answers that satisfied. Watching the news coverage, however, watery images playing across the screen, his mind began to formulate plausible but wild theories.

He hit a couple of buttons on the remote, which allowed him to split the television screen into a four-block grid. In each grid was a different news station and location, New York, Paris, London, Tokyo. The locales may have varied, but the images were eerily similar, hammering rain, slithering snakes, and attacking sharks and barracudas. Any water creature that could come on land did so in frighteningly large numbers—toads and frogs, salamanders and newts, and caecilians. Then there were the crocodiles—twenty-three crocodilian species in over ninety countries, including islands like Cuba and Madagascar.

"Gods, Assefa. It's worse than I thought. Why are the gods doing this?"

In silence, they watched the same type of scene play out the world over, with news reporters, meteorologists, and political leaders groping for an explanation.

Through it all, the religious leaders were the ones who had the most to say.

"End of the world."

"It's a sign from God."

"God is cleansing the earth of evil."

"All is the will of Allah."

"It's karma."

The scenes shifted, reports coming in from every corner of the world. The same sentiments were echoed from the streets of Miami to the halls of the Vatican to the shantytowns of Mumbai. Report after report showed mosques, churches, synagogues, and temples filled with people, overflowing with worshippers and mourners alike.

As he watched, Assefa discarded one theory after another until only one remained.

"This is what they want." He pointed to the flat-screen television mounted on the wall above the entertainment center. "In people's darkest hour they turn to faith, to religion, to spirituality, even the most ardent of disbelievers."

"When Shanumi blessed me, she told me I possessed a power stronger than the gods. I didn't understand what she meant. But now, seeing so many scared and desperate people searching for answers, I think I get it." Sanura turned away from the television and to Assefa.

"What do you think the fire witch meant?"

"We talked about it yesterday, but not in this context. Free will. We chose each other, although we were quite literally made for each other. But we decided to fall in love, Assefa, and to fight for our love. The gods played no role in that. I think the same is true with religion and faith. We have free will. I don't think the gods can deny that to us." She tucked a strand of hair behind her other ear, thinking. "Perhaps they can, but maybe it wouldn't mean as much to them."

In the same way Assefa's return home wouldn't have meant the same to him or Sanura if she'd used her magic to force him to her side when he wasn't ready to be there. Assefa mulled over her words, adding Sanura's perspective to that of his own.

"So, they manipulate us into seeking them out." That sounded too right and terribly wrong in all that the supposition implied about the gods. "Fear and faith. The prophecy is all about fear and faith. We fear death and the unknown, and many of us, preternaturals and full-humans, turn to faith when we have no answers or feel helpless. Gods fear, I don't know, Sanura. Being forgotten? Not being taken seriously or worshiped by enough people? And maybe that fear makes them question the faith they've placed in themselves and us. It's just a theory. I have no way of knowing if any of this is true."

"But it makes a scary, pathetic kind of sense. We've seen it in big and small ways. Mass shootings, terrorist attacks, people tend to do two things, pray or lash out in violence. Sometimes both."

"True. But that theory doesn't help us end the storms or stop Mami Wata and the water witch of legend." Speaking of the water witch of legend, Assefa reached over and grabbed his cell phone from his nightstand. "Anna sent me an email the other day. But I haven't had a chance to read it."

While he thumbed through his messages, Sanura scooted down the bed and under the covers. Assefa gave her five minutes before she'd be fast asleep. At least now with Shanumi gone, his mate could get a good night's sleep.

His mate. Assefa would never get tired of thinking of Sanura in that way. If they survived, he planned to also make her his wife.

Assefa read. The list wasn't long at fifteen names, none of them he recognized, which meant nothing. He hadn't known the women on Najja's and Wasola's list either. His sister and Sanura's grandmother were performing their own investigation into the water witches who met his criteria and would contact Assefa if they discovered the identity of the water witch of legend.

He didn't think they would, though. Something told Assefa the witch he sought was closer to home.

"Sweetheart, look at this list before you fall asleep."

Grumbling, Sanura took the phone from his hand. "What am I looking at?"

"Do you know the women on the list?"

"They're all Sankofa water witches." A yawn had Sanura returning his phone and turning onto her side. "You've met most of them. A few were at my birthday party. Others attended the Oshun ceremony. And one you know well."

Assefa reread the list. He still didn't recognize a single name.

"Who do I know well?"

Sanura yawned again but didn't answer.

He shook her shoulder. "Who do I know well?"

"Christine. Now let me go to sleep, Assefa. I'm so tired."

Although he wanted to, Assefa didn't disturb Sanura again. He also couldn't fall sleep. He slipped out of bed, dressed, and went to see Zareb. He needed to find out who in the hell Christine Walker was because as far as Assefa knew, he'd never met anyone by that name.

Assefa knocked on the door of the guest house and waited for Zareb to answer.

A half-hour later, hot tea in hand, Assefa listened to Zareb read Christine Walker's obituary.

"Christine Walker, age forty-two, passed away on April seventeenth in Baltimore, Maryland. Funeral services will be held at Sankofa Preparatory School's Anubis Temple.

Christine Walker was born in Phoenix, Arizona to Daniel and Sharon Hays. She is predeceased by her father, Daniel Hays, and her husband, Andre Walker. She is survived by her daughter, Christine..."

Assefa sipped his coffee while Zareb finished reading. They sat across from each other at Zareb's kitchen table, light from the computer and range hood all the illumination the were-cats required.

"Phoenix, really?" Zareb snorted. "A bit on the nose, don't you think?"

"I think Mami Wata likes toying with people's lives."

"Agree." Zareb typed. "Thanks to Walker's obit, we have two more names to search."

They did, Daniel and Sharon Hays. After another thirty minutes, Zareb found nothing useful on Daniel Hays, but he did on Sharon. It wasn't much, a couple of articles in the *Baltimore Sun* newspaper from nineteen years ago.

"According to the articles, Sharon Hays was killed during a burglary."

"Gunshot?"

"No, cut throat." Zareb lifted his eyes from the computer. "Her daughter and granddaughter shared the home with the victim. They were unharmed but…"

"But what?"

"The victim was killed in her bed."

"Meaning, she didn't stumble upon the burglar in the act. He found her. With three people in the house, the perp found Sharon Hays and murdered only her."

"He?"

"Yes, he. A were-cat. I know you were thinking the same thing. Let me guess, Christine and her daughter slept through the whole thing?"

"Yeah, but there's more. The girl and her mother were taken to the emergency room because they claimed they couldn't recall anything from the last forty-eight hours."

"Memory loss. So not just a were-cat but a witch powerful enough to cast a precise mindwipe spell."

"What do you think all of this means? And why, from a list of fifteen, are we focusing on one witch instead of researching them all?"

"We'll get to the others. But Sanura said I know Walker well, but I don't know a Christine Walker."

"Maybe you do. Since becoming alpha of the Council, you've met dozens of witches, some of them water witches. Unless the woman is Sanura, Assefa, you don't tend to remember them after they've left your presence."

"Fair enough. Still, I think there's something here, especially if we're right about Sharon Hays being killed by a were-cat. I admit it's a big leap based on the sketchy details from the articles. Mike was around back then. Maybe he remembers something that could help us."

Assefa glanced at the time on the stove. Midnight. The detective would still be awake. Grumpy but awake.

He called.

"Are you and Sanura roasting marshmallows and swapping horror stories? Why in the hell are you calling me about a cold case?"

"It was never solved?"

"No arrests. No suspects. No clues." A deep, heavy sigh. "The detectives on the case were stumped. They had no leads. For a while, they thought the daughter might have had something to do with it since there was no evidence of forced entry. But that went nowhere. Christine was sweet and beautiful and completely devastated by the murder of her mother."

"You sound like you knew her."

"Not at the time. Shit, Assefa, some people have the worst luck. Her husband left her, her mother was murdered by some phantom burglar, then she gets cancer and dies, leaving her kid with no family to take care of her."

"I thought Walker's husband was dead."

"I don't know where the asshole is. All I know is that Christine got a declaration of death in absentia. Makena helped her with the legal paperwork."

Assefa was missing something. Anna had placed an asterisk next to the names of the witches who were rejected by Katherine Spencer. There was an asterisk next to Christine C. Walker's name. What happened between the rejection of the child Christine's application to the private school by the high priestess and the older Christine's funeral at Sankofa years later?

"Makena knew Christine Walker?"

"Seriously, kid, why are you pestering me with twenty questions? Ask Sanura. She knows all of this. Probably not all the details of Sharon Hays's murder. She was just a skinny ten-year-old at the time. But she knew Christine, sat next to her daughter at the funeral. Sanura held her hand throughout. Funerals and weddings are the only times Sankofa opens its doors to other preternaturals and full-humans. It was a nice service. You know, for a funeral and all."

Assefa said nothing as Mike relayed details of Christine Walker's funeral and her distraught teenage daughter. The longer the man spoke, the harder Assefa's heart beat and the tighter his jaw clenched.

By the time the detective finished, Assefa wanted to put his fist through a wall. Mami Wata would pay for this. If it were the last thing he did, he would see the cruel water goddess dead.

Sanura was right. He did know Christine Walker. But it couldn't be true. Despite all the pieces, none of them amounted to her being the water witch of legend. He had no concrete evidence. All he had was his intuition, which he trusted.

"Thanks, Mike. I appreciate your help and apologize for calling so late."

"That's it? You're not going to tell me what's going on?"

No, the fewer people knew what he suspected, the better. He needed to speak with her, give the water witch an opportunity to explain.

"We'll talk later."

He ended the call before Mike could say more and didn't answer when the detective called right back.

Assefa met Zareb's eyes. They were cold and hard. He'd heard the entire conversation and was no more pleased by the potential revelation than Assefa.

"It's not her."

Assefa got to his feet. "We'll find out later today. Meet me at the garage at ten."

Zareb walked him to the door. "Are you going to tell Sanura?"

"Not until I know for sure. If I'm right, I'll have no choice."

"This is bullshit. There's no way it could be her. Not her, Assefa."

Umbrella up and doing little to protect Assefa from the wind and rain, he left Zareb standing in the doorway of his guest house, the special agent's blinders firmly in place.

Five minutes later, Assefa climbed into bed. Sanura didn't stir, not even when he spooned against her, breathing in her gardenia scent and holding her tightly.

He would see this through to the end, even if it meant putting a bullet between the lying eyes of Sanura's best friend, Christine C. Walker.

Dammit. Yes, he knew her well but, apparently, not well enough.

Christine Cynthia Garvey had better have a damn good explanation or Assefa would see her dead before she and Mami Wata had a chance to harm his mate.

CHAPTER THIRTY-FIVE

Assefa awoke the next morning to find Sanura's side of the bed empty. For a second, he thought himself in a hotel room on another case and his fire witch hundreds of miles away. Then he remembered the Ninki Nanka, his confession, their mate bond, and Cynthia Garvey.

Angry at a day that had hardly begun, Assefa dragged himself out of bed and to the bathroom for a shower and shave. He wasn't looking forward to this day. For a long time after returning to bed, Assefa watched Sanura sleep, relaxed and at peace.

Closing his eyes, Assefa stepped under the spray of hot water, letting the heat ease away some of the tension in his body. After today, Sanura might not know peace for a long time. Not if her mate was forced to kill her best friend.

Sanura and Cynthia were more like sisters than longtime friends. Sisters, just like Mami Wata and Oya. Assefa slammed his hand against the front shower wall, cracking tiles. Nothing he'd learned last night could be a coincidence. That many points of convergence didn't happen without a plan or purpose.

Lathering himself with body wash, an earthy sandalwood scent Sanura liked on him, Assefa recalled last summer's battle at the Potomac River. Assefa and Sanura, along with Zareb, Rachel, Cynthia and the Witch Council of Elders, had fought Mami Wata's snakes and funnels of attacking water. Through it all, Cynthia and Anna, the only water witches among them, went unharmed. No one believed, including Assefa, that either woman was in collusion with Mami Wata.

He still didn't think it of Anna. Did he of Cynthia? He did. Gods help him, Assefa did. Still, he could be wrong. He prayed that was the case. In the event it wasn't, though, Assefa secured his weapon in his holster and went in search of Sanura.

On a Sunday, he knew where to find his witch. Assefa stood in the doorway to the sitting room turned home office. Sure enough, Sanura sat at her desk, typing away. "I thought you said your school's closed due to the wind and rain."

Sanura swiveled in her chair, a warm smile her morning greeting. "It is. But my courses are online, and I haven't checked submissions or discussion forums since the day before I left for the Congo." An eyebrow arched as she took him in from head to toe. "Going somewhere, Special Agent Berber?"

He stepped inside the office and Sanura rose to meet him, her arms going around his neck and her lips to his. Mmm, he'd missed Sanura's morning kisses and full body hugs.

"I feel your gun and you're dressed for work." Leaning back, Sanura arched her other eyebrow. "Where are you going in this weather?"

The truth would ruin Sanura's day and break her heart. He didn't want to do either, but Assefa also had no intention of lying to her.

"Zareb and I are going to follow-up on a lead this morning. It shouldn't take but a few hours. I won't be all day if that's what you're worried about."

Her hands dropped from around him. "I'm not worried about that." Her withering look told him Sanura wasn't fooled by his vague response. "Try again."

"It's bureau business."

"Really, Assefa? That's what you're going with after I helped you with one of your cases?"

She had a point.

"The truth is that I don't want to tell you where I'm going and why."

"You can't protect me from everything."

"I recall telling you that you couldn't solve everyone's problem. But you still believe you can, although common sense should convince you of its impossibility. You may not be able to solve every problem, but you'll try all the same. I won't always be able to stand between you and harm but I'll give it my best, every day and without hesitation."

"Sometimes, Assefa, it's inconvenient to have an intelligent mate who also listens when I speak."

Despite the potential ugliness the day might bring, Assefa found himself grinning. They were true partners, mates in every way. They understood, respected, and trusted each other. As they grew as a mated pair, years of love and laughter between them, Assefa would remember this morning. He'd remember when Sanura kissed him on his cheek, returned to her chair and laptop, and said nothing more.

No anger or sadness. No manipulation or coyness. No tears or screams. Just a woman's silent acceptance and faith, which Assefa held close to his heart the entire drive from Alexandria to Baltimore.

"She's not the water witch of legend."

"So you've said for over an hour. Give it a break, Zareb. Do you think I want to be here anymore than you do?"

Thirty minutes ago, the rained had stopped, leaving behind soaked everything and gray skies.

Assefa parked his car and got out, slamming the door with a loud force that seemed to echo in the quiet neighborhood. Cars lined both sides of the one-way street and no one, except the two agents, were out.

"I know you don't. But Cynthia loves Sanura, she wouldn't hurt her. You saw the water witch in action that day at the river. She fought hard, just like the rest of us."

"I know."

"Then why are we here?" Zareb grabbed Assefa's arm, spinning him around to face the taller man when they stepped onto the Garvey's porch. "She isn't our enemy." Zareb's dark-brown eyes fell to the gun Assefa held in his right hand. "You don't need that. Cynthia's a good person, not one of Mami Wata's power-hungry minions."

How had Assefa not seen it before? Standing there, staring up at a pleading Zareb, the man's reaction to the water witch, these past few months, crystallized into a sad, unfortunate awareness. Zareb Osei, medja, special agent, and ladies' man was in love with Cynthia Garvey.

The big man probably didn't even recognize the emotion himself. But Assefa now saw, understood how love and lust could relieve a smart man of his good sense. Contradicting his friend would do nothing but start an argument.

Assefa gripped his gun tighter. "Tell me what you hear or smell from the house."

"What?"

"Your were-cat senses. Tell me what you detect coming from the house."

The three-level, red brick house was the third home on the east side of the street. The 1950s-home looked like every other house on the street with a small front porch surrounded by a wrought iron gate and matching mailbox drilled into the wall to the right of the front door. Four metal columns bolted into the cement porch with a simple S design held up the white wooden awning, off which rainwater still dripped.

He'd visited the Garvey's home several times with Sanura. Assefa thought of Eric and Cynthia as his friends and Gen as a niece. They were family, and he despised being there under these circumstances.

"I don't hear or smell anything, so what."

"Think about what you just said and that you're a damn were-cat, for Sekhmet's sake."

Assefa rang the doorbell.

"Okay, okay, shit. Yeah, I should sense something coming from the house but I don't. I guess you don't either."

He pushed the button again. "No, not since I stepped onto this porch. I hear everything behind and to the sides of me but nothing from in front." Opening the screen door, Assefa knocked, several times and hard.

Zareb turned back to the street. "Maybe they're out. I don't see Cynthia's car, but Eric's is parked in front of the house."

He'd noticed the same. They could be out together. But what was the probability that on a Sunday morning the Garveys would've piled into Cynthia's car in the pouring rain and taken a drive? Where would they have gone in such awful weather? Until a half-hour ago, the rain and wind howled and raged.

Assefa had passed few drivers on the road on their drive there. Mainly emergency crews and state troopers were out, Maryland's governor having requested people to stay inside while the danger passed.

He'd driven over countless snakes. Their slithering bodies were speedbumps on the beltway. Even now, he could hear them moving in the grass, consuming the abundance of frogs that littered the side street.

But no snakes or frogs had ventured onto the Garvey's property, which had Assefa's hackles rising.

He placed three unanswered calls to the Garvey's house phone before calling Cynthia's and Eric's cells.

"Anything?"

"No."

"Shit. Break and enter?"

Assefa already had his leg raised. With a hard kick to the left of the doorknob, the wooden door flew back, smashing into the wall. And Assefa heard none of it, but he did have his gun raised when he entered the dark, quiet house.

Zareb followed, gun drawn.

Assefa used hand signals, gesturing in the direction he wanted Zareb to go, which were the kitchen and basement.

He'd take the rest of the main level and then the upstairs.

Nodding, Zareb took point, moving with stealth and caution toward the kitchen in the back of the house.

Assefa felt like he was trying to smell and hear while underwater. No matter how hard he tried, those two senses were muted. An anti-sensory spell, Sanura had called it. It was the same kind of spell she'd cast when she'd broken into Paul Chambers's home to curse the were-cat.

Despite the slim hope he'd held out that Cynthia hadn't played them all, the anti-sensory spell made it almost impossible to believe that she wasn't the water witch of legend. What in the hell was the woman trying to hide?

He crept forward, slipping from the dining room to the living room and finally to the den. Nothing looked out of place. The home, as always, was tidy while giving off a feel of being lived in and enjoyed.

A frisson of malevolence hit him.

Assefa bounded up the steps, taking two at a time. His gun preceded him down the short hall. The bedroom he sought was on the right.

He stalked inside and came to a stop.

On the floor was a small form. Holstering his weapon, Assefa dropped beside the thin girl. Dark, glossy hair covered most of her face. Gods, her face was devoid of most color.

Taking Gen in his arms, Assefa searched for a pulse.

His ears popped, and sound and smells crashed over him, a tidal wave of senses set free.

"Shit, is she alive?"

Assefa pressed his fingers to a wrist and then her neck.

"Barely. Go to the car and grab the first-aid kit from the trunk." Zareb didn't move, his eyes on something above Assefa's head. "Zareb, dammit, focus. I need you to get the first-aid kit from the car or Gen's going to die."

"B-but Eric's…"

Assefa swore. He hadn't taken a good look at the bed when he'd entered. But Assefa had seen enough to know the man was dead. "We can do nothing for Eric, but we can try to save his sister. Now move your ass, special agent, and get me the first-aid kit."

Zareb ran a hand over his bald head but did as Assefa asked, darting from the bedroom with were-cat speed.

Gen had snake bites all over her, even to her face and feet. He gulped down vile curses but couldn't prevent the anger that threatened to choke him.

She had done this, Christine C. Walker. Damn Cynthia to hell. She wouldn't get away with hurting her family. Assefa would make sure the water witch paid for her deception

Zareb sped back into the room, the kit in his big hands. This time, he lowered himself to the floor instead of looking at the body on the bed. "Will this be enough?" He opened the red-and-white kit, revealing vials and syringes. "Do you have everything you need to save Gen?"

Gently, Assefa laid Gen on her back. Her eyes were closed, skin cold and clammy. She wore yellow night shorts and a white-and-yellow matching T-shirt sprinkled with blood.

Assefa used two antiseptic wipes to cleanse his hands before picking up one of the vials. He removed the plastic top from the syringe, stuck it in the container, and filled it until he was satisfied with the dosage.

"Hold her arm up for me. That's good, just like that."

Assefa plucked at her vein before tying a tourniquet around her arm. Zareb held her to him, stretching out Gen's slim arm to Assefa who stuck the tip of the syringe into her lifeless body, releasing the anti-venom serum.

Since the battle with the snakes at the Potomac River that buttressed his home, Assefa had taken to carrying anti-venom serum. Berber Pharmaceutical had created two serums, one for witches and one for were-cats. He'd never used either in the field before, so he had no idea how effective it would be on Gen.

"Did you call the paramedics?"

"Yeah, and I told the 911 dispatcher about the snakes."

He hadn't seen a single snake, but the paramedics needed to know what kind of scene they would be walking into.

Taking Gen from Zareb, he cradled the teen to him and lifted her from the floor. Tucked safely in his arms, Assefa walked across the hall to Gen's bedroom. It was an inviting room with eggshell white walls accented with tea rose carpet and the bed linen a darker pink. Books with titles like *Romeo and Juliet*, *A People's History of the United States*, and *An Intermediate Guide to Witchcraft* were stacked next to an assortment of CDs, pencils, and unfinished homework. The walls were plastered with a hodgepodge of posters, signifying the teen's diverse cultural tastes from Willow Smith to Taylor Lautner to Yo-Yo Man to *Fairy Tail.*

A ceiling fan circulated the air in the room as well as the delicate vanilla scent of the young witch he held in his arms. Assefa kissed Gen's forehead before placing her in her bed and pulling covers over her. He wished she'd hidden when she heard whatever it was that drew her to her brother and sister-in-law's room.

He wished, even more, that Cynthia had been the warmhearted witch he'd come to think of her as instead of the coldhearted fraud she'd turned out to be.

Taking one last look at Gen, her breathing shallow but steady, Assefa turned away and headed out of her room and back across the hall.

"Our senses are back, although I wish they weren't." Zareb stood at the foot of the bed, eyes on the dead man and face set in granite.

Assefa joined Zareb, knowing he had to look but regretting what he knew he would see, another dead friend.

Of all the things he expected to happen today, staring at the deceased body of Eric Garvey wasn't one of them. He tried to view the corpse with the detached, neutral eyes of a trained FBI agent. Tried to ignore the scents of blood and urine. Tried to shut out the sound of hissing coming from the dead man.

Moving closer, Assefa scanned the body, gliding observant eyes over Eric's blond-brown hair and to a hazel eye, open and frozen in a morbid awareness of his impending death. The other eye was gone along with most of the left side of Eric's face.

The left arm was severed at the elbow with flesh, skin, and jagged parts of the humerus bone jutting out. Though perhaps severed may be the wrong word, implying the arm was cut and removed as if in an operation or through some catastrophic accident like a car crash. But Assefa knew it hadn't been cut, no more than his eye, cheek, jaw, mouth or ear had been. Eaten would be a better word to describe what had happened to Eric Garvey.

Eyes Assefa knew were now a dark, furious shade of gold, traveled to Eric's upper torso. Like Eric's remaining eye, his chest cavity was also open. Snakes had taken up residence in the man's stomach and upper chest cavity. Bloody intestines and snakes swam together in a macabre mix of fantasy and science fiction.

"Are those snakes actually his...? Damn, they are."

Eric's intestines, through some hateful, twisted spell, had taken the form of yellow-and-black snakes, fangs long and sharp. They'd eaten their way out, tearing through whatever stood between them and freedom. Yet, freedom didn't extend beyond the bowels of Eric's body, for the snakes remained with the man, their lower half still that of an intestine.

They hissed and snapped at Assefa and Zareb, beady eyes dark and detestable.

It was a gruesome scene, not just the sight itself, although that was terrible and would haunt Assefa's dreams but the brutality of it all. Eric didn't deserve this fate. Few merited what had been done to the werecat.

Assefa closed his eyes, listened carefully, and sniffed the air. Searching. Something much bigger than the snakes slithering around Eric Garvey's gallbladder and liver had taken a healthy chunk of the man, and Assefa wanted no part of it. But he heard and smelled nothing.

He turned to Zareb. "She knew we were coming. She cast that damn spell, which we probably triggered when we stepped on the porch."

"It didn't last very long, though."

"Long enough."

"Long enough to distract us. Long enough for Cynthia to put miles between us and her."

He ran from the room, cell phone in hand.

"Where in the hell are you going?" Zareb yelled after him.

Assefa didn't stop; he vaulted down the steps and out the door. "You stay with Gen. Call Mike before the paramedics arrive."

"What about you?"

Assefa jumped into his car, the sun shining, the day hot, and god-damn snakes everywhere.

The Day of Serpents had finally arrived. And Assefa knew Cynthia hadn't fled after killing her mate.

He sped off.

"It's nice to see you." Sanura stepped aside and let in her guest. "How did you know I was back?"

"I spoke with Makena this morning. She said you returned home yesterday. After all the rain, I wanted to get out of the house, so I decided to pay you a visit. I hope you don't mind."

"Why would I mind?" Sanura smiled at Cynthia. The rain had stopped, and her sister had come for a visit.

"Is Assefa at home?"

"No, he and Zareb are out."

"Good, then it's just us girls. The way it should be. The way it was always meant to be."

CHAPTER THIRTY-SIX

Realm of the Gods

Mami Wata's eyes sparkled as did her white teeth, both beaming across the chessboard at her sister whose expression was less than pleased. "Do not look so grim, Oya, you knew who my chosen water witch was as I knew who yours would be." Mami Wata moved her queen one space to the right. "Then again, little sister, you have always picked from the same inadequate gene pool."

Mami Wata's eyes glistened even more, and her smile widened, highlighting her godly beauty to great effect. Without question, her luscious brown skin, long, wavy hair, and voluptuous form made her the physical rival of any of the other goddesses if such mortal values were of import to her. They were not, yet all the gods invariably manifested themselves into visually appealing forms to their worshippers. After all, only a follower of Apep would worship a god they found grotesque or terrifying, even if that depiction was closer to the truth.

Ra once told her there was a positive correlation between Mami Wata's outer beauty and her inner hideousness. "When one increases so does the other, forever linked, forever deadly."

Over the centuries, she'd come to savor the perceived insult.

Glancing at the dais, where Ra, Sekhmet, Yemaya and Anubis were, eyes on the scrying glass and the human dimension, she knew they too were concerned.

She'd maneuvered their last hope for salvation into an emotional cage with no easy exit. Sanura could kill her best friend, which would crush the witch and leave her vulnerable to Mami Wata's creatures of the deep. Or the fire witch could sacrifice herself for the love of her chosen sister. Either way, Oya's champion would be no more. With her defeat, Mami Wata would be free, Apep crowned King of Gods, and *isfet* the law of both realms.

"You switched families." Oya also moved her queen. "You made that decision for this very moment. You have no honor, sister."

Mami Wata laughed. "I do not recall honor being part of Ra's prophecy. Nor do I recall there being a stipulation that forbade us from changing families." Mami Wata laughed again when Oya's eyes narrowed in disgust. "Do not blame me for your lack of strategy and forethought."

Mami Wata relaxed in her chair and permitted her artificial mirth to slip away. "How do you think your fire witch would feel if she knew the reason the women in her family have only been able to birth one girl is because of you?"

Nothing in Oya's countenance altered, although the goddess should've felt guilt at her selfish actions. Wasn't she supposed to be the more humane of the two of them? Mami Wata knew that to be a falsehood. Oya desired her freedom as desperately as Mami Wata did.

And while being chained to the floor of Nun for centuries at a time did not deny them all the powers of their godly birth, Ra's faith in his misguided hoax of a prophecy had kept the sisters as unwilling pawns in the sun god's own game of chess.

Oya may have viewed the fire witches of legend as her and Sàngó's daughters, but she was no less calculating and mercenary than Mami Wata.

"You have done that to your precious fire witch. You have so thoroughly interfered with the genetic composition of Sanura's matrilineal line that their bodies are wholly incapable of carrying anything other than one girl to full-term. When Makena miscarried Sanura's brothers, did her grief fill you with glee, for you knew her next child would be your long-awaited savior? Does Sanura know she has nothing to offer her Mngwa but one fire witch daughter? That, while we sat here, watching her pitiful mate grapple with the possibility of losing Sanura in childbirth, it was all for naught."

Not that either Sanura or Assefa would live long enough to conceive a child. By the end of the Day of Serpents, their corpses would lie broken at Mami Wata's feet.

Genuine amusement rippled through her, the succulent taste of victory on her uncompromising tongue. She raised her voice, wanting all in the temple to hear. "You think me vicious and a monster. But it is Oya who is the true fiend." Mami Wata stood, naked and proud, her focus and words no longer for Oya but Ra. "You have sanctioned this duel. The continuation of a battle that should have ended long ago. You allowed it then, and you have permitted it ever since."

"Watch your tongue, water goddess," Ra warned.

Mami Wata would not be silenced.

"We have taken on form after form, over the millennia. Greek, Chinese, Norse, Incan, Egyptian, Christian, Tibetan. So many, but they are all us. Whether you choose to take the guise of Ra, Zeus, Olorun, Brahma or dozens of others you have claimed over the years, you are still the same self-serving god."

The falcon feathers on his head rustled in an absent wind, the only sign of Ra's anger. "Do you not understand, Mami Wata, without the worship and faith of mortals, we serve no purpose. So, we reinvent ourselves time and again. Mortals need not share the same belief, but they must believe. As pitiless as the initial battles between you and Oya, they served a greater purpose."

"You mean our war filled your religious coffers, stroked your massive ego and made you and the others feel needed and cherished."

"Yes, daughter." Yemaya floated to Mami Wata, blue dress of water a delicate wave of mystical power. "Without mortals, their folly, as well as their faith, we are nothing more than disparate energy seeking form, meaning, and balance."

"Balance." Mami Wata spat the word at her mother. "Nothing any of you have done since this all began has restored balance. She will not return. She is forever lost. Sanura Williams, like the others, will not, cannot heal Ra's broken and guilty heart."

"Without balance and the one who holds mortals, even gods, accountable, we will be no more. Despite what you and Apep may believe, daughter, *isfet* cannot exist without *ma'at*."

"I do not believe you."

"You have never believed. You lack faith, my child, and for that, you are an unfortunate creature indeed." Yemaya floated away from Mami Wata and toward the scrying glass. "We have permitted much, these centuries, with the singular hope of correcting our greatest sin. You and your sister are not to blame. We all are, for which we must atone." Touching the mirror, a ripple of power coursed through it, soundless and visceral. "If the fire witch of legend does not ascend, we will all suffer."

"Thanks to Ra, I have suffered much already. Centuries were taken from me because I wanted the same as the sun god as all of you. To be revered by mortals."

"You mean feared, daughter."

Mami Wata didn't see the difference.

Ra joined Yemaya by the scrying glass, watching Sanura and Cynthia. "Four feathers, water goddess. All that was left of my daughter were four white ostrich feathers. Yemaya created Oya to return balance to our realm when you proved yourself an irreprehensible affliction we had to bear. But Oya was yet another disappointment, a morally ambiguous disease, malignant yet redeemable."

Ra's toned, muscular form appeared, in the blink of an eye, in front of Mami Wata. His ancient power slammed into her, not harsh or even angry. Yet, the magnitude of it had her stepping away from the god, his power unyielding and without equal.

"The burden to restore balance to the realms has always fallen to Oya. She added to the imbalance you wrought instead of detracting from your malevolence. She should have been *ma'at* to your *isfet*. But the sky and weather goddess only brought more chaos and disorder. It is thus Oya's champion who must do what she could not. It is you and your water witch who will test her, who will take the fire witch to the edge of sanity and sin."

"No," Oya screamed. "You must not. You have taken three of them from me. My fire daughters, my—"

"They were never yours. They were always, and forever will be, mine. Each of them held a vestige of my daughter, which means they are of this realm and of me. Yet, none of them were worthy of the white feather. They did not ascend, even when blessed with a soulmate to help them carry the godly burden."

"It is too much," Oya wailed. "It has always been too much. They are but mortals, incapable of achieving what you seek."

"Then we will perish in a chaotic river of our making. But I yet have faith in the fire witch and cat of legend."

"They will not succeed," Mami Wata countered, a sneer in her voice. "The Mngwa will die, and the fire witch will succumb to her fury."

"We will see, water goddess. We will see."

"Are you sure you wouldn't rather stay inside?"

Cynthia shook her head. "I want to take advantage of the sun and nice autumn weather. It's been so terrible lately."

Sanura followed her friend as she used the path that led from the house and toward the Potomac River. Every cell in her body screamed at Sanura to not go near the river.

She pressed on. "I didn't think the rain would let up." They neared the gazebo, and Sanura hoped Cynthia would stop there, but she kept walking.

"It's a perfect day, and this is a great view." Cynthia stopped inches from the pier and the river, gazing out with an unreadable expression.

Sanura could swim. Her parents had made sure she could. But she'd never felt safe around a lot of water. And the Potomac River was a hell of a lot of water for Sanura's peace of mind.

"It's nice, but you've always liked the water more than I did."

"I'm a water witch. I wouldn't be much of one if I couldn't swim or was afraid of the water." Cynthia stepped onto the pier, her sandy-brown dreadlocks pulled back in a French braid, jeans tight, pullover shirt loose, and tennis shoes holding traction on the wet wood. "Are you coming or are you afraid of a little water?"

"A river isn't a little water, and I'm not afraid."

She was. Her mind conjured images of Special Agent Bell's half-eaten body and the freakishly large Ninki Nanka. Anything could be in the river waiting to swallow her whole. That's if she were lucky and a Ninki Nanka wasn't lurking below the surface to take a large bite out of her for risking her life on faith and friendship.

Sanura followed Cynthia onto the pier. And dammit, trust had never felt so terrifying.

Sitting, Cynthia lowered her legs over the edge of the pier, swinging them back and forth. Blue eyes lifted to Sanura. "I wanted to talk."

Sanura remained standing. Being on the pier was one kind of stupid, dangling her legs over the river was just asking to be dragged in and killed. "About what?" A cool breeze had Sanura zipping her hooded graystone rain jacket. Like Cynthia, Sanura wore comfortable jeans. But she'd opted to wear a graphite pair of ankle-length rain boots instead of athletic shoes.

Her friend lowered her eyes and turned away from Sanura, her gaze on the calm river. "Do you remember when we first met?"

"Of course, I do. You were the one who never remembered. You swore it was when High Priestess Katherine brought you into my homeroom and introduced you to the class."

"She sat me next to you. Do you know what she said to us?"

Sanura forgot little, although her memory wasn't as good as Makena's. "She said, 'Christine, this is Sanura, and she's a fire witch. Sanura, this is Christine Walker, although she likes to be called Christie. She's a water witch. I expect the two of you to become friends.'"

"I thought the high priestess was a little off. Scary, weird, all of the above. She paid me a lot of attention. Too much. I didn't like it. Her dark-blue eyes watched me as if she wasn't sure if I would steal something if she turned her back on me. And everywhere I went, you were always there."

That wasn't exactly true. Cynthia had been placed in every one of Sanura's classes and clubs that first year. More, High Priestess Katherine had taken Sanura aside, a week before Cynthia arrived at Sankofa, and made two requests of her—to not tell Cynthia about the first time they'd met and to protect the water witch, "No matter what."

At ten, little of what the high priestess asked of her had made sense. She didn't argue with or question adults, so she'd nodded and given the old witch her word. She'd kept it, too. It had been Rachel who'd mentioned their real first meeting to Cynthia, who'd stared at the earth witch with confusion and annoyance.

"I had no idea what Rachel was talking about when she mentioned us playing by the Tree of Ma'at."

"I told her I'd met a brown girl with blue eyes."

"I used to get that a lot." Cynthia laughed, but not with true humor. "Some people would stare, their eyes going to me and then to Mom."

"You look a lot like her."

"So much that I forbade everyone from calling me Christie or Christine after Mom died."

Those had been hard times for Cynthia. Sanura and her family did what they could to help her after Ms. Christine died, including taking her in. And if calling Christie by her middle name would help the grieving process, then Sanura was all for it and so was Rachel. It took a while, but once Makena and Anna spread the word to the teachers, the students quickly caught on until Cynthia had supplanted Christine on everyone's tongue.

Sanura couldn't remember the last time anyone called Cynthia by her first name. It had been on a list Assefa showed her last night, along with names of other Sankofa water witches. She'd been too sleepy to ask about the list. Now, she wished she would've.

"You never remembered our first meeting before, why do you re-member it now?"

The more they talked, the more Cynthia hunched in on herself and the longer she stared out at the river.

"I remember watching you play with your dad. His jaguar was so big yet incredibly gentle with you. I forced myself, for years, to not think about my father, about how all my friends had a dad and I didn't, about how he left us and never came back. But there you were with your father, laughing and playing and it reminded me of what I didn't have." Cynthia glanced over her shoulder at Sanura. "You were so nice to me that day. You saw me watching, came over and then pulled a fireball from behind your back. You made the fire dance until I smiled and for-got why I was sad."

They'd played until her mother had come storming across the quad, eyes teary and hands trembling. She'd hugged a puzzled Cynthia before looking at Sanura and then dragging her protesting daughter away. Sanura was sure she'd never see the brown-skinned, blue-eyed girl again.

"I loved Sam like he was my father." Cynthia turned away again, tears in her voice. "And I loved my grandmother, thought the world of her." Shifting, Cynthia pulled several sheets of folded paper from her back pocket and handed them to Sanura. "The letter was delivered to me about two weeks after your birthday."

Sanura could sense magic on the letter, water witch magic, but not Cynthia's. She recognized it, although it had been years since she'd last felt it.

"It's from Katherine Spencer. It reeks of her magic."

"I set off the spell when I read the first few paragraphs of the letter. The first line directed me to read the letter by myself but aloud. There was a business card inside the envelope. It was from the Spencer's fam-ily lawyer. When I called the firm about the letter, the attorney told me

Katherine Spencer had included the letter as part of her will. It was to be delivered to me on your birthday. She apologized for mailing it out late."

Interesting. For the spell to last so many years, the letter had to have been magically sealed by the high priestess and kept in a secure location by the lawyer. Likely a magic-laced vault.

"Is the spell the reason you remember our first meeting?"

"Yeah. But not just that. I also remember a big fight between my mother and grandmother after we returned home from Sankofa that day. Mom made me go upstairs, but I still heard them. They argued about my dad. Mom accused my grandmother of horrible things, Sanura."

"Like what?"

"Read the letter. It's a lot of speculation on Katherine's part, but I think she was right. She was also the person responsible for my memory loss and the murder of my grandmother. She confessed all, every awful detail as if I needed to know my loving grandmother was likely responsible for my father's disappearance."

Kneeling behind Cynthia, Sanura wrapped her arms around her friend as she wept. Unfortunately, Cynthia's story explained a lot, including a truth Sanura found difficult to deny.

"Were the contents of the letter the real reason you were so distant after my birthday party?"

"I couldn't face you. I didn't lie about the miscarriage, though. I would never lie about that."

"I know you wouldn't." She kissed her cheek, stood, and stepped away from Cynthia. "Have you come to kill me, water witch of legend?"

Blue eyes, wet and dark, stayed on Sanura as Cynthia pushed to her feet.

They stood mere feet from each other, quiet, assessing and deadly.

"When you asked me to say a prayer for Shanumi, is that when you knew?"

"No, but it was that day. Ever since the Sudan, I can see what I shouldn't. I see you, Cyn. I can see all of you. Your increased strength. Your fear. So much fear. Why are you afraid?"

"You should be the one who's afraid."

"I'm not. I'm sad. I'm hurt. And I'm mad as hell that Mami Wata has tried to turn my sister into my enemy."

"I don't want to hurt you, Sanura. I don't want to be here. On this pier. Near this water. Confessing the sins of my grandmother. I didn't want this. I never wanted to be the water witch of legend."

Tears fell from blue eyes, and Sanura knew Cynthia spoke the truth. Yet she was there. She'd led her down to the pier and the element that bolstered her power. Sanura had followed, afraid but holding onto faith.

High Priestess Katherine Spencer had made her promise to protect Cynthia. It was a request she should've never asked of a ten-year-old. As Sanura watched Cynthia's internal struggle play across her face, she realized the plea had been for the powerful fire witch Sanura would grow into, not the naïve and compassionate child she'd been.

"The high priestess wanted us to become friends, not to kill each other. I don't have to read the letter to know what it says. She put us together every chance she got. She hoped we would become friends because she knew this day would come. There was no stopping it, no matter what either one of us did. This standoff is our destiny. But we decide how it will end. Love and sisterhood or magic and death."

"You don't understand." Tears streamed from her, and Cynthia's raised voice had the river beginning to roil. "I have to do this. I have no choice. Gods, Sanura, please know that I have no choice."

She knew it was coming, but the wave of water still knocked her off her feet and down onto the pier.

Shaken, Sanura got up. Another wave pushed her back down, the force bashing the wind out of her.

Soaking wet, Sanura stood, green eyes on the blue ones of her best friend and sister.

"I have to kill you," Cynthia screamed.

"Then do it. If you want me dead, water witch, then take my life." Sanura thumped the palm of her hand against her chest. "I'm right the hell here. You drove to my home for this, now do it, damn you."

A third wave slammed into her, slicing through raincoat and jeans. Down she went for a third time, stomach and thigh bleeding.

Undeterred, Sanura pushed to her feet and faced Christine Cynthia Walker.

"Fight, dammit, fight."

Water spell after water spell flew out of Cynthia's mouth, hammering Sanura's stubborn body and sending her down over and again, body bloodied but hope unbroken.

Spitting blood from her mouth, Sanura stood again, drenched yet burning hot.

"Fight, Sanura. Dammit, fight me back."

"I won't. If you want me dead, then cast a spell that'll end me. I won't make this easy for you by fighting back."

"Easy? This is the hardest thing I've ever done. You're hurt and bleeding because of me. You won't fight back because we're sisters. I hate that you value that bond. I hate that you'll stand there and let me take you from Makena and Assefa because you're more concerned with saving my goddamn soul than defending yourself."

Hands of water, originating from the river, reached up and grabbed hold of Sanura's legs, tight and crushing.

"I told you, you can't solve everyone's problem. I must do this. If I don't, he'll die."

"Who'll die?" Sanura fell to her knees, the hands wrenching her downward.

Sobs wracked Cynthia. "My sister or my mate, that's what Mami Wata told me. 'You are my champion, whether you wish it or not. As such, you will kill the fire witch of legend or your precious mate will die a painful death.'"

The hands yanked, and off the pier, Sanura flew. And right into the Potomac River.

CHAPTER THIRTY-SEVEN

Assefa blew past the cars on the beltway, his Mercedes going one hundred miles per hour. He'd called the house phone and Sanura's cell phone a half dozen times. She hadn't picked up, which had Assefa gunning the car.

Yesterday, he'd relished having no one in the house but them. Today, he wished at least one of his brothers were at home with Sanura. Instead, Rashad was at school and the others at Sankofa. Sanura had dispatched the men to the school, thinking they would be of more use there than at the mansion.

She'd been wrong, although her heart, as usual, had been in the right place. No one was close, not even Ulan, who also lived in Alexandria. Chief Berber, like every agent in the Preternatural Division of the FBI, was out protecting full-humans from Mami Wata's creatures.

A guy in a white car beeped and flipped Assefa off when he cut in front of him.

He called Sanura again. No answer.

Assefa drove even faster.

Cynthia glared from the smear of blood on the pier and into the murky river. Sanura's blood. She waited for the fire witch's head to break the surface of the water. She knew Sanura could swim despite her fear of the water. So, why hadn't she returned to the surface, fire witch mad and ready to fight?

She moved closer to the edge, eyes on the river and heart pounding in fear the longer she didn't see the fire witch. What if Sanura drowned or there was something down there waiting for her. Oh, gods, what if she killed her best friend?

Kicking off her shoes, Cynthia dove into the water.

At first, she saw nothing but dark water. It pulsed hard around her as if angry. The waves beat against her body. It was then she realized how useless her magic was under the water.

I can't speak my spells. What am I supposed to do? How can I find and help Sanura without my magic?

Ignoring the fear churning in the pit of her stomach, forced herself to think what it meant for her to be the water witch of legend. More, Cynthia thought about the expression on Sanura's face when she'd hit the water—not so much surprise but disappointment ... in the woman who'd claimed to be her best friend and sister.

What did it mean to be the water witch of legend? Death perhaps but also power. *You are my earth element. You will listen to me, dammit, even under here.* With a magic level she should not possess but did, Cynthia conjured a spell in her mind, repeated it then propelled herself through the water when the river obeyed her command.

I can't believe that worked. Now, where is Sanu—oh, gods.

A nightmarish ring of Fangtooth Fish, five-foot long, crusty brown scales, and long sharp teeth a third the size of their body surrounded Sanura.

As one, they attacked.

Fireballs exploded under the water, sending fish flesh in every direction. They swarmed Sanura, fangs snapping even when they burned. Blood met Cynthia before she reached Sanura, which had her swimming faster.

Fireball after fireball erupted, lighting the river and Cynthia's path. Still, she couldn't see Sanura.

Cynthia sent a tidal wave of water power straight at the ring of chomping bodies. Large blue and black eyes turned her way and just as quickly ignored her.

She was the water witch of legend, which meant they weren't there to murder her but Sanura. Damn Mami Wata and the prophecy.

Another shock wave of water careened into the Fangtooth Fish, shoving determined predators away from Sanura. But more came out of the darkness.

Sanura fought from the inside, her fire heating the river. Cynthia waged her own battle on the outside of the ring, fighting to get to her friend. Witches could hold their breath longer than full-humans, but fire witches weren't meant to last long underneath the water. Sanura would need air soon.

Blue Pacific Viperfish, jagged, needlelike teeth that kept it from closing its mouth, swam from the depths of the river. Dozens, there had to be dozens of them, swimming in a straight line, their destination clear, the fire witch of legend.

Cynthia sent a shockwave of magic between the Pacific Viperfish and Sanura, slicing clean through them before they could join the frenzy of Fangtooth Fish.

A blast of angry heat started a fire underneath the water. More Pacific Viperfish emerged from below, followed by three big ass Frilled Sharks.

Cynthia had to do more, so she sent a knife of water at the first shark, cleaving the living fossil in two. But the other two avoided her attack.

They swam toward Sanura, who Cynthia could see. Sanura's blast of heat had destroyed the attacking Fangtooth Fish. Sanura raised her hands in front of her, directing her fire at the approaching Frilled Sharks.

The fire disintegrated them on contact.

Sanura swam toward the surface, slow and with streams of blood flowing behind her.

The Pacific Viperfish followed, snapping and losing heads when they came into contact with the fire witch. She burned hot, but the bites still got through, even if death was the punishment for harming the fire witch of legend.

More Frilled Sharks polluted the river with their violent presence. Sanura swam faster. But not fast enough.

She would die. Unless Cynthia did something, and fast, her sister would die.

Pulling from the element of her birth, she shoved her magic at Sanura. A blue ball collided with the fire witch's back, slamming her forward.

Cynthia sent another wave of blue magic at Sanura. *Water, rise and protect. Water, surround and assist.*

Blue magic engulfed red. With another spell, Cynthia pushed against the water and compelled the forcefield up, up, up.

The Fangtooth Fish and Pacific Viperfish didn't pursue Sanura and the forcefield Cynthia had ensconced the witch in. They did, however, turn their dark, murderous eyes on her.

Cynthia didn't move, wondering if being the water witch of legend, after protecting Mami Wata's enemy, still made her immune to their threat. When the first Frilled Shark knocked into her and sent her spinning, she knew it did not.

They attacked, and Cynthia closed her eyes. Her fate. The water witch of legend deserved to die. She had come there to murder her best friend. Cynthia was willing to sacrifice Sanura's life for the safety of her mate and sister-in-law. She loved them all. How could she choose? Yet she had.

Maybe with Cynthia's death, Mami Wata would spare her family. She had done as the goddess had demanded. She'd kept Mami Wata's awful secret, lying to Sanura and using their friendship to weaken the emotional morale of the fire witch.

A part of Cynthia had known Sanura, once she realized the danger she posed, wouldn't turn on and treat her as the enemy she'd turned out to be.

When the first painful bites came, Cynthia knew she would never see Eric again. Her love for him was the only leverage that could've gotten her to betray Sanura. More bites scored landed, sinking through fabric and finding skin.

Blood ran down her arms and legs, and she submitted to her death.

Crack. Crack. Crack.

Cynthia's eyes popped open. Thunder raged above her.

Crack. Crack. Crack.

Bolts of lightning cut through the water, dividing into lethal spikes of energy. Each bright, white light found a home in the body of the attacking water creatures, igniting on contact.

The water above her parted. A concentrated gale-force wind shoved the river water aside. There, on the pier, red-gold hair whipping in the wind, eyes a chilling shade of red and body crackling with magic, was Sanura in all her fire witch of legend glory.

And she was pissed.

"Get your ass up here before I have to come in there and get you."

With a quick, mental spell, Cynthia rode the wave of wind water Sanura sent her. She collapsed in exhaustion and shame when her body fell onto the planks of wood.

"You should've let the fish and sharks eat me. One of us must die."

"Shut up. Just shut the hell up." Sanura yanked her by her arms and up to her feet. Fire sparked from the edges of Sanura's eyes. "I won't let you kill yourself."

"But I tried to kill you."

"Step away from her, Sanura."

Cynthia hadn't heard the were-cat approach, but there Assefa stood at the end of the pier--gun pointed at her and eyes glowing gold with fury.

Sanura turned to face Assefa.

"It's not what it looks like."

"It's exactly what it looks like. You're wet, bleeding, and Christine just confessed."

Christine, damn. Had anyone ever said her given name with such contempt?

"Listen, Assefa, I know this looks bad, but I can explain. I just need you to lower your weapon."

Reaching behind her, Sanura found Cynthia's hand and began walking toward her mate.

The closer they got to him, the more he backed up until the women were no longer on the pier.

"Stand aside and let me end this."

"I won't let you shoot her. Please, Assefa, lower your gun."

The special agent didn't so much as blink, his glare brittle and deadly, and the unyielding hand on his gun implacable.

"You have no idea what she's done. Cynthia's not your friend. And she's damn sure not your sister. Now stop shielding her, so I can send the water witch to hell."

Assefa stalked toward them.

They moved, Sanura careful to keep her body between Cynthia and her furious mate.

Cynthia settled her hand on Sanura's shoulder. "It's my time for judgment."

"It isn't. Assefa will listen to reason. He's upset and protective, which makes him very dangerous."

"Get out of the way."

"Assefa, please. Cyn isn't my enemy. She saved my life."

"Saved your life? Why are you wet? How did you get those cuts to your clothes and body? Are you saying she's not responsible? That you jumped into the river fully clothed for the fun of it? Is that what you want me to believe?"

Assefa was scarier in human form than his Mngwa had been when he'd fought Greg Chambers's lion. He wasn't listening to Sanura, and Cynthia didn't blame him. She couldn't let this continue, couldn't allow Sanura to risk her relationship with her mate for a witch unworthy of her loyalty and protection.

She went to step from behind Sanura when Assefa said, "Before coming here to murder you, she killed her husband and sent snakes after her sister-in-law. Tell Sanura the truth. Tell her what you did to your family, you deceitful—"

The scream came out of nowhere. And it emanated from her. Cynthia dropped to her hands and knees. No, no, no. Eric was fine when she'd left the house. He and Gen were asleep when Mami Wata came to her, a huge snake around her neck and hair as dark as the goddess's soul.

She'd said she would spare Eric's life if she did as she was told. Her husband couldn't be dead. He just couldn't be. The way Assefa looked, accusing her of murder, it had to be true.

She wept. And couldn't stop, not even when she felt the barrel of Assefa's gun press against her temple.

"You killed your mate and tried to kill mine."

She trembled, cold and numb and wanting the death Assefa offered.

"Your manipulative tears mean nothing to me. Die, witch."

In hindsight, Sanura would realize how thoughtless she'd been when she'd lunged at Assefa. At that moment, though, all the fire witch saw was her mate, determined and deadly, and her best friend, crying and helpless.

Assefa would kill Cynthia. He'd splatter her brains onto the waterlogged grass.

She'd lunged at him, unthinking of how the reckless move could cause Assefa to shoot her friend. What else could she do? He wasn't her enemy. Sanura wouldn't use magic against her familiar, which left her body.

Wrapping her arms around Assefa, she held him with a force that didn't so much as have the man stumbling backward. He also didn't shoot. What he did do was growl and swear in Wolof.

"Dammit, Sanura, I could've shot you."

She said nothing, just held him while pushing soothing magical energy through their mate bond.

Tense and hard, it felt like she embraced a statue.

"Look at her. Listen to how Cyn cries for Eric. Whatever happened to him, she didn't do it. She would never hurt her husband."

Sanura ignored her shock and grief over the news of her friend's death. Now wasn't the time for grief, not when Assefa's gun still pointed at Cynthia's head.

Whether intentional or not, Cynthia smartly stayed where she was instead of running away. Running would only bring out more of the Mngwa in Assefa. He would give chase, a quick hunt that would end in Cynthia's gory death.

Sanura nuzzled his neck, kissed his cheek, and prayed Assefa could scent the truth in Cynthia's grief.

"She hurt you." His left arm came up to encircle her waist. "I can smell your blood as well as her guilt. I don't like it."

Sanura wanted to reach for his gun hand, encouraging him to lower his weapon now that he was talking. But it was too soon, Assefa's voice a low rumble of warning.

"I know. But Cyn's not a murderer. You know her. Come on, Assefa, you know she's not our enemy."

"She's a servant of Mami Wata, and she's here on her behest. For that betrayal alone, the water witch deserves to die."

This was the Berber male Assefa had warned her about, singleminded and lethal. Her protective mate and special agent, his job was to rid the world of preternatural dangers.

But Cynthia Garvey wasn't a preternatural danger. She was Sanura's friend, and she didn't want her to die.

Sanura stopped pumping soothing magic through their mate bond. That spell had always worked. In Assefa's current state of mind, the spell had no effect.

"For me, beloved. Don't kill my friend. You know what Cyn's death will do to me, how much it'll hurt."

"Unfair, Sanura."

"I know, and I'm sorry. But I have nothing else. I don't want her to die. She doesn't deserve to die. Cyn's death would break my heart."

"Dammit."

With the arm around her waist, Assefa lifted Sanura off her feet and turned them away from Cynthia. He stalked away from the pier and river.

Sanura didn't dare let go of him.

When he set her back on her feet, Assefa's golden eyes frowned down at her.

"When I left the house, you knew. Didn't you?"

"I didn't know you and Zareb were going to Cyn's home. But I did suspect that Cyn was the water witch of legend."

She thought he would be upset, but Assefa kissed Sanura's cheek.

"I know how much you love Cynthia. It's the same way I feel about Zareb. But she betrayed you, and I don't know if I can forgive her for that."

"But you won't kill her?"

"No, my stubborn witch. I won't kill your lying friend. She's safe from me."

"How magnanimous. The worthless water witch, however, is not safe from me."

Faster than she'd ever seen him move, Assefa spun around, gun arm up, and fired successive rounds straight into the body of a beautiful half-naked woman, a giant snake coiled around her body.

The bullets flattened on impact. No blood. No damage.

Assefa fired again, striking the head of the snake instead of the throat of the woman. It fell from her body and to her ankles. Dead.

Dark eyes fell to the lifeless snake before they raised to Sanura and Assefa. Angry, the woman opened her mouth just as a large wave of water crashed into her, soaking the green wrap she wore and her bare upper body.

Assefa grabbed Sanura by the hand and moved them out of the way.

On the other side of the water attack was Cynthia, madder than she'd ever seen her friend. Raising both hands, Cynthia drew more water from the Potomac River and sent it flying at the woman. Spirals of harsh river water smashed into her.

"You killed him," Cynthia screamed. More spirals of water. "You lying monster, you killed my mate." Vortices of water formed in the river behind Cynthia, her lips moving in a fast cadence, her spells coming out quick.

Waterspout after waterspout careened into the woman, who Sanura knew had to be Mami Wata.

Heaving, Cynthia's attacks were relentless, but they had no effect. Water either bounced off the goddess or she absorbed the liquid.

"We have to help her."

Assefa reloaded. He shot Mami Wata until the cartridge was empty and a useless gun dropped from his hand.

Sanura hurled fireballs at the water goddess, and she batted them away. She maintained her attack. Assefa was at her back, his hand on her shoulder and his magic fueling her spells.

Cynthia's waterspouts kept coming, drawn from the river and cast at Mami Wata.

Fire and water battled the goddess of the oceans. She'd tried to pit them against each other. Yet, there Sanura and Cynthia were, bound by their hatred of Mami Wata and the need to avenge everyone she'd ever hurt, including Eric Garvey.

Thundering water and searing fire intertwined, relentless and explosive.

"Enough!"

The breath left Sanura's lungs when an invisible hand clamped around her neck and jerked her into the air. The same was done to Assefa and Cynthia. The three of them dangled helplessly, caught in the goddess's brutal grip.

Long, dark hair ran the length of her body, a deadly aquamarine cloak of wavy fish scales.

"Did you think your inconsequential magic could hurt me? That I could be harmed by mortal weapons and paltry spells from children?"

The hands around their necks shook them, ragdolls in Mami Wata's malevolent chest of toys.

Mami Wata pulled Cynthia close, their faces almost touching.

"Your mate. That insignificant cougar was not your mate. He was one of Oya's tricks. She fooled us both when she manipulated your handfasting. You may have loved the useless mortal, but he was not the were-cat who could grant you the power enhancement required to defeat the fire witch. Worthless. When I saw him sleeping in bed, I knew what my sister had done. There was no need to spare his life. The mortal added nothing to the battle. He did, however, make a most scrumptious snack for my Titanoboa."

Cynthia cried, and Sanura wanted to as well.

Mami Wata threw Cynthia to the ground. She curled into a ball and wept for her deceased husband and the lie that had been their mate bond.

"You want to kill me, kitty cat?"

Assefa fought against the hand around his neck, claws out and gouging at unseen flesh. "We will kill you, beast."

Mami Wata laughed, the skull-splitting sound forcing Sanura to cover her ears.

"You are quite the entertaining fur ball. Full of ideals and notions of justice."

She laughed again, and Sanura's ears bled.

As she'd done to Cynthia, Mami Wata tossed Assefa to the ground. When he leaped to his feet, an invisible force drove him back down. On his back and spread eagle, Assefa roared but didn't move again.

Sanura had no idea what the goddess had done to her mate, but she didn't have time to ponder Assefa's predicament.

The hand around her throat loosened, and her body flew across the short distance between herself and the water goddess.

"We finally meet face-to-face." Mami Wata sniffed. "You smell like dung and defeat."

"And you smell like a salty bitch."

The hand around her throat squeezed.

"You disrespectful urchin. I will show you what happens when you cross a goddess. Watch."

The hand flung Sanura high into the air, where she floated on the goddess's cruel magic.

Above her, clouds parted. In the spaces between, waves of glass formed.

The first glass showed the grounds of Sankofa Preparatory School. The Witch Council of Elders and teachers were on the quad. With them were Manute, Mr. Siddig, and the alpha of each were-cat family. Hell, across the quad were three Ninki Nankas and a sea of snakes.

Sanura saw her mother form a sword and shield made of fire before her attention was jerked to the second glass.

The House of Berber loomed above Sanura. It was overrun with snakes. In front of the grand structure stood Jahi, in his jaguar form, big, black, and feral. Lines of armed soldiers shot at a forty-foot Groot-slang, a primordial snake of myth and murder.

Behind the fanged behemoth was Ulan, Omar, and Najja.

In Baltimore and in front of Cynthia's home, a Bengal tiger roared. Shotgun in hand, Mike took cover behind a truck. A black-feathered serpent coiled like a Rattlesnake but far deadlier and older than the Mesoamericans who worshiped the creature, reared up, opened its mouth, and sprayed the area with whitish-yellow venom.

The third wave of glass gave way to the fourth, revealing Rashad and a caravan of cars packed with students the leopard's age. Rashad had told Sanura he was building her an army. Was this them? Driving on I-395 South and headed to Alexandria?

Before her stunned eyes, the road morphed into an aquarium of green-blue water, swallowing the cars and college students within.

Sanura screamed as each glass revealed her loved ones fighting for their lives.

"This is what a salty bitch can do." With another jerk, Sanura was in front of Mami Wata. "Admit defeat, and I may let your mother live."

Sanura couldn't look away from the scenes of blood and death, no more than she could prevent her tears from falling.

With each defeated friend, the hotter Sanura became until she was a raging inferno of fire witch heat. She blazed in the goddess's chokehold.

"Fight her," she heard Assefa yell. "Show her who you are."

Mngwa power and love sizzled under her skin, and Sanura burned hotter.

"Come out, Fire Phoenix, come out."

Sanura exploded, her body engulfed in a hissing, snarling fire. The hand on her throat melted away, and Sanura dropped to the ground.

The fire witch lashed out, her arms whips of slashing, cutting fire.

They struck Mami Wata across the face, drawing blood and a counterattack.

A water funnel swept into Sanura, but she kept her feet under her. Fire strong and aggressive, Sanura went on the offensive. Fire whips snapped and sent the shocked goddess back.

"I challenge Mami Wata," Sanura yelled.

Fire whips to face and chest.

"On this prophesized Day of Serpents, I challenge Mami Wata."

Snap. Snap.

"Fire versus water. Witch versus witch." A stream of fire blazed from the palms of Sanura's hands into the body of the goddess. "Familiar versus familiar. I challenge Mami Wata. This is my prayer, given freely and with a faithful heart. Here me. Accept my challenge."

Through the chaos of Sanura's inferno stepped an unscathed Mami Wata.

"You filthy, insolent dung beetle. How dare you threaten me with your flames and insult me with your vulgar challenge. Your challenge means nothing to me."

"I wasn't talking to you, salty bitch. My words were for him." Sanura lifted her flamed head.

In the sky, the sun shone behind the descending being, his falcon's wings resplendent.

CHAPTER THIRTY-EIGHT

When he heard Sanura's challenge, Assefa stopped struggling against the five invisible hands pinning him to the soaked grass. One hand around each wrist and ankle as well as his neck meant Assefa couldn't budge, much less see everything going on above him.

Through their mate bond, he felt Sanura become one with her fire spirit. Finally. They were a powerful team, their combined might giving him hope. Not in their ability to defeat Mami Wata, but in their capacity to stay in the fight long enough to do exactly what Sanura had just done.

He could've kissed her. They'd planned this on the flight from the Congo, although neither knew whether Sanura would get a chance to recite her prayer or whether her challenge would be accepted.

Assefa smiled despite the pressure on his neck and diminished air to his lungs. The wings of a falcon. Thank Sekhmet, it was the actual King of Gods. He flew toward them, from his realm and to theirs. He'd come, but would he accept Sanura's challenge? If he did, the battle they'd wage would be the most important of Sanura's and Assefa's life.

Behind the sun god, Assefa's friends and family battled. The waves of glass flaunted each clash. Witches and were-cats fought hard, killing but also dying. If their plan didn't work, they all would die, not just the fire witch and cat of legend.

When the sun god landed, Assefa could see little from his vantage point, but he heard everything, including Mami Wata's shocked hiss at the god's arrival.

"Why are you here? You have never interfered directly before."

"The child of fire prayed to me. As King of Gods, no realm is beyond my reach and no prayer too small for me to answer personally if I so judge the faithful worthy of my ear and time."

"She is not worthy. And this is my battle to wage but hers to win. You said so yourself."

Anger and righteous indignation blended together in the water goddess's voice. The mix had Assefa straining against the hand around his neck, which, since Ra appeared, had loosened.

He could move his head enough to see Cynthia to his right. She sat on the grass, staring wide-eyed. When he lifted as far as he could, Assefa saw the source of her shocked expression. It wasn't the tall, bronzed god with feathers for hair and wings for arms.

Standing behind Ra was a woman covered in fire. Her entire body was made of crackling orange-and-red flames. The kind you'd see in a fireplace on a cold winter's day. If Assefa didn't recognize the magic signature of his mate, he wouldn't have known it was his witch who'd stood there.

His Sanura, but not quite. She'd transformed the way were-cats did, but not the way any witch was known to do. Was this her ascended form?

Cynthia crawled to his side. "Do you want my help? I'd understand if you don't want me to touch you."

Assefa wanted nothing from the water witch. But he did need help, so he nodded.

"A prayer from the fire witch of legend is most worthy of this god's attention. In all the centuries that I have watched from our realm not a single champion, yours or Oya's, thought to pray to me. Even better, inside her prayer was a challenge. A challenge that had not occurred to even me."

Ra sounded impressed.

Sanura seemed nervous.

And Mami Wata looked murderous.

"The other hands won't budge."

That was fine. Cynthia had managed to counteract the power of the hand around his neck. Although Assefa suspected it had more to do with

Mami Wata's split attention than anything Cynthia had done. Still, he appreciated her effort. He could at least breathe easier.

"This is my battle. Her challenge means nothing."

"Wrong, water goddess, the child's challenge means everything." With one of his large wings, Ra gestured to the four waves of glass in the sky. "She could have asked me to save them. But she did not. She could have asked me to save her mate and sister. But she did not. She could have begged me for her life. Again, she did not."

"This is not how it is done. This has never—"

"Fire versus water, Mami Wata. Oya's champion only requested an equitable battle. She is right here, willing to fight for that which matters most to her, which are the lives of mortals you threaten with your monsters. She is also willing to die for the same reason. I will grant the fire witch her challenge."

The hands around his limbs disappeared. Ignoring the numbness in his wrists and ankles, Assefa vaulted to his feet. He shrugged out of his suit jacket, tie, and shoes but made no move toward the trio.

Cynthia also got to her feet, eyes red from crying. She also stayed put. The water witch had a good sense of self-preservation. He'd give her credit though, she'd gone after her mate's murderer with all that she possessed. It hadn't been enough, no more than Sanura, even in her flame form, was enough to bring down the water goddess.

Months ago, he'd asked Sanura to help him figure out a way to kill a god. From the smug look on Mami Wata's face, after Ra's decree, Assefa knew she hadn't yet grasped what Ra just agreed to. In her arrogance, she hadn't listened to Sanura's prayer.

"On this Day of Serpents, I grant the fire witch her challenge." Ra's voice boomed, cracking the four glasses in the sky. "Fire versus water. Witch versus witch. Familiar versus familiar. This is my decree, and so it will be done."

For a second, it seemed as if the sun fell from the sky and into Assefa's backyard. The heat from the sun swallowed him, a circle of blinding magic that swept Assefa off his feet, burned away his clothes, and brought about his shift from man to beast.

He fell through a dark hole and onto a marshy field. The harsh landing sent shockwaves up his legs, but he was unharmed and not alone.

A few feet away, he watched his fire witch struggle to her feet, more disoriented from the dimensional travel than the Mngwa. He trotted over to her, and Sanura's hands of fire lifted to his face. She held his large head between her flaming hands and placed a kiss between his golden eyes.

"You're safe."

We both are, but where are we?

"A place I've only seen in my dreams and one I'd hoped to never visit in person." She pointed behind him. "That's the primordial river of Nun. This is the site of the last battle between Shanumi and the water witch of legend."

That couldn't be good for them. Ra gave, but he also put the couple at a great disadvantage. Another damn body of water and the first one at that.

Where is she?

Golden eyes saw nothing but dangerous liquid behind him and acres of marshy wetland in front. Their plan hadn't included the extra boost from a body of water. And Sanura's current physical state was a complete unknown.

How does being actual fire work?

"I don't have to cast a spell, even in my head. I think and it happens."

Who's in control?

"I am." Sanura touched the gold necklace around his neck. "For now," she added when her fingers found her promise ring. "I don't know how much this will help you here. Abubaker died in this place, and Shanumi lost her damn mind afterward. We can't end up like them."

The Mngwa had no intention of dying and leaving his mate alone. They needed to put as much distance between them and Nun as possible.

Let's get the hell out of here before—

A furious bellow emanated from the river, which had the Mngwa facing that direction. Out of the gloomy water came Mami Wata, her lower body that of a green-and-blue mermaid, her upper torso a naked woman. Impossibly long, black hair crinkled around each other, twisting and writhing as she pushed from the water. Her mermaid's tail parted to form two human-looking legs, brown and long. The green-and-blue scales slithered up toned legs and around curvaceous hips and a taut stomach, forming the same wrap of scales she'd worn earlier.

The crinkles of her hair lifted, covering her shoulders and breasts. The Mngwa knew without a doubt that Mami Wata had been the one to murder Eric Garvey. The same kind of yellow-and-black snakes that had eaten through Eric's stomach and chest comprised Mami Wata's crown of hair.

They hissed and snapped.

More of the yellow-and-black snakes followed her from the primordial river, slithering through the marsh.

I thought she was supposed to be a witch now. That's what you asked of Ra.

Sanura backed away, and the Mngwa followed.

"He said I asked for an equitable fight. I think it's a matter of perspective. This may be the water witch of legend's ascended form if she were meant to have one. I haven't ascended, which Ra and Mami Wata damn well know."

He's trying to force your ascension.

"Probably, but I don't know how to ascend. I didn't even know I would turn into literal fire when I fully joined with my spirit."

A spray of flames shot from Sanura's hands, creating a wall of fire between them and the approaching snakes and their mistress.

"My form matters not, dung beetle. Here is a lesson for you. Ra cannot strip gods of their powers. He can only lessen them. I still have far more than you and your ball of worthless fur."

Mami Wata's boasts revealed two points to the Mngwa. One, she wanted them to doubt what they brought to the battle. Two, she was afraid what would happen to her if Sanura ascended during the encounter. Razi once used the same mind trick on Assefa, a bullying tactic that had, for too long, worked.

Formidable, yes. Razi had always been a tough combatant. But not an invincible one, and neither was Mami Wata. Still, the woman wouldn't be easy to defeat, no matter Sanura's form.

The snakes are a distraction. Burn them all.

Sanura did, her flames high and loud. So high, in fact, he could no longer see Mami Wata and her hideous hair of snakes.

His witch set the marshy field in front of them ablaze. Her wall of fire magic disintegrated anything that encountered the flames.

As the fire raged, they walked backward, putting distance between themselves, Mami Wata and the primordial river that supplied her with snakes.

Waves of river water sliced through the wall of fire, dousing some of the flames but not all. From the hole the waves made in the wall, the Mngwa spotted three giant spider crabs. Their high leap over the wall had the Mngwa using his big body to push his witch backward.

From claw tip to claw tip, the beasts were twelve feet and easily stood five feet high.

Reinforce the wall. I'll take care of the spider crabs.

There wasn't much room to fight between the fire wall, the spider crabs and his witch.

He wouldn't leave Sanura by drawing the creatures away, but the Mngwa also didn't want the spiders distracting his witch. Being living, breathing fire was new for her. And their full mate bond was untested.

One of the giant spider crabs rushed the Mngwa, its speed surprising for a creature who spent its time foraging on the ocean floor and not running around on a wetland.

Bracing for impact, the Mngwa lowered his shoulder and head, and let the spider crab crash into him. With a quick move of his own, the Mngwa used his powerful front claw to smack the spider crab in its burnished-brown face, sending its head back through the fire.

He didn't have time to appreciate the swift win. The other two spiders flanked him, their pincers sharp and painful when they stabbed the Mngwa with brutality and strength.

They moved in, and the Mngwa charged the nearest spider crab. At the last moment, the cat sprang over the crab and then ducked.

A ball of fire shot through the air and right into the tough exoskeleton of one of the spider crabs.

It burned, and the Mngwa attacked the third water creature. It used the reach of its claws like a jab, keeping the Mngwa at a distance and scoring his muzzle each time the big cat drew near.

Deciding he could withstand a few cuts to his face, the Mngwa dove at the spider crab, going low instead of high. Sliding, he opened his wide mouth and clamped down on two claw legs.

The spider crab lost its balance and toppled to the side. With a hard wrench, the Mngwa claimed the two claw legs as his. Once detached from the body of the spider crab, he spat the hard shells to the wet ground.

The other spider crab still burned. The Mngwa leaped onto the creature, allowing his near seven-hundred-pounds of pure muscle to drive the beast down.

Sanura's fire didn't harm him. They were mates, bonded on a physical and spiritual level. Which was good because as the monstrosity burned the Mngwa's saber teeth tore at the highly-mineralized chitin of its armor, stabbing the exoskeleton until it cracked. With a heavy paw and deadly claws, the Mngwa ripped the barrier away and then stepped back and let Sanura's fire do the rest.

In a dash, he returned to the last spider crab, still down but trying to use its remaining claws to get to its feet.

Rearing up, the Mngwa smashed his fierce paws on the head of the anthropod, splitting its skull. He bit what was left of the head, chomping down hard with his crushing jaws.

The necklace and ring glowed, healing the few injuries he'd sustained in the short but vicious battle. He returned to his witch's side, but he soon found himself turning toward the sounds coming from behind them.

He listened, knowing he heard what sounded like scratching, maybe even digging or clawing.

"What's wrong?" Sanura glanced over her shoulder. "What do you hear?"

Not answering, the Mngwa lowered his head to the grass and began walking in the direction of the sounds. He stepped softly, his wide paws sinking into the grass and mud as he stalked the unseen prey.

Hands reached up from the wet mud and grabbed at his thick mane. Serrated blades for hands sank deep, cutting and tugging with a force that had him growling in pain and fury.

Wrenching himself away from the bladed hands, the Mngwa darted back when more limbs broke through the muddy ground. He watched, astonished, as ten sets of hands clawed their way to freedom followed by heads, shoulders, and full bodies.

White, water lily eyes stared at the Mngwa from heads made of grasses and rushes. The flowering plants formed forehead, eye sockets, chin but no nose or mouth. The rest of the body was a combination of papyrus and sawgrass. Hands and feet were sharp, sawtooth-like blades that buzzed like a circular saw.

In a matter of seconds, more of them crawled from the depth of the wetland. Eleionomae. The damn water goddess had summoned an army of Eleionomae, marsh nymphs of Greek lore.

With Mami Wata, and god knows what else on the other side of Sanuras's fire wall with her, and the Eleionomae behind them, the Mngwa and fire witch were pinned.

This wasn't good. They would both have to fight these nymphs, which meant Sanura couldn't focus solely on keeping Mami Wata on the other side of her wall.

There were dozens of them, saws whirling in a threatening arc of animated plant life. At least half of the army ran for Sanura, who had her back to them.

Watch out.

A slice across Sanura's burning back. Fire spewed like blood from the injury. The fire witch neither screamed in what the Mngwa knew had to be a lot of pain nor did she stop reinforcing the wall with her fire.

But she did encase herself in one hell of a forcefield while also working to maintain her fire wall. That was new. Prior to merging with her fire spirit, Sanura couldn't cast a spell outside of her protective field. Now she could.

The bubble of fire protection raged hot and lethal, burning Eleionomae each time one of them tried to attack her. After a half dozen bodies lay dead around Sanura's field, they stopped going after her, which left the Mngwa.

The yellow center of their white, water lily eyes tracked the big cat. With each soft step they took, water, grass, and plants were absorbed into their bodies, strengthening the creatures and adding to their mass.

"Destroy their home and send them back to the marsh."

The Mngwa didn't know how he could do that. But he caught on to Sanura's plan the minute his paws burst into flames.

Showing nothing but wicked fangs at the Eleionomae, the Mngwa took off running in a circle as fast as he could. He corralled the nymphs, who tried to shred his body with their feet and hands. But he kept running, the fire on his paws spreading to his legs the faster he ran.

Heat expanded outward and downward, removing moisture from the air and the marsh.

Without a mouth or nose, the creatures breathed through the plants and water of the wetland, which the Mngwa denied them with each lap around his self-created track.

This was what it meant to have a full mate bond with the fire witch of legend.

The Mngwa ran faster, and the sound of buzzing began to fade. By the time he slowed then stopped, Mami Wata's army of Eleionomae were on the ground, hands, and feet no longer whirling.

Without mercy, the cat of legend used his paws of fire to set each nymph ablaze, creating a new wall of fire from the carcasses of a tragic Greek myth.

"How are you fairing in there, my little dung beetle? Do you like my water creatures? I have plenty more where those came from."

He just bet Mami Wata did. Hiding behind a wall and forced into a perpetual defensive state, they wouldn't win this way. They needed a different strategy.

"You do realize the longer this battle takes, the more of your family and friends will perish at the hands of my servants. They will not stop, dung beetle, until my power over them is no more. Since you cannot defeat me, they will devour all in their path."

Sanura's red eyes shifted to the Mngwa. They were filled with tears. Their family and friends, based on what he'd last seen in the waves of glass, were likely already dead. Mami Wata's taunt served to only wound Sanura.

If she could've breached Sanura's wall of fire, she would've. Psychological warfare, that's where the goddess most excelled. The strategy had served her well.

Whatever you want to do, mate, I'll fight to the last. We may die this day, but our bond will survive.

Sanura retreated to the Mngwa's side, a hand going to his head and caressing.

"How far should I go?"

All the way. Hold nothing back, and fear no one. Not even yourself.

"I only fear losing you."

A partial truth. Sanura feared losing her heart and soul. If, by some miracle, they won, how would she cope with the loss of Makena and Mike?

"I love you."

I love you, too.

With the wave of a hand, Sanura brought the fire wall crumbling down.

And there a self-satisfied Mami Wata skulked, a monster on each side of her.

CHAPTER THIRTY-NINE

These creatures couldn't be Mami Wata's familiars. By the gods, they were massive. A Black Tortoise stood to Mami Wata's right, the body as wide as a tank. Its green-and-black top carapace shell was attached to the plastron by a thick bridge that held the exoskeleton together. However, it wasn't the large river tortoise that gave Sanura pause, but the ten-foot snake adjoined to it, merged somewhere in the tortoise's endoskeleton.

To make matters worse, a Basilisk flanked Mami Wata's other side. The crested snake had the head and legs of a rooster, the body of a dragon, including red-and-gray wings, and the tail of a snake.

Ra had a strange interpretation of an equitable battle. Mami Wata seemed to have an endless supply of serpents and water creatures at her disposal. Whereas, Sanura had no ability to conjure anything remotely comparable.

She backed up.

Don't look the Basilisk in the eye. Its gaze will petrify you.

"If you drop to your knees now, I will make your death quick but still quite painful."

Get on my back. We can't fight the three of them at once. The tortoise is slow, but the Basilisk can fly.

Sanura hopped onto the Mngwa's back, and he took off. So did the Basilisk. She could hear the flapping of its great wings above them. Blindly, Sanura hurled fireballs into the air.

The Mngwa ran, heavy paws striking the grass with barely a sound. The Basilisk pursued them.

A swift right then left. The Mngwa didn't run in a straight line. He zigged and zagged, keeping them an unpredictable moving target.

The Basilisk swooped low when it neared, its snake tail swiping at Sanura's head.

She ducked and sent a microburst at the creature, knocking the animal away from them with a concentrated burst of wind.

The Mngwa ran faster, his powerful legs taking advantage of Sanura's attack to put more distance between them and the hybrid.

Eleionomae appeared, their circular blades popping up from the ground. He jumped over some and powered through others.

As the Mngwa ran, Sanura left a trail of fire behind them.

It didn't take the Basilisk long to catch up, its dragon wings large, mighty and fast. It dipped low, wings working to keep up with the fast-moving and swift-cutting cat of legend.

The Mngwa darted to the left just as the Basilisk tried to draw parallel to them.

Sanura released streams of fire, followed by another microburst to the Basilisk's dragon chest.

The monster recouped quickly and dove at the Mngwa. The big cat cut again but stumbled when unnatural hands burst from the ground. Buzzsaws sliced his paws and hindquarters, drawing blood and grunts of pain.

With one of its tough wings, the Basilisk knocked Sanura off her cat. Tumbling to the ground, she scrambled backward, eyes closed, afraid of meeting the gaze of the Basilisk and being turned into stone.

Create a forcefield around yourself. And don't come out until it's safe.

What about you?

I don't need my eyes to fight.

She didn't like it, but she created the forcefield.

Sanura couldn't see either of them, but she could hear wings flapping. The Basilisk, more dragon than rooster, was twice the size of the Mngwa, which put the beast over a thousand pounds.

I'll track your aura signature.

Can you track the Basilisk's heat signature?

Yes.

Good. I'll get it in position then you light its ass up.

Sanura concentrated, tracking her familiar and the Basilisk. Two streams of color appeared in her mind, one gray-and-blue, the other green. Their auras twinkled like Christmas lights across the spectrum of her senses, forming a predatory pattern of chase and run.

The green heat signature was right above the gray-and-blue with gold flecks aura signature, which meant the Basilisk was very close to the Mngwa.

Sanura breathed deep, her fire body crackling with tension and anticipation.

The signatures merged, and the Mngwa howled his pain.

Sanura didn't wait. She launched a volcanic blast of fire in the direction of the green heat signature. Lightning followed the fire blast, aimed at the center of the green heat signature.

Another howl erupted, but not from the Mngwa.

More summoned spikes of lightning bolted through air. They drilled through the Basilisk with the aid of a wet microburst.

Hit the bastard again with more lightning.

Drawing from the strange environment that was their battlefield, Sanura envisioned a six-barreled rapid-fire machine gun. She filled the chambers with rounds of electrostatic discharges. A downburst worked as electric motors to power the barrels.

With a quick command, the rounds of lightning stormed from the barrels in rapid succession. She reloaded, maintaining her attack. Over and again, the electrostatic discharges came out as aggressive bolts of lightning that ripped through the Basilisk's green heat signature.

Attack, attack, attack.

The heat signature dipped from hot to warm to cool before disappearing from Sanura's spectrum.

Opening her eyes, she saw nothing but burned grass. Movement from her right had Sanura spinning in that direction. The Mngwa ran toward her, something long hanging from between his teeth.

She released her field at his approach, and the cat dropped the snake tail of the Basilisk at her burning feet.

"That's nasty."

You should see the rest of it.

"What now? Mami Wata's probably summoned more monsters to fight for her." Sanura sank to her knees and wrapped her arms around the Mngwa's neck. "Do you think they're all dead?"

She wouldn't cry. But her heart ached. This hadn't been a quick battle, and it wasn't over. Mami Wata was right. The longer it took to defeat her, the more of their loved ones would die.

"We need to finish this."

Then get on my back, and let us make our final stand.

Before they reached Nun, they encountered Mami Wata, her Black Tortoise, countless Eleionomae and another goddamn Basilisk.

They'd waited for them.

From her seat on the Mngwa, Sanura made out the water goddess's smirk. She climbed off.

Erect a forcefield around yourself. You can fight them while inside your protective field.

"That will leave you vulnerable."

I can't fight if I'm in the field with you. We'll have a greater chance of winning if we both fight.

More Eleionomae clawed their way out of the wetland, forming a wall of plant bodies in front of Mami Wata.

We have no choice.

"You'll die."

If I do, then I'll see you again in the Field of Reeds.

Tears of fire fell, and her flames raged ten feet into the air. She refused to believe their love story would end there, in a soggy dimension between life and death.

Mami Wata's army approached. They were out of time.

Erect the barrier. Now.

With a conflicted heart, Sanura raised her fire field.

Scorch everything, and leave nothing but charred remains.

Sanura formed a wind storm in front of the Mngwa. She may not be able to ensconce him in one of her forcefields, but she'd be damned if she didn't afford her familiar any protection. The band of rapidly moving microbursts would follow the cat with damaging gusts of winds as his armor.

The derecho wouldn't harm the Mngwa, but it would demolish anything that neared him.

The eerie silence of the wetland was broken by a loud scream from overhead. Sanura lifted her eyes to the graying sky. Flamed-colored wings swept over the battlefield and right toward Sanura.

The Mngwa jumped in front of her, bringing the derecho with him. The bird's trajectory didn't alter. It kept coming, and Sanura prepared for the impact.

The bird flew through the derecho shield of wind and landed beside a growling Mngwa.

Friend or foe, Sanura?

Sanura stared at the bird. It resembled a heron with its long legs and neck. Except for the flame-colored wings and deep-red beak, the eight-foot bird was a mixture of greens and blues.

Sanura knew what it was, a Benu bird. This had to be Shanumi's fire spirit she'd offered when she'd blessed Sanura.

"She's a firebird, like my Phoenix. I think, at least for this battle, that she's also my familiar." Which would explain why she'd been able to fly through the derecho without injury.

Sanura lowered her shield, then, with caution, raised her hand to the fire spirit. The Benu lowered her green-and-blue head and accepted Sanura's warm touch. "Thank you for coming. We could use all the help we can get." The spirit snuggled closer to Sanura, and she could sense the bird's loneliness without her fire witch. "It's all right, I have you now. I'm your witch for as long as you wish to stay."

The bird's head snapped up, sending Sanura stumbling backward. She shot into the air like a missile on fire and crashed into the Basilisk.

They fought. The Benu pecked at the eyes of the Basilisk, her long beak forceful and uncompromising.

Sanura raised her fire shield.

Mami Wata's army charged across the marshy land as the Basilisk and Benu tumbled through the sky, locked in a death battle.

The Mngwa ran, headlong, into the approaching Eleionomae, the derecho surrounding him. He let loose a mighty roar and plunged into the sea of nymphs, swatting them with claws and using his speed, size, and strength to great advantage.

Mami Wata road on the back of her Black Tortoise, the creature slow but moving a great distance with each long gait.

The water goddess formed spikes of water from the muddy water.

Sanura made it rain fire. The Mngwa and Benu would be unaffected, so she created more showers of fire.

Everything around them burned.

A tidal wave swept in from the primordial river. It moved swiftly, parting into two waves when it reached Mami Wata and the Black Tortoise. The rushing water went around them, reforming into an even larger wave when it was in front of its water mistress.

The wave powered over the fire on the ground, extinguishing the flames while also bringing venomous yellow-and-black snakes with it.

The snakes and water smashed into her forcefield, sending it and her back twenty feet.

Wasting no time, Sanura reinforced her field.

The Black Tortoise was on her, hitting her forcefield with its massive feet. On top of her great beast, Mami Wata sneered at Sanura while forming more spikes of water. They were long and pointy like spears, and Mami Wata threw them at Sanura.

They struck, and her forcefield shook but also held.

More spears followed, a ruthless barrage of stabbing water.

The Black Tortoise kept raising up and bringing down the force of its thousand-plus-pound body on her shield.

Lightning spiraled through the air, striking the big beast. Mami Wata tumbled off but was caught by a wave of river water.

The Benu screamed again, in what sounded like pain. She didn't plummet from the sky, which meant the ancient bird still fought.

Sanura could hear her Mngwa's roars and the constant buzz of saws.

An endless stream of snakes crawled up her forcefield, burning on contact and leaving behind slimy innards.

Sanura watched Mami Wata summon more snakes from the river, sending them to their death on Sanura's fire field.

She hurled more lightning at the Black Tortoise, but half of them struck the ground around the towering beast. Her field was nearly covered with the cold bodies of dead snakes. She couldn't see, which also meant she couldn't direct her fire, wind or lightning with accuracy. Worst of all, Sanura could no longer visually track her Mngwa and Shanumi's Benu.

"Come out and fight, dung beetle."

Mami Wata's taunts meant nothing to Sanura. While the water goddess's Black Tortoise and snakes may be cold-blooded, the bitch was not.

She had a heat signature, which meant she was, in her current form, as close to a mortal water witch as Ra was willing to make her.

Sanura found Mami Wata's heat signature, dark-blue with a tint of green. She envisioned the same machine gun as before, loaded it with electrostatic discharges, and let it loose.

Bullets of lighting rang out, a concussion of sound that shook the wetland.

Mami Wata's enraged bellow followed.

Sanura kept reloading and firing.

Tornadic winds formed above Mami Wata's heat signature and snatched up her screaming body in a whirlpool of wind. Inside the tornado lurked a binding spell.

Sanura freed the spell, a barbed wire of magic that wrapped itself around Mami Wata like a straitjacket.

Hands balled into fists, Sanura squeezed, and the wires tightened and cut.

Mami Wata's shrieks of pain and anger could be heard over the Mngwa's roars of victory and the Benu's warbles of attack.

The heartless goddess was responsible for the deaths of so many people, probably even Makena. Sanura's heart skidded at the thought of never seeing her mother again.

She intensified her binding spell.

The Black Tortoise pummeled her forcefield, but she ignored the creature.

Sanura called lightning and sent the lethal weapons into the tornado and Mami Wata's withering body.

She hadn't lied. Mami Wata was still a god, even if a terribly weakened one. For if she weren't, the beast in the guise of a beautiful woman would be dead. Her heat signature had cooled, but it still shone bright with health.

Sanura let loose another round of machine-gun lightning. She wouldn't let up, feared what would happen if Mami Wata was given another chance to summon more water creatures.

Then all went silent. No screams from the Benu. No thumping from the Black Tortoise, no buzzing from the Eleionomae, and no roaring from her Mngwa.

Frantically, Sanura searched for her mate's aura signature, gray-and-blue with gold flecks. Gods, gray-and-blue with gold flecks. Where in the hell was he?

Where? Where?

There, across the marsh in the direction she'd last seen the Mngwa fighting, was a weak pulse of heat. Too weak.

Sanura had to see what was going on, but the snakes made it impossible. Raising the temperature of her field to a nuclear level, the forcefield detonated a violent release of energy that caught the Black Tortoise in explosive shock waves.

Through the fire, Sanura saw the eviscerated remains of the Black Tortoise.

And more.

Her Mngwa.

Sanura's legs buckled, and she fell. Her flames dimmed and disappeared, abandoning Sanura to her devastation.

She could do nothing but stare at her Mngwa. His golden eyes were open, defiant.

Dying.

A giant orange-and-black serpent, its body extending beyond Sanura's range of vision, had the Mngwa impaled on one of its fangs.

She watched in mute horror as the fight and life drained out of the cat of legend, shattering their connection with an excruciating finality. Their destroyed mate bond felt like hundreds of jagged scalpels peeling back the layers of her skin and exposing the vulnerable woman underneath.

The hideous void of despair had Sanura throwing up.

Gods, no. Not Assefa. Not her Assefa.

On her hands and knees and naked, Sanura screamed and wept. They were all gone, her parents and now Assefa. Mami Wata, Ra, Sàngó, Oya, they were all responsible for stealing the pieces of her heart. Without them, Sanura had nothing.

Nothing to give. And nothing left to lose.

Sankofa. The Berbers. Her friends. All gone.

"Bring him to me." A whispered plea to the gold necklace around the Mngwa's neck.

Black-and-gray fur appeared before her. Sanura was afraid to look, but she did. Fresh tears bloomed anew at the miserable sight. He'd been torn nearly in two, the hole from the giant serpent's fang double the size of the Mngwa's head.

She touched him, fur soaked in warm crimson. Sanura expelled the lava churning in her gut. Molten rock of fury flooded her body until it seeped out of her through skin, eyes, ears, and mouth.

The lava flow covered Sanura and her murdered mate, and she shrieked her wrath and anguish.

Nothing left.

All gone.

The giant serpent hissed, Mami Wata curled, protectively, in one of its tight coils.

Sanura laid her hands on the Mngwa's head, his eyes closed in a heartrending death pose.

"Woman to fire, rise. Fire to woman, rise." Trembling, Sanura clutched at her familiar and forced the words past lips that would never again feel the press of Assefa's. "You're my soul, but he's my heart, rise. You're my soul, but he's my heart, protect."

At that word, more lava erupted from Sanura. She hadn't protected him. She should've let Assefa go. If she had, when Mami Wata came hunting for her pound of fire witch flesh, she would've found only Sanura.

"Fire to beast, beast to fire, rise. Fire to beast, beast to fire, be free."

Sanura set the body of her Mngwa on fire and watched her soulmate burn. She then lifted molten eyes and a ravaged heart to the Benu bird that circled above her.

With a bow of Sanura's head and a silent command, the Benu flapped her flame-colored wings and set the fire witch of legend ablaze.

CHAPTER FORTY

Oya ran to the scrying glass. "Not again. No, not again." She stared, in abject guilt, as her Sanura burned. "Not another one."

She cried. In the thousands of years of her pitiful existence, Oya had never wept. Sàngó appeared next to her and cradled Oya in his strong arms. He stroked her long, thick hair, kissed away her tears, but could do nothing to soothe her fractured heart.

Her consort shouldn't be there. Ra had never permitted him in the viewing temple before.

"How are you here?"

"I do not know." Possessive hands caressed the purple silk that sheathed her body. "Where is our child of fire?"

The question had Oya sobbing into Sàngó's bare chest. "The last of our daughters is no more."

"What of Sekhmet's Mngwa?"

"Dead."

Sàngó kissed her cheek then set Oya back from him. "How then are you still here in Ra's temple? Why are you not suffering at the bottom of Nun, held in its mystical chains?"

Sàngó peered over Oya's head and to the scrying glass. "I see Apep and Mami Wata."

She didn't want to look. "Is that all you see?"

"No, my love. I see a Benu standing guard. She waits."

"Waits for what?"

Oya turned back to the scrying glass. The scene hadn't altered. The last fire witch and cat of legend still burned.

She didn't hear Ra stir from his throne, but he stood beside her.

"It is not yet over, Oya. Apep interfered where he should not have. Your champion would not have killed Mami Wata. I would never sacrifice the life of one god for that of another, not even the life of the heartless water goddess. Balance, all I have ever wanted was balance."

"And the return of your daughter."

"Yes. Apep, through his cruelty and impatience to claim my throne, has guaranteed the return of his counterpart. Apep is *isfet*, war, chaos, and disorder manifested. Just as *ma'at*, truth, harmony, justice, and balance is manifested as the goddess Ma'at."

"I know, but Ma'at has been lost to us for centuries."

"Paradoxical dualism. *Isfet* cannot exist without *ma'at*. The last of my daughter, the remaining white ostrich feather of Ma'at, is there."

Ra pointed to the heap of ash that had once been a mighty Mngwa and a courageous fire witch.

From behind, Sàngó braced his hands on Oya's shoulders and spoke low in her ear. "You are still here, my love. Ma'at binds all living creatures, gods and mortals. Her very essence is reality itself, a delicate compromise between chaos and harmony and between death and life. Apep has not won."

"But they are dead."

A kiss to her cheek and another squeeze to her shoulders, Sàngó's voice drifted in her ear, bringing with it hope. "To live, they had to die. To die means they could be reborn."

Opening eyes she hadn't realized she'd closed, Oya searched for and found the Benu. The bird still stood sentry in front of the rise of ash. When something shifted inside the mound, the bird lowered her head and began to move aside the ash.

All in the temple observed, enraptured, as the Benu, using wings and beak, dug out two entwined forms. There, on the scorched ground, spooned as if in slumber, were the immaculate bodies of Sanura Williams and Assefa Berber.

Naked and gloriously made, they held onto each other as the Benu cleared away the last of the ash. Once done, she fluttered around them, arousing the couple fully with the heat of her flame-colored wings.

"This is impossible," Mami Wata screeched.

Oya thought the same. Yet there they were, reborn and exquisite.

Ra nodded in satisfaction when the couple rose to their feet, not as the fire witch and cat of legend they'd been when they'd died, but as ascended manifestations of *ma'at*.

Assefa shifted into his Mngwa. His body was rippled with muscles. Sharp, saber teeth extended far below his jaw and fire crackled across his

back, as much a part of the legendary cat as his elongated claws and black-and-gray fur.

Sanura first laid a hand on the head of her mate, her touch loving, then a hand on the head of the Benu, petting the bird with what Oya suspected was gratitude. She then burst into a ball of fire, and Oya could see nothing of her champion amidst the flames. Yet the longer the fire burned, the more Oya could see it begin to take form. Yellowish-red wings were the first definable features that emerged from the ball of fire proceeded by a flowing brownish-gold wrap with high splits that revealed long, brown legs and feet wrapped in gold Gladiator sandals.

A taut bare stomach led to breasts covered by a crisscross of light-gray material. From reddish-brown hair hung ostrich feathers, Ma'at's white feathers of truth. Sanura's ascended form was magnificent.

The flaming silhouette of her Fire Phoenix burned bright and hot around her as she lifted off the ground and flew toward Apep's giant serpent and Mami Wata.

The Mngwa and Benu followed.

Oya tensed. Despite their ascension, they could not hope to defeat the god Apep, who was darkness and disorder incarnate.

Yemaya, Sekhmet and Anubis, still in his black jackal form, crowded in front of the scrying glass.

"I feared this day would never come," Yemaya admitted. "The souls of the dead have waited too long for the physical return of Ma'at."

Oya knew. Yet Ra's expectations for the newly ascended were too high.

Sanura's ascended form approached the giant serpent, and Apep hissed, revealing the fangs that had claimed the life of the Mngwa. In one of his coils was Mami Wata, livid but oddly quiet.

Dread and uncertainty, Oya realized, had stilled the water goddess's tongue.

Fire wings swept back and forth as Sanura flew closer to Apep. Her decision not to stay out of striking range of the serpent was bold and reckless.

Apep snapped but didn't devour Sanura as Oya feared.

Plucking two white feathers from her hair, Sanura held them out to Apep, who, to Oya's surprise, reared back as if struck.

"We will defend humanity and light against darkness and death. You have been judged, serpent god, and will die for your crimes against humanity. Yet you will be reborn each day because there must be balance in the world."

She dropped the two white ostrich feathers. They floated down and were absorbed into the fiery tufts of her Mngwa. The cat began to grow. So large, in fact, his size matched that of the giant serpent.

"Benu, retrieve Mami Wata. Mngwa, have your revenge."

Sanura watched impassively as her orders were followed. The Benu swept down and captured a stunned Mami Wata in her beak, controlling the thrashing goddess by enfolding her in a powerful flame-colored wing.

The giant serpent, as Oya soon discovered, could not compare to an angry giant Mngwa. The ascended cat of legend had struck before Apep uncoiled his body. He grabbed the snake by his neck with his devastating jaws and piercing teeth while slashing at the rest of Apep's orange-and-black body with extended, lethal claws.

Even through the scrying glass, Oya could hear the shattering of bones: skull, vertebrae, and ribs, as well as the slicing of skin and muscles.

Oya's lived long enough to witness all manner of vengeance, but none as delicious and rewarding as the dismemberment of Apep.

The Mngwa flung the decapitated head of the giant serpent into the primordial river of Nun.

The lion goddess roared her Mngwa's victory, loudly and with much pride.

"You are now free," Ra said to Oya. "At times, we may have lost faith in them, but they never lost faith in each other. Sanura and Assefa are the one true pairing we have waited centuries for, and their bond will return balance to the mortal and god realms."

"We deceived them, Ra."

"Yes, but our deception helped release their divine nature. Go now, Oya, and bring them before me. I wish to congratulate Fire Phoenix Ma'at and Beloved Mngwa of Ma'at."

Perhaps he should've been awed by the presence of so many gods or even taken aback by the floating temple in a realm not meant for mortals, yet Assefa wasn't. He'd died, and then he'd been reborn.

Assefa remembered the quick, sharp prick of pain in his side, of struggling to breathe, and of fighting to live, so he wouldn't leave Sanura alone. He also recalled meeting Sanura's eyes in the final seconds of his life. That image, more than the memory of his murder, would stay with Assefa. Not because of the terror and sadness in Sanura's eyes but because of the love that stretched from her soul and to his. His death may not have been painless, but because of Sanura's love Assefa had died in peace.

With seven gods watching them, including a healed and scowling Mami Wata. Sanura clung to Assefa as tightly as she'd done when he'd shifted from Mngwa to man. She'd stopped crying at least, but the hurt of watching him die lingered, although Assefa stood as solid and as alive as he'd ever been.

He breathed in her gardenia scent and smiled. No matter what she'd become when Sanura ascended, she still smelled like his fire witch.

"It's all right, sweetheart. I'm fine now. You saved me."

He had no idea how, but Assef knew it to be true. They had a lot to discuss, and Assefa was sure Sanura was in shock. Hell, the woman had, up until Oya retrieved and brought them to Ra's temple, fire wings coming from her back. That physical transformation would shock most people.

Assefa, thankful for small gifts, didn't complain when Oya used magic to dress him in a short wrap skirt tied at the waist. Ra and Sàngó wore similar garments, white and red respectively, while Assefa's was black.

"I'm so tired, Assefa."

"I know, so am I. We'll go home soon." He hoped.

Ra strolled from the dais, watching them with a father's pride and patience.

As if she sensed his nearness, Sanura dropped her arms from around Assefa's neck and turned to face the King of Gods.

Gone were the falcon wings. In their place were arms that reached out and pulled Sanura to him. He embraced her while Sanura did a perfect impression of petrified wood, returning Ra's enthusiasm with stiff discomfort.

"Ma'at." The name came out as two choked syllables. "Please forgive this foolish god's arrogance."

"I'm not your daughter."

Ra fingered the white ostrich feathers in Sanura's hair before allowing her to slip out of his hold. "A truth as well as a falsehood. You are still Sanura, but you are also the embodiment of the concept of *ma'at*."

He lifted his hand to touch the white ostrich feathers again, but Sanura stepped back, denying the sun god. Ra smiled with understanding and disappointment.

"When war erupted between Oya and Mami Wata, I failed to foresee the long-term consequences of their battle on the mortal realm. Whenever they fought, our temples swelled. And so it went, over many years. However, the concept and reality of *isfet* grew within the hearts of mortals, and with it the power of Apep."

"Worshippers in exchange for the life of your daughter." Assefa's theory hadn't been far from the truth.

Guilty eyes met Assefa's. "Gods do not die."

"No, but concepts do, and gods can be forgotten."

"Yes, in many ways Ma'at was more an ideal of upright behavior than simply a goddess. As the war between Oya and Mami Wata raged and *isfet* expanded, *ma'at* drifted further from the consciousness of too many mortals. With each passing battle, Ma'at grew weaker until the electrical energy that had been my daughter could no longer take physical form. When she disappeared, all that remained of her were four white ostrich feathers."

"Sàngó gave me one of those feathers the day I was born. It almost killed me and made my fire spirit aggressive and hard to manage."

"Ma'at's feather must be accepted by the fire witch, but also by her fire spirit. The gift should have been absorbed by your Fire Phoenix, but she was, even as an infant spirit, willful and overly protective of her witch."

"That's because she didn't view it as a gift, and neither do I." Sanura reached out and found Assefa's hand. She held it tightly, and he sensed her anger and internal battle for calm. "It robbed me of a normal life and a father. You used us." Sanura looked at their joined hands. "Why? We didn't ask for this."

Ra transported the three of them to a large glass, similar to the waves of glass Mami Wata created in the sky above his Alexandria home. The glass revealed the primordial river of Nun.

"You were in Duat, the realm of the dead. I travel across Nun and through the city of Duat nightly. Once upon a time, Ma'at would lead my riverboat and battle Apep when he tried to prevent my passage through the underworld."

A riverboat appeared in the greenish-blue water and began to sail, passing tall Egyptian acacia trees on low riverbanks.

Sanura stiffened beside him, and he understood why. Souls were everywhere, dripping spheres of depressed, morbid light. They consumed every available space, squeezed on top of each other.

Sanura touched the haze of glass. "This isn't right. Some of those souls are hundreds of years old. I don't understand."

The boat stopped at a towering edifice of white stone with hieroglyphic writing on the slabs. The doors were closed, and none of the souls neared.

"This is the gate that leads into the city of Duat proper and to the Hall of Two Truths. When mortals die, their soul travels to Duat. The soul begins at the marshy field where you battled Mami Wata. The journey is often arduous. Apep and his underworld creatures threaten the safe passage to the gates of the city. Yet, for those who persevere and arrive at the Hall, they are granted the opportunity to live out eternity in the Field of Reeds."

"If their heart is lighter than the weight of Ma'at's white feather," Sanura said, her voice a mere whisper of sound. "Ancient Egyptian mythology I learned as a kid."

"Only myth to the disbelievers. The soul shares their life's deeds, which is then weighed upon the scales of Ma'at. Light with purity or heavy with sin, those are the only judgments. Purity leads to the Field of Reeds, yet a sinful soul is fed to Ammit, the Devourer of the Dead."

"No one is pure of heart, Ra, and most have broken one or more of Ma'at's divine principles, including us." Sanura touched the glass again. "But there are souls worthy of eternal happiness and others who deserve the second death Ammit gives them."

"You can feel the souls?" Ra questioned.

"Yes. They cry out to me, begging for judgment, for release from their suffering. This perpetual state is cruel." Watery eyes turned away from the glass and to Ra. "Is my father among the souls blocked from entering the Hall of Two Truths? Has his soul been left to wander, having no peace, even in death?"

The tears fell as her voice rose.

Ra appeared as if he wanted to reach out to her again, but the god looked to Sàngó instead, who stood next to Oya a few feet from the dais.

"I ferried Sam's soul to the Field of Reeds." Sàngó stepped forward. "His willing sacrifice, on the day of your birth, assured his entrance. That day, child of fire, the last of Ma'at's feathers judged the were-cat's soul, deeming him worthy of an immortal afterlife of joy. Your father is not among the damned."

The way the souls oozed hopelessness, distorted mucus of gloomy colors sagging against one another, Assefa agreed with Sàngó's word choice. They were damned.

"How long has the gate been closed?" Assefa asked Ra.

"Since the day of Sanura's birth. But it began closing, slowly but persistently, since the death of my daughter's physical form."

"That's not all of them." Sanura wiped the tears from her cheeks. "That's not all of the souls."

"Anubis performs funeral rites, but without Ma'at feathers, his duty has become complex."

"Impossible," the jackal god corrected from the dais but said nothing more when they turned to him.

"Yes, impossible," Ra agreed. "Without judgment, the souls can neither move on nor die fully. Some, like these, have waited. Others, aided by Apep, have created fissures between Duat and the living world."

Sanura shook her head and sighed. "I felt one of the fissures." She met Assefa's eyes. "In the House of Berber. Evil, angry spirits protected by powerful witches, that's what I felt."

Ra nodded, and the image in the mirror disappeared. "They are escaped souls from Duat, dangerous and carriers of *isfet*. The fissures must be closed, and the souls returned to the underworld for judgment."

Sanura grabbed Assefa's hand again. "We're not staying here. We're not gods, and we won't live the rest of our lives cleaning up your mess."

"No, Sanura, you and Assefa are not gods. But you are of this realm, which means as the rulers of the first-ever preternatural pantheon you have responsibilities. The fissures must be closed and the souls outside the gate to the Hall of Two Truths judged. Time moves differently here and in Duat. Twenty-four hours of your human time would allow you to judge hundreds of souls in Duat."

Yemaya spoke for the first time. "Neither of you are of use to us or mortals if you remain here. The Sankofa community has always taught and lived by the Forty-Two Divine Principles of Ma'at. The concept is strong there and will continue under your guidance and leadership. The school is accepting, integrating the beliefs of their network into the culture of the school, ancient Egyptian gods beside that of Orishas and other deities. All religious and spiritual beliefs are accepted as long as they align with the laws of Ma'at."

The Orisha floated from the dais and to Sanura and Assefa. She handed Sanura a blue-and-white porcelain seahorse. "Build your pantheon, Fire Phoenix Ma'at. This is my gift and blessing to you. Choose well, the receiver of this seahorse."

Sanura fisted the gift but said nothing, not even when Anubis approached on silent jackal feet and stopped in front of Assefa. "Build your pantheon, Beloved Mngwa of Ma'at. This is my gift and blessing to you. Choose well the receiver of this healing power charm."

A beaded, black bracelet with a silver charm in the shape of a jackal's head appeared around Assefa's wrist.

Anubis stepped away, his spot in front of Assefa and Sanura immediately filled by Sekhmet. The goddess of conquest and war held her palm to Assefa's bare chest, her lovely face stoic but her lion's eyes twinkled with respect. From where her hand touched him, a gold cartouche pendant with a solar disk above the head of a lioness joined Sanura's promise ring on his necklace.

Assefa had found the gold necklace and ring in the ashes of his remains, untarnished and waiting to be reclaimed by him.

"Build your pantheon, Beloved Mngwa of Ma'at. This is my gift and blessing to you. Choose well the receiver of this pendant."

Sekhmet rejoined Anubis and Yemaya on the dais.

Assefa watched as Sàngó, taller and darker than Assefa, walked up to him. "You have returned to me my consort. For such a gift, you have this god's eternal gratitude." Twin battle axes appeared in Sàngó's hands. "These have served me well over the centuries." He placed them at Assefa's feet. "Build your pantheon, Beloved Mngwa of Ma'at. These are my gifts as well as my blessing. One battle axe will remain with you but choose well the receiver of the second."

From behind the broad back of the thunder god were Oya and Mami Wata. Assefa's protective hackles rose, but no one else in the room seemed worried by Mami Wata's close proximity to the couple.

He didn't relax, but Assefa also didn't shift into his Mngwa and rip her throat out, which was far less than she deserved.

The water goddess stepped into Sanura's personal space, a sneer forming when Sanura's wings suddenly appeared, crimson and glowing with power.

"No need for all of that, dung beetle. I come in peace. You and your kitty have freed me from Nun, for which I am neither thankful for the embarrassing defeat nor pleased to have lost to my sister. Yet, I am bound to offer a token and a blessing, though I would rather curse you both to Duat."

"I don't want your token or blessing."

Mami Wata's grin, beautiful and smug, set Assefa at ease. For all the goddess's cruelty, it seemed, if nothing else, she was honorable in defeat.

"Too bad, I will offer both. In this god form, I possess the attributes of sex, healing, and fertility. I bless you, Sanura Wasola Williams, with the birth of healthy fire witches and Mngwas. They will grow strong, bring pride to your heart, and wreak havoc in your home with their mischief."

Sanura's fire wings vanished as she absorbed Mami Wata's unexpected gift.

"Ah, I have surprised you, which is not as satisfying as your death would have been. But I stole my sister's intended blessing, which makes up, marginally, for the fact that you still breathe."

Mami Wata laughed, and Assefa didn't care about the one-upmanship. This terrible, heartless goddess had answered Assefa and Sanura's prayers.

"You're awful," Sanura said.

"*Isfet* to your *ma'at*. When you gaze upon your children, you will know they exist because of Mami Wata. That thought will bring both happiness and annoyance because, whether you want to or not, you will be grateful for my blessing."

Mami Wata opened her hand. In the palm was a closed clam's shell. "Build your pantheon. Fire Phoenix Ma'at. This is my gift to you. Choose well, the receiver of this shell and the pearl within. It will appear when it is needed."

Saying nothing more, Mami Wata disappeared, a splash of water to Sanura's face, her mocking retreat.

Oya, who Sanura resembled nearly as much as she did Makena, lifted her hands, palms out, to Sanura.

Without hesitation, Sanura handed Assefa's Yemaya's seahorse then pressed her palms against the goddess's, whose green eyes conveyed a meadow of sorrow and a sky of gladness.

Neither woman spoke aloud. But there was an exchange, in the fingers that laced, in the magic they shared and, in the bond forged in fire and death.

It would be years later, though not too far in the future when Sanura would reveal Oya's blessing and gift.

Today, they connected, in the way of mothers and daughters. When Oya hugged and kissed Assefa's forehead, he too felt a mother's love.

One by one, the gods said their farewell and vanished, leaving them alone with the King of Gods.

"Will you sail with me tonight?"

Ra posed the question to them both, which confused Assefa. Sanura had ascended to Ma'at, not him.

"Fire Phoenix Ma'at and Beloved Mngwa of Ma'at, balance, and harmony. You are the one true pairing. Will you lead my riverboat over Nun, open the gates to the lost city of Duat, and return life to the Hall of Two Truths?" A hand rested on Assefa's shoulder. "Will you slay the giant serpent, Apep, and guarantee our safe passage?" His other hand went to Sanura's shoulder. "Will you use your white feathers to weigh the hearts of the damned souls and help them find peace in the Field of Reeds or a second death with Ammit?"

Sanura and Assefa clasped hands. Countless deaths had brought them to this place of myths, monsters, and gods. But it was their destiny of love that saved the world.

"Yes," they answered.

The King of Gods smiled and granted them an unasked-for boon.

EPILOGUE

One Month Later
Alexandria, Virginia

"We're going to be late, and everyone will know why." Sanura enjoyed the sight of a naked Assefa. She waited at the foot of their bed, sheets, and pillows everywhere, the scent of their recent coupling perfuming her skin.

Assefa sauntered to his closet and went inside. Sanura had no idea what he was doing in there. Despite what she'd said, only Assefa's clan of brothers and Najja were already there. The other guests wouldn't arrive for another hour.

Thanks to Assefa's anti-venom serum, Gen survived what could've been a mortal attack by Mami Wata's snakes. Unfortunately, she'd awakened to learn of the death of her brother. Four days later, the Sankofa community laid to rest Eric Garvey. Eric's mother and sister had flanked the inconsolable Cynthia. The pew where they'd sat had been the same one from which the sixteen-year-old Christine Walker had stared, with the same look of loss, at the casket of her mother.

Back then, Cynthia had accepted Sanura's comfort. This time, she couldn't meet Sanura's eyes when she'd offered her condolences. They hadn't spoken to or seen each other since that day. Sanura, Assefa, and Zareb had told no one about Cynthia being the water witch of legend. The men had kept the woman's secret and her name out of their FBI report to Chief Berber. They'd done it because Sanura had asked, not because they'd forgiven the water witch.

Sanura had forgiven Cynthia and still loved her like a sister. But she didn't know if they would ever be friends again. Still, she had no interest in ruining Cynthia's life and turning the Sankofa community against her. No one else needed to know the truth, she'd already lost so much.

"Thinking about Cynthia?" Assefa leaned against the door jamb of his closet. "You get this sad, faraway look when she's on your mind."

"Me or Zareb? Who would you choose?"

"I would always choose you." With a hand behind his back, Assefa came to her. "But I would never try to kill my best friend and brother."

"How do you know if you've never been put in that awful position?"

"I just do. There were other options. She could've talked to you."

Cynthia's betrayal was still too fresh of a wound for Assefa to analyze her terrible predicament objectively. Mami Wata was a shrewd goddess, leaving very little to chance. She'd controlled Cynthia by threatening all she held dear. After losing her parents and grandmother, how could the water witch be expected to not do what she could to protect what was left of her family?

Sanura couldn't fault Cynthia for loving her husband more than she loved her. No more than Sanura could forget Cynthia's half-hearted attempts at murder or how she'd jumped into the Potomac River to save her.

"You may distrust Cyn, but Zareb now hates her."

"I know." Assefa tucked a strand of hair behind her ear, which did nothing to help the riot their lovemaking had made of the rest of her hair "She's also most likely his biological mate, so they'll have to work something out."

Biological mates. That fact explained so much. Their attraction. Cynthia's miscarriages.

"I don't know if they can. Cyn's in mourning and Zareb's angry."

"Their problem, Sanura, not ours. Now sit please."

"Maybe I should grab a robe first; you look so serious, beloved."

"The way you are is fine. Besides, I'll just have to rip the robe off in a few minutes when I claim you again."

Sanura's heart quickened at Assefa's carnal tone and the thought of his fangs in her throat as they made love again. After all they'd been through, dying and rebirth, possessing the power of a goddess but also the responsibility to spread *ma'at*, they were learning to savor the moments when they could be Sanura and Assefa.

At his patient urging, Sanura sat at the foot of the bed.

Assefa knelt in front of her, one hand still behind his back. What in Oya's name was the man hiding? He took her left hand in his.

"I feel we've lived a lifetime since the day we met at Johns Hopkins Hospital. I knew from the moment I felt your eyes on my ass when I walked away from you and Mike and to the nurse's station, that you would steal my heart and bring joy to my life." He smiled at her, sexy dimple and all. "I told myself to wait until tonight's party, so I could declare my love and intentions in front of our family and friends."

Ra's gift. When Sanura and Assefa were returned to the human realm, they'd expected to find everyone they cared about dead. Instead, Mami Wata's creatures were gone and their friends and family safe.

"I hired the same band and catering company I used for your birthday party. I even ordered the same kind of event tent and asked Omar to bake you another strawberry shortcake. I invited everyone from before except for your full-human friends because I didn't want anyone to have to hide their true nature tonight."

Sanura's free hand rose to her hair. It was no longer reddish-gold but a gorgeous blend of brown-and-red. Gone were the green eyes she'd hid behind the magic of her moonstone. In their place were the similar mix of brown-and-red, although a lighter shade of red than in her hair.

Over the course of the last month, Sanura had begun to learn how to control the part of her that was Fire Phoenix Ma'at and that included the prominent white ostrich feathers. She and Assefa still had much to learn, particularly about building their preternatural pantheon and what to do with them.

With time, and together, they'd figure it out.

Assefa kissed her hand and pulled his from behind his back.

When she saw what he held in his hand, Sanura swallowed, tears and nerves.

"Then I decided I wanted this moment to be for us alone. Naked we came into this world as two and naked we were reborn as one." Assefa opened the black velvet box. "I had this made specially for you."

Tears trickled from eyes that held his, and Sanura's hand went to her mouth.

"You're my mate, and I'm eternally yours. But I'm a Berber male, and we like to have it all." He pressed her hand to his lips and kissed. "I love you, Sanura Williams. Will you do me the honor of becoming my wife?"

The sob had broken before Assefa finished his proposal. Her head bobbed up and down, but she couldn't speak, not with the lump of elation in her throat.

"Breathe, sweetheart, breathe."

On a ragged exhale, Sanura flung herself in Assefa's arms, crying and laughing. "Yes, I'll marry you."

What little air she'd regained was sucked from her when Assefa claimed her lips.

Hungry, happy kisses had Assefa pinning Sanura to the floor, engagement ring forgotten and him buried deep inside of her. Despite their enthusiasm, their lovemaking was unrushed. They kissed, eyes open and hands framing faces. He whispered words of love, and she breathed fire of devotion.

They made love well past the hour of their guests' arrival, oblivious to anyone or anything beyond their bedroom and each other.

The Benu warbled outside their balcony door, and Assefa groaned. "An eight-foot mythical bird as a pet, Sanura, really?" The Benu warbled again, an ugly sound for such a beautiful creature. "She's as clingy as a puppy and eats her weight in fish."

"Stop complaining, Benu is the best security system you'll ever have, and she's invisible to anyone she doesn't wish to see her."

"Invisible but not silent. She makes that awful noise whenever she thinks I've kept you too long from her. She's spoiled, and her warble doesn't make for good post-sex music. Anyway, did you even look at the engagement ring?" Naked and sweaty, Assefa scrambled from the bed and retrieved the velvet box.

As always, she admired his body, which was bigger and stronger after his rebirth.

He handed her the black box.

In her excitement, Sanura hadn't taken a good look at the ring. It didn't matter, anyway. He could've gotten her a ring made of vines for all she cared.

Sanura opened the box. Not a ring made of vines. By the gods, she'd never seen a ruby so red. There were three of them, surrounded by exquisitely cut diamonds. It was a classy and expensive engagement ring, which she would expect of her Assefa.

She held out her left hand, and he slipped it on. A perfect fit.

Instead of taking a shower, getting dressed, and joining the party, they stayed in bed, talking, kissing, laughing and making love.

Sanura fingered the small white ostrich feather, which now marked the place over Assefa's heart. Their same mate marks had returned with their new bodies, although Sanura's disappeared when she was in her ascended form. Neither could explain why what had started off as a ruse to protect their secret of a partial mate bond had turned into the strongest and most permanent symbols of their bond. Nor did Sanura care.

"I think we've created a terrible pattern."

Assefa stilled her roaming fingers. "What do you mean?"

"Twice I've gifted you with my father's wedding ring and both times we were naked."

"And wet."

True, once in a hot tub and once in an actual tub.

"Exactly. Now you've proposed when we were naked."

"I also put the engagement ring on your finger while we were naked. I see your point." His eyes slid to the love bites on her neck and breasts. "For the record, Sanura, you were also wet during the last two times."

She blushed and he grinned, male arrogance personified.

"My point, Special Agent Berber, is that I don't intend on continuing the pattern when we wed."

"The naked or wet part?"

"The being naked when we exchange vows part." Pushing a smiling Assefa onto his back, Sanura straddled his hips. "I love you, man and Mngwa."

"I love you, woman, witch, and goddess."

Sanura whispered in his ear. "For the record, Assefa, naked or dressed, when we're together, you always make me wet. And that's a pattern I never want to end."

THE END

ABOUT N. D.

N.D. Jones, Ed.D., is an award-winning author who has achieved USA Today bestselling status for her captivating Black Fantasy and Paranormal Romance novels. Residing in the heart of Maryland with her loving family, N.D. is a trailblazer in the literary world of Blacks in fantasy.

Driven by a passionate desire to introduce more positive, sexy, and multi-dimensional African-American characters as soul mates, friends, and lovers, N.D. embarked on a remarkable journey of her own. Determined to address this challenge, she took it upon herself to redefine the narrative.

N.D. has an impressive portfolio of series that reflect her dedication to bringing diversity and depth to the romance genre. Her works include the enchanting fantasy romance series "Forever Yours" and the contemporary romance trilogy "The Styles of Love." Moreover, she has authored three thrilling paranormal romance series: "Winged Warriors," "Death and Destiny," and "Dragon Shifter Romance," along with two captivating fantasy series: "Feline Nation" and "Fairy Tale Fatale." One of N.D.'s distinctive strengths lies in her commitment to crafting in-depth mythologies within her novels, as well as seamlessly weaving paranormal elements into the fabric of her stories. When she creates a world of witches and shapeshifters, N.D. ensures that her readers not only witness their extraordinary existence but also gain a deep understanding of what it truly means to be a part of the world of these mystical beings.

In her novels, the paranormal is not merely a background feature; it takes center stage and is crucial to the plot, enriching the reader's experience with every turn of the page. N.D. Jones invites you to join her on an extraordinary journey where Black love intertwines seamlessly with the paranormal, creating a world where love, mystery, and enchantment reign supreme.

OTHER BOOKS BY N.D. JONES

Winged Warriors Trilogy (Paranormal Romance)
Fire, Fury, Faith (Book 1)
Heat, Hunt, Hope (Book 2)
Lies, Lust, Love (Book 3)

Death and Destiny Trilogy (Paranormal Romance)
Of Fear and Faith (Book 1)
Of Beasts and Bonds (Book 2)
Of Deception and Divinity (Book 3)
Death and Destiny: The Complete Series

Forever Yours Series (Fantasy Romance)
Bound Souls (Book 1)
Fated Path (Book 2)

Dragon Shifter Romance (Standalone Novels)
Stones of Dracontias: The Bloodstone Dragon
Dragon Lore and Love: Isis and Osiris

The Styles of Love Trilogy (Contemporary Romance)
The Perks of Higher Ed (Book 1)
The Wish of Xmas Present (Book 2)
The Gift of Second Chances (Book 3)
Rhythm and Blue Skies: Malcolm and Sky's Complete Story
The Styles of Love Trilogy: The Complete Series

Fairy Tale Fatale Series (Urban Fantasy)
Crimson Hunter: A Red Riding Hood Reimagining
Bearly Gold: A Goldilocks and the Three Bears Reimagining

Feline Nation Duology (Urban Fantasy)
A Queen's Pride (Book 1)
Mafdet's Claws (Book 2)

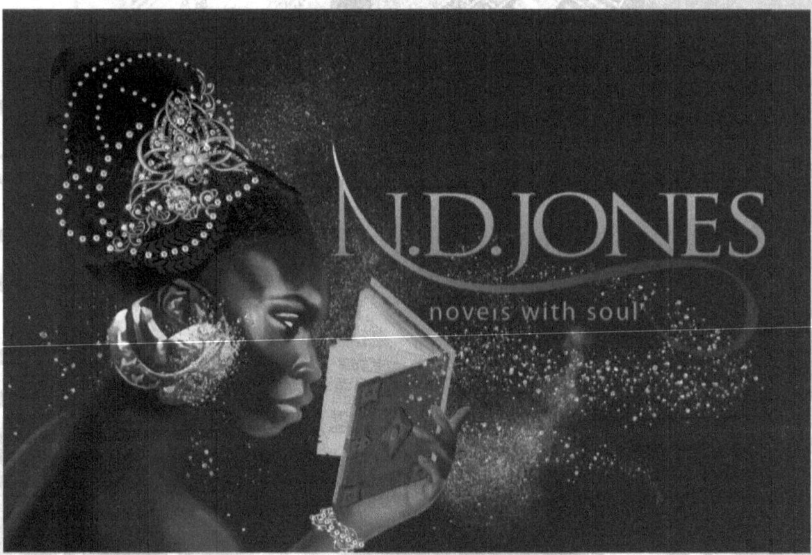
N.D. JONES
novels with soul

www.ingramcontent.com/pod-product-compliance
Lightning Source LLC
Chambersburg PA
CBHW051210120726
47905CB00004B/1060